D1372230

Mike Heppner

The Egg Code

Mike Heppner grew up in Grosse Pointe, Michigan, received an MFA from Columbia University, and now lives in Providence, Rhode Island.

The Egg Code

The Egg Code

A NOVEL

....

Mike Heppner

VINTAGE CONTEMPORARIES
Vintage Books
A Division of Random House, Inc.
New York

FIRST VINTAGE CONTEMPORARIES EDITION, NOVEMBER 2003

The Library of Congress has cataloged the Knopf edition as follows:
Heppner, Mike.
The egg code : a novel / Mike Heppner —1st ed.
p.   cm.
1. Computer networks—Fiction.   2. Computer users—Fiction.
3. Middle West—Fiction.   4. Internet—Fiction.   I. Title.
PS3608.E58 E35 2002
813'.6—dc21
2002019022

Vintage ISBN: 0-375-72725-6

www.vintagebooks.com

Printed in the United States of America
10   9   8   7   6   5   4   3   2   1

For
my parents

and
David Plante

Acknowledgments

The author would like to thank: Richard Abate and everyone at ICM, the Allan family, Linda Burnett, Nicholas Christopher, Michael Cunningham, Stephen Dueweke, Gary Fisketjon and everyone at Knopf, Joshua Furst, Gina Gionfriddo, Lauren Grodstein, Gordon Haber, Victoria Haggblom, the Henfield Foundation, Marjorie Heppner, Binnie Kirshenbaum, Richard Locke and everyone at the Columbia University Writing Program, Priya Malhotra, Adam Mansbach, Tim Naylor, Betsy O'Brien, Amber Qureshi, Paul Selig, Dani Shapiro, Suzanne Sommerville, Peter and Susan Straub, Dr. Lutz Wolff, and anyone I may have forgotten.

Special thanks to Christa Crewdson.

In memory of Georgia Hill.

Qui librum mendis undique scatentem habet,
certe non habet librum sed molestiam.
　　　　　　　　　　　　—Johannes Froben

The buyer of a book full of misprints
does not really acquire a book but a nuisance.
　　　　　—Translation appears in
　　　　　　Five Hundred Years of Printing,
　　　　　S. H. Steinberg

Contents

XXI Suckass

XXII Fuck Technology

XXIII A Brief History of the Internet

XXIV Back to the Womb

XXV Throat

XXVI Survivors

1

Back in the Day

The Nature of Systems

1989

I t had been years since a man had touched her like that. Strong hands molded her body, her hips and soft shoulders, reminding Kay of dear Macheath Tree, dead these twenty-one years. The past two decades had been hard on the woman. All she wanted now was a respectable end, maybe a nice luncheon, a kind word from the vice president. The folks from Georgetown could even send down an assistant chair to deliver a few unfelt sentiments. *Today we honor . . .* the usual bullshit. She'd heard it all before, starting at Harvard, where the youngsters from Biological Sciences had worked hard to destroy her husband's program (and what an entire department couldn't accomplish with all its collective ill will, a shattered glass stamen managed quite nicely in the spring of '68).

Yes, a kind word from the veep. Not this new guy, though. It wasn't that the poor fellow was such a simp, or that he'd fudged on his military background. But they should've known not to pick an extremist. The right-wingers belonged here, in this building. Let's keep the centrists in the White House, where they can't do any harm.

From where she now stood—head down, watching her reflection in the bright marble floor—Kay could see all the way up her dress, the pleated fringe spreading wide around her sneakers. The floors in these federal buildings were too damn shiny. Still, it excited her to watch the dress sway every time those hands pressed into her sides, fingers hot and firm against her thick cotton underwear, his knees touching hers, forcing her legs apart, so controlled, yes, we will not miss a single step, Mrs. Tree, we will execute the steps in the proper order.

"Sorry about the added security, ma'am." The young man at the northeast entrance passed her wristwatch through the metal detector one last time and gave it back to her. "Inauguration," he explained.

"That's all right." She smiled, feeling sexy as she put her watch back on in front of the guard. "I love getting frisked," she said. "It's better than having a husband."

Past security, she continued down a hallway and into an empty reception area. With the swearing-in taking place across the river, most of the Pentagon was closed down for the afternoon. Kay had known George Bush for years, and had high hopes for his presidency. The media take on the new president as some sort of bumbling idiot was a joke. As anyone who knew the real story would tell you, Bush was the *balls*. Even back in '73, it was Bush who'd urged President Nixon to ignore the Democrats, to insist upon his beloved rationale, national security, even if it meant endorsing a few indiscretions. This might not have been very good advice, but it certainly wasn't *cowardly*. It always made Kay smile, the American public's willingness to manufacture its own misinformation.

On the third floor, she caught up to Mitchell Frenkle, deputy director of the DCA. He walked carefully, trying not to spill his coffee on his way past the elevators. "Hi, Kay. Recognize the joint?"

"Sure, it never changes."

The man groaned. "Well, we like to play around with our acronyms every now and again, but what the hell."

The door to Frenkle's office opened automatically as they reached the end of the corridor. *Swissshhh . . . space age!* Kay looked over her shoulder, nervous around these hi-tech contraptions. The door closed behind them.

"Look who's here," Frenkle said. His outer office was spacious, with three secretaries' desks and a leather sofa, some magazines on the coffee table. A middle-aged man in a light suit half-rose from the sofa and shook Kay's hand.

"NSF, I'm Barney Crain," he said. "It's nice to meet you, Mrs. Tree." Christ, she thought. First the branch, then the name—these people in Washington sure have some weird priorities.

Still holding Kay's hand, Crain asked, "When are you folks over at Georgetown going to send us some decent interns?"

Kay took her hand back. "When we have some decent students, Mr. Crain." It was returning to her now, the Washington josh. Almost a form of social currency in these parts.

Frenkle broke in: "Crain is head statistician for the National Science Foundation. He'll be working with us today." He led the way into the next room and closed the door. On his desk, an answering machine fluttered its red eye—six quick flashes and then a pause. He shook his head. "I tell people to use the e-mail, they don't listen."

"Give it time." Crain tossed a pair of high-density floppies onto a round conference table and settled into his chair. Hitting Play on the answering machine, Frenkle listened to his messages, the usual Inauguration Day blather.

"Hi, Muh-Mitch? Thuh-this is Dan here." Coughing, the voice deepened. *"That's* Mister *VeePee to you, pal, heh-heh. Just kiddin' there. Luh-listen—"*

"Shut the fuck up." Frenkle deleted the message, then joined the others at the table. Crouching down, he inserted both disks into a hard drive and hit the power button. The lights dimmed theatrically as a sixty-inch monitor came down from the ceiling. On the screen, a blue image showed an outline of the forty-eight contiguous states. White lines curved from one point to another, like missiles launched and exploded halfway across the country.

Blinking at the bright screen, Crain resumed his original thought. "Telephones are so *bloody* old-fashioned, it's pathetic. Even the utility companies have wised up. I still remember AT&T, back in '64, '65, AT&T telling Paul Baran that packet switching was a doomed concept. Now they're all lining up. You'd think this was the only thing we do."

Kay tried not to listen as the two men traded inside jokes about the eggheads at AT&T. She hated computer talk. She'd been around it ever since coming to Washington in 1969, and to this day she still favored the lunchtime solitude of her office to the chatter of these swashbuckling men with their hi-tech delusions. Who among them could muster up the same passion for a Strauss opera, those last liquid moments of *Der Rosenkavalier*, say, with the voices seeking chromaticism and yet still reaching with a backwards longing for the court and parlor? Macheath always preferred Verdi to Strauss, but he and Kay never argued about such trifles. So the man had a thing for "La donna è mobile," so what? At least he had a wide range of interests. Botany, yes, of course, and glassmaking, but also Scottish literature, typography, Bauhaus art and architecture, combat theory, semantics, even cross-country skiing. He *cared* about things, you see. For all their talk of the coming information revolution, men like Frenkle and Crain were ignorant of the world beyond the network. These men craved information, but only for its statistical value. Information was something to be channeled, transmitted, systematically converted, broken down into packets and later reassembled as text and color. The last thing anyone wanted to do was *read* it.

"Kay, we're looking at an overview of the system as it stands today. I'm sure you've seen something like it before."

She pulled her glasses out of her purse, then peered up at the screen. "I don't know," she said. "I haven't been paying much attention lately."

"Kay's been too busy teaching cryptology to graduate students," Frenkle said, making it sound like an indulgence, a housewife's distraction. *Kay's been taking a pottery class on Wednesdays.*

"God, how dull," Crain muttered. "What's to teach?"

"Not much, I guess," Kay said. This was something her youngest daughter, Lydia, had never learned. Around men, sometimes it's best just to let things *go.* Leaning back in her seat, she added, "The most promising students, I pass on. I send them across the river to Frenkle."

"'Where they are never heard from again,' he laughed with insane abandon." Pleased with his joke, Frenkle cut the banter short. "Anyway. Here nor there."

"Agreed. So, Kay, to bring you up to date . . ." Crain tapped the mouse button, causing the image on the screen to fade behind a grid. "I'm sure you're familiar with the old ARPANET."

Frenkle glared across the table. "Jumping the gun a bit, aren't you Crain?"

"Old, new, whatever, we need to start somewhere." A new picture hovered across the screen, depicting the original four IMPs set up by Bolt Beranek and Newman in the late sixties. Seeing this again, Kay remembered the time, her own life back then. Things were different when her husband was still alive. Macheath's world was a world of slow communications, where one had to choose each word carefully, for every mistake meant endless backtracks, cross-outs, crumpled pages in the trash can. Had he not died in 1968, would he too have shelved such habits in favor of newer, speedier modes of communication? Had technology itself brought about this blanding of shared thought?

"As you can see," continued Crain, dragging his mouse to erase the map, "that system has since been replaced by a larger, more complicated array of nodes."

Annoyed, Frenkle set down his coffee. "You write it off so easily," he said. "Those IMPs supported our activities for nearly two decades."

"Relax, Mitch. Credit due. But we all knew years ago that the network eventually would grow beyond the capacities of any single agency. If it didn't, we would've failed."

Frenkle folded his arms. "I just want Kay to understand the topography as it stands."

The two men stared at each other, then smiled. It really was silly, in a way. This whole thing.

"Okay, Mitch. Good point." As Crain spoke, different views of the network passed across the screen. "It is now January 1989. The IMPs of the past are largely worthless, since high-speed routers—manufactured by IBM and maintained by the Gloria Corporation—provide us with a more efficient means of controlling traffic. This new development, quite naturally, will diminish the role the Defense Communications Agency plays in determining network priorities."

"Getting out of the computer business, Mitchell?" Kay smiled.

Frenkle paused to finish the last of his coffee. "We'll always be around, Kay," he said.

Crain continued his presentation. "The demographic makeup of groups using these networks will change dramatically over the next few years. With the rise of personal computers, the Net will soon host dozens—possibly hundreds—of sites maintained by unknown individuals. Security issues will become more and more of a factor. The need to keep a clear perspective on where information is originating from, how it moves along the network, and where it winds up is of critical importance."

"I sense a bottom line around here somewhere."

"Oh, she's good."

"Of course she is, Barney," said Frenkle. "It's Kay's job to see the words behind the words."

"Well, since you asked, the problem is this." On the screen, the map gave way to a drawing of an RS/6000, T-3 compatible bit processor. Flow arrows demonstrated a progression through an in point, into a computer core, and then out along a variety of links. The diagram did not indicate the size of the contraption; it could have been as tiny as Frenkle's teacup or as large as the Pentagon itself.

"What is it?" Kay asked.

"The Gloria 21169. Your key to a better future."

"It's a router," Frenkle snapped. Crain's sense of dramatics seemed to be getting on his nerves.

"It's a very bad router. Or so we think. Let me bore you with some theory for a moment." More symbols, more diagrams. The picture on the screen clarified nothing, even though Crain's tone of voice suggested that it did. "The network has always functioned as a hierarchy of layers. This is not likely to change. It only makes sense that as long as there is a network, there will be a distribution of roles. This is the nature of systems."

"Take a tip from Uncle Sam." Frenkle rubbed his nose, feinting at each nostril with a bent finger. January allergies rustled in the throats of both men.

Crain continued: "Routers are specialized computers designed to conduct the flow of traffic. Certain routers handle business within autonomous networks. Other routers are configured to serve as an interface between two distinct networks."

"The Gloria machine," Kay said, unsure of herself. She did not mind Crain's pedantic tone; while she'd worked with network prototypes for many years, she'd always utilized preexisting software and thus knew very little about computers on the bare-bones level. As a cryptographer, it was her job to scramble the thoughts of others, not to devise ones of her own. "So we've got a computer that doesn't know what it's doing."

Here, Crain seemed genuinely puzzled. "Maybe . . . but I don't think so." He set his pen down on the table. "Do you remember Bob Kahn?" Kay did; she'd seen him at MIT in the mid-sixties, and in Washington a few years later when she was hired to create a cipher for the

TCP/IP project. "In the early days of the ARPANET, Kahn outlined four basic principles central to network communications. The first three, I don't remember." He looked at Frenkle, who shrugged—*search me*. "The fourth rule was simple. There can be no global consolidation of power in a system of this size." He sighed. Through the thick, tinted windows of the Pentagon, the noise of the inaugural parade sounded dull and ominous, like the boom of an underground explosion. "It seems the Gloria router may not have gotten the message."

"I don't understand." Kay rubbed her eyes, missing the clarity of a well-lit room. "Weren't the Gloria routers manufactured according to the government's own specifications?"

"They were, but so what?" Crain grabbed a sheet of paper and sketched a diagram—positives and negatives and decimal expressions of relative proportions. In the dark, Kay could read none of it. "Look. The way the protocol's designed, a host computer sends a message. The router receives information from the host describing where the message should wind up. Based on that information, the router makes a decision. It can send the message on to its destination; it can relay the message back to the host; or it can redirect the message to another router. The important thing is this: In order for the network to operate effectively, these decisions must be made on the basis of the overall system. Each router has its own role to play. These roles were determined when the network was set in place."

"Sounds reasonable."

Crain looked back at the screen. "It *is* reasonable! That's our problem. Somehow, the Gloria router has managed to manipulate its neighbors into following a new command. And when I say 'neighbors,' I don't mean some dinky mainframe sitting in a concrete barracks five miles down the road. I'm talking about sites as widespread as Chicago, Cal Tech, Ithaca . . . This is a whole new geography, Kay."

Frenkle turned on the overhead lights. Kay felt strange at first, as if she'd just shared something intimate with the two men. "Any ideas on how it's getting around the protocol?" she asked.

"Yeah, I've got a notion." Crain's voice dropped a notch. "It's possible that by passing erroneous information on to other devices, it's able to augment their FIBs with its own forwarding specifications. Kind of the equivalent of putting yourself on the guest list. The question is, Is this something that the Gloria router is doing on its own, or is it simply responding to instructions from an outside source?"

"What's the list of suspects?" Here she could finally start to assert herself. This was Kay's world—bad men, nasty secrets.

"Well, naturally there's the usual nut jobs. I'm sure Frenkle's already got his people working on that." Reluctantly, he added, "Then there's the Gloria Corporation itself."

"What would their motive be?"

"Think about it, Kay. We're talking about a systematic inversion of the entire structure."

Kay shrugged. The way these men talked. Empty portents, all vaguely apocalyptic. "You're afraid this one tiny contraption could seize control of the whole network?" *Why not just pull the plug?* she wondered, feeling silly.

"Nothing quite so drastic as that. There's not enough room in the computer's buffer to handle that much information. Its circuits would burn out." Eyes flashing, he stared at Frenkle across the table. "But it could make some friends."

Yes, the appeal of the committed insurrectionist. The Messiah newly emerged from the desert. Kay remembered her first year in this town, back when the feds were working on the Manson case, and everyone wondered how such a despicable man could get so many others to listen and obey.

"Okay, boys." She clapped her hands together. "I'm hooked. Where the hell is this thing?"

"Ah. Good point." Crain wrote a few words on a scrap of paper and passed it to her. Frenkle studied her expression as she read the note, then put it into her purse.

"So you can see what our problem is," he said. "Just the mere fact that the thing exists poses a major security hazard."

"Have you talked to the people over at Gloria?" she asked.

"They'd say it was a statistical aberration and to think no more of it. Besides, if someone working for the GC really is behind this, I don't want them to know we're on the case."

"I don't know," Crain grumbled. "I'm inclined to go in and swing our fists around. We hold the damn contract."

"I agree," said Kay. "The arrangement you've described sounds pretty one-sided. Without our funding, Gloria would go under. Seems to me we can do whatever we want."

"Kay, you're absolutely right, but my budget and Crain's combined aren't big enough for us to hire a new liaison and reconfigure the entire backbone from the ground up." Frenkle looked pale. A good ninety percent of his job involved juggling cash around; the very thought of it made his heart race. "I want to keep an eye on things. The fewer people who know that the Gloria router exists, the better. You, me, Crain, and that's it. You want to whip something up for us?"

"You want me to shadow the Gloria Corporation?" Kay laughed. Crain and Frenkle both sat with their hands in their laps, waiting. "I'm a little old for that, aren't I?"

"That's not what I mean." Frenkle pointed at the screen. "Those numbers could lead an educated miscreant back to the source. Some of our potential enemies may have access to our code files. I don't want a single binary open to interpretation. Use a trinomial matrix, transpose it a half-dozen times, whatever it takes, but make sure we've got the information locked down."

"Now, Mitchell, come on." Kay touched the back of his hand. She knew the way these defense boys operated. At the first sign of trouble, they'd clog up the system with byzantine procedures and cold-war conniveries. But she also knew enough to realize that those same tactics wouldn't fool the typical hi-tech raider. "Look, I've been working codes for forty years. You make a stink that big, you might as well run the software over NBC during the Super Bowl. Someone bent on decrypting the information is going to spot a granny knot like that."

"All right then, Kay." Frenkle nodded judiciously. "This is why I called you down here. What do you suggest?"

Kay gave him a nasty look. *I could have had a nice lunch today.* "Mitchell, what exactly is it that you're hoping to do?" Counting on her fingers, she provided her own answers. "You want to maintain the secrecy of the router; you want to make sure that no one tampers with the equipment; and if the damned thing turns out to be an asset, you want to guarantee that no one outside of the DoD will be able to use it. Am I right?"

Frenkle frowned. "It sounds so sinister when you say it."

"Ha!" Kay touched her hair, adjusting the shape of her permanent.

What an old lady, she thought, scolding herself. "Rule number one of American government, Mr. Frenkle—if you want to keep something a secret, make it obvious." She slung her purse over her shoulder and headed for the door. "Call me when you've got a real problem."

"Kay," Frenkle pleaded, turning in his chair. "Don't let me down. I've been very nice to you over the years."

"Relax, Mitchell. I'll give my daughter a call tonight." At this, both men looked confused. Standing in the doorway, she leaned against the metal frame and said, "By the way, do you know what the new president drinks?"

Frenkle shook his head. "No idea, Kay."

She backed into the outer office. "I was thinking of sending him a case of Scotch."

"Can't go wrong with Scotch," Crain agreed.

"Takes a long time to go through that much whiskey." Frenkle smiled. "A good eight years."

"Are you kidding?" Kay laughed. "George Bush is a Texan. Four years at the most."

Waving over her shoulder, she closed the door on the two befuddled men and thought, *Thank God I won't live to see how this turns out.*

Two V
the

was a worthy cause, but
Americans came in
"The deman
months are
der and
Madri
sp

LONDON

I n 1944, communication was slow between London and Washington. Waiting for news, Bartholomew Hasse stayed indoors, keeping watch over his belongings. There were prowlers outside; looters, war-crazed vagrants. A safe under the fireplace was his best defense against burglary. The Hasse flat had suffered a few indirect hits — chipped plaster in the entryway, that sort of thing. Most of the damage was purely psychological. Madrigal, Bartholomew's English wife, took it the hardest; after all, this was *her* country. Bartholomew didn't let it worry him. Having already left one place behind, he'd grown used to sneaking out of town.

"Well, Bartholomew, our only reservation is this." The American secretary lit his cigar and picked a bit of the wrapper out of his mouth. Along with the Hasses, he sat in a candlelit room near the back of the apartment. The rest of the flat was dark. "You've worked well for us in the past," he continued. "But you are a small organization, and this is a difficult time in the war. The more we close in on Hitler, the tougher he is to defeat."

Bartholomew looked at his wife, then back at the secretary. Secretly, he worried about his business. In Germany, he'd worked under the direction of a man named Scherbius, who'd designed an early model of the Enigma cipher machines now being used against the Allies. Since coming to England, he'd helped the Brits develop their own version, called the TYPEX. In both cases, the goal was the same — to prevent enemy eyes from decoding secret intelligence transmitted via radio. It

there wasn't much money in it. That's where the

ds we'll be placing on your facilities in the coming
normous," the secretary warned. He looked over his shoul-
blew his smoke toward the dark half of the room. The sight of
igal standing next to the empty fireplace startled him. Trying to
nile, he scooted in his seat—a vague offer of some kind—but she
shook her head and turned away.

Unsettled, he rested his cigar against the rim of a steel ashtray and
handed Bartholomew a stack of blueprints. "As you know, our efforts to
nullify the enemy's Panzer corps have failed." He watched as his host
flipped through the stack. "Personally, I don't trust these rotor machines.
Our field soldiers aren't smart enough to use the damn things."

Bartholomew shrugged. "Well, sir, you have my sympathy. But everything is done with computers now. I haven't seen a code book since
1938. People are afraid of them."

"Yeah, well, I don't like it. I want those numbers where I can see
them. Right on the body of the plane." The secretary scooted forward in
his seat. "We need a consistent cipher. No one in the States knows what
they're doing. Think you can handle it?"

"I can, sir." Coming to the end of the stack, Bartholomew set the
blueprints aside. "As an Englishman and a German alike, I swear it."

Madrigal stepped to the window at the far end of the office. From
here she could not smell the smoke, nor hear the final negotiations
between the secretary and her husband. She knew it was dangerous to
stand in such a vulnerable spot, but a growing belief in her imminent
departure caused her to look upon London as a kind of dreamland in
the making. The ruined opera houses, the rubble-heaped roundabouts,
the ancient glass that nightly shook and sometimes shattered in the V-1s'
wake—soon she would resign these things to what she already thought
of as a closed volume, an overlong prelude to the main portion of her
life. This arrangement with the American would ensure an easy passage
to the States for her and her husband. The extra money certainly
helped, but it was the diplomatic protection they needed the most. Oh,
there were many things they would have to leave behind—small treas-
ures, pricey linens, a relative or two—but she would not regret their loss.

London was a dead city, almost Gothic in its scattered destruction; after months of bombing, the Nazi firepower had turned the plainest slabs of modern British architecture into amazing displays of twelfth-century detail.

The American rose from his seat as Bartholomew added his name to a list at the bottom of a contract. The secretary made a cursory show of inspecting the form, then dropped it into an innocuous envelope marked GROCERY LIST.

"Ah," he said, gathering his things. "Another contract. This war is full of 'em."

"Yes, yes." Bartholomew retrieved the man's cigar and handed it back to him. "Men are fickle. Words are not."

"Agreed, agreed." They shook hands. "That's what I love about you, Bartholomew. Your cold German logic."

"No, my friend." Still smoking, he steered the secretary away from the desk. "Things are different. I am an American now."

Mrs. Hasse excused herself and ran down the corridor. Passing a closet, she grabbed a suitcase and hurried upstairs. The bedroom was dark. Empty drawers lay in a pile next to the window. Sorting clothes into bundles, she picked out three blouses, three skirts, three pairs of underwear. No perfume, no makeup. No books.

PITTSBURGH

"Mama, why I got to stay in here, it's hot!"

" 'Cause I can't be watching when you're walking around. Now sit right there and don't be swinging your feet!"

Julian loved watching his mother work: the way she moved against the hull, squeezing the handle on the paint gun as she stood alongside a few hundred other women, each dressed in high black boots and gray jumpsuits with blue bandannas wrapped around their heads. Ten hours a day, they worked inside an old cannery, now converted into a hangar. They took few breaks, fought occasionally, but mainly ignored one another because the work was hard and exacting. The stencils they used were thin sheets of metal; the edges were sharp, and you had to wear gloves to keep from cutting your fingers. The children kept out of the way, playing among themselves, torturing the enormous insects that crept out of cracks in the cement foundation. Julian avoided the other kids, preferring his mother's company. The letters fascinated him, how they jumped directly from the stencil to the body of the plane, as if a machine had put them there. His mother was the machine. Candace Mason, wife of DuMochelle, the world-famous Jap killer of Pittsburgh. She made letters appear out of thin air, and could do it over and over again.

"Julian, hand me the *J*."

"Which one's the *J*?"

"Oh, now, you know which one's the *J*. Like your name — Julian, with a *J*. You start way up high, and then you go all the way down and you make a little squiggle."

The hangar was dark, and the ceiling was so high that Julian could barely see the iron support beams, even when he lay on his back and squinted past the bluish fog of the fluorescent bulbs. The place reeked of wet laundry and women's sweat. He could still remember the sour odor of cucumbers from those days when the cannery made pickles instead of fighter planes. Before the war, his mother used to sew at home, and he would listen to the clang of the canning machines from the steps of his tenement house two streets up and over. So much had changed since then. No men, no school. No pickles.

"Mama, what are you making?"

"Oh, Julian, you know what we're making. We're making planes to fly over Europe. Now you be quiet and toss me the *M*."

"What are you gonna name it?"

"You name it whatever you want to, baby."

"I wanna call it *One-Eye*, after Jimmy Maxwell."

"Now Julian, damn it, I said the *M*! Ain't you got sense to hold it right-side-up?"

Perched atop a steel tool rack, Julian watched the letters spring from his mother's fingertips. Her new job was mysterious, exciting. As a seamstress, she'd kept to her small tasks, sewing in the kitchen. The factory changed all that. The planes loomed over the dirty floor — vicious monoliths — and she tamed them, naming them with her paint, her letters.

She was his hero, a new Adam. He'd heard all the old stories from a white preacher who stood on downtown street corners as kids and war widows passed by on their way to the factories. Black or white, didn't matter, they all stood outdoors in the cold fall of 1944 and listened to the preacher read from the Old Testament. Adam was the first man, the namer of the beasts. With this power, he created something from nothing. I call thee—lion! Whitewolf! Devilfish! Wonderjet! Just like Adam, Candace Mason gave names to the unknown creatures. She was a powerful woman, knowing and beautiful. Julian adored her. He rarely thought about his father.

"Mama, what are you writing now?"

"Oh, Julian . . . I just don't know."

II

Dipshit,
U.S.A.

Old Man, Alone

1998

Grass on my shoes, wet grass. The steep slope, from the house to the lake. Could Mother have lived here? Nope, I would've had to do everything. *Julian, fetch the groceries.* Oh, yes, ma'am! Just sit right down, there you go . . .

It's a nice view, though. Water looks cold. You buying a new house, that's half your investment. Girl's trying to tell me, *You need to refinance.* I said, *I don't need to refinance — if you can get me zero-point-nine percent, I don't need to refinance nothing.* No sir. I got *plenny* of money. I take better care of my money than most people do . . .

Leaves are coming down early this year. I can see my house from here. The lake, the moving van, the ramp sticking out of the back, big words, bold and blocky: CRANE CITY MOVERS. Looks like a popcorn bag — remember those? — with the blue and red pinstripes, and the words HOT POPCORN always written in one square serif or another. It's a childhood thing. Summer carnivals. Of course, there were no carnivals back in 1944. I remember those days. DuMochelle Mason fights the Japs while his wife builds the bombs. That was my childhood, right there . . .

These little kids don't know. They've got no reason to worry. But when you're living in the city, then you're dealing with a whole 'nother situation. *That's* when you get it . . .

I don't even know if these people have a police department. In the wintertime, I'll probably have to stay inside. Teach myself to chop wood. What's the trick? I guess you just have to make sure you don't swing too far. Cut right through your leg. That would hurt more than a shot to the stomach. No thank you. There are other ways for a man to die at my age . . .

Whoo, wow! I need to get me some of that cream . . .

Activity, that's what I need. Get to work by seven in the morning. This sleepy street could put me into a coma. The hardware store, bags of fertilizer in the window. *Feed in back*. I'm not familiar with that design. Almost looks like a modified Caslon. Obviously done by an amateur. Americans love that stuff. And this banner—another American institution. SEPTEMBER DAYS—ALL LOCAL VENDORS WELCOME! It's a little tacky for my taste. Red's a good color, though. Not particularly seasonal, but it keeps the place in mind. You want a nice, simple presentation. Nuttin' too flashy . . .

Sun's comin' out. What time is it, anyway? I got a craving, boy. Somethin' salty . . .

Streets are quiet. Must be a school day. Maybe I'll come back on the weekend. I'll do some free sketches, drawings of the children. Having kids around always puts everybody in a good mood. I guess they must bring 'em up from the city. Youngsters on the bus, twenty miles to class each morning. I remember Boston, back in the fifties. Those schools didn't look much different than this one here. Same style of architecture. Incised Romans. The ogee line curving along the base of the L. Thick windows, cast-iron moldings. Classrooms dark and dreary. Heads down, hands on the table. Bored out of their minds. That one's not even paying attention. Eyes outside. Never seen a nigger before . . .

Our Fine Community

Simon Tree-Mould sat by the classroom window, holding a beautiful pose. His black hair capped his head with its hard, snap-on shape. He was eleven years old, a few months younger than his classmates. Important months. Phallus rising! In those days of accelerated development, the boys' shower room was a panicky place. The first time he saw another boy's dick, he almost cried. Black stuff. Disease. A punishment for something.

Yawning, he stared across the classroom, ignoring his test. Mrs. Oates kept her back to the students as she spoke to an elderly janitor. Past the window, an American flag tossed in the wind.

The janitor looked at the flag, then at the teacher. He tried to smile. "Mrs. Oates, I don't know if I can just take it down. Isn't there some sort of federal law that says—"

"Do we have to argue about this in front of the children?"

Mrs. Oates was not a woman who liked to complain, so when she addressed the janitor, she did so in a whisper, angling her body so the poor man couldn't squeeze past the door.

"I'm sorry. I'm not trying to argue. I'm just telling you that there may be certain things that I can't—"

"This is an important day for this class, and for me, and for the children. We've been doing tests all morning, and have three more to administer this afternoon. Everyone is tired. Now, this is not fair to the students. If the school system cannot provide us with a soundproof testing facility, then we're just going to have to come up with a suitable compromise."

Outside, the flag snapped; a heavy rope banged against the steel pole. The janitor rubbed his face; his tongue moved in and out of his cheek. He was a stocky guy with suntanned skin and a perpetual squint. An oily hank of hair stuck out horizontally from the side of his head. "The noise didn't bother you this morning?"

"I told you, the wind picked up just now, just fifteen minutes ago, right before I called you, and that is why we're having this discussion."

The janitor chewed on his lip. "Well, all right, I guess I'll take it down. But it seems like there ought to be a federal law against it or something."

The old man left, mumbling. Hoping to restore order, Mrs. Oates closed the door, wincing as the knob mechanism clicked into place. Turning to face the class, she pressed a finger to her lips, requesting silence. "Simon?"

"Mmm-hmm, yes?"

"Why are you looking at me? Why are your eyes not on your paper?"

"Can't concentrate."

"You can't concentrate, what's the matter?"

"The noise, the flag outside. The janitor, when he came in. And then the other thing."

"What other thing?"

"The singing."

"Singing?"

"Someone's singing."

"Singing? Where?" Mrs. Oates stared at the public address system. "I don't hear anything. This is a perfectly quiet room. There's no reason you shouldn't be able to continue with the examination."

"You can just barely hear it."

It was a lame stall, but Simon didn't care. These new assessment tests were a drag. Ultimately, he preferred the easy exams, where they'd show you a drawing of a big egg inside a box and you had to figure out how much space was left over, you know, like around the edges and stuff, and they gave you a bunch of numbers like, oh, 6, 8, 9, 22 and 213, and right away you know that it's not 213 because that's just silly, and it's not going to be 6 either because that's the smallest one, and it's also probably not 8 or 9 because how could it not be 8 and yet still be 9, or vice versa, so that just leaves 22, and even if that turns out to be wrong, well, you tried. Bonus points!

"This singing, is it coming from inside the building?"

"I don't know. It's okay. I'll try to ignore it."

These new exams, however, were a problem. Too many open-ended questions. It wasn't fair that there didn't seem to be one right way to respond to anything. Some of the questions were so long, you'd get to the end and wonder what the hell you were supposed to do next. I mean . . . *You are a slave owner in Georgia in 1861. You receive a letter from your brother (sister) who is currently in Boston attending law school. He (she) informs you of his (her) decision to fight for the Union army. Based on what you know about the time period* . . . Fuck that! Bring back the egg!

"Hey, man." The girl sitting in front of Simon turned around in her chair. "Miz Oates wants to see you."

"Wha?"

"You high or something? Two times already she called."

Mrs. Oates and the school nurse were standing by the doorway. The other woman didn't look much like a nurse, even though she wore a paper hat which she kept in place with four hairpins situated around her head like the points of a compass. As she lingered in the doorway, one of the pins caught the light and winked at Simon. A copper flash.

"Simon, please go with Nurse Wheatt."

"Come with me, please, Simon."

Nurse Wheatt held her hands behind her back as she spoke—another bad habit. The exaggerated concern, the broad body language, the facial expressions learned from a pop psychology paperback and practiced with calisthenic discipline every night on the toilet—all of this would have appealed to a second-grader with a splinter in his thumb. Simon once had a dream where he peed in Nurse Wheatt's mouth and she didn't like it.

"Where are we going?" he asked, rising in his seat.

"Your mother's come for you."

The nurse, when she talked to Simon, liked to lean over slightly and wedge both of her hands between her thighs, palms out. This was strange, since she wasn't much taller than the boy. The leaning over,

Simon thought, this must mean that I'm a kid and you're not. You're a sensitive adult who cares about my thoughts and feelings, I guess, or whatever.

"Mrs. Oates, can't I stay and finish the test?"

"I'm afraid not, Simon. Your mother needs you now."

"Well, okay."

Simon turned his paper over and followed the nurse out of the room. Over her shoulder, he could see EAT FUCK NANCY WATKINS scrawled across a series of lockers, one letter for every door; at the far end, a custodian with a red beard was busy blacking out the words with a marker.

"I'm taking you to the health clinic right now, Simon." Stopping quickly, Nurse Wheatt's shoes squeaked against the floor, producing two swishy streaks like the logo for a corporation of some kind. Sinking to a crouch, she wrapped her arms around her legs. This whole I'm-taller-than-you thing has got to go, he thought. "You just have to be brave. Everything is going to be all right."

The health clinic was a poorly lit room located between the girls' lavatory and a loading dock. The room smelled vaguely of Band-Aids. A glum boy sat on one of the beds, his arms folded in his lap and his saddle shoes swinging high above a nylon backpack. Lydia Tree watched the boy from across the room. Following the nurse into the clinic, Simon could hear the end of a muttered conversation between his mother and the unhappy patient.

"What's the matter?"

"Don't feel good."

"Your mommy's coming to get you?"

"Uh-huh."

"Can't you wait until the end of the day?"

"Got sick twice."

"Oh, why don't you just grow up."

Lydia Tree was a tall woman, thirty-nine years old. She didn't feel particularly old—didn't look it, either, and watch your mouth. Oh, there were a few concessions she'd had to make as of late. The dresses had gotten longer over time, the shoes less daring, the undergarments more functional. But overall, she liked what she saw. Years ago, she'd always worn her hair long. A versatile look. She could keep it straight for around the house or curl it for a formal occasion, not that Steve ever took her anyplace fancy. This phase lasted for many years, until one day she decided to try something daring. *Bernard, I feel naughty today, take off eight inches.* Problem was, when it finally grew back, she found that it looked different. Not bad, just different. Bernard suggested a perm, maybe some copper highlights. Lydia thought it made her look like a giant cauliflower, but her friends didn't seem to mind, and as the months passed, she began to notice similar vegetables clinging to the heads of her contemporaries. And that's when it hit her: This is what women my age are *supposed* to look like. This is thirty-nine! Even her mother, at age seventy-two—whenever the fuck she died—even Kay Tree, who was not a beautiful woman, had always managed to stand out at Republican Party mixers. And the worst thing about it, Lydia realized, was that she'd done it to herself. A kind of death, this was. Death by hair. This growing-older business would have to be watched *very carefully*.

"Oh, my baby." Seeing her son enter the room, Lydia jumped up from her seat and took hold of his hands. The cigarette hidden in her palm was damp with sweat, bent out of shape.

"Ms. Tree, would you like me to inform the principal?"

"No, that's not necessary. Not until we know all of the details. It still may turn out to be nothing. Oh, God, I hope it's so."

Simon looked over his shoulder and smirked at the sick boy. He knew that his secret was safe with Antonio Fava. Antonio's own tactics for getting out of class were revolting and crude. Oatmeal in the toilets—a striking resemblance! The acrid smell of fresh vomit meant freedom, a day away from the books, the scritch of the chalkboard, the female instructors who seemed like a cross between his mother, a television news anchor and a phantom in a mystifying dream. With all this hanging over his head, Antonio would never reveal Simon's little ruse.

"Mother, where are we going?"

"Simon, your father's not feeling well. He's resting now, in a place where people will be able to take very good care of him. He wanted me to send for you. He said he wanted to see you before . . . oh, before . . ."

Nurse Wheatt handed her a Kleenex, which Lydia used to dispose of her gum.

"Ms. Tree, you must be strong for your son."

"You've been so good to us, Nurse Wheatt. My husband and I will remember you at Christmastime."

Lydia and Simon said their goodbyes, then marched out into the hallway. Simon walked in front while his mother stayed close behind, her right hand smoothing a lock of his hair. Without speaking, they went outside and crossed the parking lot. There was a gym class on the field, playing a violent game. Like prisoners, the kids stared through the high wire fence as Simon and his mother drove away. Simon liked it when the other kids watched him. It made him feel warm under his clothes. Gazing at his classmates, he pressed one hand against the rolled-up window. "Do I have to be off book?" he asked. The passenger seat was too big for him—too deep and too cushy.

"You'll do whatever they tell you." Lydia clutched the automatic transmission, working it like a stick shift. "You know how these things go. Now what's this old fool doing in my way?"

Julian Mason stepped onto the lawn, watching as Lydia sped around a curve. His heart seemed to rock back and forth, favoring the right side, a double pulse. He returned to the sidewalk and continued past the school, the car now only a screech in the distance. Closing his eyes, he remembered the driver's face in the windshield. Her judgment of him. He tried to laugh, resolving not to take it personally. From now on, he wouldn't take anything personally. He was tired of carrying his race on his shoulders. His clothes reflected this desire to blend in, to assimilate at all costs. Jeans and a T-shirt. The words QUALITY, INTEGRITY circled the rim of the button fly in a kind of unshadowed Gold Rush font. Julian knew the hidden language of print. Walking the streets of this, his new home, he made himself available to the information. Every sentence, every phrase bannered across an awning transmitted two signals at once—the literal meaning and the visual sense it conveyed. A black-letter Fraktur swinging above the entrance to Simster's Biergarten expressed not only the building's identity, but also the old German Reich, the Gothic type now reduced to the status of novelty, rendered harmless by the easy icons of the global theme park. Passing the bar, he smiled up at the sign, ignoring the woman in the entryway. A nice design. Black paint, varnished wood. Touch of the artisan. He liked this place. Now two blocks east of the school, he wondered at the town's size. Mass communications, common in the city, seemed out of place this far off, where telephone lines and fiber optics crossed the main part of town, then vanished into the forest. The main road curved down a slight hill, and at the base of it he could see a row of detached apartments and walk-ups. A parked van sat with blinkers flashing in the street as a man made trips in and out of the building, his arms brimming with loose piles of clothes. A divorce, Julian guessed. Even the words on the side of the van underscored this impression of hasty flight: GET OUT OF DODGE TRANS-PORTATION FACILITIES written in slanted block sans serifs with tiny scores of motion streaming past each word. *Pack up your things and run,* the letters said. *Leave nothing behind.*

"Hey, you got the same idea as me."

"What's that?"

"New to town." Julian stood on the curb and slid his hands into his pockets. A dingy convertible, moving slowly, passed between the two men. A woman in the passenger seat made a face as he called across the roof of the car. "Just moved up from the city."

The car stopped, then turned at the corner. Heaving a pile of books, the man met Julian in the center of the road. "I'm not new to town. My wife and I, we've been here for quite some time."

"Oh, well, all right then."

"Yes, I'm a native of this place. Not exactly, of course. *Native* implies that I've been here my entire life, and that's not true."

"Oh, okay."

"My wife and I used to live right by the lake. The lake, if you've seen it, it's just up the road."

"Oh, well, then you got it going on."

The man lifted the stack of books and braced it with his chin. "My wife still lives in the same house. I—as you can see—I'm a bit at loose ends."

"Oh yeah, I know how that is."

Clouds covered the sun, casting a shadow over the man's face. He was tall, in his early fifties, and you could see the shape of his skull through his tight, thin skin. Wheat-brown hair had receded to the back of his head, and a stiff mustache made a broom across his upper lip. His teeth were yellow and crooked, and his blue eyes gleamed with an unnatural radiance. The overall impression was that of a normally reasonable man struggling to conceal the effects of a bad drug.

Cars passed as they spoke, slowing sometimes to stop and watch. Julian began to feel sleepy. The man lectured, one arm panning across the street; behind him, the row of apartments seemed to hunker like an audience. "So, if you're new to the neighborhood, I'd recommend that you stop off at the municipal building right away."

"Mmm?"

"Oh, yes. Let them know who you are." The man's voice was clear and strong. He seemed to be making a point of finishing his sentences coherently. "It's a small community. We like to help each other out."

Julian laughed. "Well, I could use some helping. I ain't used to"—he pointed up the road—"all this. I'm a city boy."

The man blinked, absorbing the information. Julian was aware of something artificial about the whole exchange. The blink meant something. Press to record. What's your name? Blink. And where do you come from, Julian? Blink. Oh. Blink. That's fascinating. Blink, blink.

"Well, if there's one thing I've learned from all of my travels, it's this. People who live in cities tend to find their own way. And most of them fall right to the bottom. But in a small town like this, everyone has his own identity. We all matter. There's only one barber, one tax attorney. It's like a situation comedy. We all go to the same bank."

Julian nodded, impressed. "You sound like a philosopher."

The other man chuckled. "I am a philosopher," he said. The word agreed with him in a way that Julian could not understand. They both stepped onto the boulevard. The turf was wet and it squished under their feet. "I've lapsed somewhat," he continued—a cheery song, notes for words. Stopping, he turned in the doorway. "But I'll give you some advice." Again, he laughed; his facial expression suggested that he didn't find himself all that funny. "Number one: always keep plenty of food in the kitchen. *That's* important . . ." His voice trailed off; he licked his lips, staring over the old man's head. "Number two's a freebie: just be careful."

Julian smiled good-naturedly, feeling a bit put down, not by the words, but by the tone of the man's voice.

"And number three . . . now listen."

Julian squinted, ready for the punchline.

"Never get involved with a woman named Gloria. Oh, God!" Turning, the man headed up the stairs. ". . . worst mistake you'll ever make . . ."

III

A Bad Marriage

Author's Note

We were giving a conference in St. Louis, a three-day seminar. "Wealth Through Endeavor" we'd called it—lots of speakers, lots of food, no liquor of course. Three days, Friday, Saturday, Sunday. Optional prayer on Sunday. This was 1980; we were trying to phase God out, slowly, in increments, not so you'd notice. I was the main speaker on Sunday, the prime slot. You see, I had quite a reputation in those days. I once had a woman follow me from Albuquerque all the way to the United Arab Emirates. Said she wanted to touch me.

Two in the afternoon, I take the stage. Now, back when I was young, whenever they said my name, I'd start in the back of the auditorium and run right through the crowd. That was how I made my entrance. What did this convey? This said to my audience that I was happy to be there. That I was enthusiastic about sharing their company. Here is a man in a three-piece suit. He is not stuffy. He is not afraid to show his silly side. Crowds loved it. What were they thinking? Derek Skye loves his work. He is, as they say, *raring to go*.

They were right. I loved my work.

So I'm out there. Donna's sitting right up front, holding a pamphlet in her lap. The pamphlet, like the banner above my head, reads "Wealth Through Endeavor." There's something wrong with the name. What does mean? *Wealth*. I think money. I think fat, overweight, overweight figures into it somewhere, being overweight, owning a recliner, owning a comfy chair. *Through*. A process. A changed state. Wind on skin, suggesting movement. *Endeavor.* Sounds like something a politician would say. A word you use to fill in a blank. It doesn't mean anything. It's hanging over my head.

It's at this time, back in May 1980, when I think Donna was probably most proud to be my wife.

I've done these speeches before; filling up two hours is no problem. I talk about your innate desire to succeed. You nod. Some of you cry. Why are you crying? This is neither happy nor sad, this information I'm giving you. I talk about your inhibitions, your fears. This is why you're here today. Why are you discontent? Because you are afraid. You nod. Your lips move as you commit my words to memory. These things I say, for some reason they ought to be memorized. They ought to be memorized and then laid out in numerical sequence. Number 8: Why are you discontent? Because you are afraid.

We engage in group activities. At one point a volunteer from the audience, a woman from St. Louis, stands next to me, holding a daffodil in one hand and a gym sock in the other. She's trying not to laugh. Many people in the audience are laughing, particularly the woman's friends and sponsors. I have no idea what this means. I have selected a person at random, and I have placed random objects in her hands, and she's standing there, waiting for it to start to mean something. She trusts in me completely. I size her up with a professional's eye. It is my job to find the lesson here.

On occasion, I add the word *endeavor*, slipping it into my speech whenever the sentence calls for a noun and any old noun will do. *Endeavor.* In this way, I keep you on your toes. The word exists. I can and will use it at any time.

At the end of my presentation, my wife joins me on stage and waves at the crowd. She will not wave unless I wave. Her waves are timed with mine. My arm goes up, her arm goes up, and she waits until I bring my arm back down again. She is most definitely The Wife. She has been my wife since 1973. At some point during the latter half of the decade, she became The Wife. Books were printed and sold in large quantities. Speaking engagements welcomed full houses, first in America and soon around the globe. Fame spread. In this fashion, and for this reason, Donna Skye has evolved from my wife to The Wife. She likes the definite article. It makes her feel something that I can't understand.

The spiel is now over and I have several unpleasantries to look forward to. The dinner with respected community leaders. The plane back to Crane City. From behind the stage, I can hear your applause. Why are you still clapping? I'm not going back out there. I'm not doing an encore. As I move down a flight of stairs to my dressing room, my butler presses my face into a hot hand towel, and I can feel the thing shrivel to fit my shape. My wife is changing her shoes in the far corner of the dressing room. I don't know why this is. At some point between here and the stage, we must've passed into a new realm. Her old shoes—perfectly good shoes, as far as I can tell—are no longer appropriate. Donna's like that. Her life is booby-trapped by these invisible transitions. Like she's walking down the street and suddenly orange is not her color.

"Derek, we need you for a moment." Reggie, my agent, hands me a cup of water. The cup is just a sheet of paper curled and glued into the shape of a cone, and I can feel the water seeping out through the seam.

"Derek, Steve Carlin."

"Steve." I acknowledge the man with my left hand, and with my right I crush the cup.

"Hello, sir! Nice to meet you in the face."

"Steve has something he wants to—"

"Before you go. I don't mean to hold up your departure."

Over the man's shoulder, I can see Donna moving out into the hallway, holding the old shoes in her hand, just the shoes and nothing else, for I have hired someone to carry the rest of her belongings. A woman approaches from the stairs and hugs my wife, and I can tell from twenty feet away that she's been crying. What is this about? I must've said something that moved her deeply.

". . . it's fine, but when our man from Planning called your people up north, they told us, well, okay, 'Wealth Through Endeavor,' that's pretty clear."

"You're from a financial organization?"

"Well, it's . . . it's not important. The point is—"

"He feels," my agent butts in—Reggie's primary responsibility is to translate English into English—"that he's entitled to a reimbursement for the misleading information, but what I'm trying to say—"

"I mean, I don't quite get this, because if you'd requested any of the promotional material—"

"We did, but you know, we've got a stack this high."

This Steve Carlin character, right away I don't like him. Right away I'm thinking, Whatever you want, man, I'll give it to you, just go away. Out in the hallway, a group of circus clowns are milling about, smoking cigarettes, flopping around in their huge shoes. First me, then the clowns. Perfect.

"I mean, it's Sunday, we've been here for three days, and all that time you've been taking advantage of our resources."

"We haven't been taking advantage of the resources. I borderline resent that. My men and I, we've been out in the lobby since Friday, drinking soda, waiting for the money management team to show up."

"Oh, Christ, Reggie." My agent shrinks down into his suit collar when I look at him. "This is what I'm saying. With some people, you gotta spell things out, and most folks, when they read *wealth*, they're gonna think wealth."

"Just following orders, Derek."

"This is part of the problem."

"When I see *wealth*," Steve says, "I think wealth. 'Stead I get this AA jive, and my men, frankly, they take it to be an insult." Right in my face, he sticks out his chin. Fucking little rabbit. On his glasses, I see fingerprints, like someone tried to push their thumbs through the lenses and into his eyes, which is what I'd like to do. His gray slacks are spotted with piss stains, little dark dabs. His name tag reads HELLO MY NAME IS but the space is left blank. This I take to be an act of aggression. To not wear the tag at all is one thing. To wear it properly filled out, okay. But to wear it with the blank left empty, this says negative things about the wearer.

"This is something you're gonna have to take up with Hasse Publishing."

"Who're they?"

"They're the people who run this whole thing. I don't do anything. I show up and flap my lips."

The hugging woman has released my wife and now it seems likely that I am to be her next target. "Oh, Derek," she says, pulling on my sleeve. "I've just been talking to your wife—Alexis, is that her name?"

"Donna." Alexis. Sexy name. I'd like that.

The woman stands between Steve Carlin and I, but she is so short that we don't need to make any special adjustments to continue our conversation.

". . . so I talk to these people, they send me their lawyers, I send them my lawyers. Then what happens?"

". . . what you said about 'finding your worth,' I could really relate to that, because my father—"

"I don't know what happens. I'm not sure it would be appropriate for me to comment."

"—he had a thing where for five years he was in a deep, deep depression. And as his daughter, I . . . I interpreted this as, Okay, what's he saying to me?"

I can't do two conversations at once. I reach down and take the woman's hand, hoping that will get me off the hook. She keeps talking to my vest, and evidently my handhold is all she needs.

"I'm just saying for your own future reference, you might want to consider being more specific about—"

". . . the anguish of being the daughter of a man whom I'd admired for so long—"

". . . well, fucking la di da, I need a guy to come down here, tell me what to do . . ."

A vein starts trembling on the right side of Steve Carlin's neck. I nod at my agent, and together he and the dissatisfied customer move off along the corridor. It's hot down here; bare insulation hangs in wisps from the ceiling. When the two men reach the corner, Carlin takes out his wallet and parts the folds to display the bills inside. For some reason, he thinks it's necessary to show my agent how much money he has inside his wallet. I'll hear about it on the plane, I'm sure.

Still holding the woman's hand, I sit down on a stool and rest my back against the dressing-room mirror. The big bulbs around the perimeter of the mirror feel hot above my head.

"My father just said one day, 'We're moving to Wisconsin.' And that's how it was in our family. There was never any joy . . ."

My wife watches me from the bottom of the stairs. The fact that I am holding this woman's hand does not bother her, for as the veteran wife of Derek Skye, she knows that this is simply another part of my job. To comfort. Comfort sometimes means touching. I smile, first down at the woman, then up at my wife, who I can tell is anxious to be getting back to Crane City. Me too, honey. I miss it. You and me, alone in our regular bed. The predictable sounds of the house at night.

Dinner is prime rib at a Perkins near the expressway. All of us, the group of twelve or what have you, have the same thing. Here we are in a chain restaurant, real run-of-the-mill, yet no menus are brought forth, and no one asks us what we want because that information has already been communicated to the kitchen by someone on my personal staff calling from the convention center an hour ago. How this saves time, I don't know. Why I can't take a moment to browse the menu and make up my own mind, I just don't know. Other people dining in the restaurant, good normal folks traveling without an entourage, sit in star patterns all around me eating clam spaghetti and breaded flounder, and when they drink, it's not from a common pitcher of Coca-Cola that no one wants, it's from tall glasses brimming with Mountain Dew, Orange Crush, cream soda. The glasses are bubbled red plastic, and they make whatever's inside look like partially sucked red candy.

I manage this around bites of prime rib: "Martin, what I'm hearing you saying is that the East Coast is not excited about the audio series lined up for the fall. Is that what I'm hearing you saying? Okay then. So if that's true, what I need to say is—and I'm not mad, I appreciate where everyone's coming from, you're thinking cost versus take and I understand that, but what I need to say is, this is a market we can't ignore. Every airport I go to, it's Billy Dee, *Billy Dee's Checklists of Personal Contentment,* ninety-minute cassettes, you get a free ballpoint pen, it's embedded in the shrink-wrap."

As I speak, I feel light flash against the back of my neck, and I'm surprised to discover a team of tag-alongs from the seminar taking pictures out in the parking lot. Their flashbulbs make bright globes against the glass. Fearing a rough flight up ahead, I laugh and flick ice water at my face. Good God, save me from the lightning.

As it turns out, a nasty patch over the Mississippi River forces the pilot to maintain a high altitude the entire trip, and our drop into Crane City is quite literally that—a free fall, and even one of the stewardesses utters a tiny scream as a food tray clatters inside a storage closet. The taste of peanuts is strong in my throat, and the striped pattern on the seat in front of me is making my temples throb. Despite the nausea and the frantic activity, I somehow know we will land safely. That settled, I allow myself a little fantasy, a vision of a quick, unexpected death, with the plane pitching over in an unnatural spin and the lights of the earth now over our heads where they most definitely don't belong. I turn to my wife, who is sitting first-lady-like to my right, protecting me from the fandom that has been crowding the aisle ever since St. Louis. I somehow know that in eight seconds, it will all be over. Our life together, our marriage. I have seven seconds to collect one last glimpse of my wife, my Madonna. Her knees? Not very respectful, staring at her legs at a time like this. This is the moment when the black-box device finally succumbs, and when the feds recover the tape, they will hear nothing, only a quick interruption as the engines fail and the cockpit tears apart from the rest of the plane. Donna has risen from her seat, taking her purse with her. This is how she has chosen to end our marriage. By leaving. Convinced that this disaster is somehow my fault, she now wants to flee. Her loyalty may be severed by less than eight seconds of fear.

This fantasy having come to an unsatisfying conclusion, and with the plane still looking for a runway, I pull out the in-flight magazine and flip through the pages. Under the heading MOTIVATIONAL MASTER STRIKES A NEW PATH, I notice a picture that stops me short. The man in the picture looks familiar, even though I've never seen him before: blond mustache, band of hair hugging the back of a bald head, deep eyes spraying coldwater blue through two chiseled cracks. I recheck the cover, and when I see the April '99 publication date, I realize what has happened, and that my wife is no longer my wife, and I am no longer a young guru, neither young nor a guru but rather a middle-aged crank, and this is just the kind of publicity I need, x-million travelers per day and they all think they know what Derek Skye's all about, and even the poor girl from the features department seems a bit unsure of how to phrase her questions, but I am patient with her, having already survived a year of threats and intimidations, late-night phone calls from the Gloria Corporation, and I know that quite possibly most or maybe even all of my former followers will hate me when they see what I've done. The reporter conducts her business as another woman takes pictures, and while I find this all a bit distracting, I have been assured that this method is in keeping with the informal tone planned for the article. I'm speaking like a maniac, fast and garbled. The photographer asks me to lean forward so she can adjust the folds of my collar. Her fingernails scratch the back of my neck.

"I am tired," I tell the reporter, and she writes it down. "That's the theme of this book. My fatigue. My need to jump up and scream— enough with the excuses! Enough with the, 'Well, it happened *to* me.'" The photographer pats my shoulder and I sit back up, passing gas as my belt presses into my stomach. The reporter scrunches in her seat, pretending not to notice. "As long as it happened *to* you, there's nothing you can do about it. Whatever misfortune you may have encountered in your life, ultimately you brought it upon yourself."

Having these women in my tiny apartment feels odd to me. I've been here by myself for so long now that I find it hard to interact with any company, no matter how polite or well-meaning. My apartment is nearly bare. White walls. I eat from the same plate every night, even though I own a set of four. I wash the plate after every use and set it back on top of the other three. Me and my habits. Well, I haven't been entirely alone. My ex-wife has stopped by a few times. And Scarlet Blessing, the girl. But now she's gone too.

The interviewer holds her pen against her notepad and bites her lip. She doesn't want to ask the next question. I offer her a beer and she begins to relax. "I wonder," she says, "if you think that others like you may have inadvertently contributed to a harmful mindset in this country?"

"Inadvertently?" I smile, toying with her.

She looks annoyed. She too has limits; my cute response strains her capacity, her professional need to care. Still, she says, "You know what I mean. The American mindset. We're all victims. Poor little me."

My shoulders slump as the woman takes a swig of her beer. I'm glad she's enjoying her drink, because right now I feel like throwing up, covering the windows with chunks of gore, my gore. I set my beer down on the wooden floor and say, "Yes, dear. I do. I think about it all the time. It fills me with a terror that I can't describe."

Transcript of Stiessen-Hasse Meeting, June 17, 1972

MADRIGAL HASSE: The tune. The pop song. Look at all
   the lonely people. That's my situation, right
   here.

BARTHOLOMEW HASSE: Shhh, relax, it doesn't matter,
   everything's fine. Now shut up and say hello to
   our friend, our young guest, this is—

M HASSE: Hello, I'm Mrs. Hasse. Welcome to our home.
   I'm sorry if I'm a bit frantic just now.

DEREK STIESSEN: I understand, absolutely. Is there
   anything I can—

M HASSE: No, we pay all these servants, that's why
   they're here.

D STIESSEN: Must be two hundred fifty people.

B HASSE: Tom Collins?

M HASSE: Why bother sending out invitations? Just put
   a sign out: COME ON IN!

B HASSE: Derek. Tom Collins?

D STIESSEN: Oh! Thank you. Thank you very much, sir.

B HASSE: I know it's Tom Collins because of the
   alumni, you know, the thing Midwestern threw last
   fall.

D STIESSEN: Oh yes, yes. I was just down from Ann
   Arbor.

B HASSE: But you're fully moved in now?

D STIESSEN: Well, fully as I'm ever gonna get, I
guess.

B HASSE: And now you've got—

A CATERER: Mrs. Hasse, the ice sculpture, do you want
it on the porch?

M HASSE: Are you kidding? It's ninety degrees out!

B HASSE: Madrigal, attend to that, would you?

M HASSE: What is that, George McGovern? Who can tell,
it's half-melted!

B HASSE: Here, let's walk, it's too crowded.

D STIESSEN: I brought some wine. It's in the—

B HASSE: Don't worry about that. We're just glad to
have you back in town. I remember seeing you at
the graduate seminar—when was it, '69? '70?

D STIESSEN: Not sure.

B HASSE: I thought, Here is a guy who . . . this kid's
got pizzazz, you know? You could've handled the
war. Most people your age, they couldn't have
lived in England during the Second World War, but
you could have, and that's a compliment.

D STIESSEN: Well, thank you very much, sir.

B HASSE: Now, what about this book? Here, let's keep
walking.

D STIESSEN: Well, the book—

B HASSE: Have you met my daughter?

D STIESSEN: Uhh, I don't think—

B HASSE: The one over by the pool in the rather too
provocative bikini.

D STIESSEN: Oh, I see.

B HASSE: Everyone's wearing white tuxedos, but the
kid won't bundle up. I tell her she ought to be
ashamed of herself. I'll introduce you, if we
ever get the chance. Anyway, I'm sorry I
interrupted. Let's keep moving. The book.

D STIESSEN: The book . . . I don't know what to say
about it, except it's kind of disorganized.

B HASSE: The title, what's it called? When I walk into
   a bookstore, where do I find it, in what section?

D STIESSEN: That I don't know.

B HASSE: Start with the name.

D STIESSEN: Oh. For now? The Father and the Son.

B HASSE: Kind of a religious thing.

D STIESSEN: In a way. You know, my father taught
   religious history at the University of Michigan
   before all of this . . . stuff started to happen.

B HASSE: Sure, sure. So it's a memoir?

D STIESSEN: It's more like his memoir than my own.
   I'm a little young to be writing a memoir.

B HASSE: What is it, twenty-three?

D STIESSEN: Twenty-five.

B HASSE: Okay. Well, that's still okay.

D STIESSEN: Turned twenty-five back in January.

B HASSE: The reason I ask is this. As you know, I'm a
   publisher. I've made my living in publishing ever
   since the end of the war. And as you can see, we
   haven't done too badly.

D STIESSEN: It's a beautiful house, sir.

B HASSE: And God bless the U.S.A. for that. And God
   bless Adolf Hitler—which I mean ironically,
   because if it wasn't for Adolf Hitler, we
   wouldn't be here today.

D STIESSEN: Sure.

B HASSE: No, of course not "God bless Adolf Hitler"—
   no one in their right mind would say such a
   thing. But this is American capitalism right
   here. Supply and demand. We as a people depend on
   printed materials to carry out the business of
   the day. And this goes all the way back to the
   time of Johannes Gutenberg—who was my relative,
   by the way.

D STIESSEN: Wow. He was—the microscope?

B HASSE: The printing press.

D STIESSEN: Ah.

B HASSE: Ever since the mid—fifteenth century, this is
    how it's been, and this is how it'll always be
    until the day the world goes to hell. And, not
    incidentally, this is how I earn most of my
    income, from the printing and distribution of
    such materials. Posters. Pamphlets. The sign for
    Kleinstock pork sausages hanging over the
    crosstown expressway. This is information.
D STIESSEN: Good thing to get into.
B HASSE: What's that?
D STIESSEN: Information. Big business.
B HASSE: If you're willing to diversify. People don't
    realize the technological revolution that's about
    to take place. Suffice to say that the printing
    industry is on the verge of a major shock. And
    the thing that they're planning is so wrong, it
    makes me want to spit.
D STIESSEN: Wrong? In what sense?
B HASSE: Morally it's wrong, very much so, and I'm
    not exaggerating. Listen to my philosophy, Derek.
    And if I'm speaking in hushed tones, the reason
    will soon become apparent. When you place type on
    a page, it forces you to confront the meaning of
    your words. The type is real. It's real ink, real
    paper. The words have a source. The source is
    accountable for the truth of the words. These
    messages flowing out along telephone lines,
    hurtling themselves across the country, these
    messages cannot be trusted. They come from
    nowhere. They're not real.
D STIESSEN: Telephone lines?
B HASSE: Do you now see why I'm speaking in hushed
    tones?
D STIESSEN: Abso—
B HASSE: So the point is that I've been looking for
    an excuse to broaden my range and who knows, your
    book might be the thing. I want to read it. Give

it to my secretary tomorrow morning. Or better
yet, drive back up to the house. We'll have a
family luncheon, without all these people around.

D STIESSEN: I'll certainly do that, sir.

B HASSE: Oh, and Derek. Change the name. Too German.
We'll fix it. Here, don't move, I'll grab Donna,
we'll get you kids going. Freshen your drink?

D STIESSEN: I'll do it.

B HASSE: It's all ice, tell them to make you a new
one. But come right back.

D STIESSEN: The bar?

B HASSE: Through the French doors. I'm headed this
way.

KENNETH HOOK: Bartholomew, you've got to make
yourself more available, I've been trying to hunt
you down all afternoon.

B HASSE: Ken! Hi, come walk with me. You came to
my party, this is amazing. Inviting you was a
mere formality, we never thought you'd actually
show up.

K HOOK: Gotta leave at three. My plane's taking me to
Washington, then down to Key Biscayne.

B HASSE: What do you need to see the president for?

K HOOK: Who the fuck knows. This is Richard Nixon, he
probably just needs an alibi. Anyway, you . . .
you're the man in question.

B HASSE: Is that a fact.

K HOOK: I have a picture of you.

B HASSE: Oh, well this sounds lurid.

K HOOK: What you wouldn't give just to see it, let
alone keep it off the open market.

B HASSE: I don't know, Ken, I have a pretty high
tolerance for shame.

K HOOK: Dogs beg, my friend. Dogs beg and puppies
whine.

B HASSE: Are you smiling? I can't tell if this is a
smile, or what this is.

K HOOK: You'll see. We'll work something out.

B HASSE: This picture, now what could possibly be so
    terrible that I would actually make such an
    arrangement?

K HOOK: Imagine the purest essence of evil . . .

B HASSE: Yes?

K HOOK: Okay, now imagine it's a full-color snapshot
    and I've got it in my coat pocket.

B HASSE: Again, the smile. Your facial expressions,
    you should walk around with a stack of subtitles
    pinned to your chest.

KAY TREE: You! Don't move.

B HASSE: Oh, hello! Ken . . . we'll resume, you and I?

K HOOK: Your eldest grandchild, his genitals dipped
    in bronze, this is my payment.

B HASSE: I'm just trying to reach my daughter.

K TREE: You've got a bug on the back of your shirt.

B HASSE: Well, wipe it off. What kind is it?

K TREE: I have no idea. It's blue—looks tropical.

B HASSE: I think I felt something.

K TREE: Those were my hands, my fingers. I'm running
    my hands up and down your body.

B HASSE: Look out for the *cake!*

K TREE: Why don't you—

MADONNA HASSE: Daddy, I'm cold.

B HASSE: Look, I'm sorry, I just need to pass some
    information on to my daughter.

K TREE: Oh, there—*now* he goes. Goodbye.

B HASSE: Donna, there's someone I'd like you to meet.

M'D HASSE: Can't I at least throw on a kimono or
    something?

B HASSE: You'll be fine, everyone here loves you.

M'D HASSE: But I don't understand why I can't cover
    myself properly. These men, these old men,
    they're lurking around, staring down my top, it
    makes me sick.

B HASSE: They're just expressing their warm feelings
of fatherly affection for you. Now, please . . .
just be quiet and get with the program, won't you,
darling? This young man, I think you'll like him.

M'D HASSE: Which one is he?

B HASSE: He's right there, standing on the back deck,
next to the French doors.

M'D HASSE: The "Scenes of Edo"?

B HASSE: No, no, the Frank Lloyd Wright.

M'D HASSE: Oh, yes.

B HASSE: Very handsome.

M'D HASSE: He's okay.

B HASSE: His name is Derek Stiessen. Twenty-five years
old, just graduated from Midwestern University.
I'm very impressed with his credentials. He's a
smart guy.

M'D HASSE: What does he do?

B HASSE: He's a writer, darling. He writes, ummm . . .
pop psychology, that sort of thing.

M'D HASSE: And people buy his books?

B HASSE: They will if I have anything to do with it.

M'D HASSE: If you have anything to do with it?

K HOOK: I'm still here, Bart.

B HASSE: I'll be right with you, Ken. Give me thirty
seconds.

M'D HASSE: Daddy, what are you talking about?

B HASSE: Look, never mind. Just be nice to him. He's
a perfectly decent young guy. He's been going
through some tough times lately. Father just
died. They were very close. And then his mother.
Committed suicide, apparently.

M'D HASSE: Oh dear.

B HASSE: Anyway, he's new to town and I figure he
needs some friends, what's wrong with that?

M'D HASSE: Fine, okay. How're my lips?

B HASSE: What's that?

M'D HASSE: My lipstick.

B HASSE: It's a hideous color but we'll just have to
    live with it.

M'D HASSE: Daddy!

B HASSE: Ah, Derek, hello, I see you've managed to
    find that drink.

D STIESSEN: Yes, sir, no problems.

B HASSE: Yes, well, hello, wonderful. Oh! This is my
    daughter, Donna Hasse. Donna, Derek Stiessen.

M'D HASSE: Hi.

D STIESSEN: Very pleased to meet you.

B HASSE: Donna's, umm, she's been staying with us for
    the time being, just kind of doing her thing.
    Well, I don't need to speak for her, I'm sure
    she'll tell you all about it. Look, kids, I've
    got some business to attend to, so why don't you
    two mingle and I'll be back shortly. Oh, and
    Derek, don't leave without seeing me first.

D STIESSEN: About the—

B HASSE: Tomorrow.

K HOOK: Bart.

D STIESSEN: Yeah, okay.

K HOOK: You want to check this out?

B HASSE: I hear you, Ken. I'm right on it. Donna? Be
    nice to Mr. Stiessen, won't you, sweetheart?

D STIESSEN: Oh, gosh.

K HOOK: This really is amazing.

M'D HASSE: I certainly will, Father dear.

K HOOK: Bart.

B HASSE: All right.

K HOOK: Your testicles, my picture: an even swap.

B HASSE: Here, let's go down to the basement.

D STIESSEN: Bye.

M'D HASSE: There they go. Hurry, hurry.

D STIESSEN: Busy men.

M'D HASSE: I don't ask what goes on. I don't need to
    know.

D STIESSEN: Are you here by choice? Or is this just because you live here?

M'D HASSE: Well. I live here by choice. So I guess that's the same thing.

D STIESSEN: Does your father give a lot of parties?

M'D HASSE: Oh no. My father is the most antisocial man you've ever met. We go to a lot of parties.

D STIESSEN: Do you? Do you enjoy that?

M'D HASSE: Well. Sometimes. That's how I meet people, at parties. People see me with my father, so they think, Oh, she must be okay.

D STIESSEN: Do you ever go out of town?

M'D HASSE: For what?

D STIESSEN: I don't know. I thought, maybe with Mr. Hasse, he might take you along on his trips.

M'D HASSE: Not really. Mom and I, we stay home most of the time. But we're always here in case someone needs us.

D STIESSEN: That must be nice for your father.

M'D HASSE: Oh, it is. And there's plenty to do here. I read a lot.

D STIESSEN: Are you a student?

M'D HASSE: Ha! Isn't that the same thing as asking a woman her age?

D STIESSEN: I don't know. I just thought that since Mr. Hasse was such a big supporter of the local universities, you might also . . . But, you don't?

M'D HASSE: Well, hmmm. Not to be crude, but I have no desire to do that. No. Some people I do not wish to see. We have a nice little town here. I like things right where they are.

D STIESSEN: You don't think you'd get along with the other students?

M'D HASSE: I don't know. You were a student once, weren't you?

D STIESSEN: Well, yeah, I guess.

M'D HASSE: I think I'd get along with you. You look

like you probably have a whole lot of interesting
things to say.

D STIESSEN: Really? I don't know if that's true or
not.

M'D HASSE: Daddy tells me you wrote a book.

D STIESSEN: Oh, it's nothing. I honestly think he's
getting his hopes up too high. It's just a little
thing I wrote about my father.

M'D HASSE: Well, if you wrote it, I'm sure it's very
good. Do you think a lot of people would want to
read it?

D STIESSEN: I don't know much about how the business
works. Maybe Mr. Hasse can give me some pointers.
I don't even know why I wrote it. I just figured
everyone's got a father. And most people probably
have the same questions I have. Who is this guy
who goes off to work every day, and then comes
back home and goes to bed? And then, because of
the way things usually work out, lots of times,
when you reach the age where you could actually
have a real conversation with him, well, by then
it's too late because he's probably, you know, no
longer available . . . for questions.

M'D HASSE: How much do you think you'd sell this book
for? ·

D STIESSEN: Oh, wow. I have no idea. I think probably
someone else would make that decision.

M'D HASSE: Ten dollars?

D STIESSEN: That seems a little high.

M'D HASSE: Not if you put it out in hardcover first.
You could charge ten dollars for the hardcover
version, and then bring it out again in
paperback, but for less money.

D STIESSEN: Yeah, I guess that's how they do it.

M'D HASSE: Not that I know. I'm just guessing. I
don't know anything about it. My father owns a

lot of books, two whole rooms full, but they
don't have the prices on them because they're all
old.

D STIESSEN: What kind of books do you like to read?

M'D HASSE: Just whatever we happen to have in the
house. My father, as you can imagine, has quite a
collection. Publishing is a huge business. You
should get into *that*. The books he has, they're
just for show. I mean, you don't have to read
them, they're just there because they're old. I
don't know anything about it, but it just makes
sense that when things get older, they get more
and more valuable, until eventually they're worth
so much that most people could never even dream
of buying them, and that's when they're
considered priceless, which doesn't mean that
they're not worth anything, it's just the word
that people use to describe things that are
really valuable. That's just what I've heard. I
don't know anything about what I just said.

D STIESSEN: That's really interesting.

M'D HASSE: It is! Oh, I just love books. I pick one
up and look at it, then I go on to the next one.
Sometimes I like romances, because my mom reads
them too, and we can get together and talk about
the ones we both read, "Oh, I liked this one,"
"Oh, this one wasn't so good." The best ones
always take place a long time ago, in a far-off
land, or maybe with people different than the
ones here in Hedgemont Heights. Even the
coloreds, the slave-ship romances, because when
you read about their struggles and how they breed
and sometimes fall in love with the man who runs
the plantation, then you can get a sense of what
these people are really like. I like to learn
about all sorts of different people. Coloreds—oh,

and also the Indian books, those ones are really
exciting! I probably sound like a real idiot,
don't I?

D STIESSEN: No, of course not. I think it's good that
you're interested in . . . a variety of things.

M'D HASSE: I'd really like to read your book. I bet
you could sell it for fifteen dollars, even.

D STIESSEN: Well, we'll see. That'd sure be nice.

M'D HASSE: Would you like to see the library?

D STIESSEN: Oh yeah! That'd be swell!

M'D HASSE: I'll take you inside. Don't be shocked by
all the Mother Marys lying around. My parents,
they're not originally from America. When they
first came over, they really got into religion in
a big way.

D STIESSEN: Yeah, well, that sometimes happens with
people.

M'D HASSE: That's how I got my name, obviously.

D STIESSEN: Donna?

M'D HASSE: It's actually Madonna, but I changed it
when I got my driver's license. Madonna always
makes me feel like a statue, like someone who's
already dead. Not like a real person, y'know?

D STIESSEN: I think it's beautiful. It's unique.

M'D HASSE: No, you're just saying that because you're
a gentleman. And anyway, you're not to call me
that. Donna will do just fine.

D STIESSEN: All right then. Donna it is, and Derek
for me.

M'D HASSE: Donna and Derek. My, aren't we getting
along nicely! Here, I'll show you the library in
a minute. Let's go upstairs.

The Favorite Scarf

1980

The scarf was not one of Derek's favorites. Thinking it over, Donna realized that her husband did not really have a favorite scarf. This was wrong, she felt. A man should have a certain scarf that he values over the rest. This is what it means to be an adult. To cherish things. A treasured set of mittens. An old slicker. Derek did not appreciate the importance of objects. Walking the floors of their three-level apartment in North Crane City, his eyes would dance and hover over the furniture, not seeing, not caring. Donna sometimes imagined the inverted reflections of stock figures creeping over the lenses of his reading glasses. Derek had that look, the look of a man forever watching prices rise and fall.

So, lacking a preference of his own, Derek generally left such decisions to his wife. This was fine with her. She enjoyed dressing her man. Whenever she saw his picture in bookstores and airport terminals, it made her happy to know that she had picked out his clothes herself, and could go right upstairs and pull the same shirt out of the closet, while the other women could only stare at the facsimile, the $2.99 imitation in their hands. With loving eyes, she inspected the cover of his latest publication. *If I Say You Can Do It—You Can Do It!* Such long titles. Well, that was the business. She remembered the picture on the back jacket. She had chosen the tie that morning—another sleepy nine a.m. photo session. Rooting through the closet, she said, "Derek, you wear the yellow one." Derek held out his hand and took it from her.

So this was Derek's favorite scarf. She'd found it under a pile of junk in the basement—old college textbooks, ice skates, unfamiliar boxes that seemed to originate from a previous owner. Couples and their garbage. The Skyes had been married for seven years. Their apartment was too small and soon they would have to move. She missed her old home in the suburbs. Nothing against the minorities, but there were too many of them. Still, she was certain that she'd never go back to Hedgemont Heights. The business would win, as it always did. This was best for everyone. In a roundabout way, she was very happy.

Donna wadded the scarf and hurried upstairs. Derek would need his favorite scarf. *He would appreciate this thing she had done for him.* Swiping up her car keys, she glanced down at the kitchen counter, where a book of note paper sat near the telephone. For Derek's thirty-third birthday, she'd purchased an expensive answering machine, though she normally turned it off during the day because her father did not approve of it. Bartholomew Hasse did not approve of a lot of things. He believed all telephone conversations should remain the personal property of the party placing the call. He believed that once a voice was committed to tape, it could never be removed, no matter how many times you recorded over the original track. Thinking it over, Donna relented and agreed to use the machine only at night. Mr. Hasse regularly contacted his daughter in the morning, when Derek was out of the house. Since his requests sometimes crossed the line of what a disinterested third party might consider prudent, she was willing to keep their conversations a secret.

The drive to the convention center was short, just a few blocks down River Street and then north through the commercial district, where the road ran a tight course between buildings. Donna generally stayed away from her husband's lectures. In many ways, they led separate lives. Her friends, in general, were not his friends. Hers were mostly old high-school acquaintances, but as Donna was not yet thirty, she supposed that this was not so unusual. Few of these women had ever lived outside of Hedgemont Heights, and they all thought her quite brave for staying in the city. She tolerated their admiration, shrugging off questions about pickpockets and curbside parking. It was their pity she could not stand. Her friends all had children, and she did not. Their husbands, like their fathers before them, were all successful in a harmlessly anonymous sort of way. They were lawyers and surgeons and advertising executives, and no one out in the great world beyond gave a damn about what they said or did. They were competent functionaries: dependable, loving, accepted by their peers. Derek was a superstar. He traveled ten months out of the year, and made regular appearances on the Johnny Carson show, and once an apparently demented woman sent him a refrigerated parcel in the mail, and inside the box was a glass tube containing her most recent ovulation, along with a note reading: PLEASE DEREK SKYE IF YOU COULD JUST FERTILIZE THE CONTENTS OF THIS TUBE WITH YOUR SEED AND KINDLY SEND IT BACK TO ME SO THAT I MAY PLACE IT INSIDE MY UTERUS DEREK SKYE I WANT TO BEAR YOUR CHILDREN AND I PROMISE NOT TO DISTURB YOU AGAIN NOR WILL I EVER ASK YOU FOR MONEY!! Derek did not have many friends. He had agents, admirers, handlers, contacts, accountants, partners, advisors, secretaries and drivers. And one wife. This made Donna feel very special. She craved the power of the definite article.

A well-behaved mob jammed the lobby of the convention center, filing in awkward clumps through the revolving doors. A black maintenance man with a pear-shaped afro and wiry sideburns stood smoking near the entrance. Hiding her purse under her jacket, Donna asked for directions to the Derek Skye Action for Life Seminar and Hot Lunch Buffet. Tossing his cigarette into a bucket of mop water, the man pointed at the escalator and said, "Well, you gonna wawna ride up to the fourth flow-uh, 'n' then you gonna wawna make a right turn, past s'cur'ty, 'n' then you gonna wawna open a door, mark Conference Room T, 'n' then you're all set." She smiled, marveling at this other language.

Pushing through the crowd on the fourth floor, she stared at the mob of young women who had turned up to hear her husband speak. During the first years of their marriage, she'd never questioned Derek's loyalty. There were temptations, yes, but he was faithful and that was the end of it. Something else bothered her about these people. Why couldn't they appreciate their many blessings? Life in the United States was good enough. Donna knew from her own experience that things could only get so bad. She had a solid man, a safe home, a decent upbringing and many more years left to live. These women all had children and she did not, yet she loved her marriage even as the months went by with more blood and no babies. So what was *their* problem?

"You look like you come alone, like me."

A middle-aged groupie emerged from the crowd, holding a half-crumpled box of Pop-Tarts. Stepping sideways, she blocked Donna's path with her body. "I told my husband, it's for our own good. You come or you don't, either way." Pleased with herself, she pushed an unbaked Pop-Tart into her mouth.

"You must be here for the couples retreat," Donna said. Pressed up against the edge of the balcony, she looked down at the mass of men and women streaming up the escalator. Patient, hopeful faces, fresh from the fights.

"Only one left!" the woman bragged, thumping her chest. "I done all the rest. I was at the one they had last winter. They give you a rock, say 'Break it.'"

"Oh, I know that one. It's not really a rock."

"It's not really a rock. And then they give you the booklet. Check, check, check. I told the man, 'I can't do this sort of thing.' They don't care, they'll throw you right in."

"I guess I've never seen the one with the booklet," Donna said in a soft, halting voice. The booklet. Derek's idea. Standing beside this proud fanatic, she felt oddly at a loss. Tell me about my husband, she wanted to say. What's he really like?

"Give you a booklet," the woman repeated as they crossed the reception area. "You get a check for every person you say hello to. They check it themselves, so they know you ain't cheating. They're real disciplinarians about it."

By this time, they'd reached the front of the crowd, where a line of guards kept the people from storming into the auditorium. Near the door, a woman carried a hand-drawn poster: Derek the Great, rendered in neon Magic Marker. Donna recognized the man in the picture. Everything matched up—his mustache, his deep-set eyes. Yet this was not her husband. This was a totem, a satanic Kewpie doll. And these women had stolen him, taken his spirit and projected it as something garish and candy-colored. The real Derek was dark, covered with bruises. She'd held the real thing, held his soft, leather-burnished genitals in her hand, and they were not orange or purple or shocking pink; they were his own color, Derek-dark, the color of their strange marriage.

"I hope these meetings are helpful," she said, taking her eyes away from the picture.

The woman frowned; her lips were gummy with jam. "They're helpful if you keep coming back and buying the books, and then you gotta get the tapes. I got 'em all. I listen to 'em sometimes when I'm outside, doing things. I stand out by the garage, make sure the neighbor kids don't jump on the roof or nothing. That's when I listen to 'em. It's like watching two birds with one stone, or whatever."

"I've heard the tapes. The man has a beautiful voice."

Saying this, Donna remembered her husband's voice. Smooth. A practiced cool. *Honey, help me with this.* Derek and his speeches. *Here, get me a glass of water. I can't speak when my throat's dry.* She smiled. She wanted to be near him. She wanted to run her fingers along the hard veins on the backs of his hands. She wanted him to be perfectly quiet while she did this.

"They're okay." The woman popped a fresh tart into her mouth. "I get my health care to pay for 'em. Hell, yeah! My husband thinks it's wrong, he thinks I'm pulling a fast one. He was out two years on a broken cheekbone, this ain't no different."

Donna gave the woman a strange look. *My husband,* she thought. Sneaking away, she felt the urge to proclaim herself, to stand apart from the rest of these lonely and desperate people. Just ahead, she saw a young couple purchasing two cups of soda from a concession stand. Coming closer, she smiled and offered her hand. "Hi there, I'm Donna Skye. I'd like to thank you for coming to my husband's lecture."

The young woman nodded, still holding both sodas. Her body was long and thin, like a flame drawn toward the ceiling. Her partner was less thin, less handsome; his neatly trimmed beard was a bad choice, aesthetically speaking, and his blue eyes gleamed tentatively, as if waiting for someone to take his picture.

"Wow . . . wee." He looked around, feeling cocky. "Boy, they know how to treat you right around here, unh?"

"Steve, take your drink." The woman nudged him in the gut with one of the cups, spilling a little on his shirt.

"Door-to-door service."

"Steve, she's trying to be polite, so why don't you take your drink, before it gets on my vest."

"Oh, right." The man took the cup and absently set it on the counter. "I'm Steve Mould, ma'am. Hi there." He started forward with his hand, then, catching himself, made a fist.

Donna laughed. "Hi, Steve."

"And this is my fiancée, Lydia."

"Very nice to meet you." Lydia curtseyed with her head.

"Okay, hi."

"Wow and double wow." Steve's barrel chest swelled with a contented sigh.

"When I saw you two together, I figured you were newlyweds. I guess I wasn't too far off."

"Steve"—Lydia spoke out of the corner of her mouth—"don't leave your drink on the table."

"Oops!" He reached for the cup. "Sorry 'bout that."

"We're going through the early stages," she added, winking at Donna. "I'm systematically rebuilding his brain from the ground up."

Steve smiled thickly as the others laughed at him. Donna liked this woman. She admired the way she seemed to steer her man from one thing to another, guiding him with a sure hand. Donna wondered what Derek would do if she tried that technique with him. *Honey, stop. Just leave the glass where it is.*

"It takes awhile," she said. "Derek and I were a little shaky at first, but we got used to it." Yes, the early years. Hard times for newlyweds. Derek and Daddy on the verandah. Nice gray suits. Open briefcases, papers fluttering in the wind. Donna sitting behind the closed French doors, bouncing a plastic birdie on a racket. Derek's knuckles on the glass: *How you doing in there, kid?*

The sound of the convention center filled her ears—a rush of present noise. Steve was saying, "With a fella like that, he's gotta be making a quarter-mil easy."

"Steve. Don't be rude."

"It's not rude. I'm saying he's doing great. What's rude about that?"

"It's the kind of thing that people don't talk about."

"Doggone."

"Well, it's okay." Donna smiled, her voice descending a short scale.

"I should be so lucky to shine the man's shoes with my tongue."

The mob near the entrance scuttled back out into the waiting area as a lone usher opened the huge double doors.

"Looks like the line's moving." Donna glanced over the crowd. "I'll let you folks get a seat. But don't you forget, now, we've got a couples' cruise coming up in the fall."

"Oh, yeah?" Steve scratched his beard, casually considering the ramifications. "I think I can find some time off."

Lydia yanked his hand away from his face. "Steve, if my mother finds out you've been blowing our money on expensive cruises, she'll take back that allowance so fast you'll never pee straight again."

"Well, I just won't tell her then, what do you think about that?" Bright eyes. "This is my family, my business. I'll do whatever the heck I want to. Enough of this noise." Turning to Donna, he said, "If there's any way, ma'am, I'd really like to meet Mr. Skye."

"Steve." Lydia moistened her fingers and dabbed at his forehead. "Your hair."

"I know that's a lot to ask."

"Your hair's sticking straight up."

"I don't know if he works that way. I mean, I know they do it with the pope sometimes, if someone just wants to speak with him in private."

"Your hair. Hold still. You look like a homeless person."

"An audience, they call it. That's what you get with the pope."

"It's not that formal." Donna opened and closed her jacket, fanning her face. "He's a very nice man."

"I think I'd make a good impression. I'm just out of college, see, and I'm really interested in work and . . . work-related activities."

"That's great." She hesitated, seeing her husband's stern face. You said *what*? "I don't know if he can help you out with that."

"I mean, I'll do whatever it takes. I've got skills like all get out. You betcha."

"Honey, you look like a raving lunatic." Lydia brushed his scalp with her fingers. "Where's my comb? People will think you're demented."

Bored already, Donna began to drift away from the couple. "I'll see if he can spare a minute or two," she said. Waving goodbye, she snuck through the crowd and followed an escort down a ramp to the backstage door. A fat woman dressed in tight dungarees stood just inside the entrance, swinging a flashlight, casting a bright arc across the carbon-black wall. Donna blinked as she moved toward another beam, then another, lights swaying like a team of illuminated pendulums, wildfires leading her to him. Opening the door to an unmarked dressing room, she found her husband alone, reviewing the words of his speech. He stepped away from the mirror. "Honey."

"I brought you your scarf," she said, drawing it out of her pocket.

Stark lights hid Derek's dark eyes under a heavy shadow. His nervous hands ran across the countertop, finding a bottle of prescription pills. "I'd rather have some warmer weather." He twisted the bottle open. "Think you can help me out?"

"What?"

Disappointed, he wadded his tongue against his lower lip. "Never mind. It was a joke. You didn't get it."

"Tell me."

"I was saying, if you could . . . change . . . the weather. Oh, I don't want to be here. I *don't* want to be here." Leaning away from the mirror, he blinked at his own tired reflection.

"So, come home with me."

He looked over his shoulder. "You know I can't do that," he said. "The promoter is squeezing me for everything I've got, and don't tell anyone I said that."

This was what she loved about her husband—his bitterness. The rest of the world knew the man's easy side, but the darkness belonged to her alone. Drawn to it, she stepped across the room and pressed the scarf against his cheek.

He backed away. "Don't," he said. "That thing's filthy."

Donna laughed, then squeezed the scarf and held it in her fist. "How did this get so wrinkled?" she asked, touching his sports jacket. It looked old and out of style, something a college professor might wear.

"It was my father's. He wore it around the house. Like Glenn Gould. With the hat and the long coat. Even in the summertime."

"Which one is Glenn Gould?" she asked, thinking, *Personal assistant? Legal secretary?*

"He's a piano player," Derek snapped. "Look, do me a favor. Take a quarter, there's a soda machine at the end of the hall, can you get me a Canada Dry? Just a Canada Dry, nothing else. I don't think my throat's going to make it." He gave her a coin and slumped against a post in the middle of the room, already exhausted.

Donna's fingers closed around the quarter. She repeated the words to herself—*Canada Dry*—and left the room. Out in the hallway, she found the soda machine and dropped her money into the slot. A motor inside the machine grunted, pumping freon in and out of the refrigeration unit. Smiling, she pressed the button marked Sprite, then pulled the cold can from the base of the machine. It opened with a satisfying *crack*—metal shearing metal.

Break

1989

After sixteen years of marriage, Derek and Donna had finally decided (he'd decided and she'd gone along with it) to move out of Crane City. Big Dipper Township offered every luxury Derek had denied himself until now: clean country living, a huge house on the water, no neighbors, a decent school system (not that it mattered anymore). To Bartholomew Hasse, the decision represented much more than that. Derek had no idea what he was getting into. Kay Tree lived nearby; not Kay herself, but Kay's daughter, and that was bad enough. The battle between the old and the new had started to shift. By the end of the decade, he'd seen the Internet grow from a small, academic enterprise to something more pervasive, more tied to the world economy. The federal government was interested. And now Derek! This was a betrayal. Trapped in Hedgemont Heights, he needed a new acolyte.

Whenever they'd discussed it—Derek sitting on one end of the dining table, Donna and her father on the other—the same issue always came up. Derek had received an offer from the Gloria Corporation to conduct a series of lectures—the usual corporate rah-rah he'd been dishing out since the seventies. Drunk on three glasses of wine, he snarled, "Gimme a break, Bart. I could care less about the GC. I'm just trying to do a little consulting work."

Bartholomew kept silent as Donna argued on his behalf. "My father has given you so much," she said, glaring at her husband. They'd all dressed up for dinner; with her thick brown hair stacked high, a pair of pearl earrings dangling from her chewy little earlobes, she looked privileged, easy to damage. "You owe him everything. Your career. Me."

Derek zeroed in on his wife; he'd hardly touched his lamb steak, which was served in a fancy green pesto sauce by Bartholomew's live-in cook. "You agreed that the move would be good for us. Do you think that I don't care about our marriage?"

"No, Derek, I don't think that." She was crying again. *Tactics,* thought Derek. *Ignore it.*

"Well, all right then." Satisfied, he went back to his dinner. Between bites, he pointed at the old man with his knife. "I won't let this guy ruin everything. We'll go to the country. He can't hurt us there. He's too old to make the drive."

Bartholomew smiled at Derek's bluster, at the pigheadedness of it all. Big Dipper Township was only an hour away, and the Hasse family had many servants. Chauffeurs. Messengers. Strongarms. Then there was Donna. She would be faithful. She would not forget her old home. Bartholomew might have kept her sheltered in her youth, but at least he'd made her take driving lessons. *You never know when you might not have a man to depend on,* he once told her, thinking mainly of himself.

"We won't talk about it anymore," Derek said. He ate aggressively, chewing with his mouth open. "We're moving. And tomorrow morning I'm going to call those people up at the Gloria Corporation, and I'm going to take that contract."

Finished with his dinner, Bartholomew folded his napkin and left it on the table. This kind of nasty chatter had been going on for months now. There was no point in talking anymore. He'd already made his decision. The Hasses were a family of craftsmen. They'd built their legacy out of print and paper, going all the way back to the time of Gutenberg—five centuries' worth of profit and protest and inky hands. That line would not be sold out to an invisible organization bent on dismantling the great tradition with their elusive grid of fiber optics and subterranean pipelines. Nothing would change. Information would remain something physical, something you could *touch*. Bartholomew would see to it.

IV

Another Not-Very-Good Marriage

The Tree with
Four Trunks

1998

When the folks from Gloria presented Derek with the pin back in 1989, his first thought was, Hmmm, well, attractive, but what is it? He could never understand the logic behind these corporate logos. He remembered the Lake Charles Human Resources Center from whatever year it was, seventy-something. Those were the folks who'd tried to make a fortune renting out physical-fitness trainers to oil companies and the like. Modeled after the old Japanese business notion—you know, the company that works out together works well together. Didn't fly in America. Anyway, Derek got some good money out of them for a few years; in fact, they were his first really big contract, not counting the few local engagements he'd managed to book through his father-in-law. He could still remember their logo, a massive torso bench-pressing a skyscraper with each hand. What was their slogan? *Get a lift out of your business? Move your butt, not your bottom line?* No, it was the whole *We Can Work It Out* concept, with the Beatles tune as the tie-in. Not a bad idea—would've worked if they'd spent a little more time shoring up their resources, then waited another year to go public. But the Gloria insignia was different. It wasn't abstract. It was too intricate, too strange for symbolism. This object existed somewhere in the world.

A tree, that's what it was. The fella from Gloria told him it was an elm and Derek took his word for it. Fan-shaped leaves grew together in a bunch: could've been anything—a maple, an oak . . . hell, even a cactus. What Derek noticed—what he was *meant* to notice, clearly—was the trunk. Trunks. Four of 'em. Almost like a Masonic emblem. Staring at the pin on this September afternoon in Big Dipper Township, he wondered if he'd joined a business or a brotherhood.

Come to think of it, those endless battalions of Gloria liaisons *had* been rather persistent about persuading him to honor his final commitments. He'd been firm about saying no, but they'd been equally firm about sending progressively higher-placed representatives south from Ann Arbor to convince him not to quit the gig so thoughtlessly. Derek was a legend in the business. No one liked to see him go. Still, no amount of money was worth the pain he felt every time he hosted an employee retreat or kicked off another three-day motivational weekend. All those faces looking up at him, their mouths forming desperate phrases, Heal us, Make us whole. The freaks of the world would just have to understand. Having left his wife, Derek now imagined long trips, sudden disappearances. So typical, the wayward husband who heads north to the Yukon, never to be heard from again.

This was probably the best solution overall, this tiny flat, still within screaming distance of his old house. The smallness of the place appealed to him. The spartan environment would help him to focus on the new book. He would keep the walls bare as well; the diplomas and honorary degrees would stay in their boxes. The books, too—thirty-eight of them, ranging from the 1973 first edition of *The Father and the Son*, all the way up to the latest compilation, *The Skye's the Limit*, dreadful thing, all rehashed junk from Derek's mid-eighties heyday. Remember *How Do I Like Me Now?* Oh, and what about *Why Does It Hurt When I Do This? . . . Don't Do That!*, or *Love, Hope, and Twelve Other Really Big Words?* A thick cardboard box, sealed once with staples and again with masking tape, would hide them all. That alone would solve half of Derek's problems. The other half was another issue. Modern technology was making it hard for a man to walk out on his wife. Whether he traveled to Tibet or just two blocks down the road, Donna would find him. Magnanimous in his betrayal, Derek hoped that by staying in town, he might at least save her a few bucks on the long-distance bill. He could do that much for the poor girl.

"That I had to find out from Reggie Bergman. This is what pisses me off, Derek."

"You could have just dialed my publisher. I've got the same listing."

"Oh, you know I never call those people."

"Well, that's your problem, not mine."

Derek held the receiver against his chin as he shuttled dishes from the study to the kitchen. The telephone cord snarled and kinked around the jack; Donna's voice crackled with every shake of the loose connection.

"There are some things that Reggie Bergman doesn't need to know."

"What, that I'm here two days and you're already getting me on the phone? This is not secret information, Donna. This is something Reggie could've worked out on his own."

"You're turning him against me, aren't you?"

"He's my agent. He has nothing to do with you."

"Friends for how many years? How many dinners have I supervised? Menus planned, seating arrangements . . . the seating arrangements alone, I've spent a year of my life figuring out where to put Reggie at the table."

"Yes, I'm a horrible person. I owe you everything, Donna, I really do. My career, the house. Even my bad attitude."

"Don't say those things."

A plastic teacup fell from his arms and bounced without breaking against the floor. The cup was part of a child's play set needlessly purchased in the optimistic summer of 1983; not wishing to deprive Donna of her good china, Derek had assembled his kitchenware out of such odds and ends.

"Don't say what things?"

"Don't say those things in that tone of voice."

Giving up with the dishes, Derek focused on getting off the phone. To him, his voice sounded steady and reasonably self-possessed. To her, it sounded cold, premeditated: his television voice, she once would have said with love in her eyes.

"So what you object to is my tone, my sarcasm. The fact that I'm actually trying to be serious doesn't matter."

"You're so sure of yourself. So sure this is what you want."

"I'm not, honey. I'm not sure of anything. This is something I never planned for. Feeling this way. Feeling apart from you. Looking at you and wanting to go away."

"You're killing me."

"Yeah. That might be what I'm doing. I don't know, Donna. I don't feel like I can talk to you about it. Not for a while, anyway."

"When, then? I'll be forty-eight years old in a week. I'm just supposed to sit here and stare out the goddamn window?"

"I'm trying to think of something profound to say. It's not coming."

"It's all got to be on your time, doesn't it?"

Donna wandered across the brick patio, pacing a crooked line between the beach and the back of the house. The reception on her cell phone sounded clearer out here than it did indoors.

"Donna, it's like this. I'm in a position where if I say one thing, you're going to think, 'There, he doesn't know what he's talking about,' but if I try to explain it, then it's going to sound like—"

"I don't care what it sounds—"

"—like I'm so noble, I'm doing the noble thing, and this is just because I don't want to hurt you."

"There's something wrong with saying I love you?"

"Yes, there is. In this situation it's very counterproductive. This is where we are, I'm not going to renege, I'm not going to rationalize it or ask for your pity because I don't want it. It's just . . . I did what I did and it's over and I'm not going to give you any more ammunition to fire back at me."

"You made a commitment when you married me."

"Yes, I did."

"You made me give up my entire life, and now, at this late stage, I'm not equipped to start over and suddenly be an independent woman."

"Jesus, Donna, you make it sound like you're two years old."

Donna continued down to the edge of the water. The loose sand under her feet was hard to walk on, and she was wearing the wrong shoes for it.

"This is our world, Derek. Couples! All our friends are married, they all have kids—which is another thing you couldn't do—and now you want me to face that whole nightmare by myself. The divorcée. There she goes."

"It's been done before."

"Not by me it hasn't. I want my family back!"

"Good God. Did I do this to you? I never would've married you if I thought you'd become so goddamned *clingy*."

"You never would've married me if it wasn't for my father, and you know it. I was the big prize, part of the arrangement, and I'd like to think that over time we grew to love each other, but I guess I'm wrong."

"You're not wrong. I love you desperately, Donna, and I want you to drop off the face of the earth."

The line went dead. Donna sat for a minute, shoveling the sand into little humps with the heel of the telephone. She imagined Derek trapped inside the receiver, a snared beast. Carried away, she saw herself lofting the phone into the water, Derek sinking to the bottom, naked and huddled against the flood, braids of colored wires hanging from the walls of the chamber, water rushing through the perforated mesh, round holes, portals, gushing shafts of foam. Catching herself, she tugged on the antenna and pressed a button marked LT. The phone rang once, then chirped and picked up.

"Donna, sweetheart," Lydia said, once she'd finished hearing her friend out. "Here's what you do. Let me hand off my list of activities. We'll split it up. You do half and I'll do half. You'll feel a lot better."

"I don't want to do all that. Actually, right now I feel like bringing a bottle of wine upstairs and sitting in the bathtub all night."

"Don't start drinking. Worst thing you can do. Activity. We'll have lunch. Tomorrow."

"That sounds nice. But not in town. Let's drive down to Vega. He'll walk in and I'll lose my appetite."

Lydia hated hearing Donna whine like that. That's all it was: whining. Everything Lydia said, there was a purpose, a clear statement of intent. You obeyed, you didn't obey, that was up to you. Call it her Washington upbringing—this need to dart in precisely defined directions. From her mother, she'd inherited a certain impatience for womanly virtues; Kay *mattered* in a way that most women did not.

Driving along a straight country road, Lydia conducted herself with a mechanized efficiency, each limb doing its own thing. Neither hand touched the wheel as she reached over to flip through the pages of the script in Simon's lap. The script was heavily annotated with instructions scribbled in Lydia's own hand, directions to slow down and enunciate. Simon's mouth moved, skimming the words.

"Your husband—let me say it, darling—your husband is a bastard."

"I can't believe that."

"I don't even know if it's true. It's just a thing to say. He's gone, he's a bastard. That's just the way you're going to have to look at it from now on. Otherwise, what? You're sitting there in love with a man who doesn't care."

"You really think he doesn't care?"

Lydia sighed, flipping back to the beginning of the play. The sound the pages made reminded Simon of stage wind—the director standing between two curtains, waving a bright sheet of aluminum, his face conveying a look of terror, willing emotion to the kids in the chorus. Eyes dark and empty, he stared at the script as the car shot over the expressway. The monologue was about a fifteen-year-old delinquent growing up in Tennessee in the 1870s. *Having lost two brothers in the Civil War, the character considers his love for Rachel McCree, the alchemist's daughter.* Interpreting the lines, Simon decided to use his dumb voice.

"Look," said Lydia, "you need the speech. I need to give you the speech."

"What's the speech?"

"The speech is not for the phone. The speech is for one-on-one only. Tomorrow. Until then, I've got to go. You wouldn't believe."

"Lydia, I envy you. Your beautiful son."

"My beautiful son is sitting right next to me and he's learning his audition piece, and I swear to you, Donna, if he doesn't get a callback this time, I've already got an open letter to the town council all typed out and you can look for it on the front page."

"God. See, that's what I mean. You're so committed to Simon's well-being."

"Shit, we're in the parking lot and he hasn't even done his makeup yet. Goddamnit! Donna, I'm hanging up."

"Tomorrow, at—"

"Gotta go!"

Lydia parked in front of a giant, lozenge-shaped structure of steel and reinforced concrete. There were no other buildings around, only brown fields and a long, straight road running east to the highway. Hatchbacks and station wagons waited in the lot, with empty spaces left in between, as if their owners were suspicious or afraid of each other. Lydia dropped the phone and a mess of keys into her purse and rolled out of the driver's seat. Simon followed his mother past the other cars, leaving fuzzy handprints on the hot metal and glass. She glanced up at the building—

klutzy fifties architecture, orange and mint-blue paneling, paper-doll chains taped to the windows. Amateurs, she thought, shaking her head. No one respected the glory of the theater anymore.

About thirty kids had showed up for the auditions. The high turnout was understandable, given the rumors of talent scouts from Hollywood, each tale prompting visions of instant, catch-free success. A large basement room served as the rehearsal site, a dark place with varnished walls and a hard green carpet poorly glued to the cement floor. Lydia stepped on the boy's heels, steering him by the shoulders, showing off all the angles. The other mothers frowned at her, and she returned the look. She went way back with these people, and for the most part the relationship had not been a happy one. If they objected to her assertive tactics, it was only because they were not aware how much was riding on her son's success. How could they be? They were provincials, strictly small-time. Even the director was little more than a third-string hack. Peter Wayne Zachary: yeah, there's a name to remember. Barely thirty, he was—in Lydia's opinion—far too young for the job, although his quite blatant homosexuality did have a certain risqué charm. It angered her, how he encouraged even the most inept of her son's rivals, those Hedgemont Heights brats who compulsively auditioned for everything in the tricounty area, their résumés designed by a team of professional consultants. The mothers were the worst. Jewish bitches in pantsuits of black cashmere. Glorified whores drowning in their own sense of entitlement. They, like the director, did not respect Simon's unique gifts. His look was too eccentric, his delivery too distinct. There were only a few people in the business whose talents matched Simon's own. Sydney Pollack, maybe. The guy who did *Rain Man*. But not this Fuck.

"*'I'll run away from here.'*" Simon stood in front of the director as the other kids waited their turns—stiff shoulders, feet splayed in first and third. "*'I'll go someplace where they ain't never gonna find me.* He cries.'"

"Simon, I hate to interrupt—you're really doing a super job—but where it says 'He cries'? You don't need to say that."

"I don't?"

"No, that's something else. We'll work on that later."

"Well, then, how do I know—"

"Well, do you see those little bendy lines, right where the sentence starts? Those are called parentheses—"

"Will you let him get on with the piece?" Lydia produced an unlit cigarette from her sleeve and thrust it in the director's face. "It's his interpretation of the material, and you've no right to question him on it."

"Lydia, I'm just trying to help the kid out here."

"No, what you're doing is you're humiliating him in front of the other children, and that's discriminatory and I'm not going to stand for it."

"You're—I'm sorry, you're right . . . Simon dear?"

"Simon, continue with your reading."

"Yes, please do. It's perfection personified."

Lydia continued to stare at Zachary even as her son resumed his performance. Seen through the lenses of his glasses, the director's wandering eyes seemed without anchor, like two fighting fish caged in neighboring tanks.

"'*They say Mack Winslow is hiring gunners for a new run out west.* Thumps his chest with the palm of his hand. *I could do that. I ain't too young.* Crosses to dee ess ell and points at the audience.'"

"Oh my my."

"'*It's a new world. This country just gets bigger and bigger every day.* Spits.'"

"Connie, can you get me a soda from the machine?"

Lydia snapped her fingers, breaking the cigarette in half. Sensing a scene, the other children looked up from their scripts—a vapid pose, old toys with the batteries worn down, frozen in stupid positions. One child, wanting to make a special impression, had worn a cowboy hat and tin spurs; a rawhide strap, knotted at the chin, clutched at the boy's throat.

"Mr. Zachary, may I speak to you in private?"

"Well, by all means, that's my job, that's what I'm here for. Connie? Never mind about the soda—will you stay here and take notes on little Simon's sterling performance?"

"What do I—"

"You, Simon, just give your lines to the nice lady in the blue pants while I go out and have a chat with Mummy."

"Starting with . . . here?"

"Yes, starting right there where it says, 'Printed on one hundred percent recycled material.'"

"That's quite enough, Mr. Zachary."

"And be sure to read every single word."

"Simon, we'll be right back."

"Every word is vital to the meaning of the play."

Lydia held the door open for the director, a nasty little dig. In this town, life between adults worked on a point system: one for me, none for you. Moving into the hallway, Zachary hid his hands under the folds of his sweater. His posture was bad; pissed, he slouched against the wall. "What, shall we go upstairs? We can discuss this in my office."

"Now listen," Lydia hissed, "you know as well as I do exactly what's going on here, and it's going to stop, and it's going to stop this minute unless you want this whole thing to blow up right in your face."

"First of all, I want to know what gives you the right to come in here and sabotage my auditions? I have a whole roomful of kids out there waiting to go on, and we've already spent five minutes indulging your pathetic little fantasy."

"You've been nothing but rude to that boy since the moment we arrived, and I don't know what your hidden agenda may or may not be, but I do know that my child is on the verge of tears and I won't tolerate it any longer!"

"Good, maybe he's finally getting into character, instead of saying 'He cries' every time—"

"Why must you be so nasty to us?"

"Because your son has no talent for the stage, and he's a terrible waste of my time!"

Lydia smiled as she gazed down at the floor, finding humor in the ratty tassels of the man's loafers. "That's what they always say to the best ones, before they're discovered. Before they're appreciated for what they are. Then they all come slinking back with their hands out."

"Yes, well . . . I have news for you, Lydia. They sometimes say it because it's true."

"Look, you fucking queen—"

"Oh, *aren't* we just the biggest bitch of all time?"

"We are skating ever closer to lawsuit land, Mr. Zachary. I suggest that you revise your ways."

The director opened his mouth to speak, but nothing came out. The sounds of an afternoon ballet class practicing in an upstairs studio shuffled across the low ceiling.

"All right." Lifting his glasses, he rubbed the sore bridge of his nose.

"Okay, Lydia. I'll tell you what I'll do. If you promise to shut up and accept my final judgment, I'll pass Simon on to the second round at five. Now, I won't guarantee he'll get the part. I am still the director here."

"That's understood, Mr. Zachary. I'm not looking for trouble."

"All right, then. But I will say one thing. I'm doing this entirely to appease you. I conduct my auditions fairly and without bias. Every child gets an equal chance, and because you've forced me to make an exception for your son, another young boy will have to go home disappointed."

Lydia opened the door to the rehearsal room. Her son's voice came back to her as a thing both awesome and in need of protection. "The only boy I care about is Simon Tree-Mould."

"'Someday I'll come back and show them all—'"

"Well, that's perfectly clear."

"'—no one pushes Shep Lawson around!'"

"Simon! Great news!"

Clapping his hands, the director continued past the foyer. Lydia stopped under the threshold, then turned and hurried upstairs and out to the parking lot. Warm air baked the pavement. Standing in front of a hand-lettered sign—AUDITIONS TODAY!—she dialed her husband's work number. Steve sounded short of breath when he came to the phone, his thin voice straining against the clang of a cash register. Having learned over the past eighteen years how to recognize his wife's most volatile moods, he limited his responses to *yes dear* and *I will* and *sure* and *fine* and *okay* and *yes dear* and *yes*.

Paper

Lydia Tree
Topics in Modern Science
Winter Term
3-26-79

Weather affects everything. It's everywhere, it's in the air that we breathe. Imagine that. Just think about that for one second. Every breath that you draw into your lungs is influenced in some fashion by what the weather is like outside. If it's a cold day, your breath might be cold as well. If it's raining, well you get the idea. Weather can be dangerous too. Planes crash. A foolish person goes swimming in the ocean. It is a peaceful afternoon, but because this person has not taken the time to consider the unpredictable nature of weather, she is struck dead when a storm blows in from the coast. This causes great grief and inconvenience for her family. So as I have shown, weather is a part of everything we do. And this is what makes the job of the National Oceanic and Atmospheric Administration, or NOAA for short, so important. I happen to know a good deal about this organization, because I lived in Washington D.C. for eight years. I know that we're not allowed to talk about our personal lives in these research reports, because this is a Science class, and Science deals with general matters, like gravity or the way things taste. So if you want to flunk me for not following the assignment, all I can say is oh well. I can't help it when certain professors use unfair standards to evaluate their students' work. That's not my problem. It's just not. And I know you stole my bag.

This concludes the introductory portion of this essay. I will now move on to the next paragraph.

This term paper will examine the subject of weather, or more specifically, the ways in which weather data is collected and distributed around the world. I have studied this issue for two reasons: A, because it was assigned to me, but also B, (fill in later). Did you know that nearly forty percent of marine advisories issued by the National Weather Service depend upon readings taken by the National Oceanic and Atmospheric Administration Data Buoy Office? I didn't before I looked it up. I did _not_ know that. The short way of saying the National Oceanic and Atmospheric Administration Data Buoy Office is the NDBO. The letters stand for National, Data, Buoy, and Office. This is known as an acronym. The dictionary defines "acronym" as: _a word formed from the initial letters or groups of letters of the words in a name or phrase._ This is a direct quote from the dictionary, which I just copied out word-for-word.

ANALYSIS

The NDBO came under the command of NOAA in 1970. This is the impressive part that I really

researched, so get ready. FACT: the first weather
buoys were twelve meters across and are still in
use today, although they are gradually being
replaced by smaller aluminum hulls. FACT:
aluminum, unlike steel, does not corrode, nor does
it interfere with the homing devices inside the
buoy's payload. These buoys are moored with
strands of various lengths and of various
materials. Thick chains keep buoys restrained in
shallow waters while links of polypropylene and
nylon help to secure larger buoys in depths of up
to 6,000 meters. Not all buoys are confined to deep
sea and coastal regions. The nearest one floats
less than a hundred miles to the north and east of
our beautiful campus, but you can't see it because
it's hard to find. Newer models called Drifters
have recently been incorporated by the NDBO.
Drifting buoys are primarily used to study large-
scale changes in the environment. They were first
used to record climatic data as part of the Global
Atmospheric Research Program, or GARP for all you
bureaucrats out there.

I just read a book about a person named Garp,
and the author pictured on the back cover sure
looked handsome. I always thought that writers
were scrawny little guys with strange sexual
fixations. He must have some other problem.

We have not yet begun to scratch the surface of
this fascinating topic. Let's talk about history
for awhile—is that okay with you, Dan? You don't
mind if I call you Dan, do you? Doctor Dan. Dan
the Man. Is that what your wife calls you? No,
your wife probably calls you Captain. Hey, Cap.
You probably sit around the house with a sailor's
hat on. When I get married, it's not going to be
like that. My boyfriend is going to be an

International Businessman, and we're going to live on Manhattan—not in Manhattan, but on Manhattan, because Manhattan is an island—and when we host parties, they're going to be really serious parties where no one smiles, and if you don't like the dessert, you're dead. No one speaks to you for the rest of your life.

By the end of the 1980s, ultra modern computers will replace the old buoy system, leaving thousands of sailors out of work, which I think is sad. At any rate, the NDBO may wind up taking over all services on the east coast, particularly if we can manage to get the Democrats out of the White House. The computerized system will be just like the buoy network already in place, except totally different in a variety of complicated ways. Now a Man of Science such as yourself might want me to elaborate on this last point. But quite frankly, I'm just not in the mood. I'm very angry with you right now. You should give me a passing grade on this paper, because I tried, and also because I never physically attacked you, which you could at least say something nice about.

Professor's Comments: B+. *You argue your point with precision, and your knowledge of the subject is impressive. So impressive, in fact, that I feel unable to provide you with any more useful instruction. May I recommend that you take a day this week to visit the Advisory on the fourth floor and inquire about transferring into an adjacent section, one better able to accommodate your unique skills. This, of course, is simply a suggestion. You should do only what you feel is best. Good luck, Daniel Kind, Ph.D.*

Sheesh

1998

I t was just a case of too many things going on at once, and I kind of
blew my top. Not proud of it, but that's what I did. I can only be pulled
in so many directions. First there's Lydia. She always calls when she
knows she's going to get me on the sales floor. That's part of the game,
the game we all play. I say, look, I have an office, why not call me there?
Wouldn't that be a lot simpler? Right in the middle of talking to Jim
Carroll, she gets me. He's bopping around, stinking up the joint. Steve,
he says. Store's looking pretty good. This is from the guy who changes
my quantities every month without telling me. Ooh, he's a treat. I tell
him okay. Matter of fact, I say, it looks *dang* good, and we're going to
keep it that way. So he goes, gets a clipboard, says he's got some display
tips he wants to show me. I say fine, I'd like to hear 'em. He says okay, go
grab a clipboard. So I go grab a clipboard! What the heck else am I supposed to do? That's when the phone rings. Sometimes I think, when she
calls, she doesn't understand there's actually some sort of activity going
on, and it's called work, and it's a little bit important. Aah, I don't know.
Women. You can plug 'em in but you can't get 'em to go.

Oh, and the other thing. This girl. Let me back up. This girl. She's a
cashier. Colored girl, by the way. Which is okay. She's not really obvious
about it or anything. You just gotta be careful. All right. So she puts
some candy on the counter. A little dish, puts it out—take one. Now,
this is with Jim Carroll, who's the Visual Merchandiser for the entire
zone, not to mention the guy who's probably going to make Senior Veep

soon as we go worldwide, standing right there, looking at this dish, think-ing I don't know how to manage my own store. So I go up to her. Tal-Ahnka, I say. That's her name. Your guess is as good as mine. Tal-Ahnka, let's work this out here. We don't sell candy, we don't even sell this dish, what am I supposed to do when someone wants to buy the dish? She says it's her dish. Someone wants to buy the dish, they can talk to her. So now that's where we've got to go, down that lovely primrose path. Now I've got to be the bad guy because I happen to care about my customers' well-being, their safety for God's sake. What happens when a little kid comes in—mommy look at the candy—takes a bite and bam, he's on the ground, my god he's choking, how could you do such a horrible thing, I go to prison for the rest of my life and that's the end of that. See, that's where your managerial jurisprudence comes in. The blacks, they don't appreciate this sort of thing, and I mean that with all total respect. But I'm trying to be pleasant and I'm trying to be professional, so I just say now Tal-Ahnka, I've asked once nicely and I've given you a chance to respond—see, with some people, you gotta go through all the rigma-role or else it's lawsuit time. So I tell her look, that candy is gonna go, and that's all there is to it, and I'm not messing around with it anymore! Enough of this noise, man! That's what I said, word for word. A real good, slick kind of an answer, I thought.

So you're starting to get the idea, I think, why I darn near blew my top.

Came dang close.

And it doesn't help when my customers start getting in on the act. That really ticks me off. Some dumb broad butts in while I'm having a private conversation with my cashier, just walks right up and says why don't you lighten up on the girl, she's only trying to be nice. Isn't that a hoot and a half? This lady's telling me how to run my store, that's great, that's just what I need with Jim Carroll standing right there, senior VM for the whole doggone kit and kaboodle, and this woman's gonna tell me how to handle my sales staff. As if she's worked a single day in her life. I wanted to say look, ma'am, when you come home at night and it's time to make dinner for your family—you've got your meat and your vegeta-bles all laid out—do I come over and tell you what to do, how to cut the meat properly or boil the potatoes, that sort of thing, do I do that? No, I don't, I don't think so, so here's an idea, why don't you just respect my thing and I'll respect yours and we'll all be happy. See, some of these women, what happens is, they meet some guy, they're twenty years old, she's looking dynamite, she's got the dress up to here, and the guy falls for it and boom, it's over, she's set for life. They got a word for a lady like that, and I'm not going to say it, but you know darn well what I'm talking about. Ooo, I was hot. But instead I just said, ma'am — I don't remember word for word, just . . . ma'am, something something, I appreciate your input, so on and so forth, but we do have certain regulations which we have to follow, and if there's anything I can do to make your shopping experience more pleasurable, please let me know. But the way I said it, she could tell. What I was really saying was, you miserable woman, don't you ever come into my store again and start bossing me around. That was the message, loud and clear.

Next thing you know, Jim Carroll comes up, gives her a stack of coupons. Oh, we're sorry if we've inconvenienced you in any way. I'm standing right there, I'm the stinking store manager, now I look like an idiot. I call him over and say Jim, what are you doing to me here? That's twenty, thirty coupons, two hundred dollars' worth, what am I supposed to do with my Gold Club customers? Jim laughs, says tough tooties, you work on your sales skills. Work on *my* sales skills? That's a kick in the pants, right there. This is the guy, back in '95, we're waiting in line, you you 'n' you — *they didn't pick me!* That's how those people operate. Oh, I can dig it. No problem, buddy. I'll get out of your hair. I know when I'm not wanted.

It was just one of those days, man, when it seemed like everything was going against me. I get back to the stock area, it's a mess, no one bothers to put the stuff away. Fire inspector stops by, I'm out on the street. These kids wouldn't care, half of 'em are still in high school, what do they know about safety codes, they're too busy thinking about what Jimmy said to Ricki, meanwhile I'm digging through boxes, saying hey guys help me out here. Scarlet's the only good one in the whole bunch. Older gal, twenty-two, twenty-three, real sweet girl. And beautiful. I mean, if I was fifteen years younger. Heck, ten even. Kind of on the petite side, maybe five-foot-one. Says she's a dancer, but who knows. That's usually code for something else. You go on over across the river, they got gals like that who take home five hundred, a thousand a night. Even the name's perfect. Scarlet Blessing. Does that sound like a porn star or what? Heh. No, but Scarlet's a real nice, intelligent young lady, and a pleasure to work with. Kind of quiet, studious. Does not have a boyfriend so far as I know, but I'll tell you, the guys sure do look at her, you can't hardly help it. Half the time I keep her out back doing paperwork 'cause otherwise we'd never get any work done. A woman like that, with the legs and all . . . you get one of those in the sack and you might not get up again. I go into the break room, she's sitting there with one leg up on the counter, she's got the dress wide open and you can see all the way from here to Toledo. I mean shoot, I almost dropped my sandwich. We get to talking, hi how are you, you know, the usual crap. I'm her boss, naturally she's gonna be a little bit flirtatious. Older man, more experienced—you learn to brush it off. We're sitting there, eating. I tell her, you know, you've been working out really well here as a sales associate, why don't you talk to Karl Becker down at Personnel and sign up for the trainee program. That's real money! I don't tell her how much 'cause I don't want her to know how much I make. Women hear that, right away the sonar goes up. Soon as I cleared forty grand, man, I stopped talking. But a girl Scarlet's age could easily be running her own store in five years. Gotta take advantage of those opportunities. That's when you go for it, when you're young. And if you're a good-looking gal, then all the better, because the world just *stops* for beautiful women. I mean, take me—I would hire Scarlet *dead on the spot* over some other gal. But she's not interested in that. The young kids don't think about these things. At that age, you don't know. If it feels good, do it! Hey man, I'm all for it. Get it out of your system. Nothing wrong with being idealistic. Until you're twenty-seven. Then it stops.

So, twenty-two, twenty-three. She's still got a few years left to go. Good kid. Reads all the time. Derek Skye this, Derek Skye that. I'm sitting there, looking at the back cover—I want to say something but I figure if I give her the Skyes' home number she might feel obligated to return the favor, and I don't want to put her in that position. Women, they interpret everything as, you know, you're trying to seduce them. So I just play dumb. She reads a few sentences out loud. The Derek Skye philosophy. It's okay, but some people get too into it, and they kind of lose their minds. I'm thinking why don't you read the monthly sales sheet if you want to get motivated about something. Still, I was pleasant about it. I just finished my snack and went back out onto the sales floor. Nice girl, but a little on the kooky side. That happens a lot with these beautiful types. They get guys coming on to them all the time, thirty marriage proposals a month, and they start seeing the world in a weird kind of way.

Five o'clock rolls around, I'm all set to take off. Right before a zone visit, I've got to get some sleep. You got Cam Pee, who's only the CEO of the whole cotton-picking organization, coming over with a bunch of advertising executives, said they wanted to use my office. I'm no fool—I said sure, go ahead, whatever you need, man. I know how lucky I am even to be here, the way I was going, working four jobs a night, trying to keep Lydia in diamonds and pearls, pushing a broom, selling cotton candy at the circus, shelving books at the public library—got to be a real drag. I feel sorry for the kids today. It's hard! Even for the smart ones.

What I'm saying is, I think I got it pretty good.

This ain't bad. This ain't half bad.

For a guy of my skills. I'll take what I can get, man, I know what it's like out there.

My dad, good ol' "Barndoor" himself, thought I was the biggest idiot known to mankind, bet he never guessed I'd be making forty G a year, got a beautiful wife, a son just turned eleven now, a nice house, a bunch of junk in the basement I don't even look at. I mean, *yeah!* This is what it's all about!

Lord of all you survey.

The only thing I don't like is the commute. I'd prefer living closer to town, not that anyone cares. Kay Tree, may she rest in aytch-eee-double-toothpick. Didn't even ask us if we liked the place. Just take it and smile. Hey, I've got no problem with that. Free house, heck. I know when to keep my mouth shut. It just makes for a long drive, and by the time I get home, I'm usually pretty tired, and it would be nice to occasionally have a wife sitting there ready with dinner on the table, but I guess that would be too good to be true. What she does with her time, I have no idea. Actually, I'll tell you exactly what she does, she pulls Simon out of class and carts him down to these crazy casting calls, all these batty housewives standing in line, thinking their kid's gonna be the next Telly Savalas, meanwhile poor Simon's scared out of his pants, he just wants to stay home and play ball with his buddies. I know how it is. I get home, the lights are off, the cat's going nuts, should've been fed three hours ago. I think, fine. I'm gonna pour myself a soda and sit down. I don't mind! Not this guy. I can *take* it! I'm sitting around, watching TV. Nice TV. Nice sofa. Everything's real good. Know what? I'm gonna take my shoes off. Six o'clock, I start making supper, I've got the whole meal prepared, the pasta, my mother's recipe, it's getting cold, an hour goes by before they finally show up. *Where were you?* No answer — they just head straight for the food, and no one says hi or even asks me how my day went. It's enough to make a guy feel like he just doesn't matter.

Dinnertime was another lovely thing. Let's all get in a fight! That's just what I need to round out the day. I don't like to go to bed with Lydia mad at me — two a.m., she wants to apologize, well I'm sorry too but I got to get some shut-eye, I got Cam Pee pounding on the door at ten in the morning, and if I'm not bright-eyed and bushy-tailed by sunrise, I'm gonna be out of there faster than a ton of bricks. Jeezo-pete, use your *mind*, lady! We're passing the salad around, she starts in on me about this television commercial they're putting together down at Corporate, like I've got some direct line running straight up to the nineteenth floor. *Yeah Mr. Pee? Hi, this is Steve Mould over at Store #731, we met once, I was standing in a crowd of, oh, I don't know, eight million other people, you happened to look over for, gee, must've been about one point two seconds, anyway, my son, he's a cute kid, his mother wants him to be in the company's next commercial, you're only sinking something like six trillion dollars into the campaign.* Yeah, that's a great idea, if that doesn't get me canned I might as well torch the store, run down the street screaming with my hair on fire. Finally, just to get on with it, I said all right, I'll do it, I'll take care of it in the morning, let's just eat. No, she says, I don't like the way you said that, don't talk to me that way. I say what is this junk? I come home, I want to see nice happy faces and this is what I get. My kid's staring down at the plate, all set to cry, his mother's pointing at him with a knife like she's going to stick it right in, I say don't point that at him, she says a dirty word, Simon asks to be excused, I don't blame the kid, I say sure, go, do what you gotta do, then Lydia gets on a rant about how he hasn't finished his supper, I say what do you care, you've been nagging him all night, oh but we can't have that, now I've hurt her feelings, let's go, the big eyes, the pout, everything just the way we like it, and that's when she says all you ever think about is your job, you don't care about me and you don't care about your son's career.

That's it. I just blew my lid, man. I said—this is what I said, word for word. I said I'm fed up. I'm fed up, I can't even stand it anymore, and if he wants to be excused, then that's his right as a man of the house, and if he doesn't want to eat his supper, then that food's going right straight down the garbage disposal, GOSHDAMNIT!

And I don't curse. Ever . . . at . . . almost at all.

Threw my napkin down. Better believe it.

Now I can't talk to my son. Lydia doesn't care—she's got her purse out, writing a check. Got the pen in one hand, she's eating with the other like there's no tomorrow. I said heck, enough of this screwing around, people getting angry at each other for no reason. I'll tell you what, I'm gonna clean up, shampoo my hair and work on the train set for a few hours, just see if I don't. Now she's not talking to me. I'm trying to keep the mood as light as possible. I say what on earth are you doing, you know, just making mild conversation. She doesn't even answer, just holds the check up, puts it about two inches in front of my face and says here. No, I don't play that game, lady. Not my style. You've got your money, I've got mine—I get it. If the ol' lady wants to buy my family, she can move to another cemetery. Just don't screw around with my son. I hardly ever see the kid anymore. He spends most of his time with his mother. They're usually out with people I don't know, going to one function or another, I'm totally out of the loop. It's like, hey guys, I'm here too. Just once, wouldn't it be great . . . everyone's in a good mood, and we go out to get some ice cream or check out a movie? I mean, that would be dynamite and I'd be all for it, but it doesn't look like that's going to happen any time soon. My old man, now. He *ruled* that family. No question. It was his way or the highway, and if you didn't believe it, he'd bust you right in the chops, boy. Good ol' "Barndoor" Mould, man. Hard. As. Nails! 'Bout the meanest guy in the world. Hoooo, I didn't argue with the man, I just said yes sir, no sir, watched my P's and Q's and to this day I'm still grateful to him for giving me that particular kind of upbringing, I mean it really worked out for the best. Heck, if it wasn't for him, I'd probably still be sweeping floors, making three bucks an hour, Lydia would've taken off by now and I never would've had the chance to experience firsthand what it's like to have a child of your own, which is something that, if you haven't been through it yourself, I can't hardly explain how wonderful it is. The best is when they're still babies. I even like the crying. It's just noise. The back talk is what I can't stand. Once they start talking, once they start saying words. That's when it gets rough.

And one more thing. All you men? Watch out. 'Cause once the baby's born, that's when the woman changes. And that's just totally a fact.

The Terrorist

I Want Some Answers

http://www.eggcode.com

FACT: The Internet is a diverse place. Very little binds us together, except for our—perhaps random—decision to visit this site. That said, let us celebrate what little we *do* share! All across the country, roads join our cities, connecting families with businesses, churches and schools. The traffic jam is part of modern Americana—long waits, angry faces, construction cones on the highway. The naive reader would accept these inconveniences as simply the price we all must pay for smoother roads and faster commutes. Good-natured fools would hardly suspect the federal government's true intentions, the insidious motive behind every blocked lane, every orange flag. Ah, yes. The Egg Code knows, though we have been threatened under pain of death to keep our silence, to protect those who would do us harm. For this reason, we would ask our subscribers to please excuse the bits of conjecture and allusion. It is for our own personal safety that we must hide behind such clever subterfuge.

The history of the road extends back to ancient times. With the greater speeds and braking capabilities of the automobile, modern highways required a better means of guiding fast-moving traffic along a set course. Two competing technologies grew out of this need; of the two, most engineers preferred concrete over asphalt. This method held on into the postwar years, when freeway construction was at a premium. It was in this context that the United

States first established the U.S. Interstate Highway System—or, as it was originally called, the National System of Interstate and Defense Highways.

The reader might wonder what a transcontinental series of roads had to do with defense in 1956, but the answer, sadly, is everything. This was the height of the Cold War, when federal agents envisioned a network of military convoys shuttling weapons to the suburbs. Well-connected, the American people stood strong against the Russians. The defense rationale had another, perhaps more cynical purpose. In those days, scientists believed that the only way to obtain federal funding was through the Defense Department. This phenomenon was certainly not unique to the United States. England and France were both reluctant to establish major road-building initiatives in the aftermath of World War II, and in both cases it was the military argument that finally won the day.

With the money finally in place, the U.S. Interstate Highway System began digging across America. It was definitely a learn-as-you-go operation. Thousands of miles of ineptly laid road eventually had to be torn up and reconfigured, pushing the project well past its tentative 1971 completion date. Frustrated engineers—their eyes still glassy with visions of bold "Freeway of the Future" campaigns staged at World's Fair conventions—had not anticipated such high speeds, such chaos on the roads. Neither asphalt nor concrete had provided any real solutions to the titanic demands of twentieth-century mass transportation. Moreover, as the eighties became the nineties, the federal government showed signs of withdrawing support from the project. The Interstates were a financial bust.

At about the same time, an interesting discovery was made, namely that bitumen—critical in the formation of asphalt—was a natural by-product of petroleum. The other major by-product just happened to be *gasoline*. Whammo! Faster than you can say "heinous misuse of appropriations," road commissioners throughout the states, in concordance with their federal bosses, recognized the beauty of the system. As the demand for gasoline increased, the production of bitumen likewise increased, lessening the cost of purchase and deployment. The fact that asphalt was considerably less resilient than concrete was an added bonus. Faster wear increased the need for maintenance. Cars stuck in slow construction zones burned more fuel than cars cruising along a slick road. More gasoline meant more bitumen meant more asphalt meant more construction meant more gasoline. A perfectly closed circuit. An economist's dream.

Only one question remained. Where would the money come from to pay for all this? For our answer, we must return to the Roman Empire, to the golden days of a statute known as the corvée. The corvée, unpopular in its time, was a kind of tax paid in the form of enforced labor. At this very moment, officials in Washington—with the full cooperation of representatives from all fifty states—are busy drafting a plan that would reinstate the corvée as an option to heavy taxation. Because it would be "unconstitutional" to demand this kind of service from its constituents, all the government can do is offer it as a handy alternative, knowing that the only people who will take the bait will be members of the lower class. They will also try to make us feel grateful. Can't pay your taxes? Grab a shovel! We at the Egg Code refuse to participate. This is imperialism of the highest order, and the only reason why we haven't burned our 1040 forms in protest is that it's just so fucking clever.

The Fear of
Being Touched

1998

Shirtless, Olden Field stood at the edge of the lake and stared out over the horizon. His face was clean-shaven, his lips sienna, his hard and bony chin marked by a slight groove in the middle. Long black hair blew over his shoulders. A tendon in his neck throbbed with energy, a constant pulse. At age twenty-nine, he'd given up on everything—junk food, television, regular sex—in exchange for a well-conditioned body, tight muscles, the ass of a quarterback. Living alone in Big Dipper Township, he saved his words like pennies, resting his voice for days at a time. His longest conversations were rehearsed bits of patter, the same five or six themes revisited in endless cycles. He was even quieter around women, choosing never to discuss his strange occupation. Left to guess, most interested young ladies—and most were, indeed, interested—pictured him spread across the pages of a Manhattan fashion magazine. *Olden on page 48, shirt torn, belt loose. The clothes are for sale, by the way.*

A big crappie cartwheeled over the lake, striking the water with its tail. Overhead, a line of warblers raced toward the horizon. Thick clouds brooded in the sky, standing apart like guests at a funeral. Olden peeled off his shorts and stepped into the water. Crossing his legs, he dropped to the muddy bottom. Water filled his ears. He opened his eyes and saw long weeds and flecks of debris illuminated by something pale and green. His own hands looked puffy and distorted. Standing up, he swiped his hair back and tasted the water on his lips. A big shrub rustled near the far shore. He'd disturbed the boy, evidently. The naked boy. This happened sometimes, always around dusk. The child belonged to the couple across the lake; he'd grown bolder over the past few weeks, staying outside for minutes at a time, far from the secret place where he'd stashed his clothes, his balled-up socks and red cotton underwear. Olden's hard-on was an automatic response. Remembering his own childhood, he felt drawn to proto-freaks such as these: troublemakers in the making. He wanted to be the boy, to be naughty and alone like the boy. Following his erection out of the lake, he stepped back into his shorts, then started up the hill to his cabin. The trail was rocky, and it hurt the bottoms of his feet.

At the top of the hill, he peered across the basin, the steep slope of pines running all the way down to the water. With its rough stones and empty windows, the tower in the middle of the lake recalled the turret top of a submerged fortress. Its vaguely medieval architecture suggested a castle built centuries ago. Over the past three years, Olden had proposed many theories, none of them conclusive. An old utility station. The crumbled remains of a massive stone bridge. But a bridge here, in Big Dipper Township? It would have to be enormous, an absurd waste so far from the city. So, neither a bridge nor a castle. A mystery. Olden's little obsession. He planned his days around this pointless ritual. Every evening, he paid his respects to the enigma, then turned and walked home. The walk, the look, solved nothing. Feeling the shadow of the tower at his back, the same thought always troubled his mind. I did not come here by choice. I was brought here by an outside force. A man named Bartholomew Hasse gave me this place, and now he is dead and my father is still not free.

Home again, he stepped through the wide-open door and instinctively made his way past the heaps of junk on the floor. Olden's one-room cabin was an assertion of the solitary lifestyle; seen from the road above, it resembled an abandoned summer cottage. The cement foundation sloped toward one end, causing him to sleep at an angle, his head lower than his feet. Semen stains embedded in the rumpled comforter gave the sheet a flaky texture, like mica. Tattered blankets led in kicked swirls from the mattress to a computer station near the far wall. The computer, currently in sleep mode, was always on. Electricity, much more important than water or decent insulation, was never a problem; a power generator stashed next to the desk guaranteed his system a sure supply. Built essentially from spare parts, the circuitry approximated the configuration of a Spark 20, albeit with a few extra features not available outside of the business market. The Spark was a UNIX device, functioning under a Solaris 2.5 operating system, with 256 Mb of RAM and a pair of 20-gigabyte fast and wide scuzzy drives. The showpiece was a Reduced Instruction Set Computing Processor, far more elegant than the high-profile Pentium. Because of the success of the Pentium chip's widespread marketing campaign, many of Olden's customers specified it in their service requests. His clients were mainly business folks who liked to check up on the stock market while their wives downloaded recipes from the Martha Stewart page. Their interest in the technology did not extend past the consumer level. One of the reasons he'd been so quick to accept Mr. Hasse's offer back in '95—despite the obvious questions about Hasse's own relationship to Martin Field—was his growing intolerance for hi-tech poseurs such as these, cocksure morons with too much power on their hands. The peasants were taking over, crowding out the intellectuals with their chatrooms and their user-friendly interfaces. Plotting from afar, he'd resolved to inject just enough fear into the system to render the whole thing useless.

Not that he considered himself much of an insider. Quite the opposite. In fact, he hated computers—the specs, the endless upgrades, the byzantine bits of lore. That was what had driven him away from the scene all those years ago. Because of who he was—his technical background, his father's work for the computer science department at Stanford in the 1970s—he found himself unable to engage in any conversation that didn't ultimately return to the same tired subjects. The early days of FTP. The fine points of packet switching. The best ways to infiltrate a PBX. It all seemed so beside the point. Like a surrogate hobby, this fascination with gadgetry acted as a substitute fix for people with no real interests. Of course, speed was the main qualitative distinction, the factor that finally determined your place in the crowd. Olden's RISCP was fast enough, but fast enough for *what*? Now almost thirty, he'd developed a new taste for slow pleasures. Stacks of damp, warped books made pillars on either side of his bed. They were his protectors, guarding against a national need for quick and easy satisfaction. For three years he'd educated himself by going back to the source, circumnavigating the user-friendly synopsis. A little bit of fiction, but only lengthy, dense works, novels whose proud agendas bordered on the academic. *The Glass Bead Game. Atlas Shrugged.* He liked the idea of the intellectual willingly sequestering himself from the rest of society. Screw you, peasants! Lacking a point, fiction seemed indulgent and narrow-minded. The bumbling misadventures of the individual. Olden was more interested in the general than the particular. Armed with evidence, his bookshelf described mobs, howling throngs of thugs, the world as he saw it. *The Mass Psychology of Fascism. Extraordinary Popular Delusions and the Madness of Crowds.* None of these books were easy to read. For Olden, they represented three years' worth of sheer effort. Apart from the crowd, he'd joined the ranks of the brilliant and the self-educated. Books were his way of resisting the circuits, the phantom fingers of the twenty-first century working past the zipper of your fly, turning, twisting, trying to get at the goods.

Feeling sleepy, he reached for a cup of coffee, cold dregs left over since morning. The battle could wait, at least for another few hours. Tonight he'd attend to other matters. Groping about for something to wear, he pushed past a windsurfer standing against the wall, the skeg cutting into the rotten floor. He'd owned the board for years, although he rarely went out anymore, even with the lake so convenient and the weather nice in September. Nearby, a steamer suit lay in a derelict slouch, and he squeezed a chunk of it between his thumb and middle finger. Thick, like whale fat. Well, the same idea really. The safety of skin. Chugging his coffee, he put on his clothes, then went outside to his car. The keys, already hanging from the ignition, were cold as icicles. The bald tires struggled up the hill to the main road. Pausing at the intersection, he checked his look in the mirror. *Olden on page 39 — pants in charcoal, rust, and parchment.* Yes, he thought. Keep it quiet. Lie low. Take advantage of the country.

The Divine Ray
of Inspiration

"What have we been talking about all night?" Derek Skye held his hands over the lectern, fingertips touching, thumbs flexed, pointing at the ceiling. "We've been talking about stress. We've been talking about what you can do as an individual to remove stress from your life." He stepped around to the side of the podium, taking the microphone with him. In the audience, Scarlet Blessing watched with an intensity that singled her out, even in a crowd of three hundred. She'd deliberately chosen the third row, although she'd arrived early enough to have her pick. She couldn't sit too close. The aura, the sheer force of the man.

"Here's a question," he said, whipping the cord. His voice sounded hoarse this late in the evening. "You've heard the expression 'the survival of the fittest'? Who's heard it? You've heard it? You've heard it?" A scattering of hands. "Well, the fact of the matter is, it's *not* the survival of the fittest. Historically speaking, the groups that have survived have been those groups best able to *manage time effectively*." He went back to the lectern and fished for a pair of reading glasses. A prop. "The ancient Greeks have a phrase for it which roughly translates into *motivation plus dedication divided by time awareness equals bliss*."

Scarlet nodded, her lips moving—*motivation plus dedication*—but then the words ran out and she could only shake her head, comprehending nothing beyond the awesome fact that she was here and so was he. Her feet marched in place, mashing her gym bag under her heels.

The bag contained her leotard, her jazz shoes, a bottle of Motrin, a split of champagne, a full change of clothes, three hundred and thirty dollars in cash, an array of contraceptive devices, a portable cassette player and two tapes (Walter Gieseking's recording of the Debussy preludes and *Sabbath Bloody Sabbath*), dental floss, a roll of athletic tape, an expensive calculator, a loaded .22 revolver, three Sooper Seller gift certificates from Living Arrangements, half of a chicken-salad sandwich and a copy of Derek Skye's latest compilation, *The Skye's the Limit* (wrapped in a T-shirt to keep the jacket from getting smudged). Hot and sweaty from the long day, she stuck her nose under the neck of her shirt and smelled. Old apples. She disgusted herself, the smells she made. She wondered what Derek smelled like. She wanted to smell his hair. His neck. Behind his ears.

"Gratification. Who knows the word? You know it? Who knows it? It's a big word. Who can say it for me? Let's all say it. Can we? Can we do this? Better yet, let's spell it. Can we spell it? Who can do that? Come on. Let's all spell it together. Let's go. G-R—good—A—*good!*"

A police siren passed the conference center, a faint swirl and then silence. No one looked, no one cared. Even with the interstate closed down for construction, Derek had still managed to draw a sell-out crowd. As he ended his presentation—fifteen minutes ahead of schedule—Scarlet stood up and pushed her way to the front of the room. A few dozen admirers were pressed against the podium, asking for autographs. Reaching the stage, she could feel her legs begin to tingle—a strange sensation, similar to the special buzz she sometimes felt in dreams, the weightless place inside her mind. Only the others held her down, the mob, their voices calling out questions that sounded so small and ordinary compared to hers.

"Derek, hi, my name is—"

"Yeah, hi . . . I'm sorry—"

Face. Skin. White!

"My name is Scarlet and I—"

"I'm sorry, I've got to go—"

Muh-mustache. Chin, neck. Shirt colla—

"I just have a—"

—collar, blue shirt, wrinkles, dark lines moving.

"—got to get to my car, I'm sorry."

The crowd parted as Derek hurried out of the room. The round end of Scarlet's gym bag nudged her in the belly. A big hand blocked her way—spread fingers, the spaces in between. She sagged, giving up. Trash on the floor. Shoes—all different! Still, he had seen her. He had wanted to respond. Oh, these damn people . . .

Refusing his escort, Derek fled down three flights of stairs to an underground parking garage. Doors on every level cautioned against entry; yellow tape wrapped around the push bars made bright warnings, snaky zags of toxic color. Wanting only to get away, he tripped the alarm on the basement floor and scurried past a security light. The siren sounded against the cement I-beams as he climbed into his car and drove off, hearing the siren, then hearing only the noise of a carnival, the low roar of the people on the streets. What a night. Well, a necessary ordeal. One last chance to check his resolve, to say goodbye to the scene. Staring out at those hungry hopeful faces—eyes eagerly swallowing the icon—he was reminded of why he'd left in the first place. They loved him. They loved a monster! Something verging on sadism made his hands go tense on the wheel. Pedestrians swarmed the crosswalks, looking for bars, places to piss, and he hated them, he wanted to mow them down, to feel their bones turn to mush under his wheels. They would pay. They would pay for their love. His followers were fragile things, overly ornate creatures too elaborate to survive outside of the greenhouse. What would they say when he finally revealed his true self? At least one might go over the edge. And *then* what?

Turning right to avoid the interstate, he found himself caught in the congestion of a narrow side street. A stoplight near the center of the block exploded, spraying hot glass across the road; ladies in nice dresses hurried away from the lamppost, stepping carefully to avoid the mess. As he veered into the left lane, a group of drunks muttered and shook their fists. Two men straddled the yellow line, waiting to see which way he'd go. Their faces were hidden; a neon slash winked across the lenses of the shorter man's glasses. Derek checked his mirror and saw the man's middle finger, stiff and proud in the dim light. He nodded, accepting his punishment.

Gray Hollows lowered his hand as he stepped over the curb. "Meatheads," he said, grinding the broken glass under his heel. "The world is full of 'em." The urge to add something sarcastic swelled and went away. Past the corner, his friend continued, moving easily through the crowd. Gray raced to catch up. Together, they entered a shady vestibule; their shoes crunched and clacked against the sticky floor tiles. A fat man eating a hot dog casually checked IDs by the door. Embarrassed, Gray pulled out his driver's license. The man in the photo was smirking, looking off to one side, lips parted in an interrupted remark.

"Remember this dump?" he shouted in his friend's ear. "Back when we were in school, this place used to be a cannery." Olden nodded, then turned his shoulders, pressing through the mob. Gray followed, speaking the whole time, changing his voice according to the fluctuating ratio of men to women. "This is what we do now, this is the thing. 'Oh, wow, here's this condemned building, let's turn it into a nightclub, kinda rustic, kinda dangerous, glass on the floor, bums passed out in the doorway, aw, yeah, cool, it's right on the water, can't you see, prime property, we'll hire a couple of derelicts to piss on the carpet, get that authentic vibe going on, if the customers complain, we'll take a hammer and knock their teeth out.'"

The bar was a circular counter with one woman covering the whole shift. Out of breath, she ran between the customers, stretching for money, taking orders over her shoulder. Olden pointed at the bar and slipped her a ten. Regardless of his plans for the evening, he never liked to run a tab. Too much to remember. Quick exits, no obligations. He needed his freedom.

"Hmmm, Gray. I don't know." He frowned, hooking an empty stool with his foot.

"Sure! Advertising 101!" Gray slumped onto the stool. The leather cushion settled under his weight. "What I say goes, fuck it, I tell my boss over at Enthusiasms Inc., 'Hey, West, I got an idea for a new campaign,' he drops a half-mil into my lap, 'Don't spend it all in one place,' the worst that can happen is we go out of business, two weeks later I'm back on unemployment where I goddamn belong."

Olden smiled. His long hair hung over his face, a dark curtain. "I don't know, Gray. You've got a lot of power at that place. You should use it. Look." Reaching across the counter, he grabbed a cocktail napkin and tore it into halves and quarters. "Here's your client," he said, holding up a square. "'We've got this business. Help us to reach our customers.'

You prove to the client why you should be trusted. The pamphlets, the fancy brochures. The type." He pointed. "Don't forget about the type. You tell them what they want to hear. Then you go home and you do what you feel is right. You come back the next day." Another square. "'See. I did what you wanted.' They believe you."

Gray slammed the rest of his pint. "I'm not looking to get away with anything, Olden! You know what it's going to take to get me out of there? Those people own my ass, I'm telling you. You talk to my father up in Battle Creek about it, he's probably got the next twenty years of my life all mapped out!" Still shouting, he pointed randomly at the stranger sitting next to him. The other man scooted away, guarding his drink. "Sheer incompetence. That's my only chance. A major screw-up. Otherwise, I'm dead. 'Cause I don't belong up there, stuck with those idiots: 'Ooh, Gray, pretty cool guy' . . . Yeah, fuck *you*. This is all marking time, you know that. You know I haven't given up. *You* haven't given up either."

"I've given up on everything, Gray. That's why I live in the country."

Gray removed his spectacles and tightened the screws with his thumb. Without his glasses, his face looked extra-large, swollen in spots, almost hydrocephalic in its strange design, starting wide and tapering toward the bottom.

"Art-school rejects, that's you and me," he laughed, replacing his glasses. "When the academics don't like you, you know you must be doing something right."

Olden shook his head. "I like everyone."

Oblivious, Gray plundered on, holding up a rolled five for another beer. "Sanctioned mediocrity, that's what I always used to say—and goddamnit, Olden, I believe it now more than ever. Let some of those college pansies with their phony liberalism and their arrogant ideals work in advertising for two weeks, then we'll see what happens. Ah, yes—the *artist*! The divine ray of inspiration! Lick my balls."

Olden listened without looking, keeping his eyes fixed on the woman behind the bar. Relaxing between customers, she adjusted the hang of her floppy tie, pulling on one side, then the other, pressing it smooth to save the changes. "I think you romanticize things too much."

"Romanticize what?"

"You've always known what you wanted to do with your life, Gray. That's wonderful. You should be grateful. Most of us are lost."

Still staring at the bartender, Olden reached between his legs and fixed the tilt of his hard-on. In recent months he'd forgotten all about women, how they walked, spoke, their different gestures, the course of their strange logic. He wanted to talk to one, just to watch the thoughts pass from one thing to the next. Hearing Gray's voice, he rubbed his eyes and focused on the sound, trying to distinguish the words from the background din.

". . . I should be grateful that I wasted my entire childhood parked in front of a word processor—'Ooh, he's so cute, he thinks he's Truman Capote, *Herbert, where's the Instamatic? Get a shot of his feet swinging under the table*'—meanwhile all the other kids are busy throwing rocks at each other and masturbating to the chick in the life-insurance commercial, HA HA!"

Olden selected a toothpick from a jar of three hundred and held it between his fingers. His gestures seemed designed to mislead, to deliberately override the listener's better sense.

"Think about it, Gray. You're a writer. This is what you want to do. Okay. There are certain steps you have to take if you want to succeed. For example. I am someone who might be able to help you. Now what does this mean? This means that no one knows who I am. You do, but you don't say anything about it. It's not in your best interest that anyone should know this part of the story. What I do, I'm a person who can take a message and put it someplace where everyone's going to find it." He wiggled the toothpick. "The message, we say, in this case, is that your product—it could be a story, it could be a piece of music, it could be something as simple as an *idea*—is a desirable commodity. There. It's done. It's out there. Now I go away." No more toothpick. "We act like, oh, it just happened—but it didn't just happen. I put it there."

Giving up on the bartender, Gray unrolled the five-dollar bill and set it on the counter. "And then what?"

Olden tucked his hair behind his ears. The bartender looked up, stubbed out her cigarette and walked over to the beer pulls.

"Well, this is all just speaking hypothetically," he said, shrugging, "but I'm working on a little project that you might find interesting."

"What project?"

Olden didn't answer, just smiled as the bartender filled two pint glasses with expensive bock. She set the drinks in front of the men and shook her head, rejecting their money.

Olden tasted his beer. "Remember this name," he said, nudging the woman's hand with his glass. Her fingers curled around his palm.

"What name's that, honey?" she asked.

Olden lingered, then took his hand back. "The Egg Code," he said.

She wrinkled her nose, puzzling it out. "Egg Code, let's see . . ." Looking up at the ceiling, she tapped a ballpoint pen against her throat. "That's amaretto . . . and Drambuie . . ."

"No." He raised his half-empty pint glass, toasting the girl. "That's not it at all," he said.

Coming Together

It was still early when they left the bar, so they followed the crowd to a nearby theater, where free shows played from nine to eleven. The theater was small, and the floor rose at such a steep angle that you could put your feet on the seat in front of you without bending your knees. It reminded Olden of a lecture hall, or maybe a dissection room: white and clean, camera trained on a splayed lizard. Tonight the stage was bare, with only a few mirrors running along the back wall. Gray shifted in the darkness, making the whole row of connected seats shake on a spring. Olden breathed into his hand. Not so bad. A few beers, an hour drive and he'd be all set to work until morning. The city made him nervous—too many people, too many schedules to coordinate. Out in the sticks, he could make his own hours. An easy lifestyle. In the city, he saw the proof of his own wildness. Every multiplex, every three-story strip mall revealed his basic inability to *get with the program*. The women were nice, and they all seemed to like him, but overall he preferred his solitude. Even Gray was starting to get on his nerves.

But then the dance began, and something changed. An instant reversal, for as soon as Olden saw the girl, he wanted only to look at her, to watch her body move. She danced in the center of the troupe, a leader of sorts; the other performers gave her space when she needed it, space to shine and rock. The music was loud, an electronic mix, and it boomed from speaker to speaker—a bit more, really, than this crowd expected. The people in the front row covered their ears and crossed their legs and smiled tolerantly, waiting for it to end. The choreography slashed in violent thrusts across the stage. The women were more daring than the men, and they threw themselves down from the scaffolding, striking the ground with a terrible force. The first thing Olden noticed about the girl was her hair—pigtails, an innocent touch, so out of place in the midst of this awful rite. She was small, barely five feet tall. Fat, grinning cheeks, pale, pockmarked skin, pitted across the forehead. Her eyebrows were thick and dark, and they joined at the bridge of her nose, her eyes hidden in cinch-folds of happy wrinkles. But it was her body that Olden watched, for it amazed him—the violence inside, the strange contrast between the sweet face and the angry gestures. Her body was a super piston, machine-made, ultra-efficient in the way it reached and tore and swatted. Flat feet banged the boards, bent legs stepping with leaden effort, then flexing to kick the air. He admired the way she'd trained herself, knowing that his own body could never do those things. This was a skill, a secret that she knew and he didn't, and in that secret he saw another life, years of dreams and discipline, an ambition similar to his own except in the course it took, and he respected her for this, respected her for being so good at one thing. As her hips swiveled in a wide bop, he thought about the work involved, the complex terminology, the words used to describe this and that, words unfamiliar to him but a part of her daily routine, common to the point of habit (like checksums and sequence numbers, only not . . . not *quite*). He wanted to stay there, to learn more. Onstage, the dancers divided, came back, bowed quickly. Olden clapped, staring at the girl.

"I don't think that's going to help my hangover," Gray said, rubbing his temples as the lights came up and the audience moved toward the exits, embarrassed by the incongruence between their own lives and the bigness on the stage. Stepping over the back of his chair, he hurdled the rows, lifting one leg, then the other.

Olden stayed in his seat, thinking. An elderly couple slowed the traffic, clotting the aisle with their tiny waddle. A teenager made a gun finger with his right hand, held it up to the back of the old man's head and pulled the trigger. Olden waited for the crowd to pass, then met Gray out in the lobby. A circular sofa surrounded a steel post in the center of the room. Gray was in the middle of saying something sarcastic about an advertisement hanging over the concession stand. Olden tuned the words out, hearing only the cadence of sounds, the jesting rise and fall.

"Let's stay," he said, finding a space on the circular sofa between two heaps of children's coats. "I want to meet the dancers."

Gray slid his hands into his pockets as he paced around the sofa. "Tiny clothes," he muttered, inspecting the jackets, the lightweight windbreakers, yellow and red. He seemed to be pitching ideas to himself, searching for an angle, a satirical point-of-attack. "The shelf life is ridiculous. Six months and it's no good. This is part of the psychology. In this way, we will train you to buy, to become dependent upon the consumer culture. We, meaning corporate America. Fashion! Today, tomorrow and the next day. That's what the third-world countries know that we don't. The children go naked. The children go naked, and once they're sixteen years old, they get a little tunic and they're all set. HA HA! No more *buying*."

A group of kids ran into the lobby, screaming, swirling their fists, each clutching the same neon doodad—a free souvenir, evidently. A few tired adults followed behind—mussed hair, coats dragging, the worn-out remnants of parental authority.

Olden stood up and stepped out of the way, watching the swarm of children, their munchkin bodies darting in chaotic directions. He wondered about the underlying principle behind all of this apparently random activity. If child A equals child B. His father would know. Peering down the corridor, he saw a few of the performers mingling with the parents, answering their questions in an even, professional tone, poised like representatives for some worldwide youth organization. The girl with the pigtails was standing with her arms around two of the men. In her street clothes, she seemed even further removed from himself, a real woman instead of a prop, instead of a two-dimensional phantasm, a woman who owned more than one pair of shoes, more than one shirt, a fully accessorized human being, a complex and remote *other*. There she was. He wanted her to be not-perfect. He would love her more for these imperfections. Weird habits. Things to apologize for. Oh, Christa *always* does that. Christa—where did *that* come from? Generic dreamgirl. No, don't think of her that way. Keep the name open. Only truth, only true things. Let her come to you. Stay empty. Start with nothing.

"I saw you!" The girl was pointing at Olden, who just stood there, marked, unable to move. Kissing each of her partners once on the cheek, she kicked her nylon gym bag down the hallway until it came to a stop against the foot of the sofa. "You were sitting up front," she said, hoisting the bag.

"You can see from onstage?" he asked, liking her voice, liking it all so far.

"Not too good." She reached between her legs and pulled out a wedgie. "With the long hair, though."

"Oh, yeah, right." Olden touched his hair, suddenly remembering it, finding it strange for some reason. *His* hair. She'd noticed his hair. Why not?

"I like it when guys do that. With the hair. It looks sexy."

He smiled, she smiled. The whole thing was real nice. Looking over her head, he nodded at the two male dancers, who stood leaning against each other with their arms folded—sizing him up, sure. Well, fine. Guilty until proven innocent. Not a problem. Olden saluted and they waved back. H . . . i.

"You must be real tired, after all that," he said.

"Not too." She shifted the bag, working her arms through the wide straps.

"I really liked the show."

"Oh, thanks."

"You want to have a drink with me?"

"Oh, sure, yeah, let's go."

The girl waved goodbye to her partners. One of them said, "Scarlet, gimme your cigarettes." Scarlet, then? Olden tested the name out in his head, trying a variety of pitches—the bored purl, the sexy shout. Hi, Scarlet. Let me ask Scarlet. Scarlet, where's my wallet? Sure, Scarlet. Scarlet's not here, can I take a message?

Passing the vestibule, they saw Gray standing by the entrance, watching the children pile onto a short yellow bus. A chaperone manned the door, scooping the air with his left hand, moving the kids along.

Olden nudged his friend in the gut. "Come on," he said, his arm now around Scarlet's waist. They looked good like that. A nice height ratio. Him and her. "We're going back to the bars."

"Okay," Gray stammered. His tongue felt pasty, his brain slow to react. Shaking his head to clear the fog, he followed Olden and Scarlet out into the chilly night. "I can do that," he said, keeping a few steps behind.

The Meet Market was a dreadful place: club tunes and boys and girls writhing on spiral staircases like in a television dance show. The three of them waited in line, then took a booth by the front door, where the music wasn't quite so loud. Olden and Scarlet sat together arm-in-arm while Gray stayed on the other side, stirring his vodka with a bright red straw. Yellow foam leaked from a big rip in the upholstery, and he picked at it until finally the fabric caught and the seam split along the edge. Embarrassed, he covered the hole with his jacket.

"Cheap place anyway," he muttered, chugging his vodka down to the ice. "Adds to the effect. Graffiti on the tables, probably done by a professional, some hired hand—oh, make it look authentic, use real curse words, 'Jimmy loves Cathy' and the whole bit, signed by the artist, collect all five, lookit, this one's different than the other but it's all bullshit, HA HA!"

Scarlet rubbed Olden's thigh under the table, but talked mostly to Gray, cupping her hand around her mouth, almost burning her chin on the hot orange of her cigarette. "I think graffiti is cruel," she said, dragging on the filter, making the ash go bright. "When they do that to trees. Or even if it's plastic. Then that's just as wrong, because you're still killing a living thing."

Gray wadded up a napkin and dropped it into his empty glass. "Ah, but by that same logic, what about this table?"

Scarlet looked down at the nondescript slab of wood. Already she'd lost track of the argument. She wanted to talk about something else. Cars. Magic spells. "It's kind of a cruddy table," she shrugged.

"Why are we talking about this?" Olden asked, his own little contribution. Scarlet laughed and touched his cheek.

"Let's drop it then, baby." A curl of smoke hovered between her lips, not moving, maintaining its wave-shape. Putting her hand back under the table, she looked at Gray and said, "Oh! Do you like baseball?"

Gray stared for a moment. "Wait," he said. "I still haven't made my point yet."

"Oh, about the . . ." She blunted her cigarette in the tray and coughed without covering her mouth—a loud, phlegmy hack. "Well. What?"

Gray looked at Olden, his eyebrows bobbing over the ridge of his glasses. "Can I make my point?"

"Sure, make your point, Gray," Olden said, keeping an eye on the crowd.

Gray moistened his lips. "Look . . . all I'm saying is . . . people spend *way too much time* talking about . . . things that . . . don't necessarily have anything to do . . . with anything."

"Right." Scarlet, trying to be nice, smiled and lit up another cigarette. "You know?"

"Oh, totally."

"And the problem with that is . . ." Gray slowly tipped forward, his mouth wide open, trying to sneak up on the next word, to take it between his teeth. "I completely forgot what I was going to say."

They stared out at the growing crowd, feeling trapped inside their little booth by the bodies and the noise. A group of young guys—all dressed in nice slacks like men in a pants commercial—stood right next to them, talking about a pornographic movie; it was impossible not to hear the graphic details, what she did and then what he did to her. Olden was embarrassed, mostly for Scarlet's sake, though if he knew her better maybe he wouldn't have felt that way. Slowly, a new feeling came over him, and he imagined his left arm as a giant bird's wing, draped protectively around her shoulder. Over the past three years, he'd conditioned himself against this sort of thing. One name—Gloria—stood for all the other women in Olden's life. Now he wasn't so sure.

Gray stood, jangling his keys. "Got to run."

"No," Scarlet said, but she offered her hand anyway, letting him go.

"Sure." He waited for the expected line, the speech about driving home drunk, but neither Olden nor the woman said a word, so he added, a bit maliciously, "You two lovebirds."

The couple moved closer together, thanking him for his endorsement. Turning, he waved over his shoulder. On his way out the door, he saw a woman standing in the entryway, trying to take an octopus costume off over her head. Foam tentacles waggled on strands of fishing line. A circle of people stood nearby, watching apprehensively. Gray approached the woman and said, "Do you need a hand?" but she didn't respond, so he crouched down and peered inside the eyeholes, blow-holes, whatever you call 'em, and he repeated, "Do you want me to pull?" but she just sniffled and told him to go away.

So, home again. Gray moved his car to avoid getting a ticket, then walked the six blocks back to his downtown apartment. A stack of take-out menus and Christian literature made a slippery mess on the entryway floor. A squashed roach decorated a tiled mosaic near the elevator—big guy, with distinct entrails like rodent guts, not just an amorphous jelly but something that looked like a stomach, something that looked like a heart. The elevator bucked up to the third floor. Each floor in Gray's building had its own strange smell. His was pesticide. He leaned into the door with his key, missing the lock a few times before finally getting it right. Taking his shoes off, he followed his long floppy socks into the kitchen, where he downed a jar of pickled mushrooms and drank a beer. He looked at his reflection in the dark window and burped at it. The light on the answering machine blinked a constant rhythm, six messages for someone named Francis, each more desperate and ominous than the last. Gray stripped down to his boxer shorts and turned on his computer. The OS went through its usual sing-songy introduction as he bobbed in his seat, trying to stay awake. He wondered if he could do it tonight. Shut out the distractions, the other crap. Well, writing. A bit of a game. Just put the words down. Make something up. But lately every-thing that Gray made up sounded like bad copy, the same insincere non-sense he wrote every day, nine to six, the adman's curse, meaning nothing, believing nothing, pushing other people's products, and no room for your-self anymore. The margins between day and night were hazy; no longer could he compartmentalize, keep the BS on one side. Now it was all BS, even his own work, the big three pages per month, chapter one, chapter one, chapter one, every word of it as empty and unfelt as selling potato chips or fire insurance or—this week—orthopedic shoes. Still, in his mind he saw the character, the situation. He saw the story he wanted to tell. Then he felt ashamed for wanting to tell anything, embarrassed by his own arrogance, his vague dreams of greatness, the banality of it all; yes, even his own ambition was banal. Just do your job and shut up about it. Nothing wrong with that. But there was everything wrong with that, for he hated it, all the stupid commercials, the dip-shitty thirty-second spots, hated the whole *idea* of it—most of all, he hated himself for being good at it. And the less he cared, the better he was. Here's Gray at work, designing citywide billboard campaigns, million-dollar affairs, half-drunk, half-asleep, half-looking at the page while half-jerking-off under the drafting table. For this he was rewarded. When would it end? Probably never. Promoted endlessly, up and up, ever closer to that great grave in the sky.

The phone rang. He stumbled into the kitchen and picked up just as the answering machine began to kick in. His heart banged against his chest. The usual fear. Late-night phone calls. No bad news, just the terror of the sudden noise, the secret voice on the other end.

"Francis?"

Gray cleared his throat, going for an effect. "N-no, this isn't Francis."

The voice jumped over a tiny hurdle. Tears. An intense situation—but someone else's. "Who's this?"

"This is Francis's friend." Gray looked at the fuse box, the scuff marks over the baseboard, the calendar on the wall. "Rick."

"Rick, I don't know you, but could you please tell Francis to call his mother as soon as he gets in."

"Let me get a pen." Gray didn't move, just kept looking at the calendar, searching for a random date. The ninth. Gets its own box.

"His father's in the hospital."

"I'm writing it down."

"No, he's got the number." The voice faded, speaking to someone else. In the background, he could hear an institutional din—a busy hallway, PA announcements, a man sobbing violently. The woman returned, less frantic now, already on to the next thing. "I've got to go."

Gray listened for the click, then hung up the phone, went back to the computer and wrote: *Francis hated his name. Hated the ambiguity of— is he a boy? or a girl?* Ah, maybe, he thought, closing his eyes, but when he woke up it was six a.m. and the computer had gone to sleep, dropped the file, forgotten already, a new noise on the streets, loud trucks in the courtyard and early cops shouting, "Move the junk!"

The Morning After

Some dreams are third-person dreams and others are first-person dreams. This is a first-person dream, meaning that it is not a movie but rather a physical experience. The meadow is a finite land, and it curves around a circular border. There are trees here, but they are pink, and their leaves are hard and geometric. The smell of grass seems artificial, as if sprayed from a can. Scarlet wears a pale nightgown, nothing underneath. The grass is wet and it sticks to her feet. Though she is running, she feels at ease, drowsy even. She can see her legs pumping, two limbs joined to the rest of her body. With each step, she feels the ground slipping away. This is what she remembers, this sensation. This is what she knows has happened in the past, in her waking life. She knows this movement with her whole body, and as her feet leave the earth, she can feel herself accelerating toward the high bursts of pink vegetation—up and up, into the cannonfire! Her pigtails branch out from either side of her head like the wings of a corkscrew. She travels by instinct; she identifies her destination and soon she is there. Glowing birds scatter at her approach. They leave their hidden homes and race toward the curved edge of reality. The dream switches briefly to third-person, showing the same pattern but from a distant perspective. Her journey from the ground to the sky splits into a series of still images. Numbered reference points correspond to handwritten descriptions, highlighting important steps along the way. The whole process, explained at last.

.　　.　　.

In the morning, Scarlet's body felt weighed down, returned to its natural state.

"Good morning." Olden was already awake, watching her. His raised knee made a teepee under the sheets. The bedding hung to one side, exposing the scribbles of hair streaming from his navel to his groin.

"I love these sheets." She gripped the mattress, fingers clutching at the bedspread. "Where did you get them?"

"I have no idea."

She smiled, still waking up. A slow thought formed inside her brain. "They're so *guy*. When my father was in recovery, my mother wouldn't sleep with him, so he bought a cot and set it up in the basement. I remember going down to see him. His sheets were plain white, like in a hospital. Scratchy. He hated that place."

"Your father." He rolled onto his stomach and the sheet followed. "You still keep in touch?"

"Oh yeah, they're both cool now." Dismissing the subject, she rubbed her nose on the pillowcase. "My father's a really beautiful guy. Even back then, we always used to hang out. Every night I'd bring him silly little presents, like tiny dogs made out of pipe cleaners, and then we'd play board games for a few hours before it was time to go to bed."

"What games did you play?" he asked, liking the trivia, the silly details.

"Whatever." She shrugged and the sheets fell over her shoulders. "The usual ones. Whatever was cool at the time. I think Mastermind was big back then. We were a pretty normal family." Lying on her back, she looked up at the ceiling. Mildew stained the plaster yellow in places. She wanted a cigarette but the pack was too far away. "I always wondered how he managed to sleep down there. The cot squeaked every time you moved, and the basement was cold and gross, and there were these black bugs that came out of the drains as soon as you turned off the lights. Maybe he *didn't* sleep. It only lasted a few months. I guess that's probably the best way to get sober."

"It sounds like my father's room."

She turned her head. Her cheek was wrinkled from where she'd slept on her hair. "Your mother and father, they don't sleep together?"

"My mother's out of the country most of the time. And my father . . . is traveling as well."

"Ooh, a little orphan!" She grinned. Her teeth were small and square. "That's so cute."

"I like having you here," he said, holding her wrist. She dug her elbow into his side, coming closer.

"I like being here."

One whisper, then another, and then the whispers turned silent, and now their lips were together, a pink twist, pulsing, never the same shape twice. Pulling away, she raised one leg and braced him between her knees, fumbling with his penis, finding it, making it fit. She did this without unnecessary deliberation—almost a chore really, grab-it-'n'-go. Olden lay still, letting it all happen to him, staring only at her left hip, the outward curve, the dip toward the center, a gray shadow, and he reached out and put his thumb there.

"I like it in the daylight. Seeing you."

"Much better."

Cupping his hands around her tight dancer's bottom—warmth coming from the crack, also moisture, thicker and more adhesive than perspiration—he kissed her violently, holding her tongue between his teeth, threatening to bite. They turned over, slipping halfway off the mattress. The toes of his right foot touched the cold floor. Scarlet's breasts sagged, melting into her chest. Red skin outlined the space above her heart.

"I love it when you do that."

"What's that?"

"When you pull up against my clit like that."

Olden exaggerated his stroke, wanting her to feel it, but it was all a bit stagey and soon she started to laugh. Smiling, he laid his palm flat against her chest and said, "Your heart's beating."

"So's yours."

"I love your body."

"Touch it then," she breathed, feeling the wall behind her.

He touched her right armpit where her skin was rough with new hair. The hidden ducts made a fibrous ball that rolled against his finger, then his tongue.

"You like that?"

"Yeah. Go harder. Pound it."

Half in love, they fucked. Outside, black birds flashed past the window, a dark square divided into four equal sections. The day was clear and crisp. The air smelled of wood fires, someone making pancakes. High above, squirrels raced in panicked circles. A human voice strained against the sounds of the country.

Hot and tired, they lay together in Olden's bed with the white, manly sheets wadded up at their feet. The floor was a trail of clothes. Three used condoms sat like desiccated bugs under the nightstand. Scarlet went to the window and looked out. The light made pretty splotches down her back and legs; her spine was a dark line, curved. Turning, she crept back to bed, pointing at the computer as she passed. "Aren't you afraid of someone stealing that thing?"

"Not out here."

Still thinking about something, she found a comfortable spot next to him. "You have your own business?"

"I do a lot of things."

"You don't have to tell me."

"No, I want to tell you. I want to tell you everything." Retrieving the sheets, he pulled the covers up around their shoulders. "I actually do have a real job. You probably can't tell, judging from the way I live."

"I like it here," she said, smiling optimistically. "It's like camping." Hands pressed against her stomach, she considered making breakfast—a warm breakfast, cooked over a campfire. Oatmeal and bacon. Hungry men, holding their plates.

"I used to live in South Crane City," he said, speaking to the ceiling. "I've been here since '95. A friend of my father owns the house. Owned. He died last year. Big executive in the publishing industry. He insisted I come up here. Rent-free. I guess he figured that anything was better than letting the place fall apart."

"What were you doing in Crane City?"

"Going to school, wasting time. I'd learned a lot about programming from my father. He was a mathematician back in the seventies. He worked with some of the biggest names in computer science. Vint Cerf. Bob Kahn. You probably don't know who they are." He looked at her and she shook her head. Good, he thought. Thank God you don't. "So when I graduated from Midwestern, I figured it was probably my best shot. I did all sorts of things. Web-page design. Private consulting. I configured LANs for local businesses. I couldn't take it for more than two years. Most of my friends were computer geeks. We didn't have much to talk about."

"So you quit."

"I quit. I got a job working for a construction company. Best job I ever had. Got in great shape."

"I can tell," she purred, using her sexy bordello voice, but he didn't notice, just kept looking at the ceiling. The ceiling was very interesting to him right now. Tiny craters. Goosebumps.

"I spent forty hours a week in the library. I didn't have a girlfriend, I didn't have much of a life. It didn't really matter. Instead I read books. I read medical dictionaries, obscure Eastern European novels, a two-volume history of Denmark. It was hard work. The books I read weren't dumbed down for the masses. That's when I realized: Information *should* be difficult to understand. It should be inaccessible to the general public. Everything else is bullshit." He closed his eyes and brushed against Scarlet's cheek, touching softly with the tip of his nose. "I'm tired of this stupid democracy." He moved down to her throat, speaking between kisses. "Life was bad enough without the World Wide Web. Now every ignorant fuck's got an opinion."

"So?" She felt his hair, combing it out with her fingers.

"So when it was time to move out of the city, I decided to do something about it." The words sounded empty to him; he was quiet for a while, thinking about his project, his silly little game. Egg Code. Big deal. But the Egg Code was just a ruse—an advertisement, really. His Web page stood for a greater purpose. The goal was physical, dangerous, immediate. The Egg Code only suggested an ideology, a rationale for future wrongdoings. He knew it, and they knew it too. Feeling better, he prodded her hip with his hard-on. She shifted a bit, making room.

"I think it's great that you know so much about it. I like a guy who knows stuff. Most guys don't."

"Most guys you know, what are they like?" He tongued her nipple, a hot rumpled pill. This amazed him—hearing her voice, sucking her breast. The voice, the nipple. Something vast.

"Dancers, mostly. People I work with. Everyone else, I know from school or else from the seminars I go to—sharing sessions, that sort of thing."

"What do you share?" He stopped kissing her and sat cross-legged in bed. His erection seemed silly now, tasteless even, and he hid it behind his raised knees.

"At the sharing sessions? All kinds of things. We play this game where we stand in a circle—ten, twelve people—and we're all holding hands: boom, boom, boom. And everybody gets an egg. So you're holding an egg in your right hand, and the other person's got his or her left hand around the same egg, and this goes on and on around the circle"—she walked her hand around in a circle, indicating the various places—"until this other person's holding an egg in *his* right hand, and you've got it in your *left* hand, all right? So if there's, say, ten people holding hands, then the number of eggs is also going to be ten, right? But each individual person is actually holding *two* eggs, because you've got one egg in your right hand and one in your left."

"So the idea is not to drop any eggs."

"Right. And you really have to trust your partners, because if the person who's holding the egg with you decides to let go, then you have to have the presence of mind to catch it."

"Why would he decide to let go?"

Scarlet cocked her head, trying to remember how it was explained to her. One loose pigtail dropped over her eye and she winked it away. "Well, you have to understand that some of these people have gone through some pretty drastic shit in their lives, and it might not be so easy for them to hold a stranger's hand for however long it takes."

"However long what takes?"

"For someone to lose. There's no time limit. The game ends when someone finally lets go."

"Depressing game."

"I think it's beautiful." She smiled, recalling the time she played, how they'd hugged afterward and drank punch. A meeting room in someone's basement. Low ceiling. The buzz of the fluorescent panels. She reached out and took Olden's hand. "When two people make a connection, it's like holding hands. But we're doing more than that. We're holding the egg too. It's not you and it's not me. It's both of us. It's our egg."

"I love hearing you talk."

"This isn't me." She swept her hair back, holding it in a bunch. "Derek Skye wrote a whole book about it. *These Eggs Are Scrambled! (I*

Asked for Over Easy). Good title, hunh? I'll bring it over sometime. I own all of his books. I've seen him in person sixteen times."

"You're a disciple, then."

Scarlet blushed. It made him feel strange to see her react so strongly to another man's name.

"No, we're much closer than that, and he doesn't even know who I am. I've been trying to meet him for years." She stared at their stain on the coverlet, lower than she'd imagined. "I keep having this dream. I had it again this morning."

"Tell me about it." He touched her knee and she unwound around him, resting on her side.

"It's a weird thing. Ever since I was eight years old, I knew I wanted to be a dancer. That's actually late," she added, lifting her head, "for most kids. But my mother gave lessons at this special academy and I always used to tag along. Her students were all physically handicapped. Some were in wheelchairs and some had to wear back braces and some weren't really handicapped per se but their minds were so damaged that they could hardly control their bodies, and basically the whole thing was really sad and scary and awful, particularly when you're only eight and don't know what any of it means."

"Keep talking." He felt her leg, wanting only to touch, wanting her to touch him too.

Scarlet smiled—a bit dubious, but amused all the same. "Mmm, so anyway, yeah, so I'd go to these classes and watch my mother working with these kids, and it was awful and kind of beautiful all at the same time. But what I remember thinking is that if you just put your mind to it, and if you showed a little courage, then you could overcome even the worst thing." She turned her knee, making it easy for him. Hot nerves skittered like stick bugs under her skin. "Here's some poor child who can hardly move, but with a little effort he can learn how to wiggle to the music and feel the rhythm and use the floor and laugh and hum and stomp—and if that's not dancing, what is?"

"Roll over."

Sliding onto her back, Scarlet placed her arms behind her head and held them there, imagining handcuffs, silk ropes loosely tied. "And so . . ."

"I'm listening."

"I know you are. So recently I started thinking about my own life, and how I've always been blessed with good health, good friends, enough money to live on." She closed her eyes and saw it again, the old, familiar vision. "But my dream's different. It's hard to remember. I'm weightless, always weightless, and I can dance over trees and through rainbows . . . it's like I'm the pilot of my own body. My mind takes me there. I can still feel it—oh, all the time, like it's locked up inside. A part of me says it's happened already, and that I've just suppressed the memory because at first it was almost too overwhelming to understand, and the dream's only my mind telling me that if it happened once then it can happen again, and maybe Derek can help me and maybe he can't, but if there's a man alive, he's the one."

"Yes."

"I'm going to come again if you don't stop." A cold wave poured over her body; her eyes looked sad and frantic.

"Mmm. Well. I know something you don't know."

"What?"

"Who."

"Who?"

"Derek Skye."

Scarlet sat up and seized his hand, stopping it. The words, the name. An instant recognition. "You know him?"

"Well, I don't *know* him." Olden drew his hand back, afraid of her now. "I did some work for him once. Fix-ups. He just moved into a new apartment."

"Where?" Scarlet was already halfway out of bed. Her feet pressed into the mattress as she staggered toward the door.

"Well, I don't know if he—"

"Tell me. I won't give you away. I'll say that I followed him up from the city." She scurried to separate her clothes from his. "It's in walking distance?"

"Well, sure, but . . ." The words ran out, and he could only marvel at her efficient way of dressing in the morning. It must come from working in the theater, he thought. All those quick costume changes. Her uncooperative bra wriggled like a Möbius strip, defying all attempts to bring the straps and cups in order. Giving up, she chucked it onto the bed and reached for her T-shirt.

"Look, just give me the address and everything will be cool." The tight collar stretched around her head as first one pigtail popped loose, then the other. "You have no idea what this means to me. Look, look—" Reaching for her gym bag, she pulled out a spiral notebook and flopped the pages. Both the front and back covers were missing, and the wire binding had come loose at the base. "I add to it almost every day. I've got quotes from all the tapes, ticket stubs going back to '96. I even copied the picture from *My Brush with Happiness*." Olden saw the drawing flash in a rustle of ink-intensive journal entries. A head, a mustache. A nice tie.

"Okay, okay." He grabbed the sheet and wrapped it around his waist. "It's a quarter-mile down the road. Turn right, and there's a row of apartments near the end of Main. His is the one on the corner. On the corner or right next to it, I think. Second floor for sure."

"I'll ring bells." Crossing the room, she stepped into her shoes.

Olden grabbed her by the waist. "Give me a second," he said. "I'll drive you."

"No." She pulled away. "I want to walk. I need to figure out what I'm going to say."

She opened her bag and dug through it. A sock. A gun. A new element entered the picture. Olden froze; the gun looked solid, like a giant lump, with no moving parts. "What's with that?" he asked.

"Oh, I always do this." She cocked her eye, checking the bullets. Putting the gun away, she gave Olden a quick peck and loosened his sheet, pulling on the free end. The sheet made a white mound at his feet. "Hold that pose," she said, then opened the door and skipped outside. Olden brought the sheet with him as he followed her onto the step and watched her go. Her short legs pounded up the hill and over the ridge. She walks like a peasant, he thought. A wide stance. Load-bearing legs. Smiling, he left the step and paraded naked around the muddy drive, holding the sheet over his head, letting the wind take it, a surrender to something.

VI

Go Girl

Portfolio

S. Blessing (4/17/74) — Session #1 — Mar 3, '82
Attending Psych. — Drs. Wink, Taylor
Colors Selected — White, goldenrod, pink, apple green, apricot (flesh)

A man's head. It is hollow. The skull swells to nearly twice its regular size. A caption reads "Daddy likes the funny floor." A crude phallus sticks inside the figure's throat. The phallus is apple green, and the base cradles two unusually well-drawn fists. The face itself is distorted; the right eye is three and a half inches wider than the left. Inside the brain cavity, a secondary line forms an interior chamber, containing a replica of the patient's bedroom. A young girl hovers above the bed; her arms are spread wide and her mouth forms a large O — either a screaming or a yawning motif. White swirls scatter across her body, stretching out toward the far end of the chamber. They collect near the top of the dome, where another caption reads "They can't get out!"

Scarlet was asked to draw a typical scene at home with her family. When asked why her father's eyes "looked so funny," she responded, "Because . . . sometimes Daddy . . . he sees things big here, and not big here" (pointing first at her right side and then at her left). This skewed perspective is characteristic of tetrahydrocannabinol — thus the observation that "Daddy likes the funny floor." More troubling is the image of the phallus, which the patient herself could not identify. Deep traumas brought about by the unexpected sight of a parent's genitals are common in children of the preadolescent stage. The patient associates this mysterious appendage with aggression, authority and, in cases of neglect, a kind of latent violence. This is shown by the placement of the phallus inside the throat—an instrument of both aggression and parental authority—and by the metamorphosis of testicles into fists. Toward the upper quadrant, the patient struggles against an unseen force. When questioned about this force, Scarlet was surprisingly candid. "I want to go up . . . but it's all zoomy . . . and the floor tips . . . and my shoulders go wham wham . . ." This is a longing for escape, a desire to penetrate the limitations imposed by her father's chronic abuse of marijuana and other substances. The white swirls are spectral elements, extensions of the patient's emotional frustration. These same swirls are also seen pouring out of the father's mouth, a sign of parental dogmatism or (possibly) semen.

Session #4—Mar 20, '82
Attending Psych.—Drs. Wink, Murphy
Colors Selected—Gray, robin's egg, turquoise, brown, orchid

The word SMELL divides the drawing in half. In one corner, a gray cooking range hovers at a steep angle. A woman wearing a tall chef's hat attends to the meal. Looming over the stove, she places one hand on each of the two front heating coils. Wisps of smoke and flame rise between her fingers. Near this image, various tentacle-like objects hang and sway from a disembodied nose, coiling in brown loops that extend in twisted sausage patterns. The other section shows a bottle of cleaning ammonia aimed at a giant TV screen, unpropelled by any human hand as it emits a wide, misty cone. A small figure curls inside the screen, hands tucked under one cheek. The figure's long hair stands in a straight bunch, dancing away from the side of her head. The ends taper into a swirled peak; an enormous cigarette bends to light itself on a loose strand.

Acting on the instruction "Show us what you feel like when Daddy makes the smoky face," Scarlet has chosen to depict her father as a

*mindless, oppressive force. In this context, the word "SMELL" serves as a
metaphor for sensual autonomy. "I like the smell when you put your
hand up to your mouth and breathe," she says, demonstrating this
technique by pressing her nose against her palm. "And then you go, 'Oh,
I can smell my skin, and the bone inside, and they smell like brown
cookies, but before they're hot.'" The act of smelling becomes an act of
self-assertion, of passing from infancy to full womanhood. That
femininity is embodied in the form of the female cook. Unable to feel the
heat of the stove, she demonstrates a poor sense of social orientation.
Drug imagery abounds as well. Nearby, a giant nose emits a disgusting
growth of fleshy vines. These vines, which appear at first to be strands of
mucus, are in fact intestines, bits of stomach tissue heaved out in a rage
of cocaine paranoia. "Gore! . . ." the artist stammers, clearly distraught
at the sight of her own creation. Elsewhere, she assumes a more
introspective approach. The TV screen is an example of wish projection,
a desire for a more normal social order, as typified by the spray-on
cleanser. Comfort eludes the patient, even in dreams. With his illicit
cigarette, Mr. Blessing feeds upon his daughter's essence, consuming her
youth and blowing it out in clouds of narcotic gas. That this drama
should be played out within the context of television only emphasizes the
patient's feelings of derangement and psychosis.*

*Session #6 — Mar 29, '82
Attending Psych. — Drs. Wink, Blondon
Colors Selected — Red, yellow, orange, brown, violet*

A mouth gapes. The teeth are arranged on a lower jaw; they are huge
and oddly spaced. The overall color impression here is hot, summery,
the red and brown brilliance of cherry candies and fresh scabs. A yellow steak knife cuts a lascivious tongue in half. Inside each section,
we can see an intricate compartment, quite like the fuselage of an air-
plane, though sliced down the middle to reveal the seats and the layer
of steel-bolted insulation under the passengers' feet. A little boy skips
down the main aisle, carrying a bundle of big balloons. Most of the
balloons bang against the roof of the compartment, though one
reaches around and trails up the side of the page. A tiny girl smiles up

at the balloon. A heap of paperback books lies at her feet. Lastly, an old woman sits near the back of the fuselage. A pair of reading glasses hangs from her neck. Inside the lenses, we can see the reflection of her smiling face, her twisted mouth made huge by the curve of the glass. Her lips sag and fold around an empty space. The conceptual continuity of this drawing is remarkable, given the fact that the artist is only seven years old.

Not only Scarlet's most successfully executed drawing, it is also the most upbeat in character. This change of mood is perhaps due to a new acquaintance with the teachings of Derek Skye, whose book My Daddy's Different: A Little Person's Perspective *was recommended to help the patient cope with her father's addiction. She seems to have benefited greatly from the added assistance—witness the smile on her protagonist's face, the happy iconography, even the very nature of her color choices— warm shades, hot-red derivatives. The image of the divided tongue continues an earlier obsession with human anatomy, an anatomy rendered unreal by its hollow, chamber-like design. Inside, we see a cross-section of humanity, spanning all age groups, types and fashions. The young boy—a peer, presumably—takes most of our attention. The balloons are tokens of social affirmation—friendship, communion, love. Society is represented by the old woman in the fuselage—toothless now, her smile rendered benign. When we asked Scarlet to identify the woman, she only replied, "At the drug store, you go in . . . there's pills! And the old lady says 'How much?'" It seems likely that this person— whoever she is—is really just a stand-in for another, more significant figure in the patient's life. Often when we enter a new phase of development, we feel the need to deny the image of what we once were— a kind of emotional shedding-of-the-skin. Having shared the contempt others once felt toward her father's addiction, Scarlet can now face the future as a whole, strong being, unencumbered by fear, ready to love herself and others. We will have to let Mr. Skye know of his success.*

Session #7—Apr 2, '82
Attending Psych.—Drs. Wink, Brock
*Skye Visiting
Colors Selected—Goldenrod

A thick slash makes an uneven diagonal from the upper lefthand corner to the middle of the page before streaming off into a fine line of faint color.

This drawing, much less developed than the patient's previous work, reflects a distracted state of mind, caused perhaps by the presence of our illustrious guest. In the future, we will limit such visits to only those patients less prone to recidivism. In the case of young Miss Blessing, we fear we are right back to where we started.

The Plot Thickens
Somewhat

1998

The box sat on the kitchen counter in Derek's apartment, ready to go. Outside, he'd found a fresh dog turd and carried it upstairs in a paper bag. Lining the box with colored tissue paper, he opened the bag and emptied its contents. Like a pampered noble, the turd sat upon its crimson perch as it endured the closing of the lid. He weighed the package in his hands. Light. A nice present. Moving to the sink, he washed his hands in hot, soapy water, dried them, then reached for a roll of electrical tape, which he wrapped twice around the box. Black and shiny, the package resembled a homemade bomb.

He did not want to do this. The gesture seemed so puerile, so gratuitous. But it was, perhaps, the only message that Donna would understand.

The doorbell rang. Surprised, he hid the box behind the refrigerator and hurried down the steps. The observation window—an octagon, vaguely nautical—showed only the road and the woods on the other side. He opened the door and looked down. "Yes?"

The girl on the step dropped her heavy backpack and fell forward. Derek caught her by the arms, his eyes fixed stoically on the horizon.

"Mr. Skye!" The girl's voice broke. "Just the sight of you . . . I'm sorry." She fanned herself with her hand. "I almost had a heart attack."

Leaning across the porch, Derek looked both ways, checking for open doors, shocked neighbors, the inevitable look of disapproval. Recovering a bit, he said, "I'm not sure that we've . . . you're from one unit down?"

"Oh, no. God, no! I don't live here. I don't live anywhere near here."
She stepped away from the entrance and gestured toward the road.
"This is crazy, out in the middle of nowhere . . . Derek Skye! I had no
idea."

"Yeah, well." He shrugged, wedging his hands under his arms. "You
got me."

"Oh! I'm Scarlet."

She was a groupie—that much was certain. Reggie Bergman must've
leaked the address. Still, she seemed like a nice kid. He nodded sagely, a
full bow from the waist.

"Hello, Scarlet."

"Scarlet Blessing. I know, it's a hooker name, but I swear to God I'm
not . . ." She brought her hand to her lips. "Oh, shit, that was a stupid
thing to say."

"Right," he said, studying her now. There was a smell about her—cigarettes and perspiration. Her clothes were a mess, and she wasn't wearing a bra under her T-shirt. "Welcome to the neighborhood."

"No, but that's not why I'm here at all." Her words came out in a
rush. "When I heard you were here, I had to come over right away . . . I
had to, you know . . . well, you probably don't know. I just . . . can I have
a glass of water?"

Running out of steam, she bent over and took a deep breath. Derek
fanned the door a few times, then held it open with his foot.

"Why don't you just, um . . . just come on up."

"Oh, wow. This is so sweet."

He led the way up the stairs to the second floor. He moved slowly,
hearing her footsteps, wanting to hear each one. It made no sense, this
paranoia. Still, he knew his followers. They were all nuts.

"I'm sort of in the middle of a project right now," he said, tired,
halfway there. Ten more steps.

"I'm sure you are."

"But if you"—*step four*—"just need"—*focus on*—"a drink of water"—
your secret strength.

"Oh yeah, totally, I won't take up any of your time. I just had to talk
to you about, well, I mean, it's kind of weird but . . . I'll tell you when we
get upstairs."

"Fabulous."

"Wow. You wear socks. That's so cool."

"Careful, the stairs are steep."

"Do you ever come out here at night and just, like, check out the stairs?"

"No, not really."

Once inside, he filled a plastic breakfast tumbler with water from the kitchen sink, then walked across the room and gave it to her. She wrapped her lips around the rim and drank it down. "Somehow I thought, Derek Skye, he must live in a giant house, with horses out back and a built-in swimming pool, you know, but then I read somewhere about how you gave like half of your royalties away to charities and stuff, so I thought, Wow, that's kind of cool."

"Where'd you read that?" he asked, hearing a lie.

"November '96, *Midwest Perspectives*. The chick who interviewed you, was she a bitch? 'Cause she kept asking you all of these really rude questions, like, 'Oh, isn't it true that you hire people to go out into the audience and say things like "Yeah, I took Derek Skye's class and all these great things happened to me" when in fact it's total bullshit—' oh!" Another quick stop. Endless apologies. He hoped she didn't get that from him. "I didn't mean to come barging in here like this."

"Not at all."

"I thought you were like, 'Oh, God, get her out of here.'"

"Of course not." He glanced over her shoulder and checked the hall-way. It made him nervous, leaving the door open like that. Now the onslaught. Floods of madness. He retreated to the living room and she followed, unable to resist.

"It's so nice to hear you say that, 'cause the reason I ask—" She stopped and hit her head, hating herself. "Shit, I'm totally going into a negative feedback loop."

"Relax." His hand hovered an inch above her shoulder.

"I'm just a little nervous to be talking to you like this."

"Well, don't be." Irritation flickered across his cheek. "That's absurd."

"Okay. Let me do this." She grabbed the back of a chair, her courage rising, filling her chest. "Okay. Um. Samurai warriors—no!" Her hands flashed up to erase the words. "Oh, shit, that's a dumb way to start."

Derek made a fishy expression, not getting it. "Samurai . . . ?"

She nodded, vibing with him now. "Well, you know with the samurai warriors, there's always the old master, and he usually lives in a remote village, or not even in the village but way off in the mountains where you have to climb to get to his fort, and the young warriors all make a pilgrimage, and only a select few are . . . are . . ."

"Selected?"

She stopped and stared at him. "That's incredible. How did you do that?"

Derek pointed at nothing, the space next to him. "When . . . ?"

"With the word. I was about to say something, and you were able to . . ."

"Predict?"

She shook her head. "No . . ."

He wavered on his feet. No longer trusting his words, he resorted to babble. "But . . . the samurai . . ."

"I want to be your assistant."

". . . the warriors . . ."

"I'll do anything. Buy groceries. Make photocopies. Do you have a dog? I'll take care of the dog. I read a book about going to vet school once. I know how to give a rabies shot."

He wet his lips, coming out of it. "Oh! I get it. Samurai warriors. Old master, young master. Now I see." He sighed, pleased with himself, then rubbed his forehead, confused again.

"I'll work for free."

"Why?"

"Because I need your help."

"I don't know what I can do."

"You can do anything!"

"That's . . . that's wrong . . ."

Scarlet returned to the chair and curled her arm around the seat back. "Remember when you told me I should start keeping a dream journal?"

Derek stared; everything the girl said grabbed him by the throat. "Yes," he said. Stunned, he listened to the dream, the scattered way she described it.

"It's like I'm really doing it. It's like I'm really flying. Isn't that fucked up?"

Dazed, he touched the clammy top of his skull. "Some dreams can seem very real," he said. Hearing him speak, she let go of the chair, and he felt obliged to lecture. "They *are* real, in a sense. If you know how to . . . if you know how to . . ." A wave of abstractions filled his throat, and he stopped talking.

"But that's what's weird. This *really* happened." She waited for a response, and though he didn't really understand, he nodded anyway, for the whole thing seemed so sad and unlikely that he figured why not, *what the hell, go along with the fairy tale*, but when she saw his reaction—the nod, the look of approval—her manner became more confident, and at once he felt phony and hopelessly corrupt.

She continued, "The feelings wouldn't be so intense if it wasn't true. At some point in my life, I had this special gift, like a temporary power, but now it's gone, and I've got to get it back. You know how it is when a kid gets molested at a very young age, and he doesn't remember it until he's like forty or something? And in the meantime he's just wondering why he keeps having these dreams about big hairy men with ten-foot-tall penises? It's the same with me. I deprived myself of the power because it scared me, and now that I'm older, my body's trying to communicate to me through my dreams. It's trying to say, 'Hey, look, you did this thing before and you can do it again.'"

Derek waited, going over the words. Special power. Trying to communicate. This was Skye-speak. He'd ruined her. He'd killed the girl. *My God . . .*

"I'm afraid you might be disappointed in me, Scarlet." Her face changed, and for a moment he read genuine disappointment in her eyes. It scared him, and he realized that he preferred the other Scarlet— the freak, the mindless believer. Turning, he hurried back into the kitchen and pulled a black parcel from behind the refrigerator. "But there is something you can do."

"Tell me what you need." She stood soldier-like, her back straight, hands at her sides.

"Take this package." Reaching for a scrap, he drew a map of the road leading out of town; in one corner he placed an X. "Just leave it on the step," he said, handing it to her. She smiled at the box, curious. "It's a present."

Scarlet studied the map, then tucked it into her pants pocket. The folded page felt good against her leg. Picky, she straightened some knickknacks on the coffee table. She did not wish to appear nervous or uncertain in any way; it would suggest to Derek that his teachings had failed her. "And after?" she asked, moving toward the door.

"After?"

"After I'm done? Should I come back?"

He felt his mustache, thinking about it. "Oh, I really should be alone this afternoon." She looked disappointed (again! his power), so he added, "But come back some other day. We can figure something out."

Perking up, she peered across the room to a dark corridor leading to the other half of the apartment. "What are you working on now?"

Anxious, he gave her the same reply he'd given Reggie Bergman back in August. "The usual. Another book, like last year and the year before. I just go from one to the other." He caught himself, not liking his own tone of voice. "But this one will be quite different. An important work. Important to me, anyway. If you're serious about wanting to help . . . well, we'll see."

"Even if you just need someone to keep you company every now and then." Scarlet grinned, her lips spreading to show a row of perfectly square teeth. "It's always nice to have someone to talk to, especially after you've been working all day." She laughed. "That's probably the only thing I've learned that I didn't get from you."

Near the door, she bowed low, making a flourish before going down the stairs. She must be high on something, he thought. Antidepressants, maybe. This was another way Derek's occupation had ruined his life, limiting his understanding of human behavior to medications and their characteristic side effects. Returning to the window, he saw her emerge from the building and head up the hill to the main part of town. A few dozen yards away, she turned and waved at the apartment, brandishing the black box high over her head. Derek waved back. Goodbye, girl. See you soon.

As the box waited on the steps of the Skye mansion, Donna was many miles away, a good forty-five minutes south of the township and six freeway exits outside of North Crane City. Her companion was Lydia Tree, and they sat in an outdoor café, lunching on Brie and melted berries rolled into tubes of scorched pancake. The day was not going as planned. Lydia seemed distracted, and she kept her big sunglasses on during the entire meal, flashing her black bug eyes first at the maître d', then at the waiter, then at the brake shop across the road. Donna kept her hands in her lap—head bowed, eyes focused on a strawberry seed stuck to the edge of her plate. It hurt her, this inattention. Here she'd spent three hours selecting her outfit, arranging her hair, matching scarves to shoes, when finally Lydia showed up fifteen minutes late dressed in jeans and a messy shirt untucked at the waist. No one cared, not really. Other women led busy lives, but only Donna took the time to ponder the significance of unimportant things. *Took* the time because she *had* the time. Lydia treated the meal like a feeding session, an hour at the trough. Stuff it 'n' go. But Donna lingered on each sip, dreading the check, the funereal trip home. Keep drinking. Just put it on my tab.

"He's being very selfish, and he's not taking any of your needs into consideration, and the best thing for you to do is to just forget about it."

"I can't do that, Lydia. It's not that easy. We were married for . . . it would've been twenty-five years."

"Don't cry here."

Donna fiddled with her utensils, exchanging a fork for a knife. "I mean, what about you and Steve?"

"Not a good comparison." Lydia looked past the table. White flares of sunlight puddled across her glasses. "The whole relationship is different. The financial structure, everything. If Steve ever left me, he'd be destitute."

Annoyed, Donna slumped in her chair. "As opposed to me—isn't this what you're saying?—where *I'm* the dependent one. And now with Derek gone, I might as well roll up and die."

Lydia hesitated. "Well, that's a bit excessive. You'll manage. It may take some time, but you'll meet another man—"

"Oh, that's always the answer, isn't it?" Donna seized the butter knife and twirled it around. "No other possible way. First there was my father, then Derek, then someone else. I just swing from one to another."

"Well, you're going to have to do something, honey. Do you have any IRAs, anything like that?"

"Oh, I don't know," she sighed, not interested in the technicalities.

"What are you—almost fifty, right? You can't collect on your retirement unless you've got something to retire *from*."

"Money isn't a problem. I wish it was. I wish Derek would at least give me something to fight him on." Gently, she reached under the table and held her own hand.

"He's not contesting anything?"

"Nothing worth going to court over."

Lydia leaned forward. "Is he well?" she asked.

Donna laughed; the question made her nervous. "I don't know. I don't know what's wrong with him. I thought that when my father died last year, everything would get better."

She remembered those weeks. The morning Derek woke up before sunrise, rubbing his head—nearly bald even then—and she'd asked what he was doing, but he just opened the door to the balcony and stepped outside, still rubbing his head, not a hard rub, but enough to make his scalp red, and she remembered the noise it made, a rhythmic shift, round and round, until finally he stopped and pulled out a suitcase, filled it with socks, just balls and balls of socks (looked attractive, all the different colors) and he closed the case and strode down the hall, shaking her off, the weeping woman, and he turned in the driveway to say something nasty—the final fuck-off, not worth recounting—and when he started up the car, the radio was on, a Pink Floyd tune, slow and somber, *I'll see you on the dark side of the moon,* and he left it on, backing away even as her fingers clutched at the locked driver's door, and as he moved out onto the main road, the sun broke over the pines and the music changed to Hall and Oates.

Lydia pulled a plastic cutlass out of her drink and swished it around. "It was like he was waiting for the moment when he knew you were most vulnerable, and then he stabbed you in the heart."

"I don't blame him. I can't blame him."

"Oh, please."

"I'm sorry, Lydia." Fork shift. "You don't know the whole story." No! Move it over . . . here. "I did some things that weren't very nice."

Lydia signaled the bartender and ordered another round, increasing the wattage, wine for vodka. "You need to get back at that man somehow, Donna dear."

"There's nothing I can do, and besides, whatever I try, he'll win any-way. I guess the only thing left is to just move on and—like you say—find another man who's willing to put up with a fifty-year-old, half-used-up—"

"Oh, come on. The self-pitying thing is not very appealing."

"At least I don't have any kids. That's a selling point."

"Never mind the man. I just said that as an example. No, of course, everyone knows that you don't need a man."

"Especially since, hell, I've got all this money now that Derek doesn't want it."

"So? That's great! If that's what he wants, if he's that stupid, let him!"

"Hmmm. Wonderful. I'm tickled pink." Donna moved her plate a quarter-turn; the strawberry seed slipped from nine to six o'clock. "You want some of this cheese?"

"No, I don't want the cheese, and don't change the subject." Lydia guzzled her vodka tonic and slammed the glass. "Now, this man has hurt you, and you have the right to say something about it."

Donna settled back into her chair. "What can I do?" she asked, start-ing to panic. Everything they'd ordered for lunch—the drinks, the hors d'oeuvres—suddenly seemed too expensive, way out of her means.

"Write a book." Lydia pointed. "There you go. Write a book. I dare you!"

"I can't write."

"So? Whoever told Derek he could write? Have you ever actually read any of that garbage?" She paused in the middle of buttering a bran muffin. "I mean, no offense, Donna, I know that you're still very close to the man, but talk about making a fortune off of the most dopey dreck ever committed to paper. What was that one . . . ? *Good God, Don't Do It!* . . . ?"

"*Good God, Don't Jump! Getting from Suicide to the Sunny-Side in Ten Easy Steps.*"

"There! See, now you're laughing."

"It's funny."

"It *is* funny."

"Always the ten easy steps. He made everything sound like a . . ." Donna trailed off, blanking on it.

"*That's* what I'm saying. You've been the good girl for twenty-five years, very supportive, very loving, and now this is what happens. Okay—boom!—now it's your turn."

Thinking it over, Donna turned her glass, looking for a clean spot, but the rim was dirty and so she kept turning it. "Reggie Bergman could probably help me out."

"Him, anyone. This is your chance. Derek Skye is all about one thing, Donna: men."

"Oh, well—"

"No, wait. Not just that. *White* men. Read what he's saying with that nonsense. The family. Keeping the family together. Success in the workplace. Doing the right thing for your family. We all know what that means."

Donna saw the books on display. Hundreds of copies, stacked high. "*A Woman Speaks Out* by Donna Skye. *A Woman's Turn. My Turn.* Didn't Rosalynn Carter write a book called *My Turn?*"

"Nancy Reagan, dear."

"I think *A Woman's Turn* is better. It's more specific."

"No, it's *too* specific. This is what you should do."

"Oh, no." She smiled, feeling teased. "Do I want to hear this?"

Lydia removed her sunglasses and set them on the table. "A book of lore."

"Lore?"

"Legends. *Fables.* Stories collected from all around the world. Tahiti. Where was the place with the AIDS? Was that Tahiti?"

"That's right."

"We go all over. Here we are in Outer Mongolia, where the natives are busy repairing the damage from last year's flood."

"Good, that sounds good!"

"Well, and then you write the commentary at the end. We can learn a lot from primitive cultures such as these. That way you can tap into the self-help market and cut Derek right in the balls."

"Lydia!"

"The ancient clay-maker."

"Who?"

"The old lady throwing a pot. See how her hands fashion the clay . . . this time-old tradition . . . like her mother, and her mother's mother, and blah blah, whatever the bullshit. The more pathetic and run-down, the better. Guatemala. The Australian Outback. Naked children diving for pearls in the Indian Ocean. Anything but Cal and his tweed pants fucking around on the putting green." She slapped the table. "*Many Voices, One Vision*. That's it!"

"That's what?"

"The name of your book. *Many Voices, One Vision*. Get a napkin and write that down."

"Phew, this one's yikky."

"We're writing things down on napkins. We're brilliant now."

Donna scribbled the title on a cocktail napkin and held it up to her blouse. It looked good there, like a boutonniere. "But the one thing we're missing, Lydia, is that I don't know anything about third-world folklore."

"So? Who gives a fuck? Who absolutely gives a fuck? Get him back here. Let's order some champagne."

"Oh, Jesus."

"Look, Donna, listen to me. If you can read, you can write a book. If you can do research . . . go to the library, they'll show you what to do. Or, the other thing, with the computers."

"Oh, right."

"Facts at your fingertips. And what you can't find there, you make it up, it's that easy. No one's going to care whether you checked your sources when you're sitting on top of the best-seller list."

"No, I suppose that's true. I just feel like I ought to be interviewing people or something."

"You want to round up a few thousand refugees, we'll go on down to the docks and chat for a few hours . . . these people can barely talk, Donna, for Christ's sake." She paused, then undid the top two buttons of her shirt. A busboy refilled their water glasses as she held the flap away from her chest, letting the air in. "You want to talk to someone, I know who you should talk to. The black guy, the one who just moved up to the lake."

"Which one?"

"As if there's more than one. He moved in a few days ago. Right on the water. You and I, we'll both go. Safer that way."

The ladies clinked glasses, and Donna imagined the work already completed, book published, congratulations all around. It intimidated her, for she knew she *could* do it, could get the thing in the right hands, but there were so many words involved, and each one had to mean something, and that's what scared her, making meaning, making it right. Angry questions. Nasty men. *Now Ms. Skye, on page* 208 . . . Oh, I don't know. I don't remember page 208. But if she smiled, if she seemed sincere. Then they would understand. No, it didn't have to mean anything.

"We'll do it today," Lydia said. "On the way back, we'll drop by. He won't care."

"Is he young? Old?"

"Older fella."

"How could he ever—"

"God knows. So, that's what you ask. You want authenticity, here you go. I'm sure he's got some gripping story to tell about life on the streets—"

Donna covered her mouth. "Oh, gee. Now we're being silly."

"We need that champagne."

"We do." She held up her glass. "Where's the waiter?"

"Here he comes. The dark one? Here he comes."

"I wonder . . . what is he, Spanish or Italian?"

"Spanish, looks like." Lydia studied the man. The waiter smiled, approaching. An easy glide. Pulled on a string. "I wonder if he plays the guitar," she mumbled, thinking—*ask him?*

The Black Man
in America

From the attic, Julian Mason could look out across the lake, past the tower and on toward the row of mansions near the opposite shore. The trees were wine and green and bare. The elm beside the house reminded him of a begging woman, limbs outstretched, body twisted in despair. There she was: his mother, guarding the place, her dead hands scraping the window.

But Mrs. Mason never begged—she'd worked hard, just like his father and the rest of the family. These references came from somewhere else. Whose memory was this, anyway?

The attic was dark and poorly ventilated. He'd brought his office up here for a reason—fewer distractions, too much hassle to go back downstairs. Near the window, a computer displayed a lowercase *h*—an italic, a digital recreation of the old Garamond issued by Adobe in 1989. The original letter had a heavier weight, with broad terminals and a large opening near the baseline. These new forms were too narrow. In Julian's prime, typesetting machines dictated the design, and men like Goudy and Morison worked hard to meet the demands imposed by this increased level of production. Their work began on simple graph paper, and from there traveled from metal to type and from type back to paper. Yet times had changed; as Julian grew, the art form grew away from him. New fonts, new versions of old fonts, all lacked those elements formerly associated with type—lead, tin, antimony. The digital designer worked with spirits, two-dimensional phantoms stored on magnetic tape. No punches. No files. Unreal. *Press F6 to erase.*

Julian sighed, touching the screen. Balls of white packing material clung to the plastic console. A flimsy instruction manual stood open to page 4. The woman on the customer service line had been very helpful, in a patronizing sort of way. Sir? The blue button on the back? No, not there. One over. There ya go! Slumping in his chair, he stared at the receiver, waiting for her to call back, to feed him the commands one at a time. The phone was a vintage rotary dial with a top-mounted cradle. Julian loved the old shit. The circuits never went bad. The great innovations of the last quarter-century seemed designed to function only under a given set of circumstances. Each configuration of hard drive versus OS versus application versus program versus installation was a unique phenomenon — essential today, junk tomorrow. Learning the software wasn't good enough. You had to stay plugged in, addicted to the vibe. It was all too much for an old man. Sheer incompetence blocked his ambition, hiding the dream. The goal was too remote. Toward the end of his life, Julian imagined twenty-six unborn letters, monster shapes lurking in the mist. An alphabet-in-the-making. There were other types with other names — Caslon, Fournier — but Candace was different because it was his mother's name, and after Julian was gone, there would be no other way to remember her except for this.

The phone rang. Two round bells mounted on tiny pins clanged together, making an awful noise. He jumped, looked over his shoulder, then smoothed his hair and picked up the line.

"Jules, T. Kenneth West here. How're the rednecks treating you?"

"Hello, sir. I'm fine. And how might yourself be?"

"Well, Jules, actually we're in a bind, which is why I thought I'd give you a try."

"Well, all right now."

"How'd you feel about pitching a contract to Cam Pee later this afternoon? You don't have to say yes or no. If you can just give me an answer within the next ten minutes."

"I don't know the person."

"Cam Pee's the CEO of Living Arrangements. They're a regional chain of mid-to-low-end retail establishments. They're looking to spread out, go zone-wide, hit the rest of the Great Lakes. They need a new print campaign, something snappy, something poppy, something hip and now. I figured maybe you could throw something together."

"Well, now. I seem to recall a prior commitment—"

"Don't answer yes or no!"

"Oh. Okay."

"Just let me know within the next nine minutes and we'll get going."

"All right. I'll wait, then."

"It really would be a big help, Julian. Naturally, we'd pay you under the table."

"Well, I don't need much."

"Oh, that's great. You're considering it. You're neither saying yes or no. This is good news. 'Cause I'll tell you, Jules, if not for you, I gotta go to Gray Hollows, and we both know what a pain in the ass he is."

"I don't recollect the name."

"Sure you do. Gray Hollows. He was here when you were here. A real smart aleck. My frustration level is at an all-time high. We need you back."

"Oh, well, now you're trying to talk me up, sir."

"Not at all. You were a coup for us. I need to hire more New Yorkers. This town's a wasteland. Look—I'm looking out the window. Nothing! Okay: a car."

"I like it, myself."

"Two hours, max. This is free money, Julian."

"Well . . ."

"No! You're right! Just think about it. I'm going to hang up. This conversation needs to end at this point. To say another word would be to disrupt the delicate balance between forces much too subtle to describe."

"Mmmnnnnallrightsir."

"I'll only say this. You should neither consider the words *yes* or *no* with respect to this issue until the proper length of time has passed. Which would be about eight minutes from now."

"Mmmwell, you have a pleasant day then."

Julian hung up just as the bell sounded in the entryway. Hurrying downstairs, he told himself to slow down. At his age, he'd earned the right to take his time. Still, he couldn't help it; he didn't like to keep anyone waiting. The unpacked boxes in the living room throbbed blue and red as his pulse pressed against the backs of his eyes. He slid from the bottom step and skated on slippered feet into the foyer. Two women were standing on the front porch. One was nearly as tall as Julian, and she wore round sunglasses that made her face look like a skull. The other was petite, pretty; she stood apart, drifting toward the edge of the porch. He opened the door and stepped aside.

"Brother sir, good day." The tall woman spoke in a solemn voice, using inflections that seemed unnatural to her. "My name is Lydia Tree and this is my friend Donna Skye. That's Skye with an *e*."

"With an *e*," he repeated tonelessly, staring at the woman's hair. Her assertive coif—blond and stiff—recalled an elaborate headdress.

"I understand that in your culture," she said, "names are determined by a spiritual leader who blesses the newborn with an iron brand."

"That a fact?"

"Welcome to the community!" She seized his hand and pumped it twice. Her skin was cold and hard, like a wet rock. "Are you a first-time homeowner?"

"Well, I've been a renter most of my life."

"Ah, yes." She turned and looked at her friend, who was standing on the lawn, nudging an orange leaf with her shoe. "The impoverished tenement houses. Tattered laundry blowing in the breeze. Elevated trains running at all hours of the night." Patting Julian's arm, she peered into the house over the top of her glasses. "May we come in?"

He nodded and led them past stacks of unopened shipping crates, tables and chairs wrapped in clear furniture bags. He felt oddly out of place—a squatter in his own house. Apologizing for the mess, he made a few trips around the living room with a small plastic broom, then found a pair of cement pedestals for the ladies to sit on. Fleeing to the kitchen, he opened the freezer and pulled out an ice tray, twisting it, making the cubes pop. Returning to his guests, he handed the ladies two iced teas and a plate of cheese and crackers. *Damn!* Forgot the knife. *Go back?* No, later.

"This tea is positively charming," Lydia said, smacking her lips. "Did you grind the leaves yourself? No, of course you didn't. How absurd. I'm just making conversation." Glaring, she tipped back in her seat; the rest of the room seemed to lean behind her. "The reason, sir, why we've come here today is because we need some information."

"Information?"

"Donna, perhaps you'd—?"

"Oh, Lydia." The other woman fiddled with her glass, watching the liquid slosh and settle.

"Donna is writing a book."

"She's exaggerating."

"How can you exaggerate you're writing a book? Either you are or you aren't."

"Lydia *thinks* I'm writing a book. I never said—"

"Discussions were made vis-à-vis 'Do we do this thing?' and the answer you gave me was yes."

Julian let the ladies argue for a while, then asked, "What sort of a book are you writing, madam?"

"Oh. Well. Hmm." Donna blushed, stirring her drink. "It's not really a book. *If* I write it. I don't know."

Lydia broke in. "It's a collection of motivational lore. A sprawling compendium examining the belief systems of many cultures from many different lands." Her hands flashed, pitching the words. "Their varied heritage. Their spiritual convictions. Their rough-hewn ways of life. I'm just stringing words together. This is a broad overview of the sort of thing you can expect."

"I always wanted to write a book."

Lydia slapped her partner's leg. "There! That's what we want!"

"Ma'am?" he asked, wanting to take it back—whatever it was.

"'I always wanted to write a book.' See, Donna, that's your lead-off sentence. The black man in America. His noble courage. Sweating over a factory job fourteen hours a day. Picture his children."

"One child, actually."

"Naked. Swinging from a fire escape."

"A girl. Emily. Course, she ain't so little anymore."

"This is perfect. This is exactly what we're looking for."

Julian reached out to pick up the cheese, but it had glommed onto the plate, so he set the whole thing back down, plate and cheese and crackers too, a nice fan of twenty, the top one broken but the rest okay.

"I don't know that I'd be all that useful to you ladies."

"Nonsense," said Lydia, turning to her friend. "Now, Donna, you ask the questions."

Donna stopped playing with her drink. "Oh, gee, uh . . ."

Lydia snapped her fingers, three regular beats. This is the tempo, darling. "Age, birthdate, middle name."

Trying to be helpful, Julian offered, "I was born in 1936."

"Ah." Lydia brightened, hearing a hook. "Near the height of the Depression!"

"Not really," Donna moped. "Depression was early thirties, wasn't it?"

"Near the height, *near* the height." Lydia huffed on her sunglasses and wiped the lenses with her sleeve. "It's gotta be at the very top, otherwise it's no good?"

Boots sounded in the hallway—slow, even strides. A young man appeared in the corridor, adjusting the clasp of a canvas tool belt. His faded denims looked rugged, and his flannel shirt hung open to show his bare chest. The ladies stared; their heads banged together as they both reached for a cracker.

"Hello? Mr. . . . Mason?" The man read Julian's name from a yellow notepad and knocked on the wall. "I'm the electrician," he said, scanning the floor. "Door was open so I came in. You want me to check the wires upstairs?"

"Oh. Oh, yes!" Julian's slippers slapped against his heels as he crossed the room. "No, not upstairs. I mean yes—upstairs, but all the way upstairs." He pointed at the ceiling, feeling silly. "My office is in the attic."

The young man brought out a huge screwdriver and cocked the shank. "I'll find it," he said, then continued up the steps. The ladies watched him go. Tipping her drink, Lydia cupped her hand around her friend's ear and whispered, "How'd you like to put *that* in your mouth?"

Julian returned to his guests, eager to speak after the lengthy preamble, and so he talked about his childhood, the wartime factories, his mother and the other women, the bomb builders, the celebrations after Nagasaki and the subsequent rush to buy property, but by the time he got to the fifties, he noticed that several minutes had gone by without an interruption, and so he stopped, waiting for a sign, a show of interest.

"Excuse me," Donna said, coming out of a daze, "what was that?"

"When I was living in Boston." He broke a cracker in half. Dust sprayed across his lap. "That was when I was working in the shipyards."

"Before that."

"Ma'am?"

"What did you say before that?"

"Before I moved to Boston?"

"I wasn't listening to any of it."

He coughed. "Oh. All right. Boston came right after Detroit—would've been about '52 . . ." He pointed at different spots on the wall. The places, mapped out. "Before that you'd have to go all the way back to Pittsburgh, which was where I grew up."

"Pittsburgh, Pennsylvania." Donna spoke the words slowly, making the place sound exotic, Polynesian.

"That's the one. We lived there for several years, back when my father was out fighting in the Pacific."

"And he was . . . ?" She frowned, needing more. "Killed in the service?"

"No, he came back after the war and worked in the auto industry for another twenty years before he passed on."

"Damn." She sucked in her cheeks. "This isn't really . . . dismal enough, is it Lydia?"

"It's coming, Donna. I can feel it." Lydia clapped her hands, resetting the scene. "So: Boston, 1952."

Julian straightened in his seat. "Yes, so I went to Boston and got a job working on the docks. I lived in a one-room place down by the water. Just me and a little coil to make sandwiches on."

"Describe the coil," Lydia said, closing her eyes.

"Uh . . ." He made a shape with his hands. "Little thing . . ."

"Okay, okay." She swished her drink, spilling some of it. "Just give us the nuts and bolts, and we'll take it from there."

He thought about that, the nuts and bolts, wondered what to say next—the essentials, okay, just the bare statistics, leave out the details, the old heating coil, the way the melted cheese dripped onto the hot part, then sizzled and turned black, and the taste of the sandwiches, always a little charred, the same thing each day, getting up at five a.m. for a quick breakfast, the harbor visible through his broken and barred window, the sounds outside, the bells, the bang-bang of the boats in the shipyard where he worked along with a thousand or so dockhands—mean guys, liked to fight, no harm intended but you might get a busted nose, and he recalled how they passed the time, painting dirty pictures over the hulls before covering them up with gray primer, and the funny accents of the beat cops, a constant menace, old Boston rednecks striding the boardwalk, *Hey, nig-gah, why doan you go hoam ahn take ah nahp?*, streets overrun with drunks and pissed sailors, and the bar on the first floor of his building where they'd patched a blown window with a red-and-black dartboard—window was round too, you see, so the dartboard filled the hole perfectly, and motorists would drive by and try to hit the target, thump thump, darts dropping to the pavement at all hours of the day and night, particularly between two and four in the morning when he worked on his drawings, his letters, designs of his own invention, and once a month he would send them home to his mother in lieu of money—ha ha, Julian very funny, but he told her that one day he was going to join a foundry where great men still developed new alphabets—not *new* alphabets but new ways of drawing the old ones—and his mother said that if he wanted to do that with his life then he must be someone special, which he believed at the time, but then she died and the decades passed, and little happened after that: some money made, but nothing permanent or particularly important.

Heavy footsteps crossed the ceiling. The ladies watched as a bare light fixture shook overhead. A steel measuring tape dropped from the landing to the foot of the stairs. The electrician followed, retracting the tape as he went. "Sorry. Just checking how far I've got to drop a line." He rubbed his face, sweaty from the attic. "Those outlets are grounded already." He stepped out of his work belt and set it on the floor. "You've got a free jack up there. If you get around to hooking up a modem, let me know."

"Oh." Julian cleared his throat. "No, I don't believe I'll be needing any of that."

"Don't need it?" The man shook his head. "Take my advice. It gets pretty effing lonely out here. Commute's a bitch, too."

"I don't plan on—"

"Sure you do!" He pointed over his shoulder. "What about those print layouts on the second floor? Your FedEx bill must cost a fortune." Digging into his pocket, he pulled out three business cards and passed them around. "I'll hook you up. I also do custom Web-page design. You won't ever have to leave the house."

Julian read the card and folded it in half. "Well, Mr. Field, I sure do appreciate it, but I'm pretty old-fashioned."

Lydia drained her drink, then said, "It's a strange name for a computer guy."

"I'm not a computer guy." Olden took the old man's seat as Julian left to find his checkbook. "I work with computers. There's a difference."

"Do tell." She tilted her glass, mixing the ice with her tongue. A tiny trickle pooled in the back of her throat.

Olden helped himself to some snacks from the tray. "Okay, then. For example. Your product. Which is . . . ?"

She brought the glass back down. "You're asking?"

"Or you can make one up. It doesn't matter."

"Well . . ." She looked away, trying to think. Outside, a deflated basketball drooped from a dead branch. Too bad Simon never liked to play. A few sports, third, fourth grade. The expensive uniforms. Chichi fabric. The other kids. Meatheads of the world. Drinking in the stands. Everyone's an alcoholic. Simon in his goalie uniform. Drowning in equipment. Hates the helmet, keeps it up whenever the ball's not in play.

She turned away from the window. "Does it have to be a *thing*?"

"It can be anything." Olden's eyes flashed. "A thing, a person, a—"

"A person!" she said, grabbing the edge of her pedestal. Donna gave her a curious look. "A person. My *son*!" Olden squinted, not getting it. "He's an actor. I'm working on building his career."

"TV? Movies?"

"Anything! He's a very talented . . . very *sweet* . . . uh . . . he's just a . . ."

"Oh, that's perfect. We need to get you on the Net. Three thousand hits a day. There's a lot of competition out there, but I know a few tricks." He pulled a Swiss Army knife out of his shirt pocket and cut off a square of cheese, placing it between two crackers, making a sandwich. Lydia hid behind the man's business card, rereading the words, the clever design, the neat, modern type. OLDEN FIELD—NETWORK CONSULTANT. Breathing quickly, she imagined a steady process—three thousand hits a day. Total saturation. Simon-in-the-air.

"So," she said, pocketing the card. "You do this for a living, hunh? You could put it all together for me?"

Olden finished his cracker, then shrugged. "Maybe." He dusted his hands and hoisted the tool belt over his shoulder. "We might have to work out an arrangement."

Julian returned and handed a check to the electrician. Looking down, he saw the cracker crumbs, the missing piece of cheese. He blinked. Crazy day.

Lydia stood up and tugged on her friend's sleeve. "Donna, I hope you don't mind if I take you home now."

"But Lydia, our interview—"

"That's for another time." She steered the other woman into the hallway, pushing from behind. Their high heels wobbled on the hardwood floor. "I've got to get back to my son . . ."

Confused, Julian teetered after his guests. "I was just starting to enjoy myself," he said, catching up to them near the front door. Olden stayed behind, inspecting the check.

"We'll take it from here." Lydia straightened her sunglasses and stepped outside. "Nineteen fifty-two: Boston, a bar, a bunch of junk . . ." She snapped her fingers, clicking off the main points.

Donna turned and waved through the screen. "Thanks a lot, for the . . ." She stammered, then gave up, feeling like an idiot. Her friend was already waiting inside the car. The horn sounded and she hurried across the driveway. Julian waved from the porch; when the car drove off, it seemed to take something with it—something from him.

Back inside, the men toured the place. Olden took the lead, pointing out things that needed fixing. Upstairs, he used a wrench to knock the glass out of a broken storm window. The pieces fell two stories and shattered against a concrete drain. "I'll stop by next week," he said, pulling down the screen. "The weather should hold until then."

"When does winter start?" Julian leaned against the window seat and casually took his pulse.

"Soon. October's usually pretty cold. Snow, sometimes. Several feet by January." Olden dusted the glass chips from the sill. His palm glistened with fragments. "I hope you have something to read."

"Read?"

"Yeah, and snow tires. We don't mess around up here."

Julian smelled the cool air breezing through the window. "Nice change, anyway."

"From the city? Sure." Olden curled his fingers and looked at his fist. "I like it out here. Interesting people. Takes a certain mentality."

Julian stared at the young man's hand and tried to smile. "Well, I hope I got what it takes."

"Oh, I'm sure you do." Olden excused himself and used the washroom at the end of the hall. Pipes groaned between the walls. When he returned, he showed Julian his hands, which were wet and stained with rusty water. "Your plumbing's shot," he said. "I'll fix it if you want me to."

Staring at the wall, Julian imagined a fat, snaking tube, bright metal leaking at the bends and joints. "Expensive?"

"Yeah." The electrician clipped his tool belt around his waist and started down the stairs. "But we can work out an arrangement."

Behind him, Julian clung to the banister; the loose rail shook under his hand. "More than a few hundred, I'll have to think about it."

"Well, you've got my card." Olden hit the landing and waited with his arms crossed. "How about a collaboration? Your work for my work."

Julian laughed. He gripped the newel and the turreted top bit into his palm. "I don't do anything."

"Sure you do!" The young man tucked his hair behind his ears. His jaw was sharp, a steep drop. "I need an artistic director. For my Web page. The technical stuff I can handle. The rest is up to you. New format, new type."

"Well . . ." Julian touched his neck, panicked for a moment, then found a pulse. "I don't know anything about the . . ."

"Even better. We'll stay out of each other's way." The phone rang in the kitchen—an electronic sound, different from the one upstairs. The even intervals imposed a time limit on the man's words. "Full control, Julian." He spoke slowly, thriving on the opposition. Keep ringing, you bastards. "Your design."

"Just . . . I have to—"

"Your letters."

"—answer that."

He scurried into the kitchen and snatched the phone in mid-ring. T. Kenneth West's voice sounded anxious, more desperate than before. "Gave you a few extra minutes to make that simple yet vital decision."

"Oh, with the . . . mmmm." Julian traded ears, moving the receiver from the right to the left.

"My intuition is telling me no. I'm hearing a kind of no implied by your reluctance to respond."

The old man went out into the corridor, stretching the cord, keeping an eye on his guest. "I certainly do thank you for thinking of me, sir."

"This is disappointment, Julian. This is the sound of bleak, steel-gray disappointment."

"I'm sorry, sir. It's just . . ." The words ran out, and as the other man rambled on, Julian could hear another voice in his ear, a voice recognizable as the voice of his predecessors, those ancient artisans who'd created new alphabets out of circumstances, religious and political and personal. Some of them created because their lives were at stake; others, because they believed God had commanded them. For Julian, the reason was simple. His mother wanted him to do it.

VII

A Brief History of
the Printed Word

The Flow

http://www.eggcode.com

The following text was composed by the fifteenth-century German
scholar Meister Weisskopf, a contemporary of Erasmus and one of
the founders of Christian humanism, a Northern European branch
of the Italian Renaissance. Weisskopf studied in Florence, and the
classical form he employs reflects his travels abroad. Though he was
a man of some intellectual skill, Weisskopf's reputation has dimin-
ished over time, and little of his work remains. At the start of the frag-
ment, the character named Hannah approaches her mentor, whom
she finds gazing into an aqueduct. As their discussion progresses,
they walk along a path until they encounter an urchin selling teeth
to a cloaked patrol of brigands. At this point, the text breaks off.

HANNAH: Herr Weisskopf, I am glad to see that you are well, but
   I regret your absence from our weekly convocation. I have
   longed for your presence, and I had almost lost all hope.
WEISSKOPF: Hannah, my astute pupil, I knew that under your
   observation I could not remain hidden for long. May the God
   of all men preserve your judgment.
H: But why have you come here? This is a foul and fetid place.
W: Legal troubles have driven me from my chambers. The suit
   recently won against the technician from Mainz is a worri-
   some affair, and I find myself in need of a partner to help construct my argument.

H: I am yours, my professor.

W: Well put. As I am your instructor, it is only proper for me to begin with a summary of the events. In brief, then. The defendant called Gutenberg is a German subject of some advanced years, and a citizen of this town. Years past, a vicious dispute forced Gutenberg into a long exile, broken only by a brief trip across the border to beg at the coffers of a former partner, Hans Riffe. In 1438, the two men, along with the Andreases Heilmann and Dritzehn, drew up a mutual contract, keeping the terms unresolved. Within the year, the second Andreas had passed on to his true, unearthly duty, leaving a fleet of relatives to squabble over the inherited fourth. Gutenberg, destitute but never desperate, denied them their rights, and a trial ensued. In the course of the investigation, certain secrets regarding Gutenberg's activities were brought to light. During the trial, lawyers produced one hundred guilders' worth of receipts for the purchase of a new shop in town.

H: A sizable allowance for a man in debt to put forth.

W: Your comments, my dear, are largely without substance, but they do lighten the density of my sometimes abstruse text. Yes, a sizable allowance, and a strange purchase too, strange enough to warrant Gutenberg's surveillance over the next decade. By 1448, he had acquired a new associate, Johann Fust, who agreed to loan first eight hundred and then another eight hundred guilders in exchange for a share of the business. But Gutenberg was a perfectionist — an artist, if we acknowledge such a thing to exist outside of the university. He was slow in his methods, and spent seven years working on his secret contraption. Fust's motivations were the motivations of all patrons — to secure a quick return on his investment, and to create further glory for his family's name. Gaining none of these, he brought the man to court, enlisting the aid of Peter Schöffer to help in the proceedings. The court agreed with his complaint and ordered Gutenberg to relinquish his property. The defendant known as Johann Gutenberg is alive today in this city of Mainz, and yet he is without credit and possesses no means of making a living. It is the rightness of this that you and I have gathered beside this channel to debate.

H: It could be argued that Gutenberg simply received proper justice for his offense against mankind.

W: Are you making this argument?

H: If that is what you desire.

W: Let me hear it first.

H: The proposal is this. The mechanized press credited to Herr Gutenberg is an unnatural device, unnatural in that it violates the three-tiered principle of law first alluded to by the ancient Stoics and later confirmed by Saint Thomas Aquinas. Aquinas spoke of the law's division into three parts: the law of the cosmos, the natural law of man, and the positive law, that is to say, the practical application of God's will onto everyday matters of peace, war, and commerce. An ethical flow, downward in its grade, connects the three layers, and the path is always the same. The positive law will never influence the Way of God; ours is an eternal supplication.

W: Your thesis, while pleasing in its rhythms, seems to dance before our senses like a young coquette tickling an old man's nose with a feather. Its purpose is only to elude and annoy.

H: Then hear this. This structure of three does not limit itself to the law of the Creator. All structures presume a multiplicity of layers. The stability of our layered society needs these definitions to preserve the flow of reason from the cosmos to the courtroom. Our learned men distinguish themselves from the ignorance of the crowd, and in so doing, they reinforce the divisions necessary to save the Christian people from the terror of chaos. The course of learning demands a sensible direction. Like coinage, it has no value unless rare. Gutenberg's strange device will lend an unhealthy speed to what was once the slow duty of the cloistered hand, and in this way, the whole earth will drown under a pool of unwanted words. The trusty aqueduct will balk at the demands of a rising flood. None shall benefit from this democracy.

W: This is the policy you seek to bring before your tutor?

H: Perhaps. There is another view. The defense maintains that Gutenberg is a hero, an icon of the times. This new tool has launched us upon the crest of a new era. At last, publishers may edit and duplicate documents in a uniform fashion. From one centralized location, a host of reproductions may flow across the land. No longer restricted to the quartered realms of the university, this fabulous wave of information may offer its riches to all interested men. Our culture, once defined by its concentricities of knowing and not knowing, now includes the lowly peasant, newly literate, able to obtain cheap books, printed by the thousands. The kingdom is a network of machines, and Gutenberg's device is the transmitter of the flow.

W: Of course, I might suggest that the cause of the lower class should be of no interest to the successful monarch. That an ignorant and illiterate peasantry is best suited to serve the needs of our economy. The man in the field knows his scythe. He need not know how to forge the blade from iron. The issue that troubles me, Hannah, is that of choice. Who chooses these roles that society deems necessary for our survival? The one Church itself has acknowledged the free choice given to us by our common Master and Creator. To what degree, I wonder, does this mandate extend? Is our choice limited to a simple election of good over evil? Or does God intend, by granting us this liberty, to plant within our lives a tree of choice, with each branch revealing a new and crucial binary? Soldier or physician? Beggar or monk? Peasant or patrician? Informed or illiterate? Are these choices really ours to make? At what point does such social mobility mutate into sin?

H: You seem troubled. I fear for the security of your convictions.

W: A conviction is a guarded fortress, dear pupil. Slots designed to launch the shaft of an arrow are unlikely to accept a similar blow from the outside. It occurs to me that our discussion has strayed from its original premise. My concern, once reserved for Gutenberg alone, has spread to encompass all of mankind. As a nation, we should fear the impulse that causes human hands to supplant themselves with chains and pulleys. Left without this new device, languages will die; and as the language dies, so will the people. This thing that Gutenberg has done should both be welcomed and never trusted by any careful man. The truth of life is the truth of God. The machine has its own truth, and it must be censored.

H: Your warning is not irrational, for already Herr Schöffer has taken to using sacred and traditional models for his letter-forms, drawing upon familiar examples such as the texture and recasting them as cuts of lead and brass. All of the old features are preserved, the ligatures, the florid initials. It is almost as if, knowing the time-trusted preferences of the reader, the new designs have consciously sought to cultivate these allusions. We believe the attractive word.

W: Is this what we have done, Hannah? How do we represent such a grievous sin to our Father and only Maker? Jesu, Son of God, forgive us for our evil machine. Its sole food is politics, and it excretes only propaganda.

H: If there is a penance best suited to the crime, Herr Weisskopf, then it lies in the just behavior of the vigilant man. You and I, sir, we are intellectuals. God bless us for our better judgment! We must serve as filters to the flow. Like a fine mesh, we handle the current, straining away poisons and delivering only the purest element to the garden beyond. The peasants know only their thirst; lacking discretion, they will gape and swallow at anything. Our alliance is with the invisible word. The truth has other children, but they are corporeal and therefore base.

W: Your optimistic words cheer me, my sweet Hannah. Ah, but see this smudge-faced boy selling his goods by the edge of the river. Let me make a gift to you of his wares, and in so doing, reward the boy with the same transaction. If there is but a shred of flesh left on these teeth, you may take them home and boil a stew.

P.O.P.

The Seedy Side of
Office Politics

1998

Kenneth West hung up the phone. Alone in his office, he brought out a pack of cigarettes, peeled off the cellophane, then—annoyed at himself—put it back. T. Kenneth was a man of many addictions, each pursued with a meticulous dispassion that could be interpreted as a lack of involvement. One cigarette per day. One glass of Scotch. Once a day, whenever his receptionist left the building, he would cross the room and place his cock on her desk. Just long enough to feel the tip brushing up against the ink blotter. A relatively mild iniquity. No jerking off into her makeup bag, none of that. He wasn't even particularly attracted to her—a rather squat woman with sandy brown hair and a taste for gigantic wooden earrings. Still, his need for this ritual surpassed mere sexual attraction, breaching the darker realms of compulsion and insanity. All afternoon, as the receptionist's fingers flew from binder to folder to wastepaper basket, T. Kenneth West would stare across the partitions and imagine his phantom cock hovering over the desk, following her hands in a ghostly dance. A secret awareness charged the whole day with risk.

Reaching for a cigarette, he struck a match and brought it trembling to his lips. Bits of tobacco sparked red and turned black. He drew in a mouthful of smoke, held it for a moment, then exhaled slowly, letting the cloud thicken between his lips. Better now. Stubbing it out, he threw on his suitcoat and virtually ran out of the office, pausing only to smile at the secretary on his way past the reception area. My cock was there, he thought, glancing at the neat piles of work on her desk. Just fifteen minutes ago. Right where her hands are now.

Fixing his collar, he grunted at a few interns, then turned left down a narrow corridor. Gray Hollows's office was a tiny closet at the end of the main hallway, the remnants of an old darkroom. The door swung out into the corridor, leaving a foot-wide gap. T. Kenneth angled his body and squeezed through.

"Christ, why don't you turn some lights on?" He slapped the switch and the overhead panels flickered to life. Trying to be nice, he smiled cautiously at the young man. Gray was a pain in the ass, a poorly mannered, immature little jerk. But good at his job. After five years, T. Kenneth had grown to appreciate his talent for understanding the underlying crassness at the heart of any new marketing campaign. As a rule, clients detested Gray the person, yet almost always liked the work he turned in, and T. Kenneth certainly couldn't fire a productive employee just for being a moron.

"Hey, Ken, look, listen to this."

"No, you listen to this."

Gray wheeled in his seat, rocking back and forth, making the chair dance on its casters. The chair, it seemed, was a ride. A do-it-yourself roller coaster. He steered across the room, aiming for a stack of blueprint paper.

"No, wait," he said, out of breath. "This is brilliant, you'll really dig it. Remember that radio spot I wrote last month for NCC Tech, with the idiotic music going on in the background, *doo-doo-doo*, and then the voice comes up, 'Techno, it's not just another dance craze.' Figured these kids are so fucking stupid, who'd know the difference . . . remember?"

T. Kenneth stopped the chair, blocking a caster with his shoe. "Gray."

Gray pushed with his heels and the chair shot back a few feet. "Come on, play along with me, pal," he said.

Peeved, T. Kenneth stared past the man's head. "Yes. I. Remember."

Launching into it, Gray sputtered, "Great, I was thinking what we'd do is, we'll hire some kid out of MU, have him interview his buddies—just interrogate the fuck out of 'em. What do they listen to? What books do they read? Who's the big shit with the teenyboppers as of September the whatever-the-hell-it-is at one-fifty-eight in the afternoon? Then we make a list of everything these kids have ever cared about in their short and pathetic lives, every real attachment they've had, favorite songs, favorite movie stars, who cares, nothing is too important where we can't use it to sell some idiotic product, and ultimately we get the whole process so refined that every time some poor kid hears something she likes on the radio—boom!—ten seconds later we're throwing it right back in her face, and eventually she gets to the point where she can't expend a single emotion before we're using it to get her to buy lip gloss or a car phone, and she winds up staying in her room all day just totally paralyzed with fear and the sense that there's nothing she can do or think or feel that can't ultimately be corrupted and marginalized by consumerism and popular culture, which of course is the straight-up fucking truth and don't forget it, bitch. HA HA! Isn't that funny?"

"You're a . . . you're just like a spigot, aren't you?"

"I don't know that word. I don't know these fancy words you big people use."

Hefting a thin manila envelope, T. Kenneth dumped a stack of service requests onto the desk. Gray rifled through the pages and covered his head with the top sheet, making a bonnet.

"Lovely, look." T. Kenneth swiped the sheet and held it behind his back as Gray clawed at the air, pretending to grab. "I want you to know right off the bat that you weren't my first choice to work on this project."

Turning around, Gray manipulated an invisible control and piloted his chair toward the exit. "If you were a car, what kind of a—"

T. Kenneth blinked, shouting it down. "That said, you need to clean up and comb your hair and do all those nice things—"

"I'd want to be a Jeep!"

"—because you're due up in Vega at three-thirty this afternoon, which is just ninety minutes from now."

"Ninety minutes," Gray said, tapping his watch. "That's, like, two hours, man!"

Giving up, T. Kenneth crumpled the page and left it on the desk. "Just passing on the information," he muttered, walking away.

"Man, you already told me! This morning you said, 'Fuck it, I'm gonna call Julian Mason,' and I said, 'Julian Mason is so fucking over the hill, he probably can't even go to the goddamn bathroom by himself,' and you said, 'Fuck you!' and I said, 'Right now, dude!'"

"I'm leaving."

"And then you started coming after me with this, like, battle ax."

"You are now officially talking to yourself."

T. Kenneth West strode out of the office as Gray fake-cheerfully waved farewell, his right arm moving up and down like an automaton at a theme park: "Thank you for visiting *Pirates of the Deep.*" Ah, goodbye, fucker. He grinned and saluted, then put his head down on his desk. Naptime, nyum nyum. Another day wasted. Time was the big problem in Gray's life. No one cared about his own little ambitions. Lifting his head, he blared out the chorus to a Van Halen song—PA-NA-MA! PA-NA-MA-AA!—but no one came by to investigate, so he stopped singing. This shit *sucked.* The first meeting with a client was always the worst. These fuckwad business types were rarely adept at shaping their own marketing concepts. Their contradictory adjectives smacked of a certain nose-holding schizophrenia. Make it snappy, they always insisted, yet sincere. Oh, sure. Catchy yet dignified. Such naive ideals. Gray could only hope that the board of directors would have the sense to leave the matter in his hands. Grabbing his briefcase, he slunk out of the office and stepped outside. If he hurried, he'd have enough time to scribble a few sentences back at his apartment. With that in mind, he climbed into his car and left work for the day.

When he arrived at the furniture store—not at three-thirty, more like three-forty-five—the parking lot was nearly empty, and he could see bored employees standing under the vinyl awning, smoking and waiting to go back on-shift. The air smelled of diesel fuel and hot upholstery. A bright sign hung over the front door: a red signature scrawled across a blue background.

"You got the right place," a middle-aged Vietnamese man called out as he walked down a wheelchair-access ramp and pointed up at the sign. "Living Arrangements, you got it, Cam Pee, president, CEO, here we are, you the guy from downtown, you come with me."

Gray fake-smiled as he shook the man's hand. Cam Pee was dressed in a slate-colored three-piece suit with narrow sleeves that tightened around his armpits. His constant leer seemed poised on the verge of implosion. Shiny black hair flopped about as he gestured and nodded, leading the way.

Living Arrangements was, so far as Gray could tell, a flea market in disguise, cut-rate crap ferried across the Pacific from Indonesia, the Philippines. Poorly manufactured furniture in wicker and pine leaned over the main aisle—chairs on top of desks on top of dresser drawers, an overabundance of stuff. The cashiers all were young ladies in their late teens and early twenties, each lost in a private void as they stared out the windows at the traffic on the highway. Six executives from the home office formed an anxious row near the main entrance. Dressed in blue suits and mirrored sunglasses, they each blandly reiterated the same basic look of the other five. Gray could see his reflection widen and contract from lens to lens as he followed Cam Pee down the receiving line.

"Last, here, you meet Jim Carroll." The CEO introduced Gray to a tall man with high, strangely solid hair. "Jim is Visual Merchandiser for—whole zone!" he said, pointing at both men, then crossing his arms, indicating an exchange of some sort. "You two work together—tight!"

The executives laughed; odd, thought Gray—nothing funny there. Suppressing an urge to—oh, lord, *anything* . . . play *air guitar*, complete with windmills and manic fingers on the fretboard—he followed the others past the cash wrap. A hand tugged lightly on his sleeve.

"Hey, mind if I stick my fat neck in here too?"

The team of executives shifted as a new man joined the group. He coughed, smiled, waved hi.

Jim Carroll scratched his forehead, hiding his embarrassment. "Oh, yeah, this is, uhh, Steve, Steve Mould, he's the—"

"I'm the manager of this store, Steve Mould. Nice to meet you, sir."

"Yeah. He's not the manager of . . . *all* the stores."

"No, of course not."

"Just this particular one."

"My little corner of the world. Betcha."

"Steve has been kind enough to let us borrow his office while we work out our business."

Steve's big brown shoes changed clock positions as he wheeled around and pointed at the girls behind the cash wrap. "Yeah. You all just do what you gotta do, and we'll . . . hold down the fort!"

Gray rubbed his eyes. "Super," he said, resenting the associations—his life, this man's enthusiasm.

"We're all set to go. I've got a great staff working for me today, and we're gonna . . . pump it out!" Steve made a little fist and punched the air.

"Nice, nice."

"No messing around, man. We're . . . yeah. Yup."

Jim Carroll moved between Gray and Steve, blocking the conversation.

"Cam, do we want to take Mr. Hollows into the back now?"

As the executives moved across the sales floor, Steve tripped along, walking backwards, latching onto the CEO's cufflink. "It's a real pleasure—and for you especially, Mr. Pee—to have you all here in my store. Or *the* store. The store, my store, whichever the case, uh . . . may be. And I just wanted to say—"

"Steve." Jim waved his hand in front of the manager's face. The crowd moved ahead as Steve backed into a display of stacked carafes.

"If you need anything at all, sir—coffee or paper or whatever—you just let us know, because my people are fired up to be here today, and we're all just set to rock 'n' roll!"

Jim took Steve's shoulder and pulled him back a step. "Cam, Frank, Bernie, you go ahead. I'll be right there. I just got a page from Cathy in auditing. It'll take me two minutes." He waited for the others to leave, then pinned Steve against an endcap. "What are you doing here, pal?"

"Just trying to be sociable to the new ad account, Jim." A bit miffed, Steve fanned out the front of his work apron.

"Yeah, well let me tell you something—you want to be sociable, try being sociable to Cam Pee's big fat heinie unless you want a fourth-division write-up next performance review. Where do you get off trying to upstage the Big Guy?"

"Oh, Jim," Steve whispered, feeling pretty slick. "A few words, a little hello, I'm entitled to that much."

"Steve, do you realize we've choreographed this entire affair down to the last maneuver? Every single motion—planned out in advance. I'm breaking the choreography right now, just standing here, giving you this reprimand."

Steve let go of his apron. "Is that what the heck this is? A reprimand?"

"An *informal* reprimand. Now come on! We picked this site for a reason—because you're a decent manager and because your cashiers are remotely presentable, compared to those jigaboos we've got working downtown. Don't fuck it up!" Catching himself, he noticed an old woman creeping along the knickknack wall, browsing the keepsakes. He smiled professionally and said, "I think this lady has a question."

Adjusting his tie, he hurried past the double doors to the backroom. Through the circular windows, Steve could see the executives filing into his office—*his* office!—and so casual about it too, standing in the doorway, blabbing away, the usual chat, all part of the act, a stupid kids' game, twenty-seven, twenty-eight years old, MBA ballbusters fresh out of school, not one idea to call their own, but they look good and they know the talk, and that's what it takes, m'friend, that is *it* right there in a nutshell and it's too bad but it's true, American business, wave of the future, leaves the good men out on the sales floor with the batty old ladies and their stupid questions, got nothing better to do, all of her friends are dead so she has to pester sales clerks trying to make a decent living, pushing their meaningless merchandise, keeps you forty-five minutes on a three-buck sale, good God, the same ol' yaya, yes ma'am, that there is one hundred percent gen-you-wine Southeast Asian lacquer, made and manufactured in Indonesia, special keen, just 4 U.

Thriller

1984

On television, a man stands before a series of charts. "Hello," he says, "my name is Herbert Hollows. I'm a scientist. I design prototypes for the Kellogg Corporation. When someone opens a box of Kellogg's Corn Flakes, he should know exactly what to expect. The flakes must all convey the same message. Speaking anthropomorphically, the ideal flake should say to the consumer, 'Greetings. Allow me to introduce myself. I am a Kellogg's Corn Flake. Please note my familiar shape.'" The man continues past a long drafting table. Cheesy music plays in the background, something from a sci-fi movie. "For this reason, the people at Kellogg have hired me to develop six templates, six variations on a basic theme. All future flakes will derive from these primary sources."

Dr. Hollows's voice upsets you: drab, distinctly Midwestern. This is not how scientists are supposed to talk. You seek the comfort of an exotic German accent, the fruity vowels, the *v* for *w* transpositions, the lab coat, the thrilling graphs, the clipboard, the adventurous eyebrows, the gurgling beakers. You want the *font*. You want the *scientist font*. This is why it bothers you, seeing this complicated schematic hanging above a drafting table two miles north of Battle Creek, Michigan. In pencil-drawn lines and dashes, the common corn flake appears otherworldly, like a supernatural gemstone. Already you fear that you are in way over your head. Television spoils everything. You would like to believe that these things just happen, that no greater purpose informs their structure beyond a plain desire to please you, the informed shopper. Touchingly naive, you still cling to the notion that there is fun in the world. Nothing is fun, my friend. Your every pleasure is a function of rigidly formulated theorems carried out to an irreducible conclusion.

But while your unhappiness stems from these impersonal revelations, Herbert Hollows has more daunting reasons for his concern. With malicious intent, his own son responded to the advertisement in the Kellogg newsletter last fall, calling for submissions from ambitious young filmmakers. Deliberately, dishonestly, he rented a 16mm camera and scads of editing equipment, needlessly wasting a whole year's allowance. Equipment in hand, he knocked on the studio door—said he was interested in his dear old daddy's work, and Dr. Hollows believed him, flattered by the attention, not knowing that his comments would later appear in the boy's contemptible commercial. Edited down, given a cheap, ironic spin, the thirty-second spot won a special citation from the heads of Enthusiasms, Inc. "What a talented son you have," they said, shaking his hand, calling him *mister*. Those shark-eyed salesmen would never understand the real work of the engineer. If they want his child, they can have him.

Walking off-screen, Dr. Hollows leaves his drafting table and strides down the hall of his modern, prefab home. Teenybopper music rises up from the boy's room. The window over the landing shows a two-lane highway cutting across a brown field. The sky above is blue and empty. He leans against the banister and shouts down the stairs.

"What are you doing?"

"What I'm always doing."

"Well, get up here."

"I can't now."

"Yes, you can now."

"Minute."

"And don't get sarcastic with me."

Downstairs, he hears the sound of typing, then a frustrated silence. His wife, Joan, encourages these literary pursuits, and while Herbert takes a moderate pride at the boy's obvious intelligence, he cannot approve of the time wasted, time better applied to other things. When Dr. Hollows was a student, math and physics were the only subjects he considered worth studying; he read literature occasionally, taking notes and demanding a refund from the publisher whenever the author got the science wrong. And now his only son, aged thirteen, is two hundred pages into a projected million-word epic called *Walter Munch, from Morning to Night*, seeking to reinvent the Ulysses tale by grafting it onto the mundane existence of a young resident of Battle Creek, Michigan. Herbert has not read the manuscript, despite his son's urgings. These fruitless ambitions must not be humored in a child of thirteen. Dr. Hollows has known too many marginal prodigies whose lives of frustration began with a parent's unconditional support.

"Coming?"

"I'm doing something."

"Now."

"All right."

"Hup-two."

"Come on."

"Well, do it. Now. And don't get smart."

Leaving his work, Gray steps over a pile of spiral notebooks and climbs the stairs. His room is small, and he keeps it neat. A top-of-the-line Atari 2600 game console lies in its unopened box. A curl of wrapping paper sticks to the package. A chimney. A black boot (Mr. Claus is coming). Gray's birthday is on the twenty-fourth of December. He feels personally responsible for the holiday buildup. The bustle, the chaos, the Christmas vacation—but at the end, no parties and the usual number of gifts.

"I will say this in as few words as possible. I'm angry with you. I'm very disappointed in you. I don't know what to say to you right now."

"Well, I don't . . . I don't know."

Dr. Hollows hates the look on his son's face. Loose lips, open mouth—*What did I do?*—as if any of this should come as a surprise. His shirt—oh! *nice* shirt (choke you with it).

"It seems to me—and you can address this any way you see fit, because if you want me to treat you like a man, I'll treat you like a man—but it seems to me that you have no respect for the hard work I do, and if you think you can ridicule me in front of your little TV camera, then I just don't know what to say about that."

Herbert can hear the stereo playing in his son's room. Gray likes his music; it helps him to focus on his writing. On those tense weekends when the whole family stays at home to work on their individual projects, the low drum sometimes pounds against the floor of the upstairs studio. Herbert tolerates this racket without complaint. Being tolerant appeals to the doctor; these small inconveniences enhance his sense of responsibility.

"Gosh, Dad. Most people thought it was funny. My English teacher liked it a lot."

"Do you think it's funny?"

He hates the shirt. The color. Nectarine.

"Well, no. I'm sorry. I don't know why you're so mad at me all of a sudden. I'll tell the guy you don't like it, and maybe he can take it off."

Buttons. Three of 'em. One fastened, two loose.

"Gray. Are you really that stupid?"

The stereo pauses in the silence between songs. This particular record is quite popular with the kids these days. The cover shows a black man in a white suit cuddling a baby leopard. Gray's mother purchased the record while out running errands with the boy. Seeing the covetous look on his face, she offered to buy it for him, but Gray said no, not wanting to endure the thank-you ritual, the questions he was now bound to answer (what? record? artist? do? you? like? other? kids?). Red in the face, he pretended not to see as his mother brought the record up to the cash register. Grateful, ashamed, he forced a reaction; *thanx!* — he said, then eagerly unwrapped the cellophane on the way home.

"Everyone liked it. They showed it at school. They had a special assembly, and everyone sat down. Right when it was coming on, they said to wait and we'd watch it. And then it came on. And most people laughed. They thought it was funny. My English teacher — "

"Your English teacher is of a questionable persuasion."

Gray's throat feels dry. He sees his English teacher, sees his father pushing the small woman against a blackboard. The dry feeling inside his throat breaks. "She said it was really good. Mom was there."

Joan Hollows sits in the upstairs family room, pretending to read a *TV Guide*. This is what she does whenever she hears her husband yelling at the boy. Having experimented with several different periodicals, she has determined that the *TV Guide* is best suited to this purpose, thanks to the loud noise it makes when she flips through the pages.

"So this is what you're going to do. Run to your mother. Are you that much of a baby?"

"Well, I'll call the guy. I'll do it right now. I'll tell him to take it off, and to stop showing it."

He hates the shirt. Spoiled little jerk, his mother buys him everything.

"Are you so *stupid* that you think you can call a man who's in charge of billions of dollars in revenue and simply tell him to put a stop to it—because *you* didn't think, and because *you* were selfish, and because you're acting like an immature brat?"

The buttons, and the little insignia, logo, whatever they call it—a small patch, what's that, a muskrat? a tiger? some stupid gimmick, all the kids want to look the same.

"I'm s-s-s—"

"Now he's going to cry. That's an intelligent thing to do. How would you feel if I were to go on national television—'This is my son, he stays in his room all day, he thinks he's writing a *goddamn* novel, why don't we put the camera right in his face and ha-ha, isn't that funny?'"

"P-p-please."

"Do you know what my colleagues are going to say about this piece of nonsense, this idiotic, unfeeling, uncaring thing you did?"

"I'm sorry!"

"Listen to me! Do? You? Know? What? Listen to me!"

Dr. Hollows brushes his son's cheek—a symbolic slap—and goes back to his studio, pulling the door shut as the boy grabs for the knob. Gray does not want to let his father go. He wants forgiveness. His palm flaps against the wall as the space closes—now a sliver, now a seam.

"Go away. I'll be down for dinner."

Locking the door, Dr. Hollows sits at the drafting table and switches the overhead lamp from dim to bright. The pounding stops. Footsteps creep across the hall: Joan, coming to comfort, the mother smother, the easy part of the job. Dinner in two hours. Red eyes. Bills on the table. Food moving in a circle until everyone's plate is full. Staring into the video camera—his *own* commerical, now—he waits for a light to flash, then begins his explanation. He hopes you will take this seriously. He hopes you will get it this time.

The Plot Reaches
New Levels of Thickness

1998

Steve waited outside the store as the meeting continued without him. He frowned to see an empty condom wrapper lying on the front curb. The opening crew must have ignored it during their morning maintenance sweep. *Sorry, Mr. Mould, ain't nowhere it says I gotta pick up that nasty thing.* A sudden revulsion overtook him, and he felt the need to rip off his Living Arrangements polo shirt and run across the parking lot, stripped to the waist, smashing the showcase windows of the neighboring stores. Scanning the lot, he noticed a woman shuffle out of the bakery two doors down, carrying a long baguette, her legs wrapped below the knees with flesh-colored bandages. Using the baguette as a cane, she made a sharp turn and headed for the furniture store. Steve stood frozen, intensely aware of his own shadow on the pavement.

The woman pivoted in her orthopedic shoes and glared at him through a pair of blue sunglasses. "Hey, you work here?"

"No, ma'am, I don't." He spoke in a careful voice, his eyes fixed on the sidewalk.

The woman pointed with her chin. "You got the shirt on."

He looked down at his chest, then up again. "You're right, ma'am. I've got the shirt on. You got me."

She chewed on her bottom lip, making a bunch, one ugly shape, then another. "You don't work here, how come they let you wear the shirt?"

Steve's mind buzzed with alibis, half-baked excuses. There was a free giveaway. Free shirts for opening a charge account. Free shirts whenever you register a complaint. Complain, open, open, complain. Madness! Clenching his fists, he charged the woman, shrieking as he swung his hands. She backed away in a panic, finding her car, tearing out of the parking lot as he followed her down the driveway. Hands on his knees, he stood under a NO PARKING sign and caught his breath. The ground flashed a series of psychedelic colors—all red, all purple. When he looked up, he saw Gray Hollows coming out of the store, a stack of corporate literature under one arm. Steve hurried back to the entrance, intercepting the other man halfway to his car.

"Hi, I'm Steve Mould, I'm the manager of . . ." He waved at the store's awning. "Well, you know all that." His chest swelled as he leaned against one of the two limos from the home office. "Look, I don't mean to be pushy or anything. I know that you've probably got a lot left to do this afternoon."

"Not really." Gray pulled a Dum Dum from his pocket and picked off the wrapper. "Actually I'm just going home to masturbate to my collection of antique geisha lithographs."

Steve looked at the man and nodded intently. "Oh. Well, I don't want to waste any of your time. I just wanted to say, I don't know what you might have in mind for this thing you're cooking up, but my son, um, is an actor, and uh . . ." One side of his brain suddenly felt heavier than the other. "*Wants* to be an actor, I mean. Would like to be. His mother tells me he's very good."

Gray placed the Dum Dum inside his mouth and bit down on the stem. "Does he do nude scenes?"

Again, Steve stared. The words seemed remote—the talk, all theoretical. "Well, you'd have to talk to her about—"

"Don't worry about it. It probably won't come up."

"It's just that he's kind of looking to get his big break and—"

"And you thought, Hey, being the concerned parent that I am, why not use my influence as head manager of . . ." Gray frowned at the building. "What the hell's the name of this place again?"

"Living Arrangements—it's, uh, right there on the sign."

"Living Arrangements . . . oh yes, that's right. Very clever."

Steve coughed, then said: "It's, uh, it's really my wife who's asking."

The other man nodded; his voice, soft now, came from far away.

"Something about nepotism . . . it's so touching. In fact, hey, I've been a beneficiary my whole life."

"That a fact?"

"Oh, sure!" He took the candy from his mouth. "My God, if it weren't for the golden words of a certain crazed engineer from Battle Creek, I'd still be walking the streets of Crane City, peddling pages of pretentious prose to . . . portly producers from Pennsylvania."

"Neat."

"HA HA! Peddling pages of . . . Look, has this kid of yours ever worked in front of a camera before?"

Steve started to reply, then realized he didn't know what to say, didn't know these basic things about his son. "Um, my wife would have all of that information—"

"Your wife, of course. La Grande Duchesse. Knows all. Smells all."

"I can give her a call." He started back toward the entrance. "Wouldn't take a sec."

"No, no, that's not necessary. I like the element of surprise. The unknown quantity." Gray folded his arms and stared across the highway to the stores on the other side. "Theoretically, I should be able to construct a vi-a-ble campaign around your son no matter how untalented he is."

"He's really a terrific kid."

"Oh, I'll bet he is. Probably played Huck Finn in the school play, right?" He tapped his chin, mulling it over. "What the hell," he said, thinking, *T. Kenneth's gonna kill me.* "Might as well keep it in the family. I love working with children. They're such prima donnas."

Steve held a breath, then let it go. "Well, super-doop!" Laughing, he wiped his face with a handkerchief. "This was easier than I thought."

Gray's face darkened; his eyes dimmed behind his thick and ugly glasses. The moment passed, and he clapped his hands. "Well, this should be interesting. My suggestion, sir: Protect your investment, rub his feet with smooth stones and honey butter, and I'll see you downtown at the EI headquarters ten a.m. Monday morning. But don't keep me waiting! Much penalty for tardiness." Amusing himself, he slipped into a German accent. "Paddle applied to buttocks. Angry salamander attached to anal sphincter."

The two men split up, and Steve went back in the store. A few stragglers were still coming out of his office, Jim Carroll among them, Cam Pee too, a couple of worried accountants on hand to represent the views of the budget director. His room, normally a tidy little place, was a mess, with Styrofoam coffee cups scattered across the desk, the air rancid with cigarette smoke. As the room emptied, Steve smiled, nodded, looked each man in the eye. A punk from communications handed him a paper flower, then left, giggling. Jim Carroll, last to go, leaned against the sideboard. Tired, he belched and blew a fart.

"You got this mess under control or do you need one of us to stick around?" He shook his arms out at his sides, fixing the cuffs.

"No, you go on ahead, Jim. You've got more important things to do." Steve brushed a few empty sugar packets from the seat of his chair, then grabbed the phone and dialed a preset. "I'll take care of it later. I just have to call my wife."

"Oh. Well, if you have to talk to your *wife*, I can at least gather my charts."

Waiting for Lydia to pick up, Steve watched the other man slide each of his charts into a giant leather portfolio. Little creep, he thought, turning away. *Back to HQ. Leave the dirty work to someone else.* He hoped Lydia would appreciate the effort. For years, her family had treated him like a hick, like a dumb Midwesterner. *Not no more!* A little reward was in order. Maybe a bottle of wine, some late-night TV . . . without the kid. He closed his eyes, picturing the two of them dancing barefoot on the brick patio, the breeze off the lake cool on their backs, a Glenn Miller CD playing softly with the speakers angled through the sliding screen. Without her heels, Lydia and Steve were both the same height. He always wondered how other couples managed to "do it"—a tall man and a short woman, or even the other way around. With him and Lydia, it wasn't a problem. Still, eighteen years' worth of his backaches and her ever-ascending hairdos had pushed the differential toward the extremes. Not so easy anymore. Next year, even worse. The incredible shrinking man. This was what they meant by growing apart.

The phone rang inside Lydia's purse; checking her Caller ID, she put the receiver away and let her voicemail answer it. She and Donna were sitting at the head of the Skyes' circular driveway, the engine still running. Neither wanted their extended luncheon to come to an end, each fearing the solitude of the late afternoon, the soporific cocktails, the wasting of the sun. Across the lawn, a neighbor's dog prodded at the ground with its snout, its black, mucous-wet nostrils breaking the cap of a dead, dry mushroom. Lydia reached into her friend's lap and took her hand. "Do it," she said.

Donna's knees were trembling. The seat belt made an awkward skew across her neck. "I don't know."

"You can't lose."

"I *can* lose."

"How? You've already lost your husband. You have—"

"Nothing left, I know. Thank you, darling."

Lydia took her hand back and rattled her keys, the chain hanging from the ignition. "I'm just being honest, Donna. I envy your position— no obligations, nothing to hold you back."

"I want to take a bath," Donna said. Determined, she hummed a few notes to herself. She was being silly and she knew it.

Lydia made an ugly face. "What's with these baths you take, four, five times a day? You're clean already!"

"This is my life, Lydia. My teeny-weeny pleasures."

Lydia pressed a switch and all four door locks popped up with a unison clack. "Fine. Take your bath. But don't give up on me, kiddo. If nothing else, do it for me."

Donna sighed and pushed the car door open with her leg. Stepping out, she hesitated up the chipped and broken path. Derek had once mentioned getting an estimate for a new walk, but that was just weeks before the split, and since then the house and the surrounding land had continued its slow decay. She supposed that she could always round up the workers herself—no more complicated than cracking open a Yellow Pages, really—but that would mean having to negotiate over the phone with those mean old men, men who loved to browbeat women with their garbled talk of list prices and projected costs. That's why Lydia's plan was so ludicrous—the men, their stupid egos. The men would not cooperate, Reggie Bergman and his sort. They would squash the project somehow. Typical male insecurity. If anything, they feared a fair fight. His book, her book. No, the best thing for her to do was to stay put, to gladly pocket Derek's generous settlement and to stare out at the calm, never-changing lake, gin in hand, while her home and everything else she possessed gradually turned to dust.

A small black box was sitting on the porch step, blocking the door. Donna waited for Lydia's car to move down the street, then picked up the box and turned it around, looking for a return address. Breaking the seal, she reached under the flap and squished what felt like thick putty between her fingers. Over the course of the day, the contents had hardened into a gritty paste, shit-brown and ghastly. The smell was more than just repulsive; it was an insult. *His shit on her hands.* Blind with tears, she burst through the house and crossed the yard to the lake, sobbing as she heaved the package into the water. The box wobbled once on a wave, then tipped out of sight. Kneeling on the beach, she rinsed the clumpy residue from her fingers. Her arms trembled, and she could feel a dirty layer under her skin—something awful, cored away. This was Derek's gift to her. Standing up, she ran back inside, her mind racing as well, its ecstatic transactions quickly cataloging the contents of every closet, every out-of-the-way cupboard and storage shelf, neurons stretching desperately toward that remote spot, the typewriter on the third floor.

IX

Two Excerpts from *Many Voices, One Vision* by Madonna Hasse Skye

The Tale of Tsin-gah and the Secret Star

Compiler's note: This story is a variation on a tale told by thousands of Native Americans along the Pacific coast. Favorable conditions, unique to the region, have allowed the Nootka tribe of British Columbia to develop an unusually stable economy. Lavish banquets, called "potlatches," provide an opportunity for competitors to shame their opponents with wasteful gifts of goods and cash. Young girls attend the tournaments, eager to marry a champion. In this story, a girl named Tsin-gah dreams of seducing an old sun, the star god Sirius. This tale would naturally appeal to Nootka women, for whom such earthbound alliances rarely result in much happiness. (M.H.S.)

The festivities, having entered their third day, had reached a final stage. The room was hot, the deadly air relieved only by the listless wave of a wooden fan. Two men stood before the group. Their feet were bare, and they wore only denim pants, dingy blues and grays. Confident of his advantage, Bha (Number 308) turned away from his challenger and addressed the crowd. Among other things, the potlatch was a chance for the town's unmarried females to examine the year's latest offerings. For some girls, this question was a matter of simple arithmetic, nothing more. A woman in the 800s who married a man in the 400s could expect—pending the approval of the chief—to wind up somewhere in the 600 range or better. At age thirteen, Tsin-gah (Number 1,305) had already passed beyond the tastes of the village elite. Eyes down, she ignored the match, expecting nothing.

"People," Bha proclaimed. His dark gaze swept over the crowd. "All evening, this dolt has assaulted me with tales of his tremendous wealth. But my estate is not so easily won. Take as an example . . ." From a leather satchel, he removed a sheet of rolled parchment and undid the clasp. Written in gold pen, twenty-six bright letters flashed upon the page. "Do not shield your eyes. These shapes are good spirits. Working toward a unified language, the great Sequoya has provided us with the tools we need to match the challenge of the white invaders. For his sake, we should be grateful, and we should honor relics such as these."

"Is that all you have?" questioned the other man, arms folded, his chest swelling with pride. "You should take care to harness your boasts, 308." Raising his right hand, he clasped a pine amulet, the hallowed wood of his tribe. The amulet depicted the man's name in a totem of elaborate carvings. Sequoya's ready-made Twenty-Six would have reduced such filigree to a few simple scratches—the letters, Lan-Sum. Lan-Sum was dark and tall, and his hair came to a silver point in the middle. Approaching his enemy on quiet feet, he moved across the circle until his shadow touched the border. The whole village listened. "Come with me," he said, turning. "From here, we will travel to the Raven's Shoulders. There, I will claim your title."

The Raven's Shoulders was a hilly formation just above the village, rounded to the east and jagged to the west. From a distance, the land itself seemed to be a great black bird skimming the turbulent sea. The villagers followed Lan-Sum up the grade of the mountain. The night was bright with stars. The ocean magnified the moonglow, giving it back to the town as a blanket of lively milk. At the summit, a telescope straddled the space between two boulders. Bha, sensing his defeat, hid behind a curtain of long, black hair. Lan-Sum caressed the telescope, the copper band around the lens.

"As a people, we have always looked to the sky for guidance." As he spoke, his hands fine-tuned a solid gold focus wheel. "The stars are our masters, and Sirius is their King." Hearing their keeper's name, the people looked to the ground and moaned in reverence. Lan-Sum stood apart, proud of himself. "My people, come see what I have found. See our god—not as the lone warrior of ages past, but as a pair of points, a light and a dark. Fellows of the Raven, I give you Sirius—the double star!"

The people formed a haphazard line; eagerly, they cramped the space around the telescope. Standing behind a group of maidens, Tsin-gah held her breath, too scared to speak. When she reached the head of the line, she squinted into the eyepiece and gripped the ground with her toes. Filtered through the curved glass, the star Sirius was a bright point, its white the white of anger, unspeakably hot. Its black bride was a shadow against a canvas of even blacker shadows—sensed but not seen. Rejoining the rest of the group, Tsin-gah held her hand against her cheek, blocking out the right side of her face. For an instant, she was certain that if she dared to look, the mighty Sirius would reclaim her sight, pulling her up into the inverted peaks of his dark world.

"Tsin-gah, did you see?" cried a young girl, wild and foolish. "Lan-Sum can make the stars shine in the sky!"

Ignoring the girl, Tsin-gah continued on down the peak's northern slope and walked along a narrow strip of pines. Dense trees filled the valley below. It always puzzled her—this stone formation, the headless Raven. This thought, she supposed, was blasphemous, but she did not yet understand the nature of divine punishment, whether by her actions alone she would be judged, or whether her thoughts mattered as well. Stepping into the pines, she considered the possibility that this—her protracted maidenhood—was her real punishment, meted out before the body had the chance to turn fallow. It was not her fault that she was so particular, so judgmental of those occasional few who happened to seek her hand. Today, Lan-Sum would realize his dream. He would overtake his fellow, claim the title of Number 308 for himself, then set his gaze upon the next landmark, the next man to defeat. Was he now any more worthy of Tsin-gah's favor? At what point would the numbers reach the magic limit, the irreducible sum, the final proof of his honor? Never, she supposed. This system was man-made, utilizing criteria which the boundless world outside of the tribe would never respect. This was not the way of the Raven.

Reaching the far peak, she found her path suddenly give way to a sparser array of pines. Past the trees, the star god Sirius throbbed in its black cradle, sending its light down from the heavens. Unaided by the telescope's lens, she could see the star as it had always appeared to her, as a single point of light. Sirius was a bachelor, or so she liked to believe, despite the presence of the dark star, the lurking bride. If only Tsin-gah, through some miracle of transformation, could *be* that woman! Never far from her spouse, she and Sirius would dwell together in their own private patch of sky. How the girls of the village would swoon when they gazed into Lan-Sum's telescope and saw this new constellation—Tsin-gah the meek, star-bound, joined to her King.

A mesa of swirled sand covered the northern peak. Across the valley, she could see the people of her village still waiting to peer into the telescope. Regaining her bearings, she noticed a slender black object perched atop a cairn. The Raven! The great bird stared at the girl fiercely, its red eyes blinking as it held a tattered carcass in its beak. When it finally spoke, the piece of shredded flesh fell to the ground.

"I know your dreams," the creature hissed. Steam filled its mouth, rising in thick curls. "You seek to leave this place, my daughter. The men of this tribe have done you a great wrong. You do not deserve their rejection."

"It is Sirius that I desire, my lord." Tsin-gah's knees ached as she lowered herself to the earth. Sand sifted across the mesa, hurting her eyes. "Sirius is the only man who can make me happy. His blaze is the brightest in all of the tar-black sky. Men and women from all tribes worship his authority. I wish to be the one that people see— even if only as a half-hidden presence—whenever they gaze up at Sirius's flame. To be his wife, to share his happiness . . . please grant me this wish, O blessed Raven!"

The Raven stood silent for a moment, his clawed fingers chipping away at the stony ground. "Your request is odd," he said, then stooped to seize the carcass in his jaws. "And yet I know your heart is true." His wings beat once against his rocky pedestal, propelling him across the cold Pacific. The sky opened, and the Raven slipped into a fold.

Across the narrow valley, the forest shook, overcome by a violent storm. The tribesmen stood near the edge of the lower mesa. With a gasp, Tsin-gah suddenly realized that they were all looking at her. A flash of pale light revealed the terror in their eyes. All at once, the hill dropped out from under her feet. Cold wind rushed past her ears, and as the planet shrank away, the air became harder and harder to breathe. Far from home, she could see the rocky coast of the Pacific. The great patch of land beyond the ocean was surprisingly vast. Having crossed the upper atmosphere, she could no longer move, or scream, or—worst of all—close her eyes, for a thick layer of dirty ice now covered her body, freezing her joints solid. She could only accept the burn of the ice, the way it stung her optic nerves to the core. Passing planets, weird spaceships, she left the galaxy transformed into a fiery rock of combustion. Magma settled; lightning crossed the equator. She had no real awareness of her body, only a dim belief that she occupied a large space within a gigantic void. She retained her sight, if little else; she could see her own glow, its cloudy shade the milky texture of a pearl. A bright circle, bigger than the rest, pulsed in the distance. Sirius! Claimed by a rush of passion, Tsin-gah's light swelled and then cooled. She stared at him, waiting. Sirius remained aloof, an engine raging in the peak of its years. Alien. Remote. Self-sufficient. The young girl stammered. She didn't know what to say.

"Sirius!" she cried. "It is Tsin-gah, your wife! I have traveled these many light years to serve by your side. Why won't you embrace me?"

Silence. A familiar sound, a smell would have calmed her, eased her fear. But the void would yield nothing, only the sight of Sirius's bold profile, large and two-dimensional. Just then, the Raven spread its wings across the sun. So poised, the bird resembled an ungodly insignia, the corporate stamp of whatever agency had brought Tsin-gah to this doomed place.

"Raven!" she shouted. The bird moved its head in response, yawing its beak three times to show that it understood. "What is wrong with my husband? Why won't he acknowledge his beloved Tsin-gah?"

"You are Tsin-gah no longer," responded the Raven. His knobby toes flexed in the starlight. "From now on, you shall be known as Sirius B."

"But . . ." Tsin-gah stammered, not liking the cold precision of this, her new name. "How will my family know me, then?"

"You shall have no further use for them," the bird continued. "You belong to your husband. He is your reality. You are merely a suffix to his glory."

"I don't believe you," she cried, frantic now. She longed for her hands and feet, her young girl's body. "Let me talk to him. I won't listen to your lies."

Blinking once, the Raven went on: "Though Sirius seems near in your sight, he is in fact many light years away. He hardly even knows you're here. So long as you continue to live, you will never touch him, nor will you speak to him, nor will you share the slightest intimacy. You are the dying rock that makes his radiance seem all the brighter."

"Dying?" Tsin-gah wondered, aware now of her changed appearance. "But I'm only thirteen years old!"

"Tsin-gah is no more," the Raven reminded her. "Now you are Sirius B. Sirius B is a white dwarf. An old star nearing the final stages of its evolution."

"But . . . but I thought—"

"You thought you were in love." The bird flexed its wings, preparing for flight. "You saw Sirius's grand light and assumed that it burned for you. But Sirius burns for no one but himself. You are less than incidental. The only feeling others have toward you is pity. When people look to the sky, they see only Sirius, rarely his insignificant partner. You have enslaved yourself, rendered yourself a secondary being. And for this, Sirius neither cares, nor shows his thanks. Look, here, how he shines!" Raising his wings, the Raven pulled his legs into his breast, showing more of the star's white flame. "Stable. Distant. Wholly independent from you."

"But surely Sirius loves me?" Tsin-gah asked.

Annoyed, the Raven sprang up and out of view. Unencumbered by the black bird's form, the star Sirius blazed like a reckless sphere of amazement, insistently proclaiming its own superiority. Tsin-gah could not look away. This was the choice that she had made.

Commentary: Though its science may be obscure, this tale teaches us the value of properly considering a partner's credentials before signing a contract of marriage. (M.H.S.)

The Tale of Jen-teen and the Second Draft

Compiler's note: Our next story involves a controversial divorce between the Chinese emperor Jen-tsung and his neglected wife, Jen-teen. Hoping to regain the throne, Jen-teen alleged that her ex-husband had betrayed the principles of Confucian law by seeking an annulment. While her efforts succeeded in tarnishing the emperor's image, she was ultimately unable to topple his reign, which lasted for forty-one years until his death in 1063. (M.H.S.)

It had rained in K'ai-feng, and the air smelled of wet wood. Wide boards ran between the buildings. Jen-teen's hardwood sandals clacked across the busy street. She was a tall woman, and most of the ladies of the palace suspected her of being a foreigner. Then again, they suspected her of everything, from poisoning the Regent to seducing a drug merchant from Arabia. Once, while still empress, she was even accused of suffocating a child inside her womb. Since the divorce, she could not step outside without first wrapping a veil around her face. In the hot, wet months of Honan, this was a miserable way to live. As she walked past the market, she held the veil to one side, trying to breathe. Food merchants and mustachioed scamsters from the West crowded the road, selling fabulous inks at cut-rate prices. Near the edge of the fair, four Arab adolescents wheeled a lame tiger around on an iron cart. A fat, shirtless man with a red apple painted across his belly took money from the crowd, urging them to throw rocks at the tiger—for, as he said, the animal was a freak and deserved only more pain.

Pi Sheng's factory was a large wooden shanty near the outskirts of the village. A discreet sign hung over the front door. Afraid of the government, Pi Sheng preferred to keep a low profile. The world of transmutation was a shady one, filled with power-mad supplicants hoping to turn copper into gold. Pi Sheng could do without the aggravation, the weird manipulations of the palace elect, all of which operated at cross-purposes and generally ended in blood and black passion.

Jen-teen stepped onto the porch and removed her veil. Long stretches of vellum hung from the roof, bulging and snapping as fabulous letters dried in the wind. Across the yard, a mound of dung steamed inside a wooden stockade. The smell was bad and strong. Resolved, she pushed a curtain aside and entered the room. Pi Sheng was standing behind a high workbench, shaking a bottle of arsenic. He was not an old man, but many years' worth of hard living had ruined his complexion. His bald skull was flat near the top, and he used it to balance pots of mercury whenever he needed both hands to hold his tools. In this way, he resembled a mushroom—his head swollen, a hooded stem. He wore a plain tunic, the same tunic every day, and once a week he could be seen dousing it in a bucket of fresh river water, standing naked and rubbing his chin as he waited for his laundry to dry. A naked Pi Sheng was a disconcerting sight, and this afternoon, Jen-teen was grateful for the tunic. She was bothered enough just being here, having to travel incognito, having to sit in a dark and unfamiliar place without the protection of her former guards.

"Master Magician," she said, kneeling as her robes settled about her. "I come to you in secret. I trust that you will reveal this encounter to no one."

"I reveal nothing," the alchemist answered in a high, soft voice. A cloud of arsenic whirled and zoomed around the bell of a brass pot.

Jen-teen indicated the open doorway. "I have seen the scrolls hanging from the roof of your porch," she said. Past the door, a broad piece of vellum turned in the wind. "You have experience, I trust, with the art of printing?"

"A true magician must know all things." Pi Sheng moved the brass pot and blew on his fingers. "I have prepared many documents for the emperor. He shows a great interest in literature. Maybe too great."

Jen-teen nodded, her eyes glittering. For the next hour, she and the magician discussed the state of the kingdom, her own recent divorce. Her mood changed from one extreme to another. Pi Sheng listened in silence, keeping his wisdom to himself. At last, she took his arm. "Pi Sheng, you must help me regain the crown!"

"You wish to poison the emperor?" he asked, bored by it all. "It is not easy. He must drink the metal. He must believe that by drinking the metal, he will gain the Isle of Bliss. This requires deception. Only the metal knows whom it wishes to deceive. I cannot make these decisions for the metal, for to do so would cause the sky to fold."

"You misunderstand me, great sage." Jen-teen dried her tears on her sleeve. "Where in the writings of Confucius is it lawful for an emperor to divorce his wife?"

Pi Sheng felt the top of his flat head. "It is not explicit. Confucius does not render an opinion."

Jen-teen laughed bitterly. "Such is the fate of women! How could our spiritual leader condone such a thing?"

"Confucius neither condones nor condemns. He is not an advocate. The master of our people is never wrong because he is always right." Something about Pi Sheng's wry expression told Jen-teen that the man did not entirely believe his own words.

"And yet Confucius was a man. Is this right?" Her eyes flared in the gloom of the workshop. "He wrote laws like a man. His disciples were all men. He spoke to a man's world."

"This is true. And yet it is a man you seek to disgrace. A man is judged only by the laws of mankind. And the law of mankind, as spoken by Confucius, gives credence to the *chung*, the loyalty that each man holds to his own nature. If it is in Jen-tsung's nature to divorce his wife, then he is not betraying his *chung*. If he is not betraying his *chung*, then he has committed no crime. If he has committed no crime—"

"I understand," Jen-teen interrupted, raising both hands.

"I am only telling you what it says in the *Lun yu*." Taking her sleeve, he spoke, cordially now. "Confucius, as you say, was only a man. He did not speak with the inexpressible authority of the Tao."

A slow dawning lifted her head. "Who is to say, then, what is right? If Confucius was only a man, and his words only mortal opinions, then why may we not change his words to suit our own needs?"

Pi Sheng fiddled with his belt. His hand shook, and he tucked it behind his back. "Change the writings? This is a big thing, that you ask. It would be discovered. The villain would be executed for his crimes. There would be a public trial, a burning, a gruesome disembowelment!"

"No one need know," she said, making a fist. "Look. Those lawyers in the capital—I know them all! They are fools! They do not know the law. They will believe anything they read." She pushed the curtains aside and pointed at the long sheets of vellum hanging from the roof beams. The sun made a wide ray that extended all the way to the back of the room. A pile of bright red cinnabar burned in the light. The smell was dreadful, like rotten meat. She continued: "Print me a page of Confucius. Discredit the way of the *chung*. Prove that it is unlawful for an emperor to divorce his wife without cause or warning. We will drive Jen-tsung out of the capital and I will rule as regent."

"But Empress," he protested, "there is no time. I would have to recut the entire *Lun yu*, and that would take years!" Reaching for her hand, he tried drawing her back into the room, but she was already three steps down the path.

"You must try, sir magician, you must do your best." Out of breath, she glanced up at the sun and ran across the yard. Inside the factory, the cinnabar ceased to burn as the curtains swung back into place. A white, rolling gas filled the room. Pi Sheng swished the air in front of him, then turned away. The smell of sweet poison stayed for hours. He spent the night asleep on the front porch.

In the morning, he awoke and sat on the steps, meditating. A strong wind blew in from the north, and a wall of dust slammed into the side of the house. The wind carried with it the smell of manure. Curious, he walked across the field and entered the stockade. The mound came up to his chest; the smell, while strong, was not unpleasant, and he saw clear waves pouring off of the surface, a visible heat that made the air around it wiggle and bend. An idea stirred inside his brain. He pressed his palm into the mound. A hard crust gave way to a softer consistency in the middle. Wiping his fingers, he left the stockade and walked back to the factory. The day would be short and he had much left to do.

Just past the workroom, a storage rack contained several dozen hardwood slabs, each ranked according to height. The *Lun yu* was a long document, nearly eight feet tall. The excessive nature of Pi Sheng's language had always puzzled him. It seemed impractical, unnecessarily complex. If only there were a dozen symbols, perhaps two dozen, from which one could construct all of the larger meanings, perhaps the Chinese people could forge a more complete society, organized by language, a common system of letters. Instead, they were stuck with this hopelessly involved array of lines and dashes whose very multiplicity implied a kind of pointless forever. A library of image. It was all too much.

Wrapping two leather straps around the base of the slab, he heaved the weight onto his back and brought it outside. Entering the stockade, he filled a burlap sack with hunks of manure and carried it across the yard. All morning, he smoothed the dung over the slab, spreading it thin where carved characters made dark shadows in intricate bas-relief. By mid-afternoon, he was very tired. Leaving the slab to dry, he walked around to the back of the factory, where a clay oven stood like a giant turtle basking in the heat. Grabbing bunches of dead grass, he climbed a stool and dumped the fuel into a narrow slot. The heat grew; the inside of the stove was a bright red cavern. Returning to the stockade, he hefted the printing slab—now crisp with dried manure—and threw it into the fire. Bright sparks sailed across the yellow and brown field.

Back indoors, he slept for several hours, then woke at midnight. One ball of dung sat on the counter. He pressed it flat, stripping the excess with an ivory blade. Twisting the knife, he carved a few shapes, inventing as he went along. He made the shape for HUSBAND. He made the shape for WIFE. He took a breath and drank from a bowl of hot broth. He made the shape for SUNDER. He made the shape for

DISGRACE. He wiped the blade on his hip and placed it inside a wooden box.

At dawn, he pulled the slab out of the fire, snagging it with a long hook. The dung had dried considerably, but it was still relatively soft toward the middle. Dragging the blade, he made an incision between two lines of text. With a copper pick, he inserted each of the four characters: HUSBAND WIFE SUNDER DISGRACE, then dribbled a line of silt along the crack. Glad to be done with the job, he returned the slab to the oven and walked back to the factory. Hot and tired, he drank a bowl of goat's milk, then sat down on the step. All afternoon, he tried to forget about his bad deed; troubled, he experimented with strange chemicals, blends of mercury and sulfur. The clouds he made were white and wonderful, but the elixir of life continued to elude him.

In the evening, he removed the slab and let it cool on the ground. By the next day, the piece was ready. Working quickly, he spread the ink and unrolled a length of vellum across the surface. The new document resembled the old; only the details had changed. From noon until nightfall, he guarded the front door, the writings of Confucius the Great hanging above his head, drying in the hot summer wind. The Empress would be pleased.

Commentary: If nothing else, this sentimental tale reminds ladies of all cultures that despite the advance of history, women have always had to work outside the law to get their way. (M.H.S.)

Promises Made

The Concerned Parent

1998

Simon knew the answer: Andrew Jackson. Mrs. Oates had asked the question—"Who was the seventh president of the United States?"—and Simon knew but wouldn't say it because that would mean having to answer even more questions, and the kids who gave the correct response would advance to the next round, and on and on until only one kid remained, usually some freckled girly-poo—little bitch, you wanted to rub her face in the hot lunch—and Mrs. Oates would hand her the grand prize, a pencil case or maybe even a gift certificate to Big Boy's. Nancy Watkins won the grand prize last year. She dedicated the award to her uncle, who'd been hospitalized earlier in the month for a ruptured pancreas.

"Now, Simon, this is an easy one and you're a smart boy, so I'm going to give you another chance. Who was the seventh president of the United States?"

"A bucket of spackling compound."

"Oh, Christ, Simon. Fine, just leave."

The classroom was hot and cramped, and Simon was eager to go. The audition was at four, but his mother always liked to arrive early so she could fix his hair and check out the competition. His shadow made a small black blotch on the wall as he retrieved his book bag from the back row of desks. The remaining contestants stood before their classmates—the ones who'd returned to their seats. A garish sign hung over their heads, a simply drawn cartoon of an owl scribbling basic equations on a green chalkboard. The owl's handwriting was much nicer than Simon's. A long poster ran along the perimeter of the room, and it showed you how to draw the letters both in uppercase and lowercase, arrows pointing the way, but no matter how hard he tried (not very) Simon just couldn't make the letters come out right, so one day he decided to draw them backwards, against the arrows, but when Mrs. Oates saw what he was doing, she got mad and told him to do it properly, because only Jews wrote from right to left—which, she added, was not a criticism but a simple statement of fact.

An old janitor looked up as the boy pushed open the front door and crossed the lawn. His mother was waiting in the parking lot, car chugging in gear, foot on the brake. The car jounced and bucked in time to the red warning light flashing over the rear bumper. Hands on the wheel, she yelled at him through the window. Her agitation was palpable as a tightness of the lips; he could smell the worry, a certain charge in the air. Head down, he climbed into the car and yanked open the glove box. Gone were the usual amenities—the freon-filled eye patches, the exfoliating stone, the motivational phrases itemized on numbered cards, all courtesy of Derek Skye: *Your Only Competition Is Yourself*; *You Have the Right to Remain Happy*; *Smiling Is Ninety Percent of Winning*. Worried, he peered into the backseat. She'd cleaned it out; a sterile reek rose from the upholstery. He gripped the soft headrest, and the foamy cushion made a new shape between his fingers.

"Mom?"

"Be quiet, Simon."

He thrust his fists into his pants pockets, conscious of sitting there, his mother sitting there, a bad potential. "What's going on?"

"I'm trying to drive."

Trees crowded the road as the car headed west, toward the lake. Simon hated this place; its remote location excluded him from the best of the competition, those private-school kids who eternally popped up on local-access cable stations, mugging obnoxiously for car commercials and ninety-second human-interest pieces at the end of the evening news. He liked the forest, that was all. Skin on bark. The sharp things underneath. Clothes heaped in a secret spot. Looking up at his mother, he asked, "Aren't we going to the audition?"

"Those people can go to hell."

They turned down a gravel drive and slowed in front of a small cabin. Flies buzzed; a few struck the windshield. Leaving the car in gear, Lydia turned off the motor and stepped outside. Simon followed partway, then stopped. "Where are we going?"

"Never you mind."

Reaching the step, she banged on the door and, without waiting, pushed it open. The room's few furnishings were reduced to abstract shapes by the insufficient light. One of the shapes moved, grew larger, then stood by the door, the light catching it at the knees. Olden filled the entrance, dressed in swimming trunks and an open terry cloth shirt. A pair of sunglasses hung around his neck, along with a bunch of keys that sagged to his stomach.

"What do you need?" he asked. His voice sounded cracked, as if he hadn't spoken for days. Recognizing the woman, he brightened. "Hey! It's the concerned parent. By all means." He stepped aside, waving her in.

Lydia continued past the step and lingered near the door. Olden plowed through a heap of trash, stepping into the glow of a computer screen. His face looked purple, distant. A bulky hard drive lay scattered across a worktable, exposed wires lacing the pieces together, snaking up the side of a file cabinet. He sat down at the computer. "Is that your son?" he asked, pointing with his chin.

Lydia tugged on her jacket. "Of course that's him. Can't you see the resemblance? That's the look."

"What look?"

"The family look. We all look like that."

He stopped typing and gazed through the open door to where Simon had already gone back to the car. Olden saw no connection between the two, mother and child. Giving up, he said, "How old is he?"

"Who, Simon? Simon's ten. No, wait. Eleven. Just turned. Jesus. Too old."

"Now you've done it."

"Is that a problem? He could be ten. We can make him ten. It's no big deal."

"Ten's no fun. Let's leave the kid alone."

Lydia fished in her purse for a cigarette. She moved slowly, stepping around a heap of musty pages on the floor. "I suppose you really could do it, couldn't you?" She touched the back of the hard drive, where something like spilled soda pop stuck to her fingers. "Just change the numbers. Push a few buttons and that's that."

Olden offered her a match but she pulled away, snatching the cigarette out of her mouth. The matchbook turned in his hands, and instead he lit a candle. The light on the ceiling made a round, watery shape, circles within circles, brighter toward the center.

"I like to pick my moments," he said, shaking out the match. "I've already got people watching my house, keeping an eye on my utility rates. You make one mistake and the government never forgets."

Lydia glanced down at the young man's bed, the mess of sheets. Her arms formed a cage around her breasts. "Well, we don't want to have anything to do with that."

He tapped his lips, watching her. *Silly woman*, he thought. Still, time was a-wasting, and anything was better than putting his own face on the Web. "It's all perfectly legal," he said.

She laughed. *"That's* good."

They looked at each other, then smiled. Lydia pulled up a stool, dusting it carefully before sitting down. "So . . ." She gestured at the screen, the numbers, the zeros and ones. It looked like a code, something from a war movie. For the first time since coming to the Midwest, she felt like an insider, worthy of her own good name; her mother dealt in codes, and her mother was an important person. "It won't look like this, will it?"

"No, it won't look like that." Confident, he put his feet on the desk. "We'll spruce it up for the Christmas crowd."

Lydia shuddered with impatience. The best part about going online was that she could do the whole thing herself—put Simon where hundreds of casting agents from Hollywood and New York and Chicago could find him, and she wouldn't have to worry about going to auditions, because he'd always be *out there*, and anyone who wanted his résumé or his head shot could get it, whether it was two a.m. in London or ten-thirty in Hong Kong.

"The Internet is getting stiff and stale," Olden continued. "Even the Gloria Corporation is starting to spruce up its public image. I *know* these people. They're cutthroat bastards. They don't care about us. All they want is our money. Our money and our minds. We can't let them get away with it!"

She nodded, elbows on the desk. Olden spoke precisely, his hand gestures consisting mainly of knife motions—here, here, and here. Listening, she tried to match the cadence of his voice with equally imposing facial expressions. They were discussing something here. She blinked, registering the main points. I gotcha, I gotcha. Information received and processed. I know exactly what you mean.

"This is great," she said, pointing at the screen. "I need this. I need all of this stuff you're showing me. I need it to work automatically." She looked at Olden and made a baby face. "Waaahh!" she cried.

Olden winced. "Automatically, I can do," he managed. "With reservations."

Lydia clapped her hands and stood up. "Well, I'm convinced." Dropping the cigarette back into her purse, she brought out her wallet and fiddled with the clasp. "How does this work—do I pay you?"

"Wait, wait." Laughing, he brought his legs down from the desk. "What does your son do?"

"That's a silly question," she said. Olden shrugged, waiting. She sighed and gestured again with the wallet. "If you must know, he's a model and an actor, and he can make appearances, and he's experienced in all of the . . . visual arts."

"Visual arts?"

"Yes. Visual arts. Being seen. This is a huge business we're talking about here."

"Being seen is a good thing. We need people who like to be seen." Grudgingly, he accepted a few hundred bucks, then followed her to the door, stopping where a bright shaft of sunlight fell across the porch. "Just bring me some pictures—head shots, a few three-quarters. Don't get clever. I'll let you know when it's finished."

Lydia paused on the step, looking at Simon's vague shape in the backseat. "He's got a look," she said, arms folded. "That's the thing."

"I can't see him," Olden answered, standing back a bit.

"Some people think he looks Spanish."

"Yeah?"

"I think that's a good thing." She smiled, walking away, one heel catching in the mud. "It's a versatile look." Hot in the face, she climbed into the car and drove up the hill. From the main road, she could no longer see the cabin; the ridge was too steep, the woods too dense. She laughed; this was her secret, her hidden weapon. Bad things brewing in the ground. A quick gestation, then—BAM! The faces of the other women. Oh, *congratulations*, Lydia! (pretending like you don't care). Congratulations! The big concession. Oh, well, but we *all* knew about Simon! Failed sons, proper and in a row. Lydia, Brian got an A *minus* in chemistry this semester! (pretending, but you *do* care). Oh, *congratulations*, you . . . yes, but look at it, look at it, you cunt, right there!

Who Speaks
for Our Children?

http://www.eggcode.com

FACT: The history of the Internet dates back to the nineteen-sixties, when researchers working for the Department of Defense developed the world's first high-speed router. Today, thousands of these simple devices—many located in unexpected places—form the backbone of our global communications network. The protocol enabling the network to function is a two-part system, known as TCP/IP. The transmission-control protocol is in charge of maintaining the integrity of the transmitted data, while the Internet protocol oversees the routing of the message across the network. As one would imagine, the people who originally designed the TCP/IP module were quite concerned about the security of the prototype. It was for this reason that certain intermediaries, acting under the aegis of the Pentagon, solicited the cooperation of the Department of Education, then formulating its own system of standardized placement examinations. These two projects, while ostensibly dissimilar, shared a common ambition.

It should be noted that the Egg Code stands by the following account, and a comprehensive list of sources may be obtained from the pagemaster by mailing the proper postage to the P.O. Box given at the link below. A surcharge of $1,278.53 will be added as a deterrent to all but the most serious inquiries.

Subsequently, researchers from UCLA submitted a proposal to their bosses at the DoE, the contents of which—though widely bootlegged—have remained under seal for two decades. This proposal called for the distribution of booklets containing multiple-choice questions designed to evaluate a given student's intelligence. Typically, these questions offered five possible solutions, labeled A thru E. The student indicated his or her selection by darkening the corresponding oval with a number two pencil. Administrators kept their questions simple, so as to maintain the support of those Washington-based advocacy groups who considered the adherence to any academic standard an insidious form of child abuse. Having labored through an afternoon's worth of examinations, the student returned a grid of filled and unfilled ovals to his or her test facilitator, trusting the proctor to place the completed form inside a secure envelope. Weeks later, the child received a performance evaluation in the mail; these rankings, expressed in numbers of three or four digits, were assigned at random.

At this point, the DoE's authority was transferred to the Pentagon, and from there, all relevant documents traveled to a secret location near La Junta, Colorado, where factory workers fed the stacks of papers into a collating device that converted the patterns of blackened and unblackened ovals into binary code. Reduced to zeros and ones, the test results left the building disguised as subatomic datagrams, eight bytes in length. The TCP/IP protocol was safe, at least for the time being.

The connection between these two phenomena — computer networks and standardized examinations — should be apparent. According to theory, no one router is more important than the other. As with standardized testing, the aim is to render units of unlike capabilities equally proficient, and therefore unexceptional. This goal is by no means extraordinary. We at the Egg Code propose that the prevailing trend in American cultural behavior is not a democratic one, but socialist.

With regards to the future of standardized examinations, we would like to suggest a recommitment to our nation's youth by bringing an end to this harmful practice and replacing it with a newer method less susceptible to corruption and turpitude. Perhaps an oral questionnaire would be sufficient, preferably one conducted inside a secure environment routinely swept for listening devices by dogs trained to know their smell.

Night!

L ying in bed, Scarlet pulled on a pair of jeans, her legs scissoring a foot above the floor. She and Olden had gone to sleep some three or four hours ago, and now it was dark outside; when she squinted at her watch, she could only sense the time, the hour and minute hands spread far apart. She reached across the mattress and found her shirt, a cotton heap. Olden lay on his side, his boxers twisted halfway around his waist. She smiled, watching him sleep. She thought about bears, how bears slept. Bears were gentle beasts, and their noses went whoop-whoop. She would like to kiss a bear someday, right on the nose. Bears were different from people because they never took more than they needed, and they were non-violent, and they were not afraid to go naked. Nakedness is beautiful. Why are we ashamed?

Putting on her top, she buttoned it once, fixing the middle snap. Shirttails fanned in a V, framing her belly. She liked her stomach. Her navel was tiny—just a slit, really—and you had to hold it apart to see inside. Moving in the darkness, she opened her gym bag and checked her gun. The barrel was scuffed, a little mark near the hammer. Frowning, she wiped it with her sleeve and stashed it somewhere, under or next to something. Crossing the room, she banged into a chair, said "Shit!," then mouthed an exaggerated "Owie" as she turned and held her leg. She stepped carefully, testing the knee. Olden rolled onto his back and snored, his right hand draped effeminately across his chest. Walking outside, she eased the door shut and moved away from the cabin. The meadow smelled cool and bitter, the grass leaning in a soft breeze. Trees started just past the driveway. The pines were thin and not so tall. A haphazard trail led to the beach, where the waves looked bright and choppy through the woods. A tower emerged from the lake, drawing a line across the water. Scarlet stood in the center of the lawn and felt the grass under her feet. Closing her eyes, she raised her right leg and spun around, her body tracing a curve. Arms high, she turned again, both feet leaving the ground. The weightless sensation, so familiar in dreams, eluded her now; disappointed, she fell back and caught her balance. Opening her eyes, she saw an old man standing near the cabin. He waited formally, hat in hand. His face was black, his hair silver. She jumped, body tense, all fists and elbows.

The man raised his hands. "It's okay," he said. He sounded frightened. "I'm from up the hill." Smiling, he pointed at a dense patch of forest. His eyes gleamed in the darkness. "I'm a friend of the young man."

"You mean Olden?" She looked at the cabin—no windows on this side, just a solid wall. "He's asleep."

"Oh." The man backed away. "I forgot about the time. I apologize."

"Hey, who cares?" She came toward him, laughing now, hands on hips. "I don't even know what time it is."

Relaxing, he wiped his face with a handkerchief. "You must be related."

She snorted. "Oh, no. Olden and I are lovers."

"I see."

"We share love."

"Well, that's sure good."

Reaching the drive, she squinted at the old man. She moved as if hypnotized, drawn to a flower. "Where are you from?" she asked, fascinated.

He pointed again, then replaced his hat. "Just up the way."

She smiled, shaking her head; her teeth were small and spaced far apart. "But before?"

"Oh." He sighed. "Well, I've lived all over the place. In Boston—"

"I want to go to Morocco."

The old man waited, confused. "Never been there," he said finally.

"It's really a European country."

"Oh, okay."

"I'd love to see the markets."

"Lord, yes."

"But it's so expensive."

"That's the tru—"

"I don't want to take advantage of anyone." A darkness passed over her face, and she stared at the ground. "I don't want to take advantage of anyone."

He folded his hands, leaning away from the conversation. "You can get some cheap flights," he said, trying to sound reasonable.

Scarlet looked up and wrapped her fingers around his wrist. "I'm glad Olden has a friend like you."

"Oh, well, okay." He turned his arm a bit, holding a stiff position. "I hope we *can* be friends. If you could just tell him . . . about the business proposition. You tell him I'll get to work on that right away."

She let go and pressed her hands together. "Oh! You're the guy!"

"Mr. Mason, yes, that's right."

"You're the artist from New York!"

"Oh, now—"

"That's so cool!" She raised an arm and flapped her loose sleeve. "You're so, like . . . I don't even know!"

"It's been a while since I lived in New York."

She nodded a bunch of times, getting into it. "And you still paint and everything?"

"Paint? Uh, no, that's not really my thing."

She covered her mouth, amazed. "What's it like?"

"To?"

Shrugging, she gestured with both hands, scooping the words. "Just to keep going like that. And to have such a long career. Not that you're so old."

"Well, I'm getting—"

"You never hear about artists when they reach a certain age. Does that bother you?"

"C—"

"I think it's so beautiful when an older person can stay creative, like Georgia O'Keeffe, who kept working until she was like a hundred years old or something."

"Right."

"With the flowers?"

"Oh, sure!"

"I've got one over my bed. I mail-ordered it from some place out in New Mexico. They've got a museum. Orchids. *The Orchids.* Do you know that one?"

"I'm sure I've—"

"Everyone says they look like vaginas, but I think that's stupid. It's a flower, it's a thing of beauty, and we should appreciate it on its own terms without second-guessing the artist's intentions."

Julian shifted his weight, trying to keep his back straight. "I know the pictures you're talking about."

"Oh, they're *beau*tiful! And do you know how old she was?"

"Like a hundred—"

"Like a hundred years old. It's pretty incredible." She raised one leg, letting it carry her forward. "Dancers don't live that long."

Charmed, he felt a smile form on his lips. "Are you a dancer?"

The pose collapsed. "Yeah, sometimes. I'm moving away from it, you know?" Suddenly clumsy, she picked her nose, rooting deep with two fat fingers. "Do you think I could paint?" she asked.

Julian shrugged. "L—"

"Not that I would. I totally wouldn't. Because painting is a spiritual thing."

"Oh, sure."

"And I don't have that kind of spirituality."

"Mmkay."

"Do you know what I mean?" She leaned in, expecting something from him now.

"Yes, I do." Julian fidgeted, head turning, tiny degrees. "You're saying that people need to . . . get focused, and get in line with . . . one thing or the other. And sometimes you just gotta pick and choose."

She frowned, disagreeing slightly. "Not *that* so much as knowing what you want to do. And knowing what's right . . . for you."

"That's great," he said, starting to go. The hill leading up the main road was dark and steep. A short walk. He thought about his home, the tub on the second floor, the blue basin, the way the porcelain felt against his naked back: sticky, a little grab and tug.

"But what's right for me may not be what's right for you."

"That's true."

"And that's why we need to give each other the space to say, 'Okay, maybe I don't understand you. And maybe I'm a bad person. But that doesn't mean that I can't . . . '"

". . . understand . . ."

". . . understand . . . the basic . . . *situation*."

". . . where you-all coming from . . ."

"Right. Because we're all different. You're a painter. That's your gift. I could never do that."

"Well, I'm not a painter." He spoke emphatically, words stacked like blocks on the ground. "I don't paint. I enjoy *looking* at paintings. I like that very much. But I don't personally . . . work in that field." Not wanting to disappoint her, he went on: "I design things, mainly. Books and such. Various types of . . . printed materials."

"That's so cool." She grinned, entirely won over.

Julian felt something shrivel inside; this girl interpreted everything as the deepest revelation, and he felt uncomfortable and wanted to leave. "Well, it's what I've done for a while now." He laughed, trying to keep it simple. "We just gotta do our thing."

"That's so right."

"But . . . I should be heading back."

"You walked over?"

"Yes, it's just through the . . ."

They both looked into the woods. Julian's house was not visible, only the hill rising through the trees. "Oh, that's real close."

"Not too bad. But if you could—"

"Tell Olden."

"About the business proposition, yes."

"Will do. This was so cool! I'm so glad we could do this."

"Well, I like meeting with a pretty lady."

"Oh, stop." She winked and flapped her wrist.

"And I hope you get inside soon, because it's really gonna cool down."

"I love it." She smiled and shivered, elbows close, hands at her throat.

Pointing up the drive, he asked, "May I walk you to the door?"

"Oh, no, no." Letting go of herself, she fanned one leg across a spot of grass, laughing as she turned. "I've got a gun. I'll just shoot the mother-fucker."

The old man said goodbye and went away, his footsteps fading up the hill. Kicking her legs, Scarlet built to a handstand; the blood filled her cheeks, making her face feel super-inflated. She staggered for a few steps, then tipped over. Dusting herself, she crossed the yard and went inside, undressing with the door still open. Half-asleep, Olden turned in bed. He saw her shape coming toward him; reaching out, he felt her back, the soft fuzz on her skin. She kissed him once, keeping her mouth closed. "Take off your underwear," she said.

He eased to one side, both bodies shifting as he stretched the elastic, then worked it down to his feet. He watched her as he did this; he wanted to see her seeing him. Scarlet busied herself with the covers, grabbing a good bunch and pulling it over her shoulders. She wanted to minimize the space between them, to make it flush. "Hi," she said, too loudly, trying to annoy.

"Hi." Olden wedged his hand between his chest and her chest, traced her throat with his tongue, then kissed it, a tiny bite. Her neck felt muscular, almost ribbed underneath.

"My name's Scarlet."

"Hi there, Scarlet."

"Funny meeting like this."

He pressed his knee between her legs, trying to create a place for himself as his mouth opened, making an O around her chin, then her lips, her tongue, sucking it in, drinking her groan. On top now, he braced himself and looked down, the cover drooping over his head. "Your feet are dirty."

She smiled as a strand of his long hair fell across her cheek. Reaching up, she pulled out her hair bands. Her pigtails loosened and spread. "I was outside," she said, feeling between the sheets. Olden shook, all nerves. She touched his face, his chest, marking the places, the muscles inside.

He pulled off the cover and threw it aside. "Let's do it outdoors," he whispered, starting to go, but she held him there, deep in the pillows. Her face was small; there was a dark dab on the pillowcase, water or maybe blue ink.

"No. Right here." She felt down and guided him in. His cock stubbed against her ass, botching the angle. Her eyes glittered; she smiled like a proud mother, watching her child onstage. "This is all we need," she said, and he rubbed his forehead, closed his eyes and tried to go away for a while.

XI

Seeds of Discontent

The Egg Code

Olden Field is a fifteen-year-old American male of English and Norwegian descent. His father, Martin, is a mathematics professor at Midwestern University in South Crane City. His mother, Celeste, works as a glaciologist for the Joint Ice Center in Suitland, MD. She spends much of her time in Greenland, gathering information about sea ice in the North Atlantic. The research team records the following values for each sample: total concentration; partial concentrations (from thickest to least thick); stage of development (from thickest to least thick); and floe size. Arranged on the page, the figure looks like this:

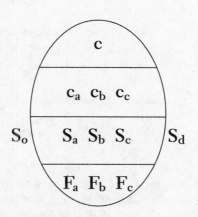

This figure is called an *egg code*.

Total Concentration (C)

Olden is a tall, lean boy, and he wears his thick black hair down to his shoulders. He attends Lance DeGregory Public High School, and is currently in his sophomore year. Last semester, he earned a 2.75 grade point average, with a B+ in Metalworking, a C- in Physical Education, a B in Physics, a B in English Composition, a B- in U.S. History, an A- in AP Calculus, and a C- in Accounting. He explains:

Metalworking: "I just . . . I don't know . . . I don't really care."

Physical Education: "That class sucked!"

Physics: ". . . And then he said, 'Why did you throw the bottle?' and so I said, 'I *didn't* throw the bottle!'"

English Composition: "My teacher is not a good person."

U.S. History: "Who gives a shit?"

AP Calculus: "Okay, okay, wait . . ."

Accounting: "I just didn't show up."

Olden stands in a record store, flipping through the heavy-metal albums. His fingers dance over the tops of the records. He picks one up and examines the back cover. One of the songs, "Angry Dream of Youth," is seven minutes and forty-nine seconds long. The album was recorded in Belgium. Olden looks at the record and thinks, Maybe I'll get this one. He puts it back.

As we ride in a commuter bus, we see Olden crossing the street on his way home from school. It is windy and he keeps his face half-hidden in the zipped-up neck of his jacket. We are thinking about something else.

The manager of a haberdashery suspects Olden of stealing a pair of suspenders. He telephones mall security and says: "Yes, I'd like to report a shoplifter . . . I'm calling from Look Sharp! in east wing . . . Yes, that's right . . . next door to the pretzels . . ."

The students stand on metal risers, rehearsing for an upcoming vocal recital. Participation is mandatory. The finale is a bombastic anthem entitled "We Are What We Are." The choir director waves her arms after the tenth bar. She points at a boy with long hair and asks, "Why aren't you singing?" A girl standing next to the boy says, "He's got a sore throat." Everyone groans as the soloists practice their gestures, removing invisible top hats and putting them back on again.

Partial Concentration (Ca)

I hate this place—hard chair, hard floor, a cold room in the basement— but at least I can talk to Mom from here, just a bunch of numbers, zero one zero one—egg codes, she calls 'em, that's what she's there to do, survey the ice for the government, a big military snow job if you ask me, just a short skip over the Arctic Circle and bammo! goodbye Moscow but hey, it's still kinda cool, the way the numbers form an egg on the page, only one number at the top, and then the others below that, the thickest and then the second thickest and then the third thickest, a bunch of stupid stuff, I just write it all down and my dad helps me convert the numbers to words, and every now and then she makes up a few figures, and if you run it through the code you can read all sorts of things like "HEY OLDEN HOW'S SCHOOL GOING PAL? LOVE MA," that sorta thing, lame I know but this is the only way I get to talk to her, it's better than nothing, nine months is a long time and Greenland is really far away, takes forever to fly there, but it's not so far in time zones so at least we're both up at the same time.

Partial Concentration (Cb)

Martin Field and his son sit in the basement of the mathematics building at Midwestern University on Saturday afternoons, and together they decode binary messages sent electronically by Martin's wife, Celeste. These messages are generally personal in nature and never exceed more than a few sentences. Martin enjoys spending this time with his son. Beyond the Internet, he and Olden have little in common, just the same last name, a few inherited mannerisms. A slight squint, a lopsided walk. A distinctive way of mispronouncing certain words. "Parochial." "Contrivance." "Entablature."

Partial Concentration (Cc)

"Hey, buddy."
  "Hey."
  "What's up?"
  "Nothing."
  "Nothing?"
  "Mmmm."
  "Okay."
  "I'm gonna get a soda."
  "Sure? Don't you want to wait?"
  "Dad, I'll be right back."
  "Okay, get me something too."
  "What do you want?"
  "What do they have?"
  "I don't know. The usual."
  "All right. I'll take a Schweppes."
  "What if they don't have Schweppes?"
  "Then I'll take a . . . 7-Up. But hurry back."
  "O-*kay*!"
  "Whoop! I just got the first packet."
  "I'm going!"
  "Hurry . . . hurry . . ."

Stage of Development (So)

Olden is telling me to stop. He says, "Don't write that about me, man." He is trying to push me away from the computer. His fist is pressed against my jaw, but I'm going to keep writing, keep putting it down even though he is not being very accommodating. Now he's kicking me under the desk. He thinks I'm not doing a very good job of writing his character. He says, "I'm not like that, man." I may have to stop soon. He's coming after me with a rock. Here he comes, closer, wow! whoops! Okay, okay, kay kay kkl;jasdfgjheuaowigafdtrfg43gf8du

Stage of Development (Sa)

Olden refuses to fight the other boy. The other boy is a few months older, a junior to Olden's tenth grade. The conflict started earlier in the day, between fifth and sixth period. The other boy ran up to Olden in the hallway and stole his comb. From there the situation escalated, and now—just a few minutes after the last bell—the whole school is buzzing with rumors and breathless reports from the front line. The boy primps by the entrance to the cafeteria, flanked by an entourage of lesser, scrawnier boys. Olden walks by the cafeteria, carrying a heavy book: *Tricks with FORTRAN.* The other boy stands in his way and says, "All right, man, whassup?" A few more students gather behind Olden, including several girls who spend their evenings kissing his picture from the '83–'84 yearbook (pages pink with lipstick splotches). For socioeconomic reasons, Olden is not officially "cute," and he will remain underground for several more years. Olden looks at the boy and says, "Do you want something?" The other boy tries grabbing Olden's book, but Olden holds it out of his reach. "What do you want?" he repeats. This is an abstract question; it flies right over the boy's head. Olden continues past the cafeteria and leaves the building. The boy's buddies converge in the middle of the hallway and say comforting things to their leader. "Man, that guy's a punk," one says. "A *faggit* punk, more like it," adds another.

Stage of Development (Sb)

They sit in the school cafeteria, these boys, ages eight and nine. Neglecting their lunches, they straddle the steel bench and reenact key scenes from this year's sci-fi blockbuster, using their three-inch-tall action figures as strange talismans to channel their dreams and delusions. A few of the action figures have plastic weapons that slide in and out of their wrists. The boys bat at each other with the weapons, their lips spurting high-pitched laser sounds as the plastic wands fold and bend and snap. Some of the boys are more particular about re-creating the scenes than others. A few insist on reciting the dialogue verbatim, while others are not quite so dogmatic. No one wants to play the princess. The bad guy is elite. A few of the boys—less aggressive than the rest—sit near the far edge of the bench, holding their inconsequential, wand-less bit players in their hands. They will never get the chance to fight.

"Hey, Olden," one of the kids says to a boy reading at the next table. Olden looks up from his book—*Fun with BASIC*—and swipes his long black hair out of his eyes. The other kid continues, "How come you never play *Star Wars* with us?"

Olden smiles and shuts the book, keeping his hand between the pages. "I don't like *Star Wars*."

The kid frowns as his cronies strike a variety of defensive postures. "Gotta like *Star Wars*," he says, holding his good-guy action figure in a heroic pose—legs spread, wand extended. "I've seen *Star Wars* forty-seven times."

"I've seen it fifty-eight times," adds another boy. Then, with a leer: "How many times have you seen it?"

Olden shrugs. "I don't know. Twice, three times." Opening his book, he adds, "You understand what you're doing, don't you?"

"What's that?" A boy makes a soft *chhhhuuuu-chhhhuuuu* laser sound, but his buddies shush him up.

"Buying all that crap?" Olden smiles as the other kid's hand tightens around the action figure's armor-plated torso. "That's the idea. Total marketing, all the way."

Retracting the wand with a practiced flick, the boy looks down at the chunk of plastic in his hand and asks, "What's marketing?"

Stage of Development (Sc)

Martin and Celeste stand in a muddy field along with a few thousand concert-goers. Everyone is drenched, even though it stopped raining an hour ago. Celeste is holding the baby on her hip. Onstage, the third band of the afternoon, Sugarloaf, is playing through a crappy PA; their one big hit is a song called "Green-Eyed Lady." The main group of the whole show—the one everyone is waiting for—is Three Dog Night. Celeste doesn't know whether or not they will stay for the entire concert. The baby is fussing, and the music seems to be hurting his ears.

A young girl with a tiny bag of marijuana tied around her neck comes up to the couple and grabs the baby's foot. "What's his name?" she asks, a delighted smile making a crescent across her face. "Olden," says Celeste, hefting the baby as he kicks away from the girl's hand. The girl grabs his foot again, but Olden twists free, thumping her in the face with his heel. Surprised, she runs off, rubbing her sore cheek. Celeste smiles and kisses Olden on the nose. "Don't let those stoners give you any guff," she says. Martin pulls a couple of wadded bills out of his pocket and shouts over the music, "I'm gonna get a drink." He returns twenty minutes later carrying two cups of warm, foamy beer. The band plays their one big hit, and the Fields walk back to the parking lot.

Stage of Development (Sd)

"Whoop!" said the nurse, wiping the spittle from the sleeve of her gown.

"Did he get it on you?" the new mother asked, smiling up at the bright ceiling tiles. A cool sponge moved across her forehead.

"Oh, sure." The nurse set the naked child back down on his mother's breast and walked over to the sink. "That's okay," she said. "All babies do that."

Floe Size (Fa)

In the dream, everything is bigger. Martin Field associates these dreams with too much drinking. "Too much" means a couple of Scotches at night. Returning the bottle to the cupboard, he creeps down the hall past his son's room. Stepping out of his slacks, he orients himself in the darkness and feels for the mattress with his knees. He falls asleep within the minute. This amazes him; reason dictates there should be a longer period of transition. Experimenting one night, he dropped the needle down on side one of *Sgt. Pepper* and then closed his eyes. The next morning, he couldn't remember the second track, couldn't remember even the second half of the first track, the song about Billy Shears. Martin finds this vaguely disturbing, this tiny border between dreams and reality.

In the dream, he sees his wife, which is not so unusual. Martin often dreams of his wife. These dreams are sometimes erotic, sometimes not. The erotic dreams make him feel ashamed, for they seem to cancel out his other feelings for her—the fact that he misses lying next to her at night, misses her help around the house, misses her conversation, her spontaneous lectures on plate tectonics and paleoclimatology, misses the censorious effect of her strong female presence. The thrill of the different. Comb your hair, son. Look sharp for your mother. But bachelors don't care. Bachelors roam the halls in their Jockey shorts and fart on the cat and pick their teeth at the kitchen table. No one to live for. So: he misses her. Then the erotic dreams come and reduce everything to simple wants. For this reason, he prefers the strange dreams to the erotic dreams. In this dream, he and his wife are stone giants, several thousand kilometers tall. The perspective is that of an eye watching the planet from a great distance away. The earth glows. Martin sees himself striding across the Atlantic. His wife sits with her knees tucked under her chin and her toes curled around the rocky coast of Greenland. Her body covers the entire island like a child perched on a milk-white pillow. Martin crouches next to her. Large rocks fall from his broken joints, crushing entire populations of Inuit and Danes. His footsteps make a booming sound, torturing the ears of the people below. For all but Martin and Celeste, this is a terrible day. The great cataclysm has begun. As he sinks to his knees, the ocean rises to touch his chin. Displaced water overwhelms the North Atlantic coast. Millions of New Yorkers die in the sudden flood. The only man left alive on the island of Manhattan is a window washer polishing the antenna at the top of the World Trade Center. Thousands of miles away, Martin reaches his arm around his wife's waist. The water recedes considerably but the damage is already done. Bloated stacks of corpses pile up in the streets. Celeste rests her cheek against the side of Martin's head. Sliding into the water, she wraps her arms around his hips, and together they swim across the equator, barely noticing the change in temperature as they reach the Southern Hemisphere and turn left at the Cape of Good Hope. A wave follows, three miles high. Chaos erupts on the coasts. The Tokyo stock market closes in a panic. The leaders of the European Community swallow suicide tablets and set fire to the state's currency. Thousands of red-eyed Africans mob the village square, raiding the poultry barns, tearing chickens apart with their brute fists.

In the morning, he can still taste the Scotch.

Floe Size (Fb)

In the morning, she is all packed and ready to go. See you in another nine months, sweetheart. She keeps most of her belongings in a storage vault near the U.S. Navy base at Thule. No point in shuttling it back and forth. Among her personal possessions—tube socks, insulated parkas, woolly mittens, heavy-duty cold medicines—she also has one nice dress for the annual holiday dance in December. Most everyone on the research team is married, and no one takes these dances very seriously. They are harmless get-togethers—forty or so scientists from the United States, Denmark and Great Britain shuffle-stepping to Glenn Miller tunes played on an ancient reel-to-reel.

"Tell me about Greenland," Martin says as they sit by the front door, waiting for the cab to come. She smiles and touches his face. They have this same conversation every year. In some ways, it is their only conversation: Greenland and what it means to me.

"It's too much to describe," she says, watching her words; the least little slip could mean nine months' worth of unmitigated bad feelings.

"Then tell me just a little part of it." He nuzzles her lap with his chin, breathing in her perfume. "Describe your lightbulb."

"My lightbulb?"

"Over your bed."

Celeste closes her eyes but the image will not come. Inventing a few details, she says, "Well, it's big. And white."

"Frosted."

"That's it. Frosted."

"Beautiful. What does it say?"

"What does it say." She focuses her mind, trying to build the lightbulb from scratch. Hmmm. A lightbulb in Thule, Greenland. A tiny thing in a distant place. She feels the lightbulb in her hand. Coarse. Chalky. It pulls on her skin. "It says . . . General Electric . . ."

"Yes." He parts her blouse between two buttons and kisses the space.

"General Electric . . . sixty watts . . ."

"That's perfect."

The cab appears at the corner, and the Fields leave the house and walk down the front path. "Kiss Olden for me," she says as he wraps his arms around her body, feeling her ribs and the soft spaces in between, thinking all the while, *I can't kiss him, darling, you'll have to kiss him when you get back.*

Floe Size (Fc)

For his sixth birthday, Olden's parents give him a giant model of the Eiffel Tower. The model is eight feet tall, and it takes Martin and Celeste over three hours to put the damn thing together. Olden stands in the corner of the room, sucking his thumb as his parents scramble about on their hands and knees, cursing occasionally, sharing an experience that he only partially understands. The purpose of the tower eludes him — not its function, for he knows what a tower is, but rather its relationship to him as a human being. He has never shown an interest in towers before. This is all his parents' doing. They have identified him with the object. Oh, Olden would like this. But *why* would he like it? What do they know? What are they not telling him about himself?

XII

The Passion
of Martin Field

Listings for the First Week of September, 1995

his fine apartment in South Crane City comes complete with a wealth of amenities. Nice location. Blocks away from Midwestern University main campus.

"I'm out of breath."

"Mr. Hasse, let me get you a chair."

Fully functional service elevator makes this a must for seniors!

"Your elevator—"

"I know. It hasn't worked since—"

"I walked five flights."

Upper level reduces street noise and enhances privacy.

"Here, sit. I'll sit over here."

Vintage furniture in all studio models.

"This chair is about to snap in half."

"I know, it's a piece of junk. Can I get you something to drink?"

"Just some soda water."

Refrigerator. Needs work.

"It may be a little warm."

"Thank you, Olden."

"How did you get down here?"

Reserved parking. Twenty-four-hour attendant.

"My driver's circling the block. I'd forgotten about the city. It's so crowded!"

"I never go out."

"Not if you're like your father. That's the wonder of technology. We can all be hermits now."

Small. Tidy. Great for students and working singles!

"Sounds good to me. I like being alone. I'm not even online any-more."

"What a surprise."

"Not really. My father's the same way. Computers per se aren't very important to us. We're more interested in the philosophies, the underly-ing abstractions."

"Philosophies?"

At Open House Realty, we believe that a happy customer is an informed customer.

"Network theory. Topology. That's what TCP/IP is all about. The nature of systems. Take any group of individuals. Within a brief period of time, a dictator will emerge. It's inevitable. Equality is an unstable element. The people demand a leader. Look at machines, and you'll see the same pattern."

Laundry room comes equipped with an array of modern appliances.

"Your father . . . was very close."

"He was close to something."

Nearby churches, theaters, and ethnic restaurants.

"And you? You're working?"

"I've been freelancing. Web design, that sort of thing. It's good money."

"But you don't like it."

Make us an offer! We want your business!

"I don't like working for morons. These MBA types understand the market, but the technology itself eludes them. They're like schoolchild-ren—even worse. At least kids know what 'http' stands for."

South Crane City School District, twice voted Best in State.

"It sounds like you need a change, Olden. Why don't you get out of the city?"

"I might. I don't know what I'm going to do."

Can't decide? Talk to our trained representatives. We'll find the apart-ment best suited to your needs!

"Olden, listen. I've got a place . . ."

The Seven Bridges
of Königsberg

1992

"I think I'd like to go home now." Martin Field rolled out of bed, found his boxers in a pile of clothes, stepped through the leg holes, then felt something heavy in both knees and sat down. His chair butted against a table, empty except for an ashtray, a set of keys, a checklist for room service and other amenities. The woman lay naked under the sheets, her feet sticking out, cloth pooling around the ankles. He spotted a small pink mole on her right leg—never noticed it before.

Donna Skye sat up in bed and pulled the sheets over her breasts. Her hair was stiff with spray, and it crushed and fanned in irregular shapes against the headboard. "I'm not going anywhere," she said, squinting at the alarm clock. "It's two in the morning."

Martin looked at the ashtray. He could read the checklist through the thick glass, a semi-transparent logo blocking a few of the words. "You've got a long drive back?"

"A long drive here, a long drive back." She turned on her side, considering the distance across town. "I could go home to my father. But not now."

No, not now, she thought, because regardless of the hour, Bartholomew Hasse would be at the door, pressing for details. In recent months, Hasse's disdain for technocrats such as Martin Field had turned into an obsession. It was impossible for him not to take these things personally. Hasse Publishing was a personal venture, born out of blood and sacrifice, and he'd smuggled it like a terrified mother from country to country and eventually over to the States, where he'd worked for decades, carrying on the tradition of Johann Gutenberg in the New World. An important tradition, reasoned the old man, because the printed word—the physical, tangible thing itself—was something that other Germans had died for. And now the last direct descendant of Johann Gutenberg was on the verge of selling the press. Something had to be done, and that something—for reasons Donna willed herself not to understand—involved screwing Martin Field. Taking the man's cock into her body, she imagined the condom as something great and impenetrable, several feet thick with nothing inside. *This is what I deserve*, she thought, faking a noisy orgasm. *This is the kind of woman I am.*

Martin toyed with his watch, then fixed the cold clasp around his wrist. "Maybe in a few days . . ."

"I don't know . . ."

"We could meet for a drink or two."

She stared at him; her eyes were hard and precise, like smashed blue porcelain. "I don't think so," she said.

The drapes blew over a crack in the sliding glass door. Outside, the sign above a service station slowly turned, flashing light across the highway. Martin scrunched in his seat, back flush up against the cushion. "This was a bad way to start," he said, the words uncertain. "For me, I feel, I would like to . . . interact with you, on occasion. But not like this."

Donna gazed at the ceiling. "It's good, though, since we're both married. And neither one of us is happy."

"I'm happy. But my wife . . . this is a hard way to live. And what does *she* do nine months out of the year?"

She looked at him, annoyed. "You think she's sleeping around."

"No, I don't."

"So you're doing it, she's not. That's *your* problem. Don't say it's her—"

"I'm not."

"—just because it's easier that way."

"You're right." Martin crossed his legs; his fly gaped, and he covered it with his hand. "I liked it, though. Meeting you. And I mean that sincerely. The rest of it . . . I'm a little nervous."

She grabbed the alarm clock and fiddled with the buttons. The hour flickered, then changed to twelve midnight. "Don't worry," she said. "I'll stay out of your way."

"Well, something in between . . ."

"No, please, just forget it. For all I know, you do this all the time."

"That's not the case."

"Oh, I'm sure." Distracted, she reset the time, trying to catch up before the minute skipped ahead. "This whole world is so weird. And the men are everywhere."

"I can't do anything about that."

She laughed and returned the clock to the nightstand. "We're not exactly the type, right?"

"I know I'm not."

Her eyes flashed. "Well, I'm not either! I never go to bars. But my husband goes on these trips that last forever, and sometimes you just want to be with another person because it's nicer that way."

"I understand."

"And I'm sure you're a great guy, but if you're uneasy about it—"

"I guess that's what I'm saying."

"Then let's just stay here for a few more hours, it'll be light out, then we'll go home."

Neither spoke for a moment. Martin felt something tenuous about where they'd left the conversation. Clearing his throat, he said, "Or we'll get breakfast, then we'll go."

"Breakfast. I can't even think about that."

He smiled and made a vague gesture, a loose spiral with one hand. "And that way you can tell me about your . . . what was it?"

"You don't want to know about me." She leaned against the head-board, letting her tits hang. "It's fine, it's no big deal, but . . . I've got a lot of problems, so, please, just do me a favor and . . . leave it alone."

"Okay." The drapes moved as cold air squeezed through the crack. Martin pressed against the textured wallpaper—coarse and splintered, like reeds chained together. "I'm sorry about this."

"Oh, goddamnit, don't apologize. *I* went up to you, remember? Women do things, sometimes."

"I know that. I'm not trying to be a jerk."

"Maybe your wife *does* sleep around."

"I don't think so."

"Maybe she does, and you know what? You deserve it."

"I'm sure I do." He slumped in his chair. The vinyl upholstery stuck to his skin, peeling away an inch at a time.

"You've never cheated before," she said.

"Please." He held his stomach. "I'm not feeling very well."

"Okay. I'm sorry." She reached over her head and fingered the wallpaper. The cheap lithograph above the bed lifted and fell, slamming face-first into the mattress. Both she and Martin jumped, but slipped quickly back into a late-night fog. Nothing seemed to matter, not even this. "It's all right," she continued. "People go through things. And being married . . . it's hard. With Derek—oh, shit. Well, that's my husband."

"That's okay. I didn't hear it."

She smiled humorlessly. "You didn't? That's good, because it's all boring anyway." She turned the picture over and studied the design, a cold abstraction, silver and copper lines. "You're boring, I'm boring."

"I am boring," he nodded. His watch felt heavy on his wrist. Reconsidering, he shook his head. "No I'm not."

"You like your work."

"I do."

The quick burst of conversation left them both exhausted, slightly confused. She snapped her fingers and pointed at the floor. Embarrassed, he fetched her brassiere from a pile of clothes. "I could never do that," she said, taking it from him. The fallen lithograph made a wet reflection above her head. "Mathematics. Numbers, problems. I'm better at human relations."

Martin's lips formed around a word. He sat there, frozen, unable to say it. She kicked the sheets away and walked across the room. Leaving the door open, she pissed in the john, then dabbed herself with a fat wad of Kleenex; he watched her in the full-length mirror inside the door. Flushing the toilet, she came back out and put on her panties. "How many sperm cells, in the average male?" she asked.

"Why? I don't know. A few million."

"Good God." She laughed, rolling her eyes.

"Why?"

"Since we're talking about numbers." She shrugged and sat down on the bed. "Are you one of those guys, with the toothpicks, and they can tell without looking—"

"No, that's different. I use a calculator, like everyone else." Self-conscious, he covered his groin. His dick felt hot and damp. "I'm more of a specialist."

"Ha! 'He said, with his pants off.'"

He looked down and saw his shorts twisted, fabric in a bunch. A sudden need pressed against his throat. "I can explain it to you."

"Please, don't. I wouldn't know."

"You might. Let me try to, anyway. I think I'd like that."

Nervous, he got up, then moved the table away from the window and placed it next to the bed. Messy sheets spilled onto the floor. Donna stood with one arm bent, left hand cupped around her right elbow. Martin spread his rumpled khakis across the gap, connecting the two, the table and the mattress. From the pile of clothes—his and hers—he found two socks, a tie, a wadded undershirt and a pair of black stockings. He placed the items on the bed, a circular assortment. Donna studied his back, the curve of his weak body hunched over his task. She felt something different toward the man. She wanted to meet him all over again, to start with the first hello.

"What's this?" she asked.

"This is a puzzle, the Seven Bridges of Königsberg, which goes back hundreds of years—"

"Oh, I see."

"Well, this is what I do." His voice was thin and shrill, like a professor's. Every word denied the situation at hand—the room, the bed, the mess on the floor. "And the whole study of topology comes from this. Because in the town of Königsberg, at that time, there were seven bridges. So, here's our seven bridges." His hand passed over the table. "And then the island, right here. And the rest is water."

"What about this?" Donna raised one of the stockings and let it drop. It wafted, finding a new position.

Martin flushed; he could smell her body. "That's where the bridge connects the island to the shore," he said, looking away. "So there's also a mainland, past the river. And the question is—"

"—how you get from one to the other—"

"Yes. How do you cross all seven bridges without going across the same bridge twice?"

"Well, that's easy."

"Okay. Try it."

She pointed at the table. "You start here, and then . . . oh." The path ran out, and her arm went limp.

"See, that's the tricky part. But that's why this is interesting. Because in today's day and age, when you've got, say, a network of computers, how do you get from one to the other, while keeping in mind that the configuration changes every fraction of a second?"

Her eyes moved quickly from the bed to the table. "So, how?"

"Well, take a look."

He returned to his chair and sat down, shivering as the cold crack pulsed behind the drape. Donna traced a path between bridges, and then another path, her hand passing in a circle. Her panties sagged, and he saw a slim shadow where the contour of her ass began. He closed his eyes. The sight of her body made him shudder—her ass, the side of her breast, the secret parts that, once seen, demanded a price, a responsibility beyond his willingness to oblige. He couldn't do it, couldn't live with this thing. Restless, he looked forward to the ride home, the mail waiting in the box, a flurry of take-out menus scattered across the stoop. Soon he would resume that life, pick up the cord left hanging for a few hours; but he couldn't do it now, not with that woman here, because some simple part of him still wanted to fuck Donna Skye, wanted to feel it, to come inside her pussy.

God, Celeste! Oh, my wife and son. Love me a little.

He opened his eyes and saw Donna working the puzzle, not yet ready to give up. He sighed, grateful for the distraction. The Seven Bridges of Königsberg would hold her for a few more minutes. The path was tangled, the theories convoluted. But like most ancient questions, the answer remained:

NO WAY OUT.

Listings for the Second
Week of September, 1995

*B*ig Dipper Township, caretaker's house, waterfront access, ten-minute walk to downtown shopping district.

"Interesting little town."

Quaint stores, chamber of commerce, winter ice festival.

"My daughter lives right around here. I own a good deal of this property."

Large lot, hidden from road.

"Do these outlets work?"

All the latest conveniences.

"I really don't know, Olden."

"Well, it's definitely a fixer-upper."

Foundation partially damaged. Needs new front door. Wood frame prone to swelling in the summer.

"Besides, you're a young man."

"Borderline. Still, I like the privacy."

Fifty miles from downtown Crane City.

"Very quiet."

"The middle of nowhere."

Bus service to schools and activity centers.

"A nice community, though. A few hundred people."

Get to know your neighbors.

"That beam is rotten. These panels—not insulated, hunh?"

"Not to my knowledge."

Extra fiberglass available on request.

"Gets cold in the wintertime."

"The trees keep the wind down."

Imagine yourself on an exotic island.

"You should *pay* me to live here."

You've got to see it to believe it!

"Olden, listen. You and I have something in common."

"I know, Mr. Hasse."

"Martin's a good man. He doesn't belong in prison."

Intimate. Cozy.

"There's a lot of good men in—"

"Well, we all know that."

"Almost a badge of honor, I'd—"

"No, of course it's not. Listen . . . your father is innocent. And I believe he'll have his sentence reduced. Not before I die. I'm very old. Just coming out here today—I'm exhausted."

Get away from those pesky solicitors!

"Mr. Hasse, I appreciate all of this. But this is a big change for me. I mean—look! It's wilderness!"

Just picture it.

"It's hardly wilderness."

"Well, no, it's not *wilderness*."

"This land is actually quite valuable. I won't tell you how many offers I've had just in the last few weeks. From some pretty strange sources, too. But I don't need the money. I like owning things."

Tired of landlords? This is your golden opportunity!

"I'll have to set up a generator. Those wires are useless."

"Send the bill to my secretary. Don't spend a dime. I made a promise to your father. He wants you to be happy."

Because if you're not happy . . .

"You want me to fix this place up, is that it?"

"I want you to live here. I want you to keep your eyes open."

"What am I supposed to see?"

"Maybe nothing. I don't know. I don't want people taking advantage of me when I'm gone."

"But your daughter lives—"

"My daughter and I don't have a very satisfactory relationship. Donna . . . is not right for this job. It's her upbringing, I feel. My fault entirely. Wealth spoils, sometimes. It doesn't have to. Personally, I find it very reassuring."

"What?"

"Money. Poverty bores me."

"Not much of a socialist, are you?"

Credit check. Must meet certain minimum requirements.

"Ah, but this is the nature of systems. Have you ever seen my house?"

"No, I . . ."

By the Balls

1993

"Now we're both criminals." Bartholomew Hasse stood in front of the living room window, nursing a gin and tonic. It was a hot afternoon in Hedgemont Heights. Outside, the backyard resembled an empty playroom, the carpet brown and tattered. He spoke without looking at the other man. "I am prepared to make a series of phone calls. Have you any idea how easy this is for me?"

"My wife is very far away," Martin said. Both men spoke in clipped tones; the words seemed transcribed, almost re-enacted. "She will be nearly impossible to reach."

"Surely you don't believe that." Tipping his glass, Bartholomew filled his mouth with cold gin, then swallowed. Standing still, he could feel his liver—a hard, glass bulb. "Isn't that the point of this wonderful technology? Easy access, everywhere. And all thanks to you."

"You really have a strange impression of who I am," Martin muttered over the back of the sofa. The room was big and dark. The light from the windows seemed to go nowhere. "I'm a simple mathematician. An on-again, off-again academic."

"I'm not impressed." Bartholomew fingered a grand piano, building a melody from fragments. "How long have you been working for the Gloria Corporation?"

"I've never worked for the Gloria Corporation." The music continued, slower now. Martin corrected himself, "Not directly. Gloria is an independent contractor. One of those outside agencies that seems to turn up everywhere. I have no idea who I was working for. DARPA, maybe. The NSF. It's all quite harmless, really."

"I don't accept that." Bartholomew closed the piano lid with a bang. "This isn't an action movie, Mr. Field. No chase scenes, no explosions. It's much subtler than that. Come next year, the RA will be in place and that will be the end of your First Amendment rights."

"I don't see the connection." Martin shrugged and looked away. This was an old argument: technology and the end of the world. Sighing, he added, "The Routing Arbiter is no big deal. The Gloria Corporation has nothing to hide."

Ah! thought Bartholomew. A loyal bureaucrat! He'd seen enough of those in his time. He crossed the room and stared at the man. Martin sat with his knees pressed together, hands folded, eyes trained on the coffee table. Bartholomew wanted to close him like a briefcase, hinges folding into halves, quarters, eighths.

"This device. It exists?"

Martin removed his sports jacket and loosened his collar. "It's possible. The routing tables offer only snapshots of a moment in time. The patterns change every tenth of a second." Rising, he walked toward the window, keeping his back straight as he passed the old man. "But there are other questions as well. The parties, the people involved. Who benefits? One man, maybe. Maybe the machine itself."

Bartholomew smiled. His eyes looked sick, overbright, like pale organs balded for dissection. "And you told me you weren't interested."

"I'm not interested."

"Yes, you are. And that's perfectly natural." He sipped his drink; the gin burned on the way down. His voice returned, upbeat now, more American. "Look—you're a scientist. Scientists explore. They test theories. That's what you did. And now—twenty years later—you're thinking: what?"

"I'm thinking nothing. Thank God it's over. Thank you for the extra incentive, a few years of high living, my little piece. But now—I have a wife, I have a son."

Bartholomew frowned and shook his head. "Your son is a grown man, so don't worry about that; and as for your wife, well, think about it, because that's something else entirely."

Martin stepped away from the window. "Meaning you'll do it, right?"

"That's right." Bartholomew pointed at spots in the air—the characters, the dots to connect. "I tell Derek, I tell your wife, I tell your family. And then this whole thing goes to hell, because some famous people are involved."

Martin blinked, trying to match his opponent's mood. "Okay, I get it. You're a cold man. You want your way. I don't have a problem with that. But your daughter. That seems a little unnecessary."

Bartholomew laughed. "Well, I hadn't thought of it like that before. Two marriages for the price of one. That would call for a celebration of some kind, wouldn't you say? Of course, you'd all have to attend— Derek and Donna, you and your darling Celeste."

Martin snapped, "Oh, you're reckless, aren't you?"

"I'm entirely out of control, Mr. Field. Old age is a wonderful thing."

Martin turned away and covered his eyes. He couldn't believe this— people who acted this way. "So. Your daughter's marriage. Her reputation. Her self-respect. These things mean nothing to you?"

"Let me tell you something, son. Donna makes her own decisions. She even gets a kick out of it. Not necessarily out of sleeping with you, for I'm sure she found it repulsive. But the whole idea of cheating on her husband. It evens the score, you know. The ego of Derek Skye is a fearsome thing."

The name settled between the two men. Remembering that night in Sparta—the sounds Donna made, the way her nipple felt between his teeth—Martin wanted another chance. He wanted to fuck her right now, to watch her having an orgasm. Even a fake one—good enough. "I've been misled," he said. "I don't deserve this." Defeated, he went back to the sofa and pulled a sheaf of papers from his briefcase. He sighed, handing over the stack. "Right now, this is the best I can do. Sixty sites, most of them privately owned. Some are more suspicious than others."

Hasse frowned at the top page. "How so?"

Annoyed, Martin explained, "Anytime you have more than one network coming together, it's a security hazard. They're called peering points. One of the biggest ones is in New Jersey."

"Where in New Jersey?"

"In Pennsauken." Reaching into his pocket, he spread a stack of color snapshots across the coffee table. "Right here, in this parking garage."

Hasse glanced down at the pictures. "This isn't good enough, Mr. Field. I want you to narrow it down."

Martin laughed, helpless in the face of the old man's single-minded stupidity. "Why?" he demanded. "Those machines were designed to recover on their own. If the idea is to reconfigure the routing tables—"

"That's *not* the idea." Hasse moved closer, waving the pages. "Listen—give me an address. A place on the map. Point it out for me."

"What for?"

"You know what for." He glared out the window. Some gardeners were working outside—red hats and polo shirts, a slogan on the back. "Somewhere out there, there's a machine, a little box. And that little box controls all the other little boxes. Wasn't supposed to happen that way, but it did. Hitler wasn't supposed to happen, either."

Martin spoke calmly, sliding into lecture mode. "No, Mr. Hasse, you're wrong. We're talking about statistics. Yes, there is an anomaly. Yes, it's on this list. No, dynamite won't destroy it. You want to destroy the Internet, then destroy the planet. Because nothing short of that is going to do it."

"Maybe it just takes a lot of dynamite."

Hearing this, Martin fetched his things and hurried away. "Leave me out of it. I'm not a thug."

"You have the easy job, Mr. Field. I pay someone else to do the dirty work."

"*This* is the dirty work." Halfway to the door, he stopped to fix the latch on his briefcase; it had swung open in his hands, but there was nothing inside, so it didn't matter. "I'm not supposed to have this information. I could go to jail for this."

The old man stared. "Yes, you could."

Martin's face turned red. Not for the first time, a feeling of injustice—of being punished for more than just his crime—weighed heavy upon his head. "What the hell," he snapped. "So could you! Why not? Let's all go."

"Highly unlikely, Mr. Field. You, on the other hand . . . maybe you need to think about it for a while." Neither man moved; unreleased tension, like fingers pinched around a balloon, grew inside the room. Bartholomew studied the pages, searching for the most likely candidate. Each location suggested a new motive—sixty different ways of concealing the obvious. All across the country, high-speed routers lurked inside office towers, military bases, bomb shelters, shopping centers. No hidden pattern, no secret design. The names themselves made no sense. Idaho Falls, Wendover, Corsicana, Montevideo. *Some are more suspicious than others.* Yes, Mr. Field, Bartholomew thought—but *why?* The list was too inclusive, the terms too vague. For now, he would suspend the search. He'd already seen enough random destruction—Germans and Italians, guns raging over Europe. Things would be different this time. One bomb, one target. A simple victory. In the end, he had to respect Mr. Field. It wasn't easy, killing your own child, even a child born of wires, algorithms, page-long equations scratched in pencil. Martin Field was a stubborn man, determined to do the right thing. But prison would change all that.

Listings for the Third Week of September, 1995

*H*edgemont Heights. Lovely Tudor estate with modern flourishes. Exclusive address, Oakmund Avenue. Forty-seven rooms, three-car garage. In-ground pool. New to market.

"Not bad for an immigrant, eh?"

"Very impressive, sir."

Serving kitchen. Wet bar in basement. Receiving entrance. Split-level terrace. Circular drive.

"I don't need this much space, of course."

"You're here by yourself?"

Eight bedrooms, ten baths. Huge yard. Room to run. Attention: large families!

"My staff and I. We just had an elevator put in. Would you like to ride it?"

"Sure."

"This is a great thing, having an elevator in your home. Look at all the buttons!"

"It's just like a real one."

"It *is* a real one! Like in an office building. But it's mine, and it's here."

"Cool."

"The whole rig—guess how much?"

"I have no idea."

Less than you'd expect. A smart investment.

"If you were to guess."

"Thirty—"

"Eighty-seven thousand dollars. But I don't care, because it makes me happy."

Can you say: splurge?

"Who put it in?"

"A professional company from Cincinnati, Ohio. This is all they do."

"Elevators."

"Not just elevators. Private elevators. Let's go up to the top floor."

Call for a guided tour.

"Okay."

"That way you'll get a sense of the whole thing. See? How the doors close. Very slowly."

Act now!

"It gives you enough time—"

"Exactly. And then look. See how the numbers go. One. Then two. Then three. And now we can either go back down or we else stay on this floor."

"I think my ears just popped."

You'll hit the ceiling!

"So this is Hedgemont Heights. Fifty years, I've been here."

Very special community. Private schools. Well patrolled. The eighth most desirable place to live in the United States (call for the complete list).

"In this one house?"

"Just about. My wife and I came over right before the end of the war."

"This was World War—"

"World War II, of course, what other war—the only war. We couldn't stay in London. England was so dependent on the United States in those days. So I liquidated. I ran a stencil company—you know what those are, don't you?"

"Sure. They still make stencils."

"Of course they do. What am I thinking? I should've stayed with stencils. Instead I got into publishing and everything was fine until these goddamn gadgets came along."

Online? Check out our Web site at www.openhouse.com. Fully interactive! Links to related sites!

"You'll be all right."

"You really think so? You're intelligent, I trust your opinion."

"These things happen. Look at the printing press. The first fifty years. Cultures died, whole languages wiped out. But as some languages died, other languages grew. The Renaissance, the Protestant movement, the rise of the working class."

"But what did that get us? More literacy, of course. But what's literacy? Does literacy imply judgment? I don't think so. Literacy equals class consciousness. Take a look at the Westernized nations. What's the first thing they teach you? How to pay your taxes."

We also have plenty of inexpensive models available. Ask about our E-Z finance plan!

"One way or another, there's always money to be made. They encroach on your territory, you encroach on theirs."

We'll meet you halfway!

"Permanent things, Olden. This is what I love. Permanent things. Quite natural for a man of my age."

Retired? How about a condo in the Everglades? You're not getting any younger!

"Nothing's permanent, Mr. Hasse. Even the Gutenberg Bible will eventually fall apart, if it hasn't already."

"Then *tangible*. Americans are obsessed with ghosts. Even their government's imaginary. We have invisible money, invisible universities, invisible shopping centers. But invisible words? Invisible words are the worst. Invisible words hide empty thoughts. Give me ink. Give me paper. Fuck technology."

"Hear, hear."

"I want a drink. How does that sound?"

"I'll go along with it."

"Will you take the house?"

"I don't know. Maybe. I'll give it a shot."

"Good kid. You need some time away. You've been through a lot."

Relax! We'll do the paperwork for you.

"What if the woods start to get to me?"

"The woods you don't have to worry about. It's the ghosts."

"Hunh?"

"Come on. Let's go back down to One."

Terms of contract may vary. Subject to owner's approval. Open House Realty is an equal opportunity employer. Ask for Sheri. Ask for Sheila. Ask for Sharonne. WE ARE NOT THE SAME "OPEN HOUSE REALTY" PROFILED ON THE NBC "BETTER BUSINESS" REPORT. *Ask for Clint. Ben Donaldson no longer works at this address.*

Prodigy

A September Stroll

1998

I t's six a.m., and Simon can hear his parents sleeping in the master bedroom. The cat is awake, as usual. She creeps around all night, suddenly present in different rooms of the house. The cat is the only family member who knows about Simon's little secret. No one else cares enough to notice.

At 6:03, he enters the kitchen and pushes open the screen door. His skin looks blue in the dawn-light. The lake is still, and some deer are browsing in the neighboring woods. His chest swells with a rush of heart-flopping energy as he flings off his pajamas and runs down to the beach. The lake is a wide-open bowl, and his feet make conical divots in the sand. An empty boat rocks nearby, a wet rope anchoring the prow. Still running, he cups his hands around his penis. Even this feels naughty. His mood changes; he no longer wants to do this. He turns and races up the jagged hill, determined now to reach the highway. This is something he cannot explain, the conflict of fear and desire he feels every time he does this thing. He wants to be caught. He doesn't want to be caught. Scaling the hill, he sees the highway's dented guardrail, then hears the clatter of a pickup truck taking the bend at forty miles an hour. He has never come this close to the road before. The thrill spools away. Turning, he scampers toward the house, finds his pajamas and quickly dresses behind a tree. Even now, he feels naked. The insides of the pajamas are gritty with dirt and twigs. Heading home, he keeps an eye on his parents' bedroom window. No light—nothing. The screen door makes a scandalous noise as he inches it open and creeps inside. Past the kitchen, the cat zooms and leads the way up the steps. Out of breath, he rolls into bed and closes his eyes. It is only now that he feels truly ashamed. He imagines thousands of security cameras nailed to the tops of every tree in the forest, recording his bad deed and broadcasting it live onto a four-hundred-foot projection screen. This has to stop, he thinks, then falls asleep.

The sleep drifts and fades, and soon his mother enters the room and tugs on his leg. Through one peeking eye, he can see the face of his digital alarm clock flashing 7:08.

Lydia yanks on a paper blind, setting the roll flapping. Obnoxious sunlight fills the room. She opens the closet and parts the clothes with both hands. Squeezing past the first layer, she gropes around, finds a garment bag and throws it at him. "Put that on and meet me downstairs."

Simon reaches between his legs for the bag. "What's this?" he asks. Through the clear plastic, he can see a tuxedo jacket, one eyelet thinly stitched, a false boutonniere.

Lydia checks her watch, then hurries out of the room. The boy is alone, wide awake and yet somewhat dazed by the commotion. Resigned, he kicks off the covers, gets dressed and stumbles downstairs to join his mother in the foyer.

"You're here?" she asks, focused on her work. Racing about, she fiddles with a camera—pointing, a few tiny adjustments—then tapes a white sheet of construction paper over the front door. The sheet hangs, slanted. "Christ, good—look, just stand right here and hold still."

Simon poses in front of the backdrop, his hair still messy from the pillow. The door inside the kitchen is open; he notices it just as his mother swoops in with a camera. He can feel his heart inside his chest.

"Damn it!" She points the camera at the floor. "Simon, hold still." The boy stands, waiting for instructions. "There!" She studies his face. "That's it. Do that." Simon frowns and looks at the ground. He hears the camera and feels hot all over.

Taking a break, Lydia skips out of the room and goes upstairs. The quiet of the place is amazing when she's gone; he can hear his father getting ready for work, running his hands under the bathroom faucet. Anxious, he tiptoes and shuts the back door.

Soon Lydia returns with a pair of reading glasses. "I almost forgot. Put these on."

She thrusts the glasses at the boy, who takes them and asks, "Whose are these?"

"Grandpa Tree's, now shut up."

The plastic stems hurt the backs of his ears. "I don't want to wear a dead guy's glasses!"

"He's dead, who cares?" She crouches, tilting up with the camera, getting a good angle. "Act intelligent. Like you're thinking about something." Interpreting these commands as physical gestures, Simon decides to wrinkle his nose. Acting does not come easily to the boy; most of the time, he has no real sense of what he's doing.

A few more clicks and the sink upstairs shuts off. Lydia curses, then takes down the backdrop and puts the camera away. The ceiling creaks. Simon feels dumb, standing there.

"Jeezo-pete, what's with the tux?" Steve Mould, dressed in his manager's golf shirt and slacks, comes down the stairs, his knees bending outward like the legs of an unwell barnyard animal. He presses the boy's cheek against his cold belt buckle, a brass medallion with the word *POP* written in tall block letters. "I'll tell ya, boy, today's the day you come into work with the ol' man! I'll show you what it's *really* about!" He smiles at his wife, his kid, the stack of newspapers on the floor. His face is still wet from the shower. Dressed for work, he resembles a delivery boy, here to do a job.

Lydia grabs her son and pulls him close. "Where the hell are you taking him?" She frowns, lines breaking across her face. "I need him today. He's mine."

Steve starts to laugh, then checks himself. "Lydia, I explained this to you. I patiently went over this with you yesterday. I'm taking Simon into work with me because he's going to be in a television commercial. I told you this twice—once over the phone, and then once at dinner."

Lydia sighs, conceding nothing. "If you have to do these things, fine, but I'd appreciate it if you would consult me—"

"Con*sult* you?"

"Yes, Steve, *consult* me. Believe it or not, I *am* a human being, and I also happen to be the boy's business manager—yes, strange but true, *me*, not you—"

"Hooo, listen to her go, I tell ya . . ." He turns his head, playing to the empty room. "Business manager, like the whole world's about to come to a—"

"Goddamnit, Steve!"

"—screeching, clanging halt."

"That's what I do, and if you think it's so fucking amusing—"

He stops, hearing it late. "*Don't* curse in front of my kid."

She smiles, voice loud, happy to win. "And don't be such a goddamn self-righteous prick!"

Steve's lips tighten. He nods, slowly processing the information. "Okay. I gotcha. I know what I am. But GAD-DARNIT—" His face prunes, turns red. He makes two fists, and his whole body seems to squeeze toward the center. "I'm the boy's father, and I'm your husband . . . and tonight we're all gonna go out and get a . . . dang-blasted *pizza*, and we're gonna have ourselves a family celebration, and I don't even care if I have to shove the cotton-pickin' thing down your whole . . . damn . . . mouth! And . . . all right?"

Lydia covers her mouth and laughs, spoiling the whole thing. Steve's expression doesn't change; emasculated, he yanks open the door and stomps down the path. Simon lingers, then follows. Something quick pounds inside his gut, like a hand lifting him up. He wants to strip, wants to show. Even as his father starts the car, unseen cameras crowd the forest, desperate for another look. The house, the lake, the beach, the tower—all belong to the same company: Simon Incorporated. The boy smiles. Nothing happens without him.

Sheesh Redux

onderful. We're driving in the car, he's staring out the window, ignoring everything I have to say. I'm making conversation, "Have you had breakfast yet?" No response. That's rude, right there. At least *look*.

I remember my old man, boy. Barndoor Mould. Would slap you *so* hard.

But Simon is . . . well, he's an interesting kid. I can't really say I understand him. That's okay, though. He'll appreciate it someday. And I don't care what Lydia says. That side of the family is overrated—Kay Tree and the rest. Some people have to work for a living. I know that store managers don't make a lot of money. But it's not *nuthin'*. You have to deal with a lot of garbage every now and then. I'm taking my kid in for the big photo shoot, this woman comes up, waving her receipt, hooting and hollering. Right there in the parking lot. I wanted to say, Look, ma'am, I understand that you're upset, and we want you to be happy with your purchase, but . . . I'm here with my son today, you know? Can't I have that? The kid already thinks I'm a creep. WHY ISN'T THIS ON SALE?! YOU TOLD ME YOU'D GIVE ME THE SALE PRICE! You know, a real . . . I won't even say the word, but you know what I mean. Some of these women, they've never worked a day in their lives, and they don't understand the proper way to do business. So I say—very patiently, very professionally, "Ma'am, that pillow is not a part of the Cumfy Cushions Sale, the sign clearly says that only floral toss pillows are on sale, that is a solid-colored toss, therefore it is not on sale, but if you'd give us your name, we'll be happy to let you know when it *does* go on sale." WELL THAT'S NOT WHAT YOU SAID! I'M NOTIFYING YOUR CORPORATE HEADQUARTERS! On and on. I wanted to say, Look, lady, why don't you get off my ass for a change, all right? That's a buncha bull! But instead I just said, "Okay, ma'am, we're very sorry that you feel this way, and because we strongly value your business, we'll make a one-time exception in this case." So I took her in and rerang her order. But I didn't smile, and I didn't give her any free coupons. No sir. I could've given her five thousand dollars in gift certificates. Heck, I could've let her walk right out the back door with whatever she wanted. I have power that most people can't even comprehend.

Those people from the ad agency, though . . . they're real professionals. I'm walking around, checking it out. Cameras everywhere. Floor's a mess. It sure keeps the customers away. Sold a couple of candles, that's all. Chump change, thanks a lot. I'm looking to clear a million two by January first—I need some *cash*. This acting business, that's where you make the money. Maybe the kid's got the knack, I don't know. His mother sure seems to think so. I don't know anything about acting, so I can't really judge. When I was in school, they had the theater department. A bunch of shows. My buddies and I, we'd sit in the back and laugh at—well, I guess you can't call them queers anymore, but you know what I mean. That's one thing that Simon's going to have to watch out for, if he's serious about this. There's a whole lot of temptations out there, and my experience is that people who go into that line of work tend to have very low moral standards. But that's just in general. I'll reserve judgment.

So I'm working, running registers, the usual crap. I look over, Simon's whispering to one of the makeup gals. Finally she says, "Simon says you're making him nervous and please leave." Okay. I can respect that. That's good, that's professional. He's working now—no horsing around with the old man. Then this Gray Hollows person grabs my arm, says let's go downtown, sign a few forms. I kind of hated leaving the store like that, but I took one of my assistants aside and showed her how to restack the armoires for the new Fall Into Fall Autumn Sales Extravaganza. They always screw it up. This particular assistant, she's one of the worst.

And I hate to say this, but I wish I could fire her for being overweight, because it's just not what you want to see when you're making a purchase. I think the way a person looks is important, and when I go into a store, I expect a certain bare minimum. No supermodels, just a nice, attractive, well-dressed woman, where you can at least see the shape. It's all a part of creating a pleasant shopping experience. But in our country you can't punish people for being overweight, which I suppose is good in the larger sense, but when I get burned by it, then I start to wonder. This sensitivity thing is getting out of hand. That's not what America's all about. If she wants a job, she oughta work in a cafeteria. Those people are *always* fat.

So we're driving downtown, fifteen minutes on the freeway. I don't know about this Gray Hollows person. The man's car smelled like just about the worst stuff you can imagine. Bananas. Rotten bananas and socks. You'd think—we're both professionals, both full-grown adults, he's invited me out on a business excursion. You'd think he'd take the time to clean the place up, maybe turn off the radio. I tell ya, if this is what passes for corporate-level material . . . a *brassiere* hanging from the rearview mirror? Yes. My jaw just about hit the pavement. A brassiere, a ceramic figure of the *Savior Himself*, with the head broken off, just a pair of legs and some bloody nails. I pointed, I said what the heck's that? Music's so loud, I've got my head halfway out the window, and you can't even hear what's going on. I wrote down the lyrics, too—I wanted Jim Carroll to know about it. This is a direct quote, so the curse words don't count: "SHE'S MY FUNKY FLY BITCH, I'D LIKE TO FUCK HER WITH MY FREAK-FACE." Now even *I* know what those words mean. Things were different when I was a kid, boy. Fourteen, fifteen years old. I had the Steve Miller Band going *round the clock*.

So we pull into the parking lot, right next to a big ol' Mercedes. These people must be raking it in. Maybe I'll go into advertising someday. Half of the guys they got down there, they couldn't be more than forty. Nice place, too. One *really* foxy gal in the front room. With the spike heels and the miniskirt. Oh lordy, my. I just about had a heart attack. *Mr. Mould, would you like a cup of coffee?* Yeah, I'll take a cup of *some*thing!

Finally, we get up to the CEO's office. Some guy with a beard. Seemed like a nice enough fella. Next thing you know, Gray starts shouting, making a big scene. That's smart, right in front of a client. I tell you, I don't know much about office politics, but I do have two eyes and two ears and a nose and a mouth. I'm standing there, feeling like an idiot. Finally I said—this is what I said, word for word—I said, "Mr. Hollows is sure doing a great job, sir, and we're all real happy about it, me and Jim Carroll and Mr. Pee." I couldn't tell, when we left the room, whether Gray appreciated my little plug. He seemed a bit aggravated. It's hard to read a man's mind when he's wearing glasses.

XIV

Book Deal

The Adam Syndrome

I realize, in writing this, that I'm probably not speaking to a group of novices. You, I trust, have leafed through at least one of my books before. It is not arrogant to assume that I have affected some small part of your life. Business clients know me from my many seminars and weekend getaways, paid holidays organized around a dubious theme. Wearing the ridiculous hat of the corporate cheerleader, I preached an uplifting message; the end of each session was an emotional ordeal for everyone involved. The platitudes multiplied—neatly symmetrical word games that sounded the same forwards and backwards. A healthy company is a motivated company. Nothing makes quite so strong an impression in the workplace as sincere enthusiasm, I said sincerely and enthusiastically. Surveys prove that a vast majority of American employers value a sense of pride and personal ethics over performance abilities and even basic competence. I held the survey high over my head and brought it down against my leg. Together we made the walls of the conference center shake with our chanted slogans and our thunderous, neo-primal, corporate-bonding war dances.

But here is my confession. No one cares if you're motivated. The word itself means absolutely nothing. Motivational speaker. More nonsense. Let me hone that statement even further. Not merely nonsense, but an utter void of sense, an emptiness of thought. For twenty-five years, I contrived and executed public seminars. That was my job. To make a pleasing noise. The truth that I have been protecting you from is a grim one. There is a controlling party in this world. You will never be a part of it. The men and women who inhabit this closed circle of power are a minority group. Many of these people are friends of mine. They don't need to take my course. Those distractions are for you alone.

This triangular arrangement of society is not only important, it is inevitable. Establish any form of government—whether left- or right-wing in nature—and in a few years, that system will coalesce into a new structure, rooted in capitalism, necessarily based upon an uneven distribution of wealth. From this trend, we may draw several conclusions. The first is that people like to own things. Without ownership, there is no ambition. The desire to possess fuels every creative act. Moreover, this same desire prevents society from falling into dependency and sloth. Given a standardized economy, the incentive is not to work more, but to work less. The wonderful thing about capitalism—and, in turn, America—is that all things are *not* equal. The surgeon earns fifty times the going rate of the average fry cook, and for good reason. The top-dollar physician—through taxes and other contributions—provides employment and financial security to low-level consumers. The surgeon—if he or she is culturally responsible—donates to arts organizations, medical research facilities, educational programs, and urban renewal projects. The fry cook spends his two hundred dollars a week on rent and food for his baby. It's nice, but it's not quite the same thing.

Which brings us to the next aspect of this whole equality nonsense, the idea that value distinctions are somehow wrong, that they run counter to the egalitarian ideals prescribed by the Constitution. Americans do not like to acknowledge that certain members of the population may be better suited to certain tasks than others. Dissenters are branded as fascists, their sometimes complicated and self-contradictory belief systems generalized and written off by the opposition as so much bigotry. This dilemma is most pervasive in our educational institutions, where once challenging programs are yearly watered down to accommodate the limitations of a student body who, in the main, clearly do not belong in college. Most professions do not require a strong academic background. By catering to the average, we deprive those uniquely talented students of the rigorous education that once produced the great minds of the early 1900s, men and women whose efforts helped make America the technological and cultural center of the Western world. In Japan, children commit suicide when they bring home a failing grade. In America, they blame the teacher for writing an unfair examination. We need more suicide, I say!

Of course, this problem arises long before students reach the post-secondary level. The sad truth is that our public school system does such a poor job of supplying young people with basic skills that universities are forced to act as surrogate high schools, nursing the troubled majority along its remedial course and cheering every minor and ultimately meaningless triumph like a couple of giddy parents taking pictures of baby's first poopie. The administrators' reluctance to discipline poor academic performance stems from the fact that parents rarely support the staff's decision to impose real and substantive standards on the struggling child. Somewhere along the line, we've forgotten the value of failure, its tough challenges, its hard yet effective lessons. Instead, we see failure as a threat, a judgment upon our own abilities as parents. Rather than encourage our children to learn from their mistakes, we scream and pout and threaten to sue the school board until finally someone from the superintendent's office sends us a form apology in the mail, an appropriately ass-licking recantation complete with a "revised" copy of our child's report card. As a result, the nation's public school system — in compliance with the demands of the American people, who, after all, pay their salaries — produces a team of graduates steeped in the philosophy that if you stamp your feet loud enough, you can pretty much get whatever you want. Graduates able to function well enough as consumers, but who lack the tools necessary to attain true financial independence. Citizens well primed for a life in the peasantry.

Here, I suppose, is where I take over, for it is precisely this climate of simulated equality, this glorification of the average, that allows me to pitch my delusional, self-congratulatory rubbish to millions of mediocrities around the world. The message I sell is simple and infallible. According to this doctrine, depression occurs when a person cannot perceive the positive forces in his or her life. Unhappy at the workplace, unfulfilled by empty relationships, we need only to change our perception to realize our full potential. What this technique amounts to is a heightened form of inactivity, a slightly belabored way of doing nothing.

Its corrective properties are nil. It's a lot like trying to cure brain cancer by wearing a hat—the cure and the disease are utterly unrelated, the prescription inept, the change merely cosmetic. This behavior—psychotic in the most precise sense of the word—is designed to distract the practitioner from the hard realities of his or her regulated fate. My dogma provides a service to you, the questing mortal. It changes your perception. It makes it easier for you to accept death, to believe that life has structure, that God actually cares about your emotional well-being. Your problems, as we have seen, cannot be solved. They are defining problems. What we can do, however, is recondition your perception of reality. No longer A, we will call it B, and once B no longer pleases us, we will move on to C, and so on and so forth. Having changed the terminology, we then gladly commit the same dumb mistakes, convinced—like medieval serfs—that our true reward lies just beyond the grave. Our sick reality festers from our refusal to see it for what it is. Is there a name for this illness? Lacking a better alternative, we will call it the Adam Syndrome—the renaming of the beasts. I believe that America is dying of it.

Skye Versus Skye

"Christ, Reggie . . . where are you?"

Voices swirl and spit. The shadow of an overpass skims across the windshield. Outside, orange and leather-brown leaves spill past the median. In the country, they are gathering for the harvest, splitting logs, testing the draw of the flue.

"Donna? Lost you for a sec."

"Are you in your car?"

"Yeah."

"It's these damn car phones."

"It's these damn I-don't-know-whats, and I think my battery's low."

Reggie Bergman shakes the phone, his other hand on the wheel. An indicator screen shows three dashes, now two, the second one flashing. Power running out.

Donna yaps, her voice small, cramped inside a tiny hole. "So, where was I? Ah, yes. The book."

"Since when do you write?"

"Since *now*, what difference does it make? The point is it's a great idea. There's nothing else like it."

"There's always something else like it. That's the nature of the business."

"Nonsense. People talk about it all the time."

"About what?"

"About the hole in the marketplace."

"There is no hole in the marketplace. This is the myth. This is what we tell ourselves. There are no holes. If there was a hole, what would it look like? I'm trying to imagine it. It's too abstract."

"Then what's the point in living, Reggie? Why don't we all just shoot ourselves right now?"

He shakes his head as the car pulls up a steep grade. "Good question."

"Just think about it, then decide. *Many Voices, One Vision*. Isn't that just the greatest thing you've heard all day? A book of collected lore."

"What do you know about lore?"

"I *know!*"

"And why does it have to be collected?"

"People want it to be collected, who cares? They're stories. You collect stories."

"Who collects stories? It's like they're bottle caps or something."

"Oh, Reggie, please stop resisting me and just say yes."

He shudders, imagining the implications. "This . . . I don't like. I'll see what I can do, but as Derek's representative, it puts me in a very difficult position."

"That's fine. Now what do you think of my chances?"

"Of what—selling it? It's sold already. Just finish writing the book, and we'll take it from there."

"Are you sure?"

"Look, Donna. Twenty, twenty-five years, I've been working. It's the name recognition. This is what sells."

"I don't want to do it that way."

"Well, that's how it's done. You want to be Jesus Christ, get yourself another agent."

The road spreads into four lanes. Reggie passes a block of shops—the town, apparently. Side streets wisp off into nothing, a few houses.

"I'm sorry. I'm just uneasy. I don't want Derek to think that I'm . . . moving in on his territory."

"But you are."

"But I don't want him to think that."

"But you are."

"But I don't want him to think that!" The car passes under a net of fiber optics. Donna's voice fades, returning with a new cadence. "Look, Reggie, I'll call you back. I want to talk with Derek about this first."

"*Don't*. You stay away from that man. Don't even call him on the telephone."

"I feel awkward."

"Feel awkward while writing your book. You asked me to represent you on this project and I said yes. Fine. Over and done. Now your job is to get a draft together so when I go down to New York, I don't look like a big *joik*, as they say in—"

"Okay."

"—as they say in—"

"You're right."

"Ah, to hell with it."

"This is great. Reggie, you're so sweet. Why couldn't I have married you?"

The old man winces and hangs up the phone. The idea of marrying Donna Skye settles inside his brain. Easing the car over to the curb, he kills the engine and surveys the apartment complex across the road. Crude battens join a series of narrow A-frames at the hip. So this is where Derek Skye lives. His client. A motherly sense of grief overwhelms the man. Only weeks ago, he could've done something about it, could've talked to the Gloria Corporation himself. Now it's too late. Tired from the long drive, he reaches across the automatic transmission and grabs a bottle of fancy water from the unoccupied passenger seat. Breaking the plastic seal, he unscrews the cap and downs the contents in one fluid motion. He can feel the water flowing directly into his bladder. Glancing at the dashboard, he checks the reading on the odometer. Fifty miles from Crane City to this place in the woods. He sighs and rubs his cheeks. He hopes Derek isn't going *eccentric* on him.

The warm autumn sun burns into his dark slacks as he walks across the street. Reggie is a man of inconsequential height, heavy within the acceptable norms. His skin is beige, almost adobe. He has aged in none of the interesting ways. Struggling to describe his appearance, a friend would mention the fact that he wears bifocals. He has lost little of his hair, though it has all turned gray, like pavement. He has recently had his teeth done—a mistake, in retrospect. They are too white, calling too much attention to the rest of his face. They are held in place by a row of steel screws driven into the roof of his mouth, an application that has distorted his sense of taste. Everything smacks of metal to him now. His oral surgeon has assured him this will not go away.

Derek comes to the door dressed in a pair of pajama bottoms and an old silk shirt. His breath is foul, the smell of fitful sleep. He hasn't shaved in several days, and his stubble has risen to meet the level of his mustache. Taken aback, Reggie glances down at the welcome mat. Derek's toenails are black with filth. The pajama bottoms are crimped and worn, and they cling to his skinny legs like detritus blown against a lamppost. Reggie wonders how long it has been since Derek last changed his clothes. It's very easy to fall into the pajama lifestyle—a real temptation for a man in Derek's position. Days and nights bleed into one another; naps become more frequent, real sleep more dear. A kind of minuteman mentality sets in. Regular meals give way to constant snacking. One notices a marked decline in the quality of one's bowel movements. The patient starts to question his ability to digest food properly. He has turned into a sieve. He masturbates constantly, and without any pleasure. The muscles are too run-down to muster a successful ejaculation. Instead, it just sort of limps out into the open, cold even as it leaves the body. Only the smell still makes him smile. Reminds him of his youth. Swimming pools and erections. A full head of hair. A future.

Reggie follows his client upstairs and into the apartment. He will refrain from making any comments. An agent's job is to encourage, to inspire. To goad, if necessary. Never to berate. He has worked with enough writers to know that self-pity is rarely in short supply. He must remain optimistic, for his sake as well as for Derek's. After all his hard work, he cannot allow it to end like this.

"You'll never guess who I just got off the phone with."

"Reggie, don't mind me. Keep talking while I get dressed. My assistant's due any minute now."

The agent smiles, finding a spot on the sofa. "You're working with someone? That's wonderful."

"Well, we'll see. She's young."

"I'm glad to hear you're working."

"I'm sure you are, Reg. So. This person?"

Derek steps out of his pajamas and strides bare-assed across the room. From the closet, he takes a pair of khakis and a lavender dress shirt, the collar buttoned around a hanger. A thick blue vein stretches across his right buttock. His legs look spindly and long. Reggie focuses on his own glasses, trying not to notice.

"Huh? Oh. Oh! Donna called. Out of nowhere, Donna called."

"Lovely. Let me guess. She's writing a book."

"She told you?"

Rooting through a pile of undershorts, Derek halts in mid-reach and stares at the old man. "She's writing a book?"

"She's writing a book! She wants me to represent it."

"Oh. What did you say?"

"I said yes, sure, all in the family, why not?"

"Why not? Anything for a—"

"Anything for a buck, right. Well, I'll have you know, Derek, that I did this for you."

"For me."

"For you! This is the best thing that could happen to you."

"Explain that one to me, Reggie."

"Donna writes her book. It's terrible."

"How do you know it's terrible?"

"It's *terrible!*"

Derek sighs, giving up. "Right, it's probably terrible."

"So, she writes her book. *The Sad Poor Me Chronicles, Volume One.* Big press, we send it out, advance copies all around."

Derek fiddles with the cuffs of his shirt, trying to button them. "I don't want to hurt Donna, Reg."

"Well, having just gotten off the phone, let's just say the feeling's not mutual."

"How do you know that?"

"Why else would she write the damn thing? What other motivation could she possibly have? For twenty-five years, you were the woman's life, Derek. She's got nothing else to write about!"

"She's writing about us, our marriage?"

"No, she's writing a monograph on European economics."

"She told you all this?"

"Look. What she said and what she *said* are two different things. I'm not concerned with that. I'm thinking, How do I sell this? What angle do I take? What's my line?"

Derek folds his slacks in half and carries them into the kitchen. From over his shoulder, Reggie hears the sound of fabric shifting, first one leg and then the other. The refrigerator door opens. Glass on steel. A desperate glug. The refrigerator door closes. The audible silence of day.

"So. Skye versus Skye. It'll make for an interesting publishing season."

"That depends, Derek. On you. If you're planning on sitting out for the summer, well, then that's different. If not . . ."

"I'll have something together."

"Excellent."

"A few more months. You'll see." Derek returns to the living room, his fly open, his belt loose. His lips are orange with fruit juice. He smooths his shirt with the knife of his hand and tucks it in place. "No tours, though. No appearances."

"Ahh, the cult-of-personality bit. I like it."

"I'm not making any more speeches, Reg. I'm done with that. One more book and I'm through. A few last thoughts."

Reggie crosses his legs and scans the apartment. He hates this—not knowing where to look. "Derek, you're only fifty-one. This is an old man's game. You're just getting started. We might need to work on your presentation, that's all. The wizened coot. Mad eyes. Long, snowy beard. People will listen to you, now that you're older. You're what they want to see."

"I've never had a problem with people not listening, Reg. Remember that woman from California, the one who stuck her face up to a belt sander? She's walking around with no nose, no mouth . . ."

"I don't remember."

"I remember, Reggie—*me*. Every time we went out west she was there, at the conferences, the intervention weekends, anytime we got anywhere *near* Sacramento. Then I get called down to the hospital . . . she's sanded her face off . . . wants a private audience. I show up, her sister's there, a couple of quack lawyers—these two Jewish guys, fucking arrogant—"

"Could you see her face?"

"She had no face, Reggie, this is what I'm telling you."

"Everyone's got a face. She had, maybe, no facial features."

"Okay, no facial features."

"No ears, no nothing."

"She had ears. She didn't get that far back. But no eyes, no nose, and no mouth."

Reggie looks ill; a sour weight pulls on his lips. "How repellent was that?"

"It wasn't repellent at all, it was just odd, seeing her like that, with everything gone."

"And she said what?"

"Nothing—she couldn't communicate except with these colored cards that she kept holding up, you know, like . . . blue meant something. There were about a half-dozen cards she could choose from."

"How did she know which one was which?"

"I don't think it mattered, Reggie. The sister—"

"Oh, she was the one—"

"Yeah, running the scam."

"Trying to say, you know, you encouraged her or whatever."

"Something like that. It was disturbing, but that was about it. Wasted two days of my time."

Derek finds a pair of loafers and clip-clops across the room. Reaching the far window, he turns the vertical blinds. Bands of light become bands of dark.

"That's absolutely awful, Derek. How can a person sand off her own eyes?"

"What do you mean?"

"I mean, it's . . . it's impossible."

"No."

"Sure! You know. The stalks."

Derek's stare is cold and dull. "I don't know the stalks. The point is . . . that's neither here nor there. What I'm saying is, I've been doing this for a long time, and it's too long, and I'm tired of it, and after this one last time—that's it! No more!"

"This is temporary. I can see it in your eyes."

"You can see what in my eyes?"

"That this is temporary."

"What is there that suggests to you this is temporary?"

"It's just a sense that I've got, that you've been thinking this over and you're feeling very discouraged right now for whatever reason, but . . . that . . . this is temporary."

"Okay, so it's temporary."

"See! It *is* temporary."

"No, I'm just conceding the point because I don't want to talk about it anymore. What I'm telling you is very simple. You'll have a book come springtime, and from then on I expect to be left alone."

Reggie grips his elbows, a full-body clench. He is trying to look thoughtful. To him this means frowning. "Is this a good frame of mind for you to be writing?"

"This is a perfect frame of mind, Reggie. For what I'm doing."

"What are you doing?"

"Well, I'll tell you right now, Reg, that . . . you're not going to like it."

"I'm not?"

"This is a different kind of book. Unlike what I've done before."

"Different is a problem."

"Well, that's too bad."

"Are you trying to wreck your career, Derek?"

Derek snaps, raging: "My career is . . . a lie! My career is . . . a fiction! And if I want to do something . . . either unconventional or maybe a bit reckless . . . then that's up to me! If nothing else, if I get to say one true thing to people—"

"Oh, one true thing. What horseshit is this?"

"One true thing—"

"Derek, I am not going to allow you to destroy in one foolish act everything we've been working toward since NINETEEN SEVENTY-THREE when your father-in-law—"

"Ex-father-in-law."

"—ex-father-in-law came up to me and said: *Reginald. Do it.* And I said *okay*."

Derek presses his hands to the sides of his head. "So you're not going to do this for me, is that what you're saying? You're unwilling to . . . execute your role as my legal representative . . ."

"I am unwilling to do something I don't believe in. I believe in Derek Skye. I've believed in Derek Skye. For twenty-five years. That's a long time. Maybe too long?"

A bell rings, and the two men turn toward the door.

"Let me get that."

"I'm leaving anyway."

"Reggie?" Derek stands in the way, searching the old man's face for reassurance.

"We'll talk later. Really, I've got to go."

Downstairs, they bump into a girl—short, barely five feet tall, with brown pigtails that sit on either shoulder like a pair of fancy epaulets. She holds a heavy canvas sack between her ankles; a pink ballet shoe spills ribbons through the zipper. Her outfit is that of the proverbial madwoman—white rubber sneakers, black tights, a flimsy dress stained in batik patterns of purple and orange. Novelty buttons urge a desperate message: KISS ME; LOVE GOD; I ❤ ARTICHOKES. Her round sunglasses are blue and mirrored, something a Deadhead would wear. She chews gum like a child trying to push out a front tooth, a kind of anxious wadding of her tongue against the roof of her mouth.

"Hi, Derek. Wow, you're like—here."

"Scarlet, this is my agent, Reggie Bergman. Reggie—"

"Oh, my."

"Hi, Reggie."

"—this is my new assistant, Scarlet—"

"Oh, God, listen to him."

"Scarlet . . . Scarlet, did you ever tell me your last name?"

"Scarlet, yeah, hi, how you doin'?"

"Lovely. We were just . . . what were we doing?"

"Oh, I don't know. Doing those crazy things that guys do. Scarlet, what's your last name?"

Scarlet pulls her dark glasses down the bridge of her nose. Her eyes are dark, marred by a lack of sleep. "My last name? Hmmm. My last name. My last name is a strange, wonderful, awesome and mysterious thing."

"Oh. I guess that answers my question."

Reggie holds his briefcase against his chest and twists sideways, trying to squeeze past. "Right, well, I've gotta head out."

"Fabulous. That's really fabulous. Reggie."

"That's right."

"That's such a cool name."

"Well, thank you."

"I mean . . . that's a *really* cool name." She smiles, her eyes beaming. "It's just totally a name that a little kid would have."

"Right."

"I mean—that's cool! That's totally great. That's great that you're keeping up with that."

"Mmm-hmm."

"It's great that you're, you know, keeping in touch with that part of you . . . that little kid part of you that we always forget about but it's always there, you know? Even when you get older and more distant from the things that are really important . . . doesn't matter. It's all good. It's like one day you just realize—wow, this is wild . . . this is what life's really about . . ."

Reggie nods, making excuses as he shuffles down the path. "Right, well . . . it was very pleasant meeting you, and I'll just . . . let you two do your business. I've got to get back to the city."

"Nice, nice. Doing that crazy commute thing. I know how that is."

Derek leans in. "Reg, give me a call. Next week sometime."

"Will do. Bye, Derek—bye, miss."

Scarlet waves as the old man climbs into his car and drives away. Taking her bag, she turns and climbs the stairs. Slowly, Derek follows; he stalls before entering the apartment.

In the kitchen, Scarlet flips through a few cabinets, then opens the refrigerator, searching for some magic ingredient. "Can I make you something to eat?" she asks. From the freezer, a thick white mist curls around her head.

"No thank you."

She closes the door; the mist rises, lingering near a vent. "Man, you *do* need an assistant. When was the last time you went grocery shopping?"

"There's some money in the drawer by your hand. Maybe you could pick up a few things."

"Gotcha. Ten four. I would be more than happy to do that, sir!"

"Excellent. Use your own discretion."

Scarlet paces the room, pointing, counting it out. "We'll start with peanut butter. That sounds about right. You need peanut butter. And just regular butter too. Several different kinds of butter. Anything else?"

"I don't believe so." Feeling awkward, he sifts through a pile of mail on the table. Head down, he speaks to a manila envelope. "Thank you, Scarlet," he says. "I'm glad you stopped by."

She smiles and shrugs. "Hey, anything you need. I can do ironing, I can take care of the kids—but you don't have any kids, do you?"

"No, I don't."

"Well, I can still do it, just in case. Let me see. I can type. I can take dictation, so if there's ever a time when the inspiration's really flowing, and you can't write it down fast enough, feel free to, you know, impose on my secretarial skills."

"That probably won't be necessary."

"No, I didn't think so. I just thought I'd mention it. I'm sure your writing is so personal, you know, like . . . 'one-on-one conversations with myself' or whatever, and I'm totally cool with that, so anytime you need me to just get lost, that's totally fine."

He garbles a few empty words of gratitude, staring at her feet. Scarlet's eyes glow; his voice fills her throat with a weightless energy. Slowly, she rises, standing en pointe. "I'm writing that down," she says, then taps her head. "Soon as I get home."

"What?"

"What you just said."

He tries to remember what he just said—something about the groceries, yeah, and be sure to get a receipt for the returnables. This scares him, how his words seem to imply more than they mean. He blinks as his mind gropes for something reasonable to say. "You're a very special girl, Scarlet . . . you're a . . . duuhh . . ."

"What?"

"I forgot."

"Don't worry about it. Look, let me go get your groceries and I'll be right back."

Her sneakers squeak as she takes the stairs in twos and bursts through the front door. Crossing the street, she skips past a few cars, trusting in her own ability to avoid disaster. This man has made her feel untouchable. Upstairs, Derek watches through the venetian blinds, then smiles with the pleasure of a new thought. Blessing. That's the girl's name. What a pretty name.

XV

Virus

Z

Ever since late September, Julian had been working on his letters, making them ready for his big commission. It was a lonely job. He worked quickly, churning out the major alphabet in little more than ten days, adding the dingbats and diacritics the following week. After this job was complete, he would take a long vacation. He was tired. His clothes stunk. He'd forgotten how to live like a human being.

Only one thing stood between him and his goal. The Z. Could not do it. It seemed like a simple task, on the surface. A line. A slash. Another line. Even so, a growing hesitation kept him from finishing the job. Obsessed, he began to dream of letters, giant, anthropomorphic letters that crowded him in his sleep, a gang of twenty-six.

"HA!" scoffed the Z, its beak pecking the space above the old man's head. "I laugh at your inability to comprehend my inherent complexity." The Z spoke in a canned voice reminiscent of Mexican banditos. "You think—LIKE FOOL, you think—three lines, boom-boom-boom—is simple, no? AI, DIABLO! You will burn for such treachery!"

Trying to wake up (he'd dozed off at the drafting table), Julian called across the dream-space, "Give me a clue, man. Tell me where you came from."

"Ahhh." The Z paused, choosing its words. "Okay, then. You wish to know what I am. I confess. I am . . . three erect phalli, bonking madly, a great gang bang! HA HA!" The Z unhinged at its corners, then returned to its proper size. "No. I tease. Look, I don't know. A winding stream, a snake, a bunch of twigs, who cares? The important thing is this—what will you do, now that I am here?" Julian looked down at his shoes. "Keep in mind my history. Nicolas Jenson—has drawn the Z. John Baskerville—has drawn the Z. Giambattista Bodoni, the great wop himself—has drawn the Z! And now, you! I scoff at your impossible predicament!"

The old man blinked, raising his head from the table. His right cheek ached where a chunky eraser had been pressing against the side of his face. His eyelids fluttered, and soon he was back in letter-land, floating in a thick, soupy mist. A woman was with him this time—Donna Skye, of all people—and she reached up and wrapped her arms around the Z's big foot.

"Hey!" The letter reared, shaking its limb. "Who is this madwoman, clinging to my mighty abutment?" Donna tightened her grip. The tapered projectile groaned and bent, twisting one hundred and eighty degrees. The Z wailed. "Oh, you gringo bitch!" It shook its leg. "Look at my foot! The Z's serif never points down! Is a failure of my manhood, no?"

Donna struggled with the letter, trying to hold on, finally giving up as the last of her phony fingernails broke off, sending her spinning into the partly cloudy depths of Julian's subconscious. "Good," snarled the Z. Bits of busted graphite poured from its damaged foot. "Now that the she-devil is gone, you—typemaker—may restore me to my proper position."

Julian smiled, regarding the letter's altered shape. "You look good like that."

"I look good?!" The Z spat. "I look ridiculous!" Its spine twisted as it tried to nudge its dangling article back into place. "The Z's serif never points down!"

"Well, I think it looks good, and I'm going to keep it."

The irate letter howled, slashing at Julian's face with its barbed tail. "Licker of poisoned cupcakes! You would let a woman come between you and your sense of aesthetics? Pfeh! I say. Double pfeh!"

Julian woke up; the blank page before him was now covered with sketches, as unfamiliar to him as if a stranger had put them there. The Z on the page was the same Z he'd seen in his dream; even the serif looked the same, a downward pointing wedge, just odd enough to give the rest of the series a personal stamp. Like that, the job was done. His head hurt and the back of his throat felt dry—a snifter of cheap brandy was sitting on the table, the bottle open and half-empty — yet an overriding desire to show his work to his partner made him feel jubilant, almost cocky. *You the man, Julian.* Creaking down from his stool, he slid his drawings into a leather carrying case and zipped up the sides. It was a warm day in mid-October; he would walk to the place.

The lake was quiet; the vacationers had all taken their canoes and kayaks back to the city. Bird droppings covered the tower with a hard, bright crust. Julian stumbled down a steep slope of wet grass, holding his bag against his chest to keep it from jouncing around. The door to Olden's shack was open; leaves blew across the step. He went inside.

Olden looked up from his computer screen and smiled. "Julian, hi. You look like you've been busy."

The old man opened the carrying case; a leather smell rose and then sank. "It may be more than you need," he said, hefting the pages. "I got excited."

Clearing a space, he left his work on the computer table. Olden gave a cursory look to each of the drawings. "Good, yeah, this'll do." He pushed his chair aside and opened a plastic box, lid flopping on a bad spring. The inside was a clump of lightbulbs and bunched wires, circuits under glass. He arranged the pages, then nudged a jury-rigged switch. The box filled with blue light.

Julian laughed weakly, looking for a place to sit. Standing there in his corduroys and his old blazer, he felt hopelessly genteel, out-of-date. "I don't know if you're in a hurry," he said, edging toward the desk. "There are some things that I'd like to call to your attention . . . tiny things, but . . . there's a little quirk in the Z that I'd—"

"Little quirks, cool, I like little quirks." Olden stared into the hot light. A bright bar traveled under the glass, grunting as it passed. "I have my own little quirks too."

Julian slid his hands into his coat pockets. "I know . . . with *most* photocopiers—"

"I'm not photocopying it. I'm scanning it into my program." Job done, Olden gathered the pages and handed them back to Julian. "They may look wonderful on paper, but they won't do me any good unless they're in here." Hands on the keyboard, he struck the same button a half-dozen times. "It's a fundamentally different medium, Julian. The foundries have been digitizing since the sixties, but they've always used old models—the latest Bodoni, another rehashed Jenson. Type must evolve, like everything else."

"You know a lot about typography," Julian remarked, nodding automatically.

"Enough to write this." Rooting through a pile of junk, Olden pulled out a ratty notebook and tossed it across the room. Julian caught the notebook and turned it over. "There," Olden said. "The first installment. I wrote it in honor of our collaboration."

Finding a light, Julian damped his lips with his tongue and began to read. The essay was remarkably thorough, tracing the first post-Gutenberg experiments with Gothic type to the end of the incunabula period, the dominance of the Roman font, the French advances of the 1500s, the refinements of Baskerville and Fournier, the reactionary elitism of William Morris and Co. A rather amazing piece of scholarship. It was wonderful. It was horrible. Terror-struck, he slunk for a few steps, then dropped to the bed.

"I'll probably cut it down a bit before I put it online." Olden combed his fingers through his hair. On the screen, a capital A grew, stretched to an unnatural size.

"You're a very good writer," Julian said, rereading the first few sentences. His eyes scanned the page; he couldn't look at it anymore. "There's some . . . factual inaccuracies—"

"There's a *lot* of factual inaccuracies."

He blinked and tried again. "I just happened to notice . . . reading this over . . ."

"The world is an imperfect place, Julian."

"Just . . . here . . . where it says . . ." He squinted at the page. "Oh yes . . . 'in 1735, renowned English printer John Baskerville, proclaiming his homosexuality to a shocked community, began producing a series of erotic woodcuts under the alias of Jonny Foote-Sauce . . .'"

Olden laughed, enjoying what he'd written. "I'm willing to bet that a good ninety to ninety-five percent of the people who read that will believe it's the straight-up fucking truth."

"But . . ." The word streamed; Julian's logic seemed quaint, based on a lame premise. "Children will see this. Students. People who need the information."

"Look, Julian . . ." Olden spoke reluctantly, not expecting Julian to understand. "The whole point is to make people *think*. There's too much blind faith in this country. Even our paranoia's way off-base. We're paranoid about the wrong things. We should be paranoid about ourselves."

The old man smiled, somewhat reassured. "I just want everything to be cool . . . like you say."

Olden scowled. "Don't you know anything about the Internet, Julian? These people don't play around. Let me take you out on a road trip someday. You should see what the Network Access Points look like. They're fucking concrete bunkers! MAE-West, MAE-East, no one knows where the hell they are." His lips twisted, the look of a mindless wonk. "'Oh, the Sprint NAP is in Pennsauken, New Jersey!' *Sure.* Where in Pennsauken? Just follow the fucking barbed wire."

"NAP?"

"The big peering points, the links to the backbone." Rising, he began to pace. "And those are just the major centers. The routers are everywhere! Inside repeater towers, in the middle of the ocean, riding shotgun on the backs of satellites. Cyberspace is not a figment of our collective imagination. It's real. Actual wires are involved."

Calmer now, he returned to his desk. Julian watched from the edge of the bed, then, feeling like a nuisance, excused himself and hurried home. *The Golden Girls* was on television—a funny one, too. He sat in front of the TV with a beer and a bag of potato chips and just laughed and laughed and laughed.

All night, he dreamed of letters.

Your Tax Dollars
at Work

The story of urine has fascinated researchers for generations. In recent years, urine testing has become the method of choice for detecting illicit substances in the bloodstream. As employers across the country continue to enforce mandatory drug examinations, the questions arise: Why urine? Why now? What's the deal? To fully understand the extent of our government's wrongdoing, one must first know a few things about dendrochronology—that is, the analysis of growth rings found in the trunks of perennial, wood-bearing plants. While the connection may not be obvious at first, the Egg Code would like to point out other links between apparently unrelated phenomena, links which—once unearthed— reveal a secret history of Western philosophy, religion and political thought. Video teleconferencing and the transoceanic button trade. Granulated sugar and the rise of the indentured servant. We cite only the most pedestrian examples.

Tree rings are formed when contrasting cells produce a series of colored bands, each marking a year's growth. Dendrochronologists use specialized drills—called increment borers—to pull samples, slender cores of soft wood cut along a horizontal plane. The Department of Defense has developed its own device, inferior to the European models, but required by federal law. As a result, the International Tree-Ring Data Bank must contend with thousands of tree cores ruined each year by faulty equipment.

What is the solution? The answer, as it turns out, is urine. Urine contains nitrogen, which acts as a special solvent, balancing the negative effects of the drilling process. The way this works is very complicated. Back in the mid-1980s, the demand for urine skyrocketed. Responding to this need, the Reagan Administration—in concert with subversive elements within the Hollywood entertainment industry—launched a multi-agency "war on drugs," a cynical sham whose only purpose was to make mandatory drug testing a nationwide standard. Make no mistake, people: all they wanted was the urine. Following a series of staged screenings, handlers loaded the urine into giant tanker trucks formerly used to transport soy milk between the coasts. Under the cover of night, the urine arrived at an abandoned quarry pit near La Junta, Colorado, where a team of dendrochronologists set upon the awful task of dunking and drying, a smelly job made worse by the bitter stink of corruption.

At this point, our story breaks down into a clouded tale of half-truths and misrepresentations. Let's go back to 1943, when a researcher named Bruno Huber published a paper on the degrees of similarity among various trees within the same growing zone. Huber termed this factor *Gleichlaeufigkeit*, or "running similarity." He quantified his research by using a binary code, a massed sequence of ones and zeros—the same principle behind our modern-day computer technology. This point was not lost on the Gloria Corporation of Ann Arbor, Michigan, current administrators of the network protocol for North America. Working through a liaison at the National Science Foundation, the Gloria Corporation reinserted the core samples, causing the trees to warp around new growths of wood, and thus enabling it to hide its own security codes in the Gleichlaeufigkeit of the doctored landscape. In other words, whenever you look at a grove of trees off the side of the expressway, what you're seeing is not a natural formation, but rather a manipulated structure designed to conceal a binary code. Any questions? Take a look at the pledge pins next time you crash a GC think tank—you'll see what we mean.

Creative Bullshit

"Put it on." Scarlet pointed at the wet suit lying heaped near the closet. She and Olden were both naked; they'd already begun to make love, and he was loath to stop now. Eyes closed, he tried to ignore her, but she said, "I want to feel the rubber on my hands. I want to feel your ass like that."

He slumped, then pulled out and crept across the room. The wet suit was a big mess, with the zipper jammed, the sleeves turned inside-out. She watched, laughing as he worked the suit over his legs.

"There's a zipper here," he said, trying to walk with the thing half on, the stretchy fabric binding his knees together.

"That's okay."

"No, but it's in the way."

"So leave it unzipped."

He tried that, tried a few positions, then finally gave up and yanked on the zipper, pulling it up to his chin.

Disappointed, she stared at the ceiling. "Well, that's no good."

Olden slid back into bed. "How did we get naked to start with?" he asked, one arm curled around her waist.

Squinting, she traced a few points in the air, mapping it out. "I came in the door. And then you said 'Hey.'"

"Oh, yeah. Right. I remember."

She smiled, touching him. "With that hard-on, which looked so good at the time."

He sat up and turned toward the door, already thinking about something else. She found a shirt—one of his—and put it on like a robe. Looking at her bare legs, Olden noticed a bruise above one knee. *I wonder about you*, he thought, then undid the snap of the suit, leaving it loose at the neck. "Here—check this out." Rising, he went behind his desk.

Scarlet slowly turned her head; her eyes scanned the ceiling. "I wish you had a guitar," she whispered.

At the computer, Olden typed a few words, then stopped. "A guitar?"

"Or anything. Even a banjo. But those are hard to play."

"Mmm, I'm sure . . . okay, look." He motioned to her, and she crossed the room, still thinking about guitars, wooden guitars with fat bodies, big holes you could stick your fist right through. A hollow rattle, the sound of something inside—a pick, or maybe a quarter. She dropped and sat in his lap. "This is it," he told her.

Recognizing something in his voice—a cue, a rising cadence—she stared and said, "Oh, wow."

The image on the screen changed. Olden pointed, finger tapping the glass. "That's where the kid goes."

"What kid?"

"The pictures of the kid. I showed you." He grabbed a stack of Polaroids and handed them to her. Flipping through the pile, she picked out a favorite and held it up. "I like his hair," she said. Then, touching his cheek: "I like your hair."

He kissed her fingers. "Other than that, it's all set. At least for a few weeks. Then we revise."

"This means a lot to you, doesn't it?" She played with a strand of his hair, tucking it behind one ear. "I think that's so great."

He waited for a moment, ignoring the screen. A nasty impulse pressed against his throat, and he asked, "What's so great about it?"

Her hands fluttered. Big lips hushed around a soft voice. "It's great that you're doing what you want to do."

The feeling drained away. "Okay," he muttered and went back to work. As he typed, neat words spooled across the screen. Scarlet whispered a few to herself, making it halfway through the first sentence. "Gee, you're so smart," she said.

He nudged her. "You're not even reading it."

She stopped, getting annoyed. "I read some of it. I'll read it all. Look—"

"No, don't read it." He waved his hand in front of the screen, then held up one of the pictures. "See? That's the idea. Without the kid, people might take it too seriously, which I don't want them to do. I don't want them to take it *seriously* per se, I just want them to recognize something in themselves—the fact that without the kid, they might actually *believe* this crap, the way they believe every other unsubstantiated bullshit theory that's out there."

She nodded, hearing the rhythm but nothing else. "Did you always know you wanted to do this?"

"You ask me that about everything, dear."

"I do?"

"Yes. That's your favorite question."

She shrugged, hurt. "Oh, okay." Her hands formed a box—the soft spot inside. "It's just 'cause . . . I'm curious."

"I know. I like it." He kissed her hard on the cheek. "Look, why don't you help me out?" He shuffled through some papers and uncovered a tattered notebook.

"What's this for?"

"Write something about the kid. A little introduction. I'll put it on the page." He raised one knee, pushing her off. "Do it in longhand, and I'll type it in. More creative that way."

Scarlet skimmed the Polaroids. To her, the boy looked hard and breakable, like a porcelain doll. "Oh no, I—"

"Do it." Olden blinked twice, staring at the screen. From behind, Scarlet studied his hands, his stiff back and shoulders. She wanted to do something nice for him. Stepping away, she made a little circuit, then came back. "Thank you," she said, hugging his neck.

"For what?"

"For letting me do this. That's so—"

"Hold on . . ." He tensed, striking the keys. She waited, but it soon became apparent that Olden had forgotten about her. Giving up, she found a place on the front step and began to draw. The broken cement felt cold against the backs of her legs. From where she sat, the driveway expanded, leaving a flat patch of dirt. The trees stood politely at a distance—orange leaves, a spangle of rust. The lake glittered as a breeze flapped the pages in her hands. She thought about the boy, the kid in the pictures. She liked the kids at MU, the ones who came to the weekend shows, troops herding backstage to meet the dancers. Yucky lunches in crumpled paper sacks. Sitting cross-legged on the lobby floor. Hands raised, one at a time. Me me me! Easy questions, shy faces. But Scarlet didn't want a child of her own. Not yet. Maybe in a few years. One kid—a friend, somebody to hang out with. Girl or boy, but quiet, happy to stay at home. No "Yes, Mom, No, Mom." A cool vibe. Laid-back parties, kids singing, playing puppets, getting high. Love everywhere. She imagined the boy, using the picture as a guide. She doodled a bit, wrote a few bad sentences, then started a new page. For ten minutes, she listened to the words, writing them down until finally the voice ran out. Closing the notebook, she walked inside, wiping her feet on an old rag. Olden did not look up, just nodded, eyes steady on the screen. Scarlet carefully placed the notebook on the desk and went back to bed. The sheets were cold, bunched to one side of the mattress. The keyboard made a loud sound, but pleasant, like rain. She closed her eyes and pressed her stomach—hands flat, fingers spread—and imagined someone inside, a proper little gent pacing the walls of her stomach, waiting to get out.

"Hey, you." Olden smiled at the screen. He paused to wipe his face. "What's up?"

She looked away, feeling patronized. "Maybe I'll go home," she said, remembering the long trip back, fifty miles to Crane City. She wanted to see someone else for a change. Too much time spent in the same dull room.

"I think you missed the last bus." He stretched, cracking his back against the high part of his chair. "Looks like you're stuck with me."

Starting a new screen, he sat for a while, the wet suit pinching his knees and elbows. An idea began to form, the vague beginnings of a story. Already, these Egg Code entries were getting harder to write. This was a tough job, coming up with creative bullshit. It had to be obvious without being too obvious; funny without being *just* that. Olden didn't regard himself a harmless revolutionary. The opposition certainly wasn't harmless; the men who worked for the Gloria Corporation were danger-ous for the simple reason that most Americans would never think of them that way. *Terrorists* were dangerous, sure—assassins, dictators. But not bureaucrats; not the brilliant demigods who owned and operated the Information Superhighway. After so many years of good living, the American public had grown comfortable with the idea that democ-racy—democracy and the responsibilities that came with it—was expendable. As peasants once bought the lie of religion, Americans now bought the lie of information, the illusion that because the Internet allowed for a certain "interactivity," it somehow meant the network was an extension of the consumer himself, reflecting his choices and person-ality, and therefore all other freedoms—the freedom to *work*, for God's sake, to take control of one's life—all those privileges that once had been unique to the United States no longer mattered, since now you could shop and chat and do all this *neat shit* online. The whole thing made Olden want to vomit. Slowly at first, he began to type:

"*The Story of the Man Who Melted into His Wetsuit.*"

He stared at the title, then made a quick outline in his head. "*A true tale. Our first story comes from Northern California, where a windsurfer and part-time accountant named Billye Daye was discovered roaming the beaches of Crescent City early one morning by a pair of naturalists. Mr. Daye, 35, suffers from a rare skin disorder. Researchers from UC Berkeley have been studying the disease since the late 1950s. Dr. Wayne Teal com-ments: 'Certain skin types are more sensitive to rapid changes in atmos-pheric conditions than others. In instances of high heat and humidity, the skin produces an acidic secretion—called Polymicroniphate—that may react in hazardous ways to other substances. In Mr. Daye's case, a trace amount of Polymicroniphate produced just enough thermal energy to cause the suit to bond with his epidermis. Surfers and divers should take caution when approaching the water, and they should always observe all dietary guidelines appropriate to persons leading an active lifestyle.' "*

He saved the page, then entered Scarlet's little blurb into a new col-umn, scanning for mistakes. "All done," he announced. Hearing noth-ing, he asked, "Scarlet?"

"Still here."

He smiled and crossed the room. Lying sideways, she moved her legs, giving up a corner of the mattress. "Are you bored?"

"No." She sighed, her voice curling at the end.

He touched her arm, reaching inside the shirtsleeve. "No more work today."

"I don't mind. I like it when you work."

"It's not boring?"

"No, Olden, it's not boring." She moved away and heaved her gym bag onto the bed. "Let's have a cigarette." Digging through the bag, she found a pouch with some rolling papers and a lump of shredded tobacco.

They stepped outside, Olden with his wetsuit slit down to the navel. She heaped the tobacco as he shished the papers between two fingers; one piece spread, and he pulled it out. "I'll do this part," he said. "You do the rest."

Together, they assembled their little cigarette, then smoked it on the step, three good puffs before the hot part steamed and went out. Olden coughed and thumped his chest. "Whoa. It tastes like fiberglass."

Scarlet dropped the butt onto the ground. Flecks of tobacco sifted away, streaming into the wind. She pressed her cheek against his shoulder. "Where are the deer?" she asked.

He pointed at the ridge, the high road. "It's October. They're usually up a ways."

She nodded, playing with his zipper. "I wish that animals could talk. That would be so cool."

Olden stood and walked away; what sounded charming to him a few weeks ago now just seemed stupid and naive. Past the drive, he turned to look at his house, the trees bending overhead. He held his hands behind his back and pressed, rubbing away the strain of the past few months. A huge sigh escaped, then turned into a laugh, a loud bit from some dumb song, just the melody with the words changed to la-las.

Scarlet waved across the lot. "Why are you singing?"

Olden sagged, energy drained. "Because I'm incredibly tired."

He walked back, and they both entered the tiny cabin, arms linked, her fingers on his zipper, tugging, *There baby, take it off.*

XVI

Promises Kept

The Fall Campaign

1998

Living Arrangements In-Store Promotion: Version #1
(16 × 20 color glossy, P.O.P., cash stand, vestibule)
The boy sits with his legs crossed, his silk shirt parted at the waist.
His expression is knowing and mischievous, a "let's play" look.
Merchandise pictured: San Rafael Overstuffed Loveseat, $650;
SleepyTyme Slippers, $13; Ortega Glassware, $28 set;
Gordon Knit Wrap, $85; Hunny Bee Rag Rug, $16;
Wrought Iron Fireplace Tools, $48; Toy, $8.
Copy: "It's a cold night and I'm all alone.
If you were here with me, we could get extra cumfy
on my new overstuffed loveseat from Living Arrangements.
It even folds out to make a bed! Wink wink!"
Tag: "Living Arrangements: Sexy Stuff"

Reluctantly, Simon Tree-Mould accepted the adoration of his peers. The line wound along the edge of the classroom, thirty or more students aged eleven and up, all clutching pictures, notebooks, things to sign. Mrs. Oates stood nearby, gloating over the boy. Simon despised his teacher; she was a parasite, another contemptible leech. Only his mother understood. She'd been with him from the beginning. Simon imagined his memoirs, published fifty years hence, the dedication on the front page: *To Mom.* He would devote an entire chapter to his mother's passing, describing it in somber, wounded tones. Chapter 49:

The Death of My Mother. A short chapter, more like an interlude, printed in italics. He would hire a professional to write it for him—the best of the best. *An Actor's Life* by Simon Tree-Mould (with Glorya Foxx).

"Can you make it say, 'To my best friend, Antonio Fava, good luck at tennis camp'?"

"Yeah, yeah, whatever."

Surrounded by students, Simon felt rather like a teacher himself, brought in to explain the vagaries of adult life. For his part, he hadn't been to school for two weeks. Skipped the midterms, the Civil War, the intro to algebra, the fetal-pig dissection, the field trip to the VFW shrine in Sparta. Students greeted his return with the same reckless enthusiasm that anticipates a tornado drill or a visiting puppeteer. *Simon's back. Things will be different today.*

"Simon? How did it feel to have your picture taken? And then see yourself on TV 'n' stuff?"

"Huh? Oh, no talking. I've got a sore throat."

The kids all stood stiff-backed and silent as they waited to approach Simon's desk. Fascinated, they watched as their former classmate signed autographs, took calls on the celly, posed like a *Teen Beat* heartthrob for a professional photographer. The students could no longer think of him as their classmate. He'd entered a realm far beyond their comprehension, where his movements were charged with celebrity. As they reached the desk, their senses seemed to sharpen, and a strange air filled their lungs—recycled air, alive with the glow of other people, adults in boardrooms, making big decisions, putting things on TV.

Touching his throat, Simon passed a note to one of the producers; in seconds, a glass of water appeared. His right hand hurt; over the course of the day, his autograph had degenerated into mere scribble: two dashes and a cross. He'd signed well over two hundred photos—for teachers, for students, for friends of the faculty. It was getting kind of stale. Resting his hand, he crossed his legs and patted his face with a hankie. The students groaned; they'd grown intolerant of these frequent delays. Simon smiled and leaned back in his chair. He liked this—the fact that when he stopped, so did everything else. Slowly, he made a fist. The kids waited. Nothing happened for a while.

Living Arrangements In-Store Promotion: Version #2
(18 × 18 rafter board, main aisle, secondary sight line)
The boy leans over a tall, citrus-colored drink,
his tongue touching the tip of a curly plastic straw.
His eyes communicate a message of naughty impropriety.
Merchandise pictured: Viva Las Vegas! Curly Straw, $2.25;
Barclay Counter Table, $175; Ortega Barware, $28 set;
The Beautiful Blue Danube Curaçao Drink Mix, $12;
Lip Gloss, $3.50.
Copy: "Looking for some action? Mmmm, me too.
How 'bout we blow this clambake?
I know a place where you can feel my mussel."
Tag: "Living Arrangements: Bar None"

The Living Arrangements in Vega was a bustling place—skirts swirling, high heels clacking on the newly waxed floor. Rude motorists sat in the parking lot, waiting for a spot to open up. The asphalt smelled of car exhaust and hot brake fluid. Steve Mould stared across the lot and chuckled to himself. He felt giddy, set apart from the world's problems. A dustpan, filled with butts and candy paper refuse, leaned against his hip. Standing in front of the store, he imagined the profit tally creeping toward ten thousand. A good day. If only they could all be like this.

The manager of the Tuxedo Emporium stepped outside and snapped a dusty cummerbund, holding one end, whipping it hard. "You ain't thinking of putting the rest of us out of business, eh, Steve?"

"Golly, Ben, no way!" Steve met the other man in front of a leather goods shop. It was hard to tell, just by watching them, who was kidding and who wasn't.

"You guys really need to move into a bigger place." Ben skirted the folds of the cummerbund with his pinky. "My morning gal just had to park all the way back at the Denny's on the southbound."

Steve scratched his beard: *That's your problem, schmuck-o.* "Oh, now, Ben, we're just having a bit of a rush, that's all." He looked over at the Tuxedo Emporium, the window display filled with bow ties and faggy-colored vests. "It'll be prom time before you know it," he said, walking away.

"Prom time?" the man shouted across the lot. "Six months, Steve! We'll be dead before spring!"

Great, Steve thought as he entered the vestibule; *we could use the extra floor space.* That was the way it was with these strip malls. The turnover was incredible. The building itself, the super-structure as a whole, never changed, but the sub-divisions fought constantly, each vying for supremacy as the War for the Floor extended past the Christmas rush and on into the clearance season. The battle was inevitably a stalemate, but like all stalemates, it demanded a steady involvement. Passing the cash wrap, he considered the possibilities for future expansion. An aisle banner blew and shook over his head. Each sign showed another vision of Simon Tree-Mould, the object of Crane City's sudden affections. A steady procession of high hairdos crowded the gift table, reaching for merchandise as they gazed up at Simon's moony black eyes, his young body, smooth and seminaked. Some of the pictures made Steve feel uncomfortable, but as his own sales had increased nearly two hundred percent, he supposed the best thing to do was just shut up and get over it.

Living Arrangements In-Store Promotion: Version #3
(30 × 30 window watchers, front face, side aisle)
The boy leans over a rack of weights, a towel draped around his neck.
His expression conveys a sort of randy exertion.
Merchandise pictured: Sweatin' Water Bottle, $8.50;
Secrets of the Orient Dressing Screen, $225;
Soft Summer Nites Bath Towels, $60 set; Candy Cane,
free with purchase.
Copy: "There's nothing like a day at the gym to get the blood pumping!
I bet I could lift you! Wanna try?
Here—you get on top."
Tag: "Living Arrangements: Sporty Styles"

"Mister Manager, you got company out back." Tal-Ahnka, the head cashier, sauntered over from the registers and straightened a stack of marble ashtrays with her hip. "A Mister . . . Pee?"

Steve dropped his broom. "Mister Pee?"

"Yeah." Trying not to smile, she added, "As in . . . peepee!"

"Cam Pee is in my office?" Racing to the window, he noticed the limo double-parked at the curb, the driver reading a paper. "No!" he whispered and hurried back.

Tal-Ahnka nodded. "Little Chinaman?"

Panicked, he halted in mid-stride, one knee bent, ready to run. "Cam Pee is in my office!"

"Damn, baby! You need to calm down." Returning to her register, she watched her boss scurry across the store and disappear behind a column of wicker baskets.

Past the stockroom, he tripped over a pile of untagged art prints and fell into a giant sofa bag—twelve feet tall—filled with packing foam. His knees churned the bag as he tried to stand. He felt himself losing his balance, and soon he was down again, flailing, legs spread.

Jim Carroll stooped over and picked him up by the elbows. "Jesus, Steve, get with it! Cam's half-tanked on gin already."

Dazed, Steve followed Jim into a cramped office, where Cam Pee was sitting behind the desk, removing cards from a fat Rolodex and putting them back out of order. Cam was a strange little guy—had his own odd little habits. He always dressed formally—wore a three-piece suit regardless of the weather, kept his bangs long in the front, drank like a son of a bitch but only the best and most impressive gins and vodkas, Stoli and Tanqueray. It was hard to have any real feelings for the man.

"Ohhh . . . Steve!" Cam's giant bifocals distorted his expression into something tiny and demented. Reading from a stack of file cards, he peered through his thick lenses and squinted at the words. Having encountered Cam Pee's file cards in the past, Steve smiled and waited, expecting the worst. "I was just . . . masturbating . . . to photographs of . . . your family members! HA!"

Laugh, thought Steve . . . damnit, *laugh*!

"Heee . . . that's great, Mr. Pee. That's sure great."

Cam flapped the cards, and a few spilled into his lap. "These are funny!"

"Heeh. They sure are. They're sure humorous."

The CEO pulled a rag out of his vest pocket and wiped his eyes. "You, Steve . . . you do good work!"

"Thank you. Thank you very much, Mr. Pee."

"Your son . . . make lots of money for us! This . . . is good!"

"Thank you."

"We rip competition . . . to death!"

"Whoa, boy, I'd like that."

Cam lowered his voice. "Steve. *Steven*. You need . . . big responsibility!"

"I'd love . . . I'd love a big responsibility."

"I want you to run . . . all store!"

"All stores?"

Jim leaned in. "Cam means in the district. We want to move you up to the DO. That means Vega, NCC, Hedgemont, Downriver, then over to the Cincinnati area and up to Detroit once every other week, plus your normal activities here. It's a big haul, but, you know, you've been here for a while, and—"

"Oh, wow. Jeez." Steve seized Jim's hand and shook it twice.

"It's not the kind of thing you say no to."

"Oh, heck no! No way!"

"Good, we knew you'd be pleased."

"Wow! I'm just . . . I'm . . . wow."

"Yeah."

"Multiple wows."

"You're going to want to hire a first-level assistant to cover for the extra time."

"Oh, yeah, absolutely, I'm on that. Wow . . . well, I mean who was involved in this? I'd like to thank—"

"Oh, don't worry about it. No one expects to be thanked. It's just part of . . . how we do things."

Steve reached across the desk and shook the CEO's hand, adding a little bow at the end. "Mr. Pee—thank you. Thank you very much."

"Good work, good work. I tell you—benefits!"

"The benefits?"

Jim sighed, dialing a cell phone. "Cam wants to tell you about the benefits of the new position."

"Oh, well, sure, shoot. Heck yeah."

Cam raised one hand and counted off on his fingers. "You have . . . more money!"

"Okay, well, more money's always good."

"And . . . every five year . . . ahhhhh . . ."

"Every five years . . . ?"

"You get . . . b . . . b . . . box!"

"Every five years you get a box . . . ?"

"No box!"

"Every five years you *don't* get a box."

"Every five year! No box!"

"Well, that sure sounds . . . real good."

Pleased, Cam leaned back in his chair. "You like new job!"

"Oh, absolutely! I love it! I can't even say—"

"No say. I know. You like it—with mustard on top!"

"Heh-heh. That's about right."

Retrieving the stack of file cards, Cam selected an appropriate remark and stared at the tiny script—smiling now, reading it to himself. He whispered it once, then said: "Now I *fuck* you . . . and your skanky-ass bitch!"

Steve swallowed; something warm, like a damp cloth, passed over his face. The feeling was so sudden and intense that the next few moments made no sense to him. He blacked out; when he woke up, he was on the floor, the other two men looking at him, concerned.

"Steve? What's up, pal? You okay?"

Jim Carroll removed his hand from Steve's shoulder and backed away. From behind the desk, Cam Pee offered his hanky, arm extended, legs bent in a half-squat. Steve looked around, felt the wall, felt the floor, his ass on the ground. He dabbed the roof of his mouth with his tongue. "Oh . . . I'm . . . yeah, sure!" Recovering somewhat: "You bet! I'm . . . I'm just so happy!"

Skeletons!

Gray Hollows made the trip up to Big Dipper Township in just under forty minutes. Near the outskirts, a dumpy red hatchback ran over a steel rake and blew a tire; the rubber husk sailed over two lanes of traffic, its shadow crossing the hood of Gray's car. Preoccupied, he kept moving north, prodding an old cavity with the tip of his tongue. This was how he stayed calm, by nursing on his own decay.

The road into Big Dipper Township was long and straight, channeled through a windbreak of evergreens. A strange object danced above the blacktop, its shape liquid, tossed by the wind. Gray slowed to the curb and looked over his shoulder. It was a skeleton, part of an old Halloween costume—cheap plastic, the skull lolling in mindless agreement as a necklace of silver tape held the mask in place. The wind pushed the suit west toward the highway, and Gray imagined it drifting all winter long, skirting the dead cornfields, a tall marker, stiff and black on the horizon.

Past the county line, he spotted the lake through a gap in the woods. He slowed at a narrow opening—trees leaning, making a tunnel—and turned into it. The tires spewed bits of smashed bark that mixed and whirled out of the wheel wells. Gray winced; his neck and shoulders ached from all the stress he'd been through, putting this Living Arrangements campaign together. The single-lane driveway curved down a hill, then stopped a few yards away from Olden's clapboard shack. He cut the ignition and stepped out of the car. Dragging his feet, he moved across the lawn and entered the house. Olden was taking a nap; at the sound of footsteps, he looked up from his pillow, and the two men exchanged a few mumbled words. Gray searched for a light switch, then gave up, sat down and told his story.

"This is insane," he concluded. "There's nothing I can do to offend these people. Everything's acceptable."

Olden sat on the edge of the bed, pulling on a pair of gym socks. "Americans are like that," he said. "It's a constant tug-of-war. On the one hand, we're a puritan nation. On the other, everyone's horny as fuck. So who knows?"

"There's nothing! I have the most dreadful ideas—each time, T. Kenneth West gives me a raise. Three thousand dollars for a day's work. I mean, this is awful. I'm getting *rich*!"

"You're really trying, though. I admire that."

"This Living Arrangements thing . . . I thought, This is it, this will do it, they'll can me like *that*. You don't mess with kids, I know that much. Kids and the Gestapo."

"What about the Gestapo?"

Gray laughed without pleasure. "Oh, just this thing I almost wrote last month. I had the Gestapo working at a brake shop downtown. Storm troopers rotating tires, stiff-arming the customers. Our efficient service, right? HA HA!"

Olden stood and ran his fingers through his long hair. "Gestapo. Okay. That's potentially offensive."

"Right, but instead I did this furniture store gig, and now it's too late. The world is *shit*. I'm already getting crap in the mail from American Express—free fucking platinum card or whatever it was . . . and yesterday I bought a *washing machine*."

"Spiffy."

"I don't want a washing machine, Olden! I don't want a raise, I don't want a car, I don't want a gold watch, I don't want a wife, I don't want any of it! I'm tired of the whole scene. I hate the people involved. I'm tired of women coming on to me just because I'm gainfully employed."

"How do you know that's why they're coming on to you?"

"Why else? It's the only interesting thing about me!"

Olden took a sweater from the closet and drew it over his head. A cartoon sea lion skied across his chest, leaning downhill.

"So you want to get out. Then quit."

Gray sat quietly for a moment. His reasons all seemed flippant—dumb versions of the same thing. "I don't want to quit. Where's the romance in that? Besides, if I quit, my father will have a conniption fit. Son of a bitch bastard fucking son of a bitch."

Olden stepped into a pair of sweatpants. "So you'll just have to try something else. It ought to be easy. Bring some drugs to work."

"No, that's nothing. Everybody brings drugs to work. Our GDs chop lines on the straight-edge downstairs. As long as it's in-house, no one cares. Public relations is another thing. I've got to fuck up. Hard."

Olden nodded; starting wide, he slowly brought his hands together. "I think you're going about this the wrong way."

"What do you mean?"

"Well, look. You're in advertising. It's *already* offensive. That's what people expect. No one's thinking, 'Wow, those people sure have a lot of integrity.' If you really want to piss 'em off, you need to preempt their cynicism. Don't attack the mainstream, attack the underground. Here, I'll show you."

Olden leaned over his desk and showed Gray the computer screen. Blocks of information spooled in tight columns as the program executed a smooth routine—shapes drifting, evolving, everything timed to fire in sequence. Near the top of the page, an egg revolved, then cracked apart. A boy emerged from the broken shell and sat cross-legged, his eyes radiating a kind of all-knowledge, vaguely Oriental. Gray looked at the boy, then at his lap, the dark floor between his feet. His tongue seemed to expand inside his mouth. "What the hell's that?" he asked.

"That, sir, is the Egg Code, and it's been out for, oh, I guess about a month now. I just sent some more shit to the server."

Gray swallowed; a solid shape passed from his throat to his stomach. All at once, the world seemed microscopic—one boy, one Web site, one furniture store. Still floating over the crushed eggshell, Simon Tree-Mould crept out of his squat and assumed a coquettish pose. Little faggit. Fuck him.

Olden crossed his arms, proud of himself. "I've been getting about three thousand hits a day. That's worldwide, but it's still pretty good for an educational site."

Gray squinted at the text and read aloud, "*In 1816, when the former emperor declared his allegiance to a band of proto-socialists...*" He laughed and swiped at the monitor. "Educational, right. Sounds sincere."

"It isn't. But at least it's subtle. I mean, look at it!" Olden scrolled down the screen. "This is just the first installment. One click takes you there. All the major commercial sites now have links to my Web page: Amazon, *The Washington Post*—"

"They let you do that?"

"No, but I did it anyway. I even hacked fucking *eBay*."

Gray looked back at the screen, then shook his head and laughed. "I don't know, man. Aren't you worried about the feds?"

"No. I never got along with those assholes anyway. It's not like they're not making enough money. If a few million people get nervous and decide to cancel their online accounts, that's not *my* problem. That's just good common sense. That's the system policing itself."

Dark shapes crept across the monitor, hot foxtrails of gore-red wonderglo. Gray suddenly felt very sleepy. He could feel the dimensions of his brain, the split between hemispheres where lightning frayed and spindle-backed neurons tossed chemicals over the gap. He blinked and rubbed his face. He saw himself no longer working at Enthusiasms, Inc. The old life, resumed. The priceless, long-forgotten luxury of writing every day, fifty hours a week—just like a regular job, but a job that other people respected and regarded as real work. "Gimme the address to this thing," he said.

Surprised, Olden rooted through the trash, found a scrap and wrote down the URL. "There you go," he said, laughing at his friend's stunned expression.

Gray took the note without looking. "Yeah, thanks, I . . ." The words ran out; he felt different, holding the address. "I've got a long drive back. Better head out."

Olden lifted a finger, then ducked behind the desk. "Stay for a few drinks," he said, coming up with a crumpled paper bag, something round and fat inside. "I found this bottle on the street. Fuckin' Benedictine. Brand-new. Never opened."

"Ooh, gift from the gods." Gray smiled, aware of something phony in his voice. "No, I . . . I gotta get back." He pointed at the door. "The construction. They're making you go slow now. But this weekend. Next weekend. This weekend or next."

Olden uncapped the bottle and took a swig. He frowned, disgusted; a spurt of brown syrup dribbled over his chin. "Okay," he said, gagging and laughing as he set the bottle down. "Watch out for possums."

They walked outside and shook hands. Alone again, Olden wondered about his friend's strange reaction. It wasn't the bogus information, he knew, that caused Gray to leave in such a panic. It was the boy, the pictures of the boy. Some things in this world were still unacceptable. Using a child as a sex object was one thing; but using a child as a *subversive* object was something else. It ascribed to minors an intelligence most adults lacked in themselves. Now *that's* offensive, he thought, delighted at the way things were turning out.

Promises Broken

The Price of Fame

When Lydia slapped Simon, everything changed. They stood on stage—Lydia holding the boy's jacket, Simon huddled over the script, fucking everything up, even the easy words. The other kids waiting to audition sat in the first three rows, coats slung over the chair backs. The auditorium was dark; a janitor moved between aisles, vacuuming the carpet. Lydia watched the boy's performance, then, hearing enough, raised one hand and slapped him across the face. Simon saw colors, blue and then orange. This was the only way he could understand the pain—as colors, as fluctuations of hot and cold. He could not understand that his mother didn't love him, that she hated everything about him, the failures he implied—her embarrassing marriage, her inability to live up to the great name of Kay Tree. Instead, Simon saw colors, hot colors and cold colors, orange and blue. He staggered away, not crying, just blowing his hair out of his eyes and trying to look cool.

Alone on stage, Lydia felt singled-out, the kind of desperate parent she herself had tried not to become. Driving home, she imagined horrible things happening to her son. In a flash, she saw herself cutting through his body with a long, tapered saw. The blade made an awful noise as it bit into his bones, but he did not bleed, and when she kicked the two halves apart, she found no organs, no neat compartments of divided sacs and chambers, but rather two smooth, wood-white planes of solid protein, like the split halves of a peanut. She could not stand these visions, nor believe herself capable of imagining them in such detail. Just ahead, her home appeared through the trees, a strange vehicle blocking the driveway. Cutting the headlights, she parked and started up the path, Simon trailing a few feet behind. Deep male voices—her husband and another man, Jim Carroll probably—filled the entrance as she stepped inside and hung up her coat. She hadn't expected a dinner party, was not aware of a previous engagement. This was not what she'd hoped to come home to. Steve's friends were such pricks—little men, pumped-up and pathetic. Jim was a handsome if somewhat generic-looking guy in his late thirties. His hair was dark and thick, traveling straight up in a continuation of his high forehead. Coming into the kitchen, she noticed that both men looked tired; December was a bitch, with long hours, mean women, polystyrene Santa Clauses slumped in the stockroom, buttfucking in big bags of fifty. They probably deserved a night away from the store. Lydia understood entirely, and yet she did not want him here, did not need another evening's worth of tiresome war stories, the same old rant—sexual frustration sublimated as sales goals and inter-departmental rivalries. Enough of that. She wanted to talk to Simon. She wanted to explain.

"Lydia, where the heck were you? Soup's just about on!"

"Oh, I don't have to tell you where I go all the time, do I, Steven? . . . Hi, Jim."

"Lydia." Jim nodded, holding a drink. He was still dressed in his work suit, nametag pinned upside down for a lark.

Steve wore a chef's apron over a Christmas-colored pullover, the sleeves bunched up to his elbows. "I tell ya, Jim and I had one *heck* of a day, hon—ain't that right, Jim?"

"What was it, twenty-two-fifty when we left?"

"More like twenty-four, Jim, almost twenty-five thousand dollars, jeezo-pete, gimme a little credit here!"

"And that was at five p.m."

"You're darn tootin'. I told my night manager, I said, 'The minute we get up to thirty, you get on that phone and give me a call!' 'Cause that's going on the board! That's going all the way up to Cam Pee, boy!"

"Better believe it."

"Enough of this junk about not hittin' a million dollars by January first. We're gonna hit it, Jim!"

"Betcha."

"And I ain't whistlin'—"

"No sir."

"I ain't whistlin' Dixie!"

Lydia's knees creaked as she rooted under the sink, searching for a bottle of Gallo. "Steven, you didn't use up all of my sherry, did you?"

"Sherry? What do you need sherry for? I'll buy you some sherry, a million bottles of the stuff, boy, I'll tell ya . . . we're on our way!"

"All I need is one glass, Steven. I don't need a million bottles. I need one bottle, one glass, I don't know where you hide things in this house."

Jim laughed, chugging his vodka tonic. "I think she wants a drink, Steve."

Steve dropped a wooden stirring spoon into a pan of steaming milk. "Yeah, I guess so." He looked at his wife with an insincere smile. "We'll get you taken care of, hon. Just give me a minute and I'll be right with you."

"If you'd just show me—"

"No, no, I'll take care of it. We don't want to make you unhappy."

"I'm not unhappy, I just want—"

"It's okay, not a problem, merry Christmas and the whole nine yards. Jim, I'll be right back, just keep stirring this for me, will ya?" He handed the spoon to Jim and led his wife down the hall to the basement. Out of earshot, he hissed, "Who the heck leaves these lights on all the time?"

"You're always so accusatory. Maybe you left them on."

"I didn't leave them on because I don't come down here. You're the one who does the laundry eighteen times a day, runs up the cotton-pickin' water bill till it's three thousand dollars a month."

"Oh, stop."

They took turns skipping the broken landing at the bottom of the steps. Steve threw open a strange cabinet door, the top edge cut to fit under the staircase. "Look, right where we keep the rest of the booze."

"Fine, thank you. Do you need another bottle of Absolut for you and Jim?"

"Why would we need another bottle of Absolut?"

"I'm just asking, since I don't know how long he's planning on staying. I didn't even know he was coming tonight, because it's obviously not important for me to know these things."

"Well, I'm *sorry!* Jim was nice enough to help me out with my two-by-twos and endcaps, and I said why don't you stop by."

"Fine, now he's here and everything's wonderful, so let's just get the fucking goddamn bullshit fucking thing over with."

"Look, Lydia, if you want to take your bottle of sherry and go right up to bed, be my guest!"

"Oh, don't I wish. I'm tired, I've had a horrible day, I'm upset and I can't take this anymore!" The bottle fell from her hands and rolled without breaking toward a rusty drainage grate. She covered her eyes and cried silently, her head bobbing up and down.

"Gee. Look, Lydia. Relax."

"What do you care."

"Shhh. Shhhh."

"I just want to lie down."

"I don't want you to feel like—"

"Ow, ow!"

"What?"

"Rub my neck . . . it's starting."

Palm flat, Steve touched her neck. He could actually feel the cramp between his fingers; it seemed to dart out of reach like something living underneath.

"It's just that Jim Carroll, honey . . . Jim Carroll . . ."

"Jim Carroll is the big cheese, and we all have to be nice and smile, and I understand all that, Steve. Really, I get the idea."

"It's my job."

"It's your job, that's right."

"I mean, Jim and I, we're equals now, you know? I've got to show him that I can schmooze and chit and chat and do all those good things. I'm gonna be regional veep someday. We're gonna have to get used to these people."

"Stop."

"What?"

"With the rubbing."

He took his hand away, afraid of her now. She hated this—Steve's obedience, the way he always capitulated to her wilder moods, as if womanhood were a kind of black magic, warned about in guidebooks. Giving up, he turned and carried the bottle upstairs. Voices resumed in the kitchen. Lydia's eyes stung with mascara; cursing herself, she washed her face at the laundry sink. A lock of hair fell over her forehead and danced in the gush of the faucet. Turning off the tap, she stared at the bare lightbulb hanging above the washing machine. The filament glowed like a melting skeleton, an orange construction of joints and limbs. As she climbed the steps, a bright figure floated across her vision, moving wherever she looked. Simon was waiting for her at the top of the stairs, dressed in his winter parka. She squinted and grabbed onto the rail. The lightbulb filament turned from orange to scabby red, tracing his spine, his fragile hands and feet. She felt sick. The thought of alcohol made her stomach curl.

"Mom, I'm not hungry."

"You're not? Daddy's making a good dinner."

"I wanna go out and look at the lake."

She swallowed without closing her mouth. "You won't be hungry later? You won't wake up in the middle of the night and tell me you're starving?"

"I don't know. Maybe."

The filament dissolved, leaving a dark impression. Lydia reached to zip up his jacket, then stopped, hand frozen, palm buzzing with awful memories, skin slapping skin. Her hand, his cheek. She glanced at the wall and saw her purse hanging from a brass hook. Rooting through the bag, she found her wallet, a trifolded husk of leather, heavy with change, credit cards arranged in a staggered column like wide steps leading up to a fantastic temple.

"Fine, darling. Go play. Here. Take some money."

"I'm just going outside."

The twenty-dollar bills felt slick between her fingers as she counted out a stack of ten, passing the bills from one hand to the other. "You always need money. In an emergency. Or maybe you'll spend it later. The next time we go downtown, darling. You'll see something in the window and you'll want to buy it, and you won't even have to ask me first because it's *your money*. See? Look at all this money Mommy's giving you. Mun-eee mun-eee mun-eee mun-eee."

"Wow, thanks."

Simon took the bills, counted them quickly and put them in his pocket.

Lydia felt calmer now, instantly better. "And there'll be more money in a few days, because you know what?"

"Christmas!"

"Christmas, right! I've bought you so many nice things for Christmas, darling, and even if you don't like them, you can take them back to the store and exchange them for money!"

"Cool!"

"You could be a very rich little boy. Do you know how much money I've spent on your Christmas presents, just this year alone? Over four thousand dollars, darling. Which is a lot of money, but I do it because it makes me very happy, and because you're such a sweet kid."

"Neat!"

"Go play, love."

"Gee, thanks! Thanks a lot!"

Simon popped out the back door and walked to the edge of the yard, a few hundred feet away. He could see the house from here, but it was small and partially blocked by the bare winter forest. A thick moon mist covered the land with its milky, luxuriant soup. The cold ran up his legs—a pleasant sensation, like Christmas and extra-long vacations. This was the kind of cold that made you more aware of yourself, that made your genitals shrink and your nipples hard. Rushing forward, he saw the tower across the lake, black against the moon-filled sky. He felt drawn to it—a tower amidst the trees, the only one of its kind. There were times when Simon felt like the only boy in the world. Then another feeling came over him with a fury so awful and abrupt that he wanted to cry. He wanted to be naked. His heart thrust against his chest as he pulled his jacket up over his head. He felt out of place, the only person compelled to do this thing. He imagined all sorts of lewd tortures as his fingers worked to free the buttons, the zipper, the tight laces knotted twice. Naked now, he looked at himself, his tiny penis hanging from a smooth place between his legs. Hopping up and down, he smiled as it bobbed from its root. He remembered those times late at night—mashing it with his hand or against a pillow. Whatever happened next was something so bad—like wetting the bed or crapping in your underwear—that he always stopped, afraid of the end result. Standing on the frosty beach, he wanted to shit in the sand, but his bowels were empty and he couldn't pee either because his dick was too big for peeing. He wished he could lick his own penis. He wished he could put it inside his mouth and then bite it off, wedging it between his teeth and the inside of his cheek until finally it grew out from under his tongue like a piece of potato root.

Still naked—wherever he'd left his clothes, he couldn't find them now—he crept back to the house, where he could hear the sounds of his parents yelling at each other. The cold returned to him after the excitement of the past few minutes. Now he wished to be indoors, alone and in bed. The house seemed so cozy inside, so nice, so *civilized*. He could see directly into the dining room, where his mother and father sat at either end of a long table, jabbing and sparring with bright butter knives while the man with the high hair concentrated on his meal, twirling the spaghetti with obliged intensity. A seam ran along the middle of the table, marking the place where the two halves came together. Simon always liked to jiggle the seam, teasing it with his knee until the night when the joint gave way and a bowl of lobster bisque fell into his father's lap, and Steve jumped up and screamed something like "DAG-GON-IT!" and his face was red and there were tears standing in his eyes as the oily stain spread across his lap and the bowl fell to the floor, and the soup was so hot that Simon could see steam coming from his father's pants, and he could remember how his dad had labored over the stove, saying things like "Mmm, boy, this is gonna be gooooood," tasting it every two minutes and smiling that slow smile of his, the shape of his smile curling around the curve of the spoon—all that forgotten now as Simon nudged the table, just enough to make the plates shake, and his mother would probably say something like "Simon . . ." in her low warning voice, but no one would actually *do* anything about it, and so he would continue, subtly ruining the dinner until the dessert course arrived—but instead the hinge snapped and the bowl tipped over and drenched Steve's lap with a great clapping splash, and his first facial expression—his facial expression at the *moment of impact*—was a stiff-necked look of white-faced terror, body lurching to grab the empty space as he jumped up and screamed "OW! DAG-GON-IT!" and from across the table his mother threw down her spoon and said, "Now you're in trouble."

Simon moved closer to the window, the voices becoming more distinct:

"Lydia, what are you talking about? You were the one who told me to put a good word in for the kid."

"Did you even look, Steven, did you even consider—"

"Of course I did!"

Big globe lanterns made distracting splotches upon the glass; from outside, Simon's parents resembled strange demons with normal bodies but glowing circles for heads.

"Those posters, those signs in that store are so patently sleazy—"

"Well they are and what do you want me to do about it . . . dag-DAMN-IT!"

"Steve, I feel like I'm intruding."

"No, Jim, you sit right there, this is something we all need to hear. Now my wife—"

"Oh, Jesus."

"Lydia, will you listen to me! Now, my wife, Jim, for months, months and months and months . . . 'You talk to Cam Pee, you set it up.' That's what she said. R-right here, where we're sitting. And I said—FINE!"

"No, you did not say fine."

"I said FINE! because I wanted her to be happy, which is all I ever try to do." He tossed his knife and fork at his plate and patted his beard with a napkin.

Lydia glared at him. "I expected you to use some discretion, Steven. I expected you to use your head."

"That's not what you told me. You said, 'Whatever it takes, whatever it costs, I don't care.'"

"Those commercials are pornographic!"

"Steve, I'll just . . . you know, some other time."

"Jim, no, come on."

"Jim, what do you think? The ads. On the TV. Do you have an opinion?" Lydia leaned across the table, pointing at Jim with her fork.

On the spot, he stammered, "I think they're . . . doing a swell job, Lydia, I don't know what else to say to you here."

"That's *my* son, Jim!"

"Lydia, I know. And he's a real talented kid. We all just love him downtown."

"Well, ain't that fucking great!"

Simon felt his father's anger as he stood and banged his legs against the edge of the table. "Hey, now. Wait. Wait right there. Do not—Lydia?—when we've got guests—"

"Oh, please . . ."

"You can say WHATEVER YOU WANT TO ME—"

"Fuck it, Steve."

"The language is just about to make me . . . POP M'TOP!"

"Steve, I'm just gonna go."

"Jim, no!"

"Jim, please. Have some more pasta."

Simon returned to the shadows, watching as the man with the high hair left the house and drove away. Slowly at first, he reemerged, showing himself, not caring anymore. His nakedness was a constant surprise to him, something he rediscovered every few seconds. His dick pulled him along, past the window where his parents argued and threw things at each other. He opened the door; a dark window showed his reflection—a pale outline with nothing inside. He pressed his belly against the glass. He wanted to rub it, to rub the whole building with his dirty parts. Losing his nerve, he hurried into the foyer. His parents' voices carried from the dining room, following him up the stairs, spiraling high above the landing and shooting down the dark corridor to his bedroom, where they accumulated at the foot of the mattress in a train wreck of muffled noise.

"I want those ads gone tomorrow! Tomorrow morning, Steve!"

"Now how the heck do you think I'm gonna manage that? Go up to Cam Pee . . . 'Oh, I'm very sorry, sir, my wife, she's a little temperamental—'"

"Why the hell not? Why can't you say that? Blame it all on me. I *am* temperamental."

The voices roared like furnace fire inside the heating vents as Simon pulled a heavy comforter over his head. Dirt from the muddy trail left a grit that collected between the sheets.

"Lydia, are you . . . are you even using your head? Are you even using your *mind*? What do you think I got this gad-darn promotion for? That's an extra nine thousand dollars a year!"

"We don't need the money."

"*I know we don't need the money!* I know we . . . goshdamnit I know! None of it! The . . . why even go? Why even go, Lydia, why do I do it, why do I bother?"

"Listen, if you want to play man of the house, you're not gonna—"

"It's . . . it's all *stupid!*"

"—you're not gonna hold *my son hostage* just so you can feel like—I DON'T CARE!"

"Lydia, just *stop*."

"OH, SHUT UP! SHUT UP SHUT UP SHUT UP SHUT UP!"

"What? *What*?"

"SHUT AAAAAAAAAAAAHHHHHHHH—"

"I'm trying to have a civil conversation—"

"I HATE YOU! I HATE YOU! Unnnnhhhh. Unnnnhhhh. Unnnnhhhh."

"I'm *trying* to have . . . I'm trying . . ."

Turning over in bed, Simon kissed the pillow, then licked it, mashing it with his lips until it changed shape, became another pair of lips, also kissing. Moving his right hand between his stomach and the mattress, he felt his penis and found that it was warm and hard and standing flat against his belly. He rubbed the shank with his thumb, forcing his face deeper into the pillow, each kiss torn away, twisted.

"Steve. I'm sorry."

"Look, Lydia—"

"Don't. Please."

"Can I just say one thing?"

"One thing."

Simon licked his palm and wrapped it around his dick. His skin felt tight at first, then slid easily as his hand pumped the shaft. Strange tingles danced across his belly like big spider legs, and he knew that soon he would have to stop. The tingle was a curtain, spreading sometimes, flashing silverfish glimpses of the space beyond. Reluctantly, he removed his hand and rolled onto his back, staring out the window, but the moon was on the other side.

"It's gonna get better, Lydia. Things look kind of crazy right now. That's just the price of fame. Give it—"

"Okay!"

"What?"

"That was your one thing."

Polymicroniphate

1999

Julian Mason slept through New Year's, the big football games, the first few days of drifting snow and ice on the shingles. He closed his eyes, saw a gravestone, then changed the year from 1998 to 1999. The numbers created a balance, perfectly in line with the year of his birth. For days he contemplated the tombstone, substituting 2004 and 2007 and 2016 with mixed results. He thought about his work with Olden Field—a dismal way to end his career. Candace was a woman, Julian's dead mother, but now *Candace* was a typeface—big words gone electric, spelling untrue things, outright lies, real facts altered as provocations. It cheapened her, this stupid egg code; he'd reduced his mother to the level of accomplice.

Cooped up one morning, he put on his once stylish Members Only jacket and trudged through the cold, picking his way down a snowy hillside to where the other houses—most of them unoccupied for the winter—clustered around the frozen lake. Olden was standing next to his tiny shack, chopping wood, stacking it against the crumpled foundation. An open pit burned a few feet away, heat licking a ring of black melt. "Julian." He fanned the snow from the ax with his bare hand. "Those shoes, they're not doing it for you."

Julian looked down at his slick leather wingtips. He felt sloppy and pathetic. "These?"

"You need to get yourself some construction boots. Heavy-duty. The weather gets nasty up here." He pointed at some power lines lacing black strands across the sky. "Thank God for mass communications. You need to check your e-mails every now and then. I sent about a half-dozen messages last week."

"I never use the thing."

Olden hefted the blade and split a chunk of maple braced between two logs. "Now, Julian, that's silly. You can't afford to think that way. How old are you? Sixty, sixty-five?"

"Sixty-three."

"Sixty-three. That's a good age. A man's age." Unnerved, Julian stood away from the ax, the silver swish, the heavy wooden collision. "I'm looking forward to being sixty-three. See, if you were ten years older, I would've said okay."

"Okay to what?"

"To your attitude. That crusty-old-man shit. But dude, you've got, what, twenty years left?"

Julian stared at the backs of his hands. The veins were thick and prominent, making his skin look purple in places. "That would be . . . very optimistic. Black men, we don't usually—"

"Twenty years easy!" Olden set down his ax, planting the blade in the snow. "Okay, fifteen. But that's a long time!"

Julian looked toward the lake and saw the fifteen years stacked up— something finite, compact enough to contemplate as a single unit. He swallowed. "I think I would like to stop doing this. This thing. If it's all right with you."

"Stop doing what?" Olden asked, his voice different now.

"Our little project. I'm not comfortable. I feel like I'm doing something wrong."

Olden laughed and shook his head. "Julian, man. I don't know . . ."

Julian spoke quickly, making excuses. "Well, I'm sorry, sir, and I feel very badly about this because I should've asked more questions at the outset, and I understand you were trying to do me a favor, and I appreciate it . . ." The young man's expression remained solemn, unconvinced. Julian's voice rose high like a woman's, and he saw his mother yelling from the front step—*Julian, you bring the broom over here, don't leave it there, that's right, you take the broom, there you go, all right now, you my baby.* "I know that it's not what you want to do, but I have my own sense of . . ."

"Ethics?"

"Right."

"Ethics, personal values."

"Yes, of course, but don't misunderstand me. All I'm saying—"

A strong wind blew over the sagging rooftop. The fire collapsed, then collected itself under a burst of black smoke. Olden held up both hands: *Wait.* "Look, Julian." He straddled the woodpile and sat down; the logs shifted, forming a more solid shape. "You're one of the good guys, man. We're doing people a favor here. Everything we as Americans have erected around ourselves—all this *scaffolding*—is an illusion. There's not a damn thing in the Egg Code that's real. And we did that, Julian. You and me. We made it all up. The phony facts, the crazy paranoia. So if *this* is wrong . . . then maybe *this* is wrong too." He made a box with his hands and placed it in different locations. "And this and that and the other. And then maybe people will stop believing everything they read."

Julian looked at the ground, the black footprints leading across a white field. He felt spun around, talked into something. "I don't know what you're saying."

Olden patted the old man on the shoulder. "Listen, I've got to run a few chores. What are you doing today?"

Stacking the last of the firewood, he got his keys from inside the house, and together they drove thirty miles south to the outskirts of Crane City. By the time they reached the mall, it was noon and the parking lot was full. Inside the main shopping area, bodies congregated around a fountain, its twenty-foot-tall geyser making a shimmering, jungle-canyon sound above their heads. A woman stood with her two children, laughing and munching on a Nutty Buddy as one of the kids pretended to control the other like a marionette. Olden led Julian to an illuminated sign marked HOW TO GET THERE, then pointed at a bookstore on the second floor. Upstairs, there were fewer customers, a more select breed. The music inside the bookstore was loud and belligerently sophisticated—the Goldberg Variations, but only the fast parts, played on a synthesizer by Kitaro. Near the back wall, fat and skinny books crowded the shelves. Olden picked one and skimmed the pages.

"Look at this, Julian." He pointed at a sentence, but just as quickly closed the book, as if by reading it one might miss the point. "This is what the Internet can't do. You can't boil this down, can't reduce it to the mindless essentials."

"Well, that's the truth." Julian scanned the wall of books and tried to look impressed.

Olden replaced the book on the shelf. "This is what I'm working to save. Nothing dumbed down." He made a face, impersonating an idiot. "All you really need to know about organic chemistry in six easy steps—kiss my ass! Nothing is easy, Julian. Intelligence is a gift. Not everyone has it."

"No, I suppose not."

"What do you think?"

"I think you're right." Julian hesitated; everything he said seemed to underwhelm the young man's expectations, so he added, "I guess I understand what you're trying to do now."

"Yeah?"

"Basically you're just trying to send a message . . . that we all need to reach out and take a step back." More comfortable now, he looked at his watch, thinking, *I need to go to CVS.*

Disappointed, Olden wandered away, drawn to the noise up front. A college girl sat near the magazines, her legs draped over a leather armrest. Smiling at her, he felt a quick longing for Scarlet. It seemed odd that someone he knew so intimately could also lead a separate existence, could shit and eat and play with salt shakers and maybe even buy a wok. He would call her someday, maybe later in the month. Too much to do. This was the price of idealism, the penalty for refusing to work for the government. Every spare moment wound up getting sacrificed to the big cause. Near the registers, where shoppers gathered around magazines devoted to their own special interests, the thought occured to him: *I need a hobby.* Picking up a windsurfing magazine, he browsed the slick, glossy pages. Near the centerfold, a column of text streamed over a photo of a wet suit, limbs arranged in an action pose, knees bending, braced against the wind. Olden read the first sentence, then the next, stopped, started again.

WET SUIT WARNING. Researchers from the University of California at Berkeley have discovered a strange skin disorder related to certain brands of wet suits, such as the one pictured here. According to Dr. Wayne Teal: "Some skin types are more sensitive than others. The body secretes an acidic compound—called Polymicroniphate—that reacts in hazardous ways with certain substances." Dr. Teal refers to the case of Billye Daye, a windsurfer and part-time accountant who was rushed to Crescent City General Hospital earlier in the year. Dr. Teal continues: "In Mr. Daye's case, the rubber content of the wet suit produced just enough thermal energy to cause the material to bond with his epidermis." Dr. Teal cautions that while this phenomenon is uncommon, all persons in the windsurfing community should be on the alert for any unusual rashes or abrasions. Thanks to staff writers at WWW.EGGCODE. COM for their helpful contributions.

He dropped the magazine, and it slid under the base of the display rack. He wanted to make them all disappear, to hide every single issue behind bookshelves and under doormats and inside empty wall cavities. The lie grew, spreading across the store and out into the concourse. The whole process seemed corrupt. This was the moment, the time of the great transference. In this way, the Egg Code had created its first fact.

Olden roamed the aisles, amazed by what he saw. Numbered signs itemized the contents like merchandise at a drugstore, *nasal spray after-shave foot cream*, except here it was art and architecture and poetry and eastern philosophy. He could smell the paper and the glue of the bindings, and it made him feel ill, for he'd always thought of books as perfect, incorporeal things, untouched by the filthy hands of the peasantry, bold conceptions hatched directly from the minds of great men and transmitted across the centuries for the benefit of a certain few. He now realized his awful vulnerability, his complete reliance on the dictates of commerce. He wondered what greater damage he could have done, given the chance. It was too easy, for Christ's sake. Hands trembling, he picked through the remainders, pulling out a random volume, a hardcover first edition of *Mathematics the Fun Way* written by some cat with a made-up-sounding name. There he saw weird fractals fanning out in

dizzy spirals, multi-arrowed flowcharts indicating the basics of topologi-
cal thought, great sinusoidal waves analyzed as a function of x and y . . .
but where was the proof? Sure, there were *proofs*, proofs on every page.
But where was the proof for the proof? This was the curse of the times.
Every opinion carried the same weight, for there was always proof out
there somewhere, some unnamed source willing to support the most
crackpot theory, and the worst sin of all was to suggest that one idea was
better than the next. An overabundance of alternatives—this was life at
the dawn of the third Christian millennium. Glass beads everywhere.

Reaching the front of the store, Olden leaned against a display table
and gaped at the stacks of new books. One display in particular caught
his attention—a black-and-white photograph of Donna Hasse Skye
dressed in a tweed blazer, cut to fit a man. The picture emphasized the
angle of her jaw, the sharp but not unattractive wrinkles common to
middle age. Take me seriously, the picture said. There's nothing remotely
funny about this. Brown and orange print spelled the name of the book—
first in English, then in Chinese, then in Arabic, then in Russian, then
in . . . the whole thing reminded him of those signs downtown telling
you not to smoke in forty different languages. A few words made a pitch
along the bottom half:

> From noted spokeswoman Donna Hasse Skye comes this
> touching compilation of tales from around the world,
> brought together in one beautifully rendered volume. Many
> of these tales have never been heard before outside of their
> native lands. Listen as Ms. Skye recreates the legends,
> dreams, and aspirations of our diverse planet. Much more
> than just a collection of stories, *Many Voices, One Vision* is
> a powerful sermon to the world, an inspiring travelogue that
> teaches even as it entertains.

Cautiously, he lifted the top copy and stared at the cover. It was a
slender volume, little more than a hundred pages. Inside, a small picture depicted Ms. Skye uncomfortably presiding over a table of curios,
odd bits of smashed pottery and ancient shattered skulls. The presentation looked second-rate, as if she and a team of ghostwriters had pumped

out the draft in a couple of days. Olden raced through a few chapters, appalled to find Native Americans of the Northwestern Nootka tribe quaintly traveling to the stars, mighty Aztecs guarding fabulous temples, huddled Chinamen muttering cryptic doggerel and bowing endlessly like minor characters in some turn-of-the-century epic. One cliché after another. Disgusted, he smuggled the book under his jacket, then left the store and leaned against the mezzanine rail. One flight down, he noticed Julian standing in front of a CVS, a little bag in his hands. The vast concourse shrieked with the demands of angry commerce. Olden dropped the book; as it fell, the dust jacket separated from the cover, floating lightly, sinking at a slower rate than the heavy weight below.

When Good Things
Happen to Bad People

The Thickness of the Plot
Attains Critical Mass

No one noticed her outfit. Not the promoters, not the people from the publishing house. Not that the outfit was the most important thing. The outfit was definitely *not* the most important thing. The most important thing was the book, the concept. She would have to speak about the book now, as if having to write it wasn't bad enough. Reggie Bergman had warned her the next few months would be awful. Awful in what way? Reading the reviews was awful. Reggie screened out the worst ones. The one that called her an empty-headed twat, she didn't get to read. The one that panned *Many Voices, One Vision* as "the latest example of a wealthy, well-heeled white woman attempting to alleviate her own feelings of guilt by paying lip service to a quaintly impoverished third world" likewise escaped the highlight reel. "Well-heeled" was not a compliment. Unbeknownst to herself, Donna Skye had become the reigning queen of the decadent upper class. The rich bitch of the year.

Donna sat near the edge of the main stage at the Channel 5 news station in downtown North Crane City, sipping tea and crossing and recrossing her legs behind a thick wooden counter. A high turban hid her hair under a wrap of brightly colored folds, peach and grape soda and nectarine. The woman at the store had showed her how to tie it in the traditional manner, used for hundreds of years by the ladies of the Niger River valley. Donna had never worn a turban before. She found it disconcerting, the sensation of her hair twirling high above her head. She tried to picture her silhouette, the outline of a woman wearing a turban. She couldn't do it; all that came to mind were bizarre geometrics, abstract ice cream cones, birds with odd beaks. Nothing remotely resembling a human being.

Not that anyone noticed the turban anyway. No one paid attention to the small things anymore. *Donna, you got your bangs cut. Donna, you look* so *nice in taffeta.* Wherever she went, people only wanted to talk about politics, the social agenda of mainstream conservatives, the changing dynamics of African and Eurasian cultures in a global society. And their questions were so angry! Sitting in this television studio, she could sense the contempt of the other panelists, the way they fiddled with their clip-on microphones, then took notes and passed them back and forth (but never to her). One man—a black professor from Midwestern University—leaned back in his chair, arms crossed, and whenever Donna said a few words, he would sit forward and make a face, as if condescending to listen. Hurt, she wiped her nose and looked toward the side of the stage. They all hated her.

"Well, Mrs. Skye's doing her best. And I suppose, in a way, she should be commended for reaching out . . . as it were."

"But ultimately you feel . . . what?"

The professor shrugged—a blasé whatever. "I just feel it's silly. I mean, here you have a woman—in all respect, a white woman, I'm sure she's a very nice person—but unless you've been in a certain *situation*, then there's no way you can . . . reconcile the . . . various ramifications . . . So that's my problem."

The host looked at the camera. "We're talking with Professor Jakob Objobway, Dr. Leon Felt from the Mrs. John W. Woodbridge Center for Cultural Research, and best-selling author Donna Hasse Skye, thank you all for being here, I'm Diane Montgomery and this is *Shockpoint*. Ms. Skye, Professor Objobway has just called you a silly woman . . . uhh . . ."

"Well . . ."

"Them's fighting words, ain't they?"

Donna squinted into the hot beams of the overhead spots. This seemed like an unnatural way to have a conversation, with everyone generally facing the same direction. She wanted to look at the woman head-on, wanted to say *no no, this is all wrong, who cares why I did it or what I did, someone else wrote most of it anyway*—but instead she stared up at the production booth and said, "I just think that the book speaks for itself."

"But the book does *not* speak for itself, ma'am. No, see . . . what we've got here—"

"Professor Objobway, you disagree."

The professor's eyes became heavy and indulgent, a fat little look. "I'm not saying I disagree, I'm just saying that when you've got a person who . . . may be of one type or another—and I'm not saying that's what's going on here—but if you take a look at it, what you're seeing is a selective series of . . . inadvertent . . . parallels, that may or may not contradict . . . the corresponding sequence."

"Leon Felt, get in here."

Dr. Felt's white, furry eyebrows pressed together as he yanked on his corduroy sports jacket. An orange STOP CANCER button chinked on a loose pin. "Yeah, I think that what the man is saying is . . . historically, this is the pattern! Go back to the earliest American settlers, back to the time of the pilgrims, with the boats and the ships. Take a look at England in the nineteenth century at the start of the labor movement. You've got guys pushing carts up and down the hill saying, 'Hey, buddy, help me out here!'"

"Right."

"So this is how it is. And it's inherently corrupt, and that's how it's always been and how it'll always be until God do we come. But—"

"No, what I'm saying is—"

"Professor Objobway, and then I want to get back to Donna Skye."

The professor crossed his legs, showing a pair of socks with strands of bright tinsel woven into the fabric. Something about the socks made Donna want to slip though the floorboards and hide between the insulation until the interview was over. They seemed so wild, so *other*. She should have known better. She should have put them in her book.

"Thank you. All I'm—you know, my point is very simple. This isn't about . . . see, you all are trying to make this an issue of *this* versus *that* . . . and that's all well and good, but what I'm saying is, if you've got one person, and he's going around saying one thing, and then you've got another person who, for one reason or another—"

"Now wait a minute—"

"—when you—"

"Wait, now you just said something very significant there."

"Professor Objobway, then Donna Skye, then I'm going back to Dr. Felt."

Professor Objobway sighed; his wrinkled forehead swirled in tight convolutions of disapproval. Donna did not like this man. So arrogant. So quick to judge. If only they could all be like Julian, with his modest sense of humor and his old-world etiquette, his wavy gray hair that reminded her of those old movies from the fifties, with the black butler who always drank whiskey but never too much, and if it was a musical he usually sang a song about pretty young girls—never trust 'em, baby, cuz you'd best believe she's gonna bust you up and break your heart. Best believe. Julian said things like "best believe." When Donna thought about the man, some inner reserve spilled away, and she felt less built-up, less constructed from parts.

"Thank you," the professor continued, pleased. "I think that what you have to look at is the fact that we're all talking about *different* things."

"Right."

"And until we can get to the point where—see, I've known people who have *never* been economically independent."

"Professor Objobway, you're saying economics is the issue."

"Not economics per se, but economics versus capital versus . . . unfair representation, or *unequal* representation, in a changing society."

"Sure, sure, that's the bottom line. Now: Donna Skye." Diane Montgomery stared at Donna across the stage. "We've been hearing a lot of things today. We've been hearing Donna Skye is a sheltered, well-to-do white woman who has no business writing about non-European cultures. We've been hearing Donna Skye doesn't know what she's talking about. We've been hearing Donna Skye is a bad writer. So . . . how 'bout them apples?"

Donna tried to smile. "All I can say is, I've received a lot of mail from people all around the country—"

"See . . ."

"—and they've all been very nice."

"Dr. Felt, then Professor Objobway, then I'm going back to Donna Skye. Leon?"

"Yeah."

"Help me out here, pal."

Dr. Felt mopped the sweat from his forehead. "Look, you can't separate one thing from another. In all my years of private counseling, this is the thing I've learned. I mean, this is what's going on right now with the Palestinians, which . . . we could talk about that but we won't. All I'm saying is, when you take a position on a public issue, then you better damn well know how to get from first to second base, otherwise you're gonna be left with a bunch of bombed-out buildings and everyone standing around, saying, 'What happened?'"

"How does that affect—"

"Now, wait, look, there's a corollary to this, because there's a very real danger that creeps in whenever people start pointing fingers, saying you did it, no you did it, no you did it. I mean, that's why in 1933 you've got the Marx Brothers having to beg up and down Broadway for union scale, while meanwhile crosstown you've got John Barrymore playing craps with the Italians and tossing twenty-dollar steaks into the ocean."

Diane Montgomery leaned heavily on one hip, tucking her right leg between her skirt and the seat cushion. She flashed her note cards and shrugged, and suddenly this was all very, very funny to her. "The Marx Brothers, the PLO, and a bunch of twenty-dollar steaks . . . Donna Skye, what the heck is going on here?"

"I think if the woman—"

"We're gonna take Ms. Skye, then Professor Objobway, then I'll go to Leon Felt for the final word. Donna?"

"Yes."

"This is the situation. The book stinks! A million and a half copies on the shelves and you're looking at yourself like oh-my-god, what did I do wrong, and meanwhile half of America is out there waiting and wondering, what is she going to do next, and the *pressure* . . . the pressure has got to be unreal."

"I just wanted to see if I could do it."

"Mmm."

"I'm not a professional writer."

"And we're not saying we don't like the book."

"Good point. Leon Felt."

"I liked the book. I bought it for my niece, who's in the hospital."

The session finally ended at a quarter to three, and Donna left feeling grateful for the two-hour tape delay. The producers would edit it down, cut out the bad parts, insert some fancy-shmancy special effects. The words weren't important—publicity mattered, nothing else. Even contempt was a strong sales tool. The more they hated you, the more likely they were to buy, and buy big. The exchange of funds for goods gave the consumer free license to hate the thing consumed. They owned her. One by one, unit by unit, they snatched up her soul. At last she knew what it felt like to be a kept woman. Twenty-five years with the great Derek Skye were not enough. Donna had to learn the lesson for herself. The pain of celebrity. Driving back to Big Dipper Township, she thought about those long years, how he'd seemed to age at an extraordinary rate. She remembered one day in the late seventies, watching the dawn play upon her husband's naked back. Squinting in the early-morning haze, she noticed a splotch of yellow no bigger than a quarter nestled between two vertebrae. The color reminded her of chicken soup. She thought she knew Derek's body so well, every speck, the subtle shades of cream and tan. The shock she felt was that of adultery, the hurt of the betrayed spouse. She touched his back and he woke up. "What are you doing?" he asked. "This stain . . ." she muttered, not completing the thought, and as the ball of her thumb rubbed against his spine, she could feel the friction, the heat between bodies, and eventually Derek grew annoyed, for this was not how he wished to start the day, and he barked in protest and jumped out of bed, his buns jiggling as he stormed into the bathroom, reemerging twenty minutes later all dressed and packed for a weekend conference in Phoenix. The theme of the conference was "I Can't Believe I'm Real!!!" but for Donna it was a weekend of loneliness and worry. She paced the house for hours, clutching her elbows under the sleeves of her baggy sweater. She couldn't sleep for fear that Derek might have cancer, and the thought scared her because this was the late seventies and she still loved him very much, and she even made love to him once near an open hotel window because he wanted to (even though she didn't). Now, returning from the city, Donna knew what the yellow splotch was. It was not cancer; it was celebrity. This was what fame did to a person. Derek had learned that lesson, and now it was her turn. This was a setup, an intricate scenario contrived by the man who had loved her, who had tried so hard to give her a baby that he would come inside her, three, four times a night, his face stern with determination. He loved her, and now he wanted to destroy her. The very thought made Donna's hands go tense on the steering wheel, and she pulled off to the side of the road and stopped for a while, watching the light snow flutter across the windshield, each flake melting in the heat of the defroster. Driving again, she passed the lake at a fast speed and turned north onto the main street, away from her house. Derek's apartment looked cold on the inside; frosty spindles broke in the space between panes. She ditched the car and hurried up the steps of the complex, almost running into him outside his unit, his hands wrapped around a silver trash bag. Five months had passed since she'd last seen her husband. Derek's sunken eyes scared her—they seemed like a skull's eyes, and all she could think about was death and the horror of old age and bodies rotting in the tomb.

"I have to talk to you!"

"Donna, you—"

"Get out of my way!"

"Let me . . . Christ, let me put this down." He set the trash beside the door and followed Donna into the apartment. "What now? For God's sake—"

"Why didn't you tell me?"

"Stop screaming."

"I'll scream if I want to and I don't care!" Walking around to the back of the sofa, she picked up a pillow and threw it at him. "Come on . . . what is this? This stupid place, this is where you live—and you don't even call me!"

"Oh, Donna, come on." Annoyed, he lingered near the door. With Donna in the house, he could feel himself reverting to a kind of behavior he'd done his best to forget.

"They told me everything would be fine. They said things would be great, just do it and everything will be wonderful, and I said fine . . . and you didn't do anything!" Finding a place on the sofa, she shoved her hands under her legs and rocked forward, touching her breasts to her knees. "Come home to me!"

"Forget it."

"I hate it and I'm alone!"

Something rustled in the next room, and a smallish girl with pigtails came creeping out of the darkness. Donna jumped up, enraged. "Oh my God. What is this little thing here?"

"Oh, Donna, don't make me—"

"Who is this slut? In my husband's house—"

Scarlet stepped warily, her arms held in front to fend off any dirty assumptions. "Sorry, I'm just going."

Derek stood between the two women. "Don't . . . let's not get angry, this is stupid. Scarlet Blessing, this is Donna—Donna, we know all about it—"

"*I* don't!"

"—my assistant."

"Ah! He goes for the twenty year old! How nice!"

"Don't be silly."

Scarlet sighed, heaving her gym bag over one shoulder. "No, I would think so too, Derek—even if, you know, I'm really twenty-four, but whatever."

"Oh, I'm *sorry* . . . she corrects me, with the fresh mouth!"

"It's okay, I'll just head out."

Derek snapped, "Scarlet's staying. Scarlet, you're staying."

Scarlet slid both arms through the gym bag straps as the others stopped to take their bearings, for this was all a bit too much at once, what with lost wives running about like mad red queens and strange girls emerging from darkened bedrooms, and in the midst of it all someone had left a pot of boiling water on the stove, and from across the room Derek could hear it splash and sizzle against the coil. Scarlet leaned back, her bag pressed against the wall. Looking at the girl, Donna felt oddly aware of her own clothes, the heavy layers draped over her body— a full-grown woman, all dressed up.

"So, here's another devoted disciple." Furious, she turned on Derek. "What do you need her for?"

"She helps me."

"Helps you? Helps you with what . . . your *nice* chores, I suppose." She scanned the room and saw that the magazines were neatly stacked on one end of the coffee table, and that someone had even set out a bowl of hard candies wrapped in cellophane. "Well, that's nice—now, after all these years . . . I never helped you. Mr. I Can Do It All—and you certainly didn't even need a wife, but that was part of the arrangement—"

"Great."

"Lovely things! Oh, we'll put the chairs over here, and then the coffee table, and the bric and the brac . . . and here's the missus! Slap her down! And if there wasn't me, there was always Reggie to take care of you."

"Reggie doesn't work for me anymore."

"That's . . . that's a thing." Stopped short, Donna pressed her tongue between her teeth. The conversation seemed to change speeds, though faster, slower, she wasn't sure. "What are you telling me? You're telling me stupid things."

"Reggie's your boy now. Use him well. I hope you enjoy yourself—"

"Derek, you should sit down."

"—when they pick your heart to death."

Scarlet moved closer, touching his arm. Donna pushed her hand away and screamed, "Stay away from him!" Nervous now, she touched the fringe of a lampshade and picked at the brittle paper with her thumb. "You dropped Reggie? Why?"

"He dropped me."

"Because you knew he was working with me?"

"He dropped *me*, Donna . . . don't you even listen? When I say he dropped me, that means one thing."

"Okay, so he dropped you. I still don't know—"

Suddenly angry, Derek kicked the coffee table. "Dropped me, dropped the book. Now I've got nothing!"

"Christ. I *just* saw him! He didn't say anything."

Scarlet went into the kitchen and switched off the stove. "So this means what?"

"This means a lot of bad things, Scarlet."

Donna stiffened, hearing the girl's name. "I thought Reggie liked you," she said.

Derek stared at his wife—sadly, because an awful thought occurred to him, that maybe Donna was stupid, and this made him wonder about everything else. Blinking, he went on: "He was looking forward to this year too. He wanted to throw us together. Number one and number two."

"But he figured you'd win."

"He figured I'd win. Well, I *would* win. What the hell, Donna. Who are *you?*"

Donna lowered her head. Her turban had come undone, and she could feel it loosening, unwinding around her hair. The room was quiet, if dazedly so, and a part of her wanted to stay here all afternoon, to just be friends with everyone, even with Derek's new little confidante. All at once she missed her domestic life, and the reassurance of chores, and the lovely thrill of staying inside all day. Even the things that once made her unhappy—the condescending smiles of her husband's associates, the sense of being stared at with a kind of lewd, patronizing contempt (by *everyone*, men and women, even Derek himself)—now made her regret her new position, somehow less desirable than the first. It wasn't so bad, really, being a trophy wife. There was something fundamentally *good* about it. Donna's goodness had contributed as much to her marriage as Derek's book contracts and lectures and mail-order Super-Success Kits. No one appreciated this, of course; Derek certainly didn't. The assumptions were always negative; so much material comfort, others reasoned, automatically disqualified the beneficiary—in this case, the trophy wife—from being treated like a human being. So what do you get the woman who has everything? Love, maybe. Respect. A real place in the world.

Derek and Scarlet listened as Donna turned and, weeping, hurried out of the apartment. Self-consciously, Scarlet crept back to the living room. It hurt her, the idea that someone else, particularly another woman, might think bad things about her. "She sure knows how to get to you," she said.

"Yes, she does."

"I can tell. You're not like that. But sometimes it's hard. I'm always saying stupid stuff."

Derek looked at her—small and hunched over the coffee table. "Scarlet, you . . . are a tremendous help to me. And a great comfort, too. I'm not sure I even know why."

She covered her mouth with her hand. "Wow . . . when you said that . . ."

"What?"

"I'm totally flashing."

"Mmm."

"It's not like literal flashing . . . it's like this strange, bright blue pulsating thing."

"I'd like to give you something." Walking back into the kitchen, he rifled through the cupboards, careful not to disturb Scarlet's neat arrangement of cups and plates.

She came forward slowly, shyly. "Oh now . . . HA! You've been keeping things from me."

"No, I haven't." He reached inside the silverware drawer and pulled out a small jewelry box. Opening it, he assumed a formal voice. "It's a simple thing, but I feel—"

"Oh! It's beautiful!" She removed the pin from the box and held it up. The little bit of color sparkled between her thumb and forefinger. "Oh, God . . . this is too nice."

"If you can't—"

"Here . . . pin it on my collar."

"Oh, okay." She held the neck of her T-shirt out to one side as Derek fiddled with the pin. "Let's see if I can get the back off."

"Can you do it?"

"Damn. There! That looks nice."

"It does. Oops, I think it's upside-down."

"No, that's right. It's a tree."

Scarlet's lips made an ugly shape as she scrutinized the pin. "Oh, I see! I'm just looking at it wrong. What a cool thing. It's like a *Star Trek* communicator."

"Mmm."

"I can, like, go to the fourth stratosphere from here."

"Great."

She patted her collar, holding her hand against the pin, keeping it there. "Thank you so much! It's almost my birthday, did you know that?"

"When's that coming up?"

"Actually, it's in April, so not really that soon."

"We'll have to do something."

"No, this is all set—for my birthday. Thank you."

"That's fine." At a loss, he mumbled, "You've made me very happy."

"Oh, you've made me happy too, Derek. You always make me happy."

He smiled, then went into the living room. One hand reached, feeling for the sofa. "Scarlet, I'm afraid . . . there'll be less and less to do around here. With the book . . . not happening. Evidently."

"We'll think of something."

"There's so many things, though, Scarlet. I'm frightened even to tell you about them."

"Don't . . . we don't have to talk . . ."

Derek said nothing at first. He felt safe, standing behind the sofa—behind it or next to it. "The book is an awful thing, Scarlet. That's why Reggie left me. He was right to leave me. It's an awful thing. And now that I've written it, I'm not sure what to do with it, because it has the potential to . . . hurt a lot of people. But I need to do it—"

"You *need* to—"

"But you don't know yet, Scarlet. You don't know what you're saying. This is a terrible book. Not that it's poorly written. That's not it at all. The message is what's terrible. It's a horrible thing, in every way . . . and yet it's me, and that's why I've written it, and that's why it has to come out."

"Yes."

"Please. I have to explain."

Derek felt her hands tugging on his shirt. Her eyes were big ovals, marred only by a tiny pock near the fold.

"You don't, Derek. I'm here, I'm here with you."

"Oh, Scarlet. It's only getting worse."

"Shh. Come here. Listen, here's an idea. Derek? Just once. Let's lie down. That'll make it better."

"I—I can't, Scarlet. Believe me, it has nothing to do with . . . look, I have to do this and I have to do it now. The book I've written is an evil book. It's dark, it's evil, it's wrong—and it's *me*, Scarlet! I've never been honest like this before. *The Skye's the Limit* and all that. It was insincere. Your father, his recovery. I didn't *mean* any of that. I didn't necessarily *not* mean it, I didn't have any feeling about it one way or the other. It was a job, a job that I did for a long time, and now it's over, I'm retired, I'm alone—"

"No . . ."

"I don't even have you, because you don't know who I am, how *sick* I am. I'm an opportunist, Scarlet! I am a capitalist and a fraud! I've lied to people and I've made a fortune off it. I've lied to you! In every way, I've lied to you. This nonsense about flying. You can't fly, Scarlet!"

"Please . . ."

She backed away, and he took her wrists in his hands. "Wait, listen to me. This is important. If nothing else, you *must* hear me. You can't fly because you are a human being. Human beings can't fly—they never will!"

"I—I don't agree with that . . ." Scarlet's words were weak things, spoken without conviction.

Derek dropped her hands and walked away, fingers curled into claws, a man on the prowl. "You don't have to agree, Scarlet. Go through your whole life not agreeing, believing in the impossible. UFOs. Government conspiracies. Happiness. Take it all! You've done it before, so why stop now? This is what we believe, that everything's connected. That our little dramas *mean* something. No one's special, Scarlet! No one cares! We're mulch, fertilizer, dirt, big black clumps of it—a whole *globe* of dirt!"

"It's awful—"

"It *is* awful, Scarlet. Isn't it? And this is what I am. This is what I've been doing. And you've helped me!"

"I don't know what you—"

"You've helped me! You've been here all these weeks, running errands while I've been locked away, eight hours a day, type-type-type. What did you *think* I was doing?"

Crying now, she tried to speak, but the words escaped in tiny bursts, torn and well intentioned. "I thought . . . I was . . . helping . . ."

"You *were* helping, Scarlet! You were helping me to do it. Each word I wrote. You were the inspiration. You made it possible. Thank you! This is what I'm saying to you. Thank you for your help. I couldn't have done it without you."

"Please . . . let me . . ."

She staggered toward the front door. Derek stayed put; dumb words, like broken machine parts, spilled onto the floor. "And now I'm all alone . . ."

"I'm sorry, I've got to—"

"Truly alone . . ."

"I'll just . . . come back some other time." Working the door open, she backed out into the corridor, wanting only one last look as she waved and blew kisses. "God bless you . . . God bless you . . ."

Outside, she stumbled down the porch steps and turned right into town, pushed along by a strange force. Words softly repeated inside her—the things he said, the things she said. Through the window of a beautician's office, she could see two cats fighting while a woman sat behind the register, fishing a crushed pack of cigarettes out of her mint-blue cashier's blazer. Stopping to tie her shoes, she could hear Derek's voice instructing her on how to make the knot. Her mind seemed frozen, locked in a mode. She needed him, needed his advice. *Make a bow, Scarlet. That's it. Now push it through. You can do it.* Chest heaving, she touched the pavement and stared at her shoe, now neatly tied. It was a nice knot, with big hoops and a tight ball. Suddenly she wanted to understand everything, the real facts—the physical thing, right there. The frozen pavement bit into her skin, but she stayed for a while, savoring it—Scarlet's pain, Scarlet's fingers. This had nothing to do with Derek. Taking the cold air into her lungs, she listened as a thick fluid rumbled inside her throat. She wondered what the fluid was; thinking about it, she resolved to look it up in a science textbook when she got home. The science textbook would tell her so many things. How to fly, how to break the spell of gravity. Scientists were always proving the unprovable, defying every law with yet another law, and while people had known for years that gravity did not exist in outer space, Scarlet felt certain that someone somewhere would discover the secret number, and as soon as the final calculation was put into place, all those who believed in the scientist's work would begin to fly, and those who didn't would have to stay behind.

Climbing around a curve, she could see the lake glinting between patches of bare trees. The tower in the middle of the lake looked like just another tree, except wider around the base and brick-brown instead of ash-gray. She crossed the road and slid down the bendy trail leading to Olden's shack. The door was open, with some red fuel canisters piled near the step. Inside the room, Olden's face was still and blue as he stared at the computer screen, a power generator humming between his feet.

"Mind if I shut the door?" she asked.

Olden didn't look up. "Yeah, sure . . . don't step on anything."

Scarlet tiptoed across the room, taking a wayward course around boxes filled with green transistor boards. "Don't step on what?"

"Just . . . never mind. I'm building a new processor."

"What's that?"

"A new processor, in case I have to move this goddamn site. I've gotta use non-registered parts. I can't just walk into a CompStomp and plunk down twelve hundred bucks for a new hard drive. They'd be on me like that."

"Oh, right."

"They're probably monitoring the whole thing right now, but if I dump the page, they'd be down here by the time the last packet hits the server, so I've gotta figure out how to divert the address—"

"You want to take a break?"

Scarlet kept her bag slung over her shoulders as she fell back onto the bed. The springs whined, a sexy noise, but Olden heard only the sound of his own fingers slapping the keyboard, updating the information. "Five minutes," he said.

"What?"

"Five minutes is all, hon, then I've got to get back to work."

"Gee, I'm glad you could spare me the time."

Olden leaned forward to peer at the screen, apparently reading from some treatise he'd just written. "Go to sleep. I'll be there in a while."

"I don't want to go to sleep, Olden. It's four in the afternoon! I haven't seen you for three days."

"I haven't seen *anyone* for three days, Scarlet. Do you know what this is about? Look—"

"I don't want to look."

Revved up, he turned the monitor around until it faced the bed. "Sixty sites, Scarlet, sixty references. Sixty sites have taken my phony information and put it out over the Internet. Corporate sites too. And those are just the ones who've admitted it. Who knows how many others—"

"Oh, God, Olden, just turn the fucking thing off and go outside. There's a whole world out there—"

"Here, listen to this—"

"I . . . don't . . . care!" Scarlet stood up, and the heavy gym bag pulled her toward the desk.

"From *Ten Thousand People, Maybe More: A Tribute to Simon and Garfunkel*. Did you know—"

"Oh, God."

"—in 1969, legendary architect Frank Lloyd Wright toured with the famed rock duo, playing Fender bass and organ for a series of six dates on the West Coast."

"Right, and then the world comes to an end, right?"

"This is fascinating to me—"

"I can see where this is going."

"—particularly since he died in nineteen fifty whenever-the-fuck-it-was."

"Oh, who cares?"

Olden frowned, then spun the console back around. "That's what everyone thinks. They're just facts. Little things to play with."

"Are you going to be angry about this forever?"

He braced the keyboard between his elbows and muttered into his lap. "Maybe you don't understand. This is serious, Scarlet. Everything you read, everything you see on the Internet . . . it's people like *me* who make this shit up."

"What can you do?"

"I don't know."

"Then don't do anything! Let it go. Let's take a walk."

"Oh, *that's* a good idea."

"Okay, I'll go by myself." She hurried toward the door, then, hearing his soft, penitent voice, slowed and came back. They both looked at each other—tired, unhappy with the argument. Their hands groped across a dark space as she pressed his cheek against her stomach. His hair felt hot between her fingers—hot and thick, like heavy sand. "Oh, Olden. What are we gonna do? You're the only—"

"What is this?" He pulled away, his eyes fixed on a speck of gold pinned to her collar.

She could feel the pin against her neck, cold and sharp. "It's nothing."

"Where'd you get it?"

"Derek Skye gave it to me."

"God-fucking-damnit."

"It was just a stupid little thing that he gave me, and I'm not going to see him anymore, so don't worry."

"Shit. That's the real thing."

She wrapped her hands around Olden's neck, her desire inflamed by what she supposed was jealousy—a bad feeling, yet better than no feeling at all. She kissed him, but he did not kiss back, just kept staring at her collar. "Honey, I know what you think about him, and I want you to know I was wrong, and all that time I wasted, I want to spend it with you now."

"Christ."

"What? The pin still?"

He pointed at her shirt. "Do you have any idea what this is?"

"What? You're gonna tell me it's some sort of valuable code—"

"The Gloria Corporation, Scarlet! The fucking Gloria Corporation—it's a goddamn cult! They were the ones who picked up the DoD contract back in the mid-eighties. The makers of the Internet. The keepers of the flame. What the hell is Derek Skye doing with the Gloria Corporation?"

"He's not doing anything, Olden. Believe me—"

"You can't buy these things in a flea market. Jesus . . . and right here in Big Dipper Township. Amazing."

"It's amazing. I'm bored out of my mind. I'm going."

Giving up, Scarlet turned and stormed out of the room. Olden followed, not because he wanted her to stay, but because the rant which had been building inside now needed, like a top, to spin itself out. "The routers, Scarlet. The routing tables all go through the GC. The hardware, even the goddamn real estate."

"It hurts me, though, Olden—"

"It's the GC. Fuck Cisco! It's not Cisco. It's the Gloria Corporation all the way. Christ! My father!"

"And I thought musicians were bad."

Olden chased her down the steps. *"Scarlet!"* he called out. *"Ten to one that thing is bugged. Take it home and melt it down. I'll see you in a week."*

"Fuck you!"

He watched her disappear over the hill, then went back inside and dug around for the telephone. He hadn't used it since December, when his father called from the Steele County Corrections Facility in Sparta, the same as he did every Christmas. Following the trail of a twisted cord, he found the receiver lying under a stack of printouts. He dialed, then waited. The man who answered the phone sounded old.

"M-Mason residence."

"Julian!"

"Oh. Good day now."

"Julian. Jules."

"Hello there."

"Do you know who this is?"

"I think I do."

"Starts with an O—"

"All right, then."

Looking out the back window, Olden stared past the trees to where Julian's house rose above a brown, rolling hillock. A tall man strode across the front lawn, peering into the basement with his right hand cupped like a visor to block out the light. "Julian, can you come over for a quick meeting? I'd make it real brief."

"Oh. Well. Gee."

"Or I could come up there. Whichever."

"I don't know if that would be possible today, sir." Standing in his kitchen, Julian held back the drapes and leaned over the sink. The telephone antenna knocked against the window as he looked at the tall man now moving around the corner of the house.

"It's just . . . I think it's important that we have this talk, Julian, because to tell you the truth, I've been seeing things a little bit differently now, and I know that in the past I might've given the impression of being somewhat—oh, you know, crazed and around the bend, and—"

"Oh . . . I don't know."

"Come on, now, isn't that true?"

Julian took the phone into the hall, hoping to catch the man on his way past the living-room window. "Well . . . different strokes for different folks, sir."

"Yeah. I mean, what can I say? I should've been more out in the open, more respecting of your need to know, and I apologize for that. But it's clear the Egg Code has got to go."

"Mmmmm."

"And I don't want to do it by myself."

"Oh, okay."

"I want to take it back. I want to do it in a way that's professional, and I want you to help. I know it's a lot to ask, but . . . I gotta tell you, Julian, there's just something about that *typeface*, man. It's so *irresistible*."

"Mmm-hmm."

"I mean, don't you agree?"

"Most definitely."

Julian could feel the acid rolling around inside his gut as he studied the stranger outside. Steam came off of the man's nearly bald head, and Julian could hear his footsteps crunching across the frozen grass.

"I don't want to screw you over," Olden continued, "because I know how much time you spent putting it together. As far as I'm concerned, that's your intellectual property, and I'm going to honor it as such."

"Nice, nice."

The man drifted back to the curb, glaring up at the third floor. Light frost made a curtain along the fringe of his mustache. Deep eye sockets, lost in shadow, revealed nothing, only a dark core. Still, Julian knew who he was. Derek Skye. The famous recluse. Bit of a quack?

"It really would just be a few hours on the weekend, and I would take it from there, and you wouldn't be obligated to, you know, deal with it anymore."

"Oh, okay then."

"And I'd definitely keep the content very tasteful, because I know how sensitive you are about, you know . . . *are we misleading children?* and things like that, whereas I'm coming at it from a more academic point of view."

Julian stood shivering inside the foyer. He could feel the cold air pouring through the walls, the thin door. "No, I understand. It's just . . .

I mean, I respect it all, I respect you, and . . . everything's beautiful. But for me, my feeling is, I guess . . . it wouldn't be something . . . I would feel comfortable—"

"Shit."

"—with having to get involved with . . . at this time."

Olden sounded distracted, already onto the next plan. "Right. Okay. Sigh. All right, that's fine."

"But I really enjoyed working with you, sir."

"Well, I enjoyed working with you too, Julian. I've always had a lot of respect for you as an artist, because . . . you and people like you are really a part of . . . an old breed of craftsmanship that's basically dying out as we speak . . ."

"Well, thank you, sir."

"Anyway, it looks like you've got company, so I'll let you go, but . . . if something comes up—"

"I'll let you know."

"Sounds good."

"Yes, and you have a blessed day, sir."

Julian squinted at the receiver, then found the right button and pressed End. He opened the door and stepped out onto the front porch. The wind blew him back into the foyer; he staggered forward again, his eyes narrow, almost shut. Derek Skye, having satisfied his curiosity, now lingered at the edge of the yard, his hands on his hips. Julian let the screen door slam behind him and joined Derek on the lawn. "Can I help you?"

"I rang the bell, but it didn't work."

Julian raised his voice over the wind. "It's Derek, right?"

"Derek Skye. We met a few months ago."

"That's right."

The two men shook hands. Looking down at their clenched fingers, Julian remembered a poster campaign he'd designed in the late seventies—some charity walk for racial harmony, a black hand and a white hand, and he'd intentionally exaggerated the colors, making it bold and obvious, but here in real life Derek was really that white and he was really that black.

"I've been out of the mix for a while . . . been going through some things. A divorce and—you don't want to hear about it."

"Mmmlord."

Releasing Julian's hand, Derek crossed his arms behind his back. "How are you enjoying the country?"

"It's a . . . unique experience."

"That's about right."

"Good place for an old man to relax."

"I hear what you're saying. I'm getting up there myself, and I'm liking the solitude."

At a loss, Julian looked back toward the house. "Why don't you come on in, and I'd be glad to show you around."

"No thanks, I've got to run. I just had a few items I wanted to discuss, if you . . . ?"

"Well, sure. It's a trifle cold."

"That it is. Look, I've heard from a few people that you're a . . . what's the word?"

"A colored fella? Heh."

Derek stared for a moment, then smiled. His mustache crinkled, breaking into frosty chips. "No, well, that too, obviously that too. But . . . you're an artist, aren't you? A designer, I guess would be the more accurate term."

"Used to be, that's right."

"Book production, that sort of thing?"

"Advertising, mostly. Print work."

Derek nodded absently. "You might know my father-in-law. Ex-father-in-law. Bartholomew Hasse . . . ?"

"Name sounds familiar."

Derek shrugged as a gust rolled in from the lake. The wind filled the neck of his shirt, and for a moment his entire torso seemed to swell and then shrink. "Anyway, I wanted to ask you—"

"Whoo—that wind!"

"I'm a writer of sorts. I write . . . informational material. I've actually had a few bestsellers over the past several years."

"Oh, okay."

"And I'm kind of working on an interesting project right now."

"Nice, nice."

Derek smiled again, and Julian could see lines of tobacco red and tobacco black running along his receding gumline. It seemed odd that such a man wouldn't have taken better care of his teeth. Julian's own teeth were sore and looked like quarried limestone, but that was only natural, given his childhood.

"I'm pretty excited about it. But my publisher . . . wait for the wind to die down . . . my publisher has expressed a few reservations about the project. The usual ninth-inning jitters."

"Nice."

"It's aggravating, is all."

"They all saying one thing, whereas—"

"Right, and finally I said to hell with it. Anyway, I've got the manuscript all set to go, and I'd really like to . . . that is, I should say . . . I would hate to—"

"I'm just covering my ears."

"Mmmm?"

"I can still hear you. I'm just trying to keep my ears warm."

"Oh! Sure. Absolutely."

"Lord, it's raw!" Julian felt his lips stiffen, and he huffed a few times behind his closed teeth.

"But the bottom line—it's Julian, right?"

"Yes, sir."

"The bottom line is, I feel confident that I can cover the production costs myself and still make out pretty well. So what I was wondering is— and I'd pay you, of course, that's not a problem—but if I could just hire you to take care of the design, the cover and layout and all that—"

"And then what you got is . . . you've just got your distribution to worry about."

"Which is expensive but . . . you know, I've made a lot of money over the course of my career."

"Sure, sure."

"I mean a *lot* of money."

"Don't be ashamed."

"Oh, I'm not. I'm grateful, is what I am. I've had a good life. It's been . . . very satisfying."

Nodding, Julian tried to smile, but his lips were blue and hard, frozen around a thin space. "And now you wanna give back . . ."

"Now I want to say that was that, and now this is something else. But in a way that's professional."

"You want a nice, clear quality presentation."

"Absolutely. And that's why I think that you could do a bang-up job for me here, with your experience and—"

"Mechanical skills."

"But it's not just that."

"Oh no."

Taking his hands out of his pockets, Derek made a bold, professional gesture, swiping his hands high and wide. "I think it's a generational thing. And I feel—you know, I'm fifty-two, so we're both coming at this from a similar perspective."

"Aw . . . you're a young man!"

"Wellll . . . not so young. But young enough—or old enough, I guess—to appreciate the difference between . . ."

". . . something of today . . ."

". . . something of today . . ."

". . . versus something of . . ."

". . . twenty, thirty years ago, where the quality was so much better."

"I agree."

"Even the simplest things, like—"

"Shoes."

Derek pointed at the old man and nodded appreciatively. This was the man's great talent—to make any answer seem like the right one. "Shoes. The manufacturing quality of shoes has just gone through the floor."

"Appliances."

"Yes. And if there's something that . . . if there's anything in this world that should be of the highest quality imaginable . . . it's books."

"Thank you."

"There's no excuse—"

"Books and furniture."

"Yes, but books, I think, even more so . . ."

Meanwhile, Gray Hollows was sitting alone in his tiny office on the second floor of Enthusiasms Inc., his head on the desk, the metal edge just starting to hurt as it pressed against his forehead. The lights inside the office were off, and in the diffuse glow of the computer screen, he could see a big bug moving toward a ventilation duct. Leaning back, he picked up the telephone and dialed the number of a Ms. DuChamp, whom he'd spoken to earlier that afternoon. If he gave it up right now, they could put something together in time for the evening news. Hating himself, he stared out into the corridor, where a dying fluorescent winked, then stayed off, then suddenly switched back on, wild and bright. I've got to get out of here, he thought. The line picked up.

"Where the fuck have you been?"

"Um . . . oh."

"Oooo. Oooo. I'm sorry! I thought you were—"

"That's all right."

"Oh my God, I'm so—"

"That's okay . . . This is . . . Ms. DuChamp?"

"Yeah, yeah, it is, umm . . . hold on, give me a sec . . . *Denny, get these flowers out of here* . . . I'll be right there—"

"No problem."

"*—because I don't want them*! . . . Oh . . ."

"Sounds hectic."

Ms. DuChamp's voice came and went, talking to two people at once. "Oh no, we're one great big happy . . . *goddamnit*! Look, are you at a place where you can—"

"Yeah, I'm fine."

"Good. Why don't we start with, uh . . . get started."

"Okay. The kid's name is Simon Tree-Mou—"

"Whoa-whoa-whoa! Simon . . ."

"Tree—"

"Ho! Okay. Simon . . . ?"

"Tree . . . That's T-R—"

"Look, can you just fax it to me?"

"Oh, sure." Something shifted out in the hallway, and he covered the receiver with his hand. Like an old house, the Enthusiasms Inc. headquarters creaked at night.

"Okay, so, Simon something-something . . . and you worked with him?"

"Yeah."

"And where was that?"

"Living Arrangements." He closed his eyes, trying to stay calm. "The furniture store."

"I bought a divan there once."

"Yeah?"

"It's a really nice divan. It takes a standard-size mattress, but it folds up, so you can use it as a couch during the day, and then at night, if you've got guests, you can take it down and convert it into a sleeper. They had a different kind, with a brass frame, but I didn't like it because I thought it looked too seventies. Brass is seventies, Chablis is seventies. Ficus plants are *totally* seventies. Anyway. Simon whatever-whatever."

He shook his head and thought, *what an idiot.* Wedging one hand between his legs, he said, "Here's the address."

"I've been there. It's out by the Vega Mall."

"No, of the Web page. The computer . . . the . . ."

"Oh. Wellll . . ."

"What."

"I don't really 'do' computers."

"I see."

"I just 'do' e-mail. That's it."

"It's just . . . it's kind of central to the story."

"No, I know . . . Aw, hell, just give it to me. I'll take it down to Frank in Post."

Gray stopped, aware of a change, as if a door had been left open, letting the cold in. Already he could sense himself drifting away from the building, away from this corporate lifestyle. "Okay, it's double-u, double-u-"

"WWW. I *know* that part."

"WWW dot eggcode, one word."

"Eggcode?"

"E-G-G . . . no space."

"Okay."

"C-O-D-E."

"They always make it so long."

"And then dot com."

She did something with her pencil—set it down, or tapped it against the telephone. "Great! Got it."

"And then you'll see it right away."

"With the kid."

"With the kid and all that good stuff."

She sighed; Gray could almost smell her smoker's breath through the receiver. "It's terrible, using a young child for something like that."

"I agree, ma'am."

"I did a story last month about a kid who was chained to a furnace for three weeks."

"Yeah?"

"Chained to a furnace. With handcuffs, they did it. They had him once around the wrist and once around the ankle. And once a day, they came down with food, and they gave it to him in a dog dish. And then the rest of the time—nothing. For three weeks. They wouldn't talk to him. They wouldn't even turn the light off at night. And there was a dog, and every now and then it walked down to the basement, looked at the boy, and then walked back up again. What was the dog thinking? That's what I kept wondering, the whole time I covered that story. What was that poor dog thinking?"

"It must've been very upsetting."

"It was, but that's my job. Look, I've got to go—but listen, thank you so much . . ."

Sheesh Is Rich

ey, I've got a store to run here! That's what I *should've* said. I've got a truck out back, I've got people on the phone, some hoity-toity ditz from Hedgemont Heights, thinks she's the queen of the world, wants to know how much the brass candlesticks are—well here's an idea, lady, why don't you come down and look for yourself! My God, these women have nothing to do all day, just sit around drinking Scotch, yapping with their girlfriends, *Oh, Linda, I'm so unhappy.* I don't need that junk. I make $43,000 a year. That's *real* money! So finally I said to heck with it. Got my assistant, I said if anyone starts throwing their weight around, you get the coupon book out and you say *right what it says on the coupon* and that's it! Enough of this noise, man. I shouldn't even have to deal with this crap. If a customer has a problem and needs to speak to the manager, I shouldn't be out there pushing a broom, *Yes ma'am, I'll be right with you, just let me finish peeling these price tags off the floor.* See, that's where your cult of personality comes in. If I had a decent sales staff, there'd be enough qualified people to manage the day-to-day stuff, and I could focus on the important business at hand. Just like any other corporation.

That's the problem, man. No one gives a *crap.* I'm losing thousands of dollars, you can't even reach the checkout stand, there's too much stuff in the way—the TV crew, cameras and lights, and everyone wants to be on the six o'clock news. Cords running all over the sales floor, hanging from the ceiling. Then this woman jams a microphone in my face, starts asking questions about my son—like I know the first thing about what goes on with those people. This time it's the Internet. That's right—Lydia's latest brainstorm. Never mind that we've already got the kid rented out for the next six months. Tell *that* to Cam Pee. We're trying to sell furniture, not blow up the White House. So I tell the woman, I say this is my store, these are my people, I'm in charge of 1.5 million dollars worth of unsold merchandise, and as a licensed representative of the Living Arrangements Family of Fine Retail Establishments, I order you to get off this property . . . and *now!* She's standing between two cameramen, making her pen go in and out, hitting the button with her thumb, trying to look concerned. These stupid women with their made-up jobs. Now she wants to come up to the house, take a few pictures of me and the family on the computer. I tell her, Look, ma'am, we don't even *own* a computer! Just the one with the shoot-'em-up games, cost me an arm and a leg but Simon nagged and nagged until finally I said okay. Other than that, we don't mess around with the junk—haven't even bought a stereo in thirteen years 'cause the new ones don't play the old LPs, and all my Cars records from college are still in good shape so why bother?

But all this is beside the point. I just don't like being bossed around in my own store. That's what I said. Words to that effect. I didn't want to cast a negative light on the company, so what I said was, Look, I understand that you have a job to do, and I respect that, but as far as my son goes (and I stressed this point, for various legal reasons), the Living Arrangements company as such is completely in the dark vis-à-vis the whole issue, and we want to know the facts as much as you do, and that's that. And I don't know anything about any Egg Code, if that's what you're asking, and neither does my boss. And then I told them to leave.

I had to get that last part in, otherwise that's my job, right there. Cam Pee shows up, *Steve, can I see you in my office*, next thing you know I'm out on my rear end, Lydia leaves me with a frying pan and a tub of butter, I'm walking around in a potato sack, singing a sad song, *Buddy, you got a light*. I'm not stupid. I know how it works.

So finally things cleared out—I'm watching my sales drop, wondering how on earth I'm gonna hit five grand by nine o'clock. One of the cameramen, *one* of 'em, bought a candle. Thanks pal. Fifty cents, fifty-three with tax, like I need this nonsense. The way he did it, too. Comes up to the cash stand while his buddies are packing up, getting ready to go. Wants me to ring it up for him. The manager, the big man. I'm doing my job, *That'll be fifty-three cents, please.* They're laughing! He's got this little smile on his face. Counts the cash out, dimes and nickels and pennies. I ask him, *Do you want a bag?* Oh, yes sir, I would like a bag. All noble about it too. So I give it to him. Thank you, thank you, sir. Still smiling. You guys sell a lot of candles? This is what he asks me. Oh yeah, a whole bunch—what do you think? Of course we sell a lot of candles, I sell eighty-ninety candles a day, close to two hundred on the weekends, I sell—ah, to heck with it. I didn't say all that. It gets confusing when you're not in the biz. I had to go to a special class myself, just to learn the terminology. Three days, they made us sit in a big conference room, nothing to eat, just a plate of powdered doughnuts—got white stuff all over my pants—and the coffee was terrible, and everyone had to wear a sticky star that said SOOPER SALES LEADER, and if you didn't want to wear it, a person from the home office would pull you aside and whisper, "Where's your star?"—meaning put it on now.

It's a hard job, managing a store. Every day, it's like hand-to-hand combat. It's like that scene in *Star Wars* where they're all trying to blow up the planet, and all the planes are flying in and out of the trenches, and you've just gotta close your eyes and say to yourself, Okay, some days you're only going to sell a few dozen toss pillows, and it's going to be scary because that money's coming out of your pocket, but there are other days when you come to work thinking nothing's gonna happen, and you wind up selling a camelback sofa, or a bedroom set, and when you average it all together, you generally pull in about five grand per day, which is more or less consistent with the other stores in the region. And that's a good feeling.

The Sad Poor Me Chronicles, Volume One

The Disease
of Disease

Over the years, I've had the opportunity to visit dozens of hospitals across the country—big-city receiving centers, county generals where the RNs are all named Sallie, and someone somewhere *always* has a nephew who's retarded. On occasion, I've even had to shake the poor kid's hand. There are many varieties to this specialized handshake. There's the one where he's not really paying attention, and the only reason you're even doing it is to please the parents, who for fifteen years have been secretly wishing that the kid would up and fucking die; then there's the one where he's jerking and convulsing and chewing on his tongue, and you don't even want to touch him because you know it's just going to be embarrassing for everyone. Sometimes the boy smiles; a big, gay, meaningless smile. Mom and Dad weep, sharing a Bible. Oh, yeah, like you've *cured* him or something. You feel sick to your stomach. Seeing this boy's vacant, disconnected smile, you want to tear your voice box out of your throat, cords and all, and chuck it out into the waiting area, gore leaving a greenish trail across the floor.

Perhaps my experience has colored my judgment. After all, these sicknesses are real, they're not delusions. So why am I not more sympathetic? My own emotional bankruptcy, I suppose. There's nothing in here, folks. It's all gone. I've led a very healthy life. I should be grateful, but I'm not. I resent every sick hand I've ever touched.

Many of my clients are members of the elderly population, dying men and ladies named Walter and Betsy who need my caring words to soothe their palpitations, their nightly chills, their mounting sense of dread. Some of my patients are not so old: middle-aged businesswomen unfairly stricken with leukemia; adolescent transplant recipients lying in jaundiced wrecks on the hospital bed, awaiting the inevitable rejection. They beg me to abet their denial. I can't do it. I *have* done it, thousands of times, but only at a terrible cost to my own emotional well-being. They ask me to reveal the great meaning behind their senseless sacrifice. Because you must languish and die before your fortieth birthday, there will be eternal peace in the Golan Heights. Because of this supreme act of courage, not one more child shall suffer the pain of starvation. I say these things, and I smile, and I envelop their hands in mine, and there we sit for the better part of the afternoon, listening to the outpatients complain about the long wait to see the doctor.

Just once I'd like to tell you the truth. Before it's too late for all of us. They'd welcome me into your private room. From your bed, your marble-dark eyes sparkle. You have been looking forward to my visit for several weeks now. The prospect of touching my hand, of hearing my voice, gives you a reason to go on. Derek Skye is coming. He will make a difference. For my part, I've seen twelve others just like you this morning. You're boring! Your death is not interesting. It needs a hook, a clever twist. Flashing a tepid smile, I try to amuse you with a quick game of got-yer-nose. You do not understand. You were expecting something more profound. This, I cannot provide. Derek Skye is all talked out. My tie spills into your lap as I lean across the bed and whisper, "This is really happening. You are really dying. It's really going to hurt. When you die, all sense of awareness will instantly disperse. Put simply, you will no longer exist. There's nothing important about this. You're not being singled out for some special form of abuse. By needlessly clinging to life, you're causing your family no end of grief and financial misfortune. This is vanity, you understand. Your death is not unusually cruel or tragic. The world will go on."

This, I suspect, would be considered unprofessional. Well, so what? I declare my liberation from the "profession." I myself have never understood this fear of disease. My own death feels more like a destination than a thing to be avoided. I want to know the date. Make it on New Year's Eve. Good lord, wouldn't that be marvelous? I can see it now. The scene is New York, December 31st. A few hundred of us have gathered together at Lincoln Center to observe the holiday. On the plaza in front of the Met, a visiting company is staging a listless performance of *Aida*, an unconventional interpretation with the entire cast whizzing about in wheelchairs. We're not sure why, but, suspecting social commentary, we willfully turn and toast the traffic on Broadway with glasses golden and wet with champagne. I linger near the fountain, alone. A man several yards away is singing a snatch of Strauss, his breath counting out the meter in huffs of white fog. Midnight approaches. Men wander the length of the plaza, searching for their dates. Overhead, an illuminated clock shows the time as an aquamarine disc against the night sky. A bovine din greets the new year.

Leaning against the fountain, I stare across the plaza as my ex-wife hurries toward me. In one hand, she is carrying a long paper party horn, the kind that unravels when you blow into it. I have not seen her for many years. She is gross and overweight. Dabs of cream conceal unimaginable imperfections. I can smell her breath from here. On the first gong of midnight, she reaches the edge of the fountain. She is almost upon me. Lacking any real alternative, I spread my arms to embrace her. Torn between her mad desire and a mindless need to cele-brate the new year, she raises the party horn to her lips and blows. The paper rod extends to a great length, a dozen feet or so. In terror, I open my mouth and gape. The party horn, still unraveling, forces itself down my throat, scraping the sides of my larynx as it hooks the base of my large intestine. Time passes; a beat, then another. I can taste the paper, the glue, the ink. With a tug, the party horn begins its awful retreat, tearing my digestive tract away from its anchor, causing the whole thing to turn inside-out like a sock. I keel over, breaking my jaw against the radiating brickwork. My death comes in seconds. On Broadway and Sixty-fourth, the light changes, the traffic moves, a stack of leaflets ruffles under a bus stop. The shock recedes as my entire life dwindles to a few greatest hits.

So you see? Everyone dies, even the great Derek Skye. Celebrate your disease. It is simply your body's way of reclaiming your soul.

Closing In

Derek waited for a few days before giving the book to Julian. This was a part of the torture, the glorious torture. Making it last. Lately he'd been dreaming of tortures, various weird punishments. He remembered as a boy going with his mother to the ice-cream shop on the campus of the University of Michigan (in his legend-filled mind, there was only one). In those days, the proprietor distributed little slips of paper listing the special flavors for all the upcoming months. Derek always took more than his share, a dozen perhaps, and he'd roll them up into a horn and blow at his mother's hair, trying to piss her off. How far he'd fallen, from that to this. Now he dreamed of oddly precise, almost sterile tortures—the calm extraction of a finger, that sort of thing. His erection woke him up most nights, and he could smell himself on the sheets; a kind of hyphenated light poured through the venetian blinds, and the world outside was just a moon and nothing else.

Then one day, he decided to go for it. Leaving his apartment, he locked up and cut across the front lawn. At the end of the walkway, two long black Lincolns sat with their engines running. He squinted, trying to see past the tinted windshields. The license plates were both from Michigan, an hour to the north. The numbers lurked behind a haze, a mind-scramble of sorts. They were low-series plates, he knew that much. Government? Military? One of those. He worked his jaw in a rough, obsessive arc, considering his past. Bartholomew Hasse was dead two years now, yet his was a power that never went away. There were minions everywhere, paid lackeys from uncertain points of origin. Something dangerous followed this book—one man, or a group of men, determined to snuff it out. Never before had a cash cow like Derek so willingly gone to the slaughter. At some point, every superstar comes to the same realization: *My life is no longer my own.* Writing this book was the most selfish thing Derek had ever done. The whole organization— so much pointless bureaucracy—stood to lose millions of dollars. And all because of his little indulgence. He didn't blame them for being annoyed.

Behind him, he heard one car door open, then another. Looking over his shoulder, he saw two men standing beside their vehicles. In their black coats, they resembled junior vicars come to call on a wayward parishioner. They seemed hesitant to approach the complex. Hands behind their backs, they scanned the jagged roof line, searching the horizon for something awful and remote, some abstraction of their own inner fear. Derek gulped and wiped the cold sweat from his upper lip. They were thugs, no doubt about it. Crossing the street, he skipped over the curb and jogged into town. At the base of the hill, the men waited, one per car. Derek panicked, recognizing their uniforms; the worst possible solution became apparent, and he knew at once who they were.

The Gloria Corporation. Gloria all the way. Realizing this, he didn't know what to think. He'd told them, hadn't he? He'd sent in his letter of resignation, even made a personal appearance, *Sorry, guys, getting old for this line of work,* and everything seemed fine, a few regretful smiles, a handshake, an open offer to come back sometime soon. Of all his former contacts, the Gloria Corporation was one Derek didn't wish to alienate. They would take it too personally, see it as a philosophical rejection, whereas to him the whole setup was just another job, a dozen or so speaking engagements per year and that was that. No further commitments. He surely didn't expect to have some goddamn *ideology* crammed down his throat. Only as the full extent of the organization's interests became apparent—the fact that they'd spent the past decade forging their own semi-legal monopoly, taking over damn near every Network Access Point in the country and leasing out peering "privileges" to a few lucky subscribers—did he begin to wonder what he'd gotten himself into. Those who worked for the GC were committed enough.

Once idealists, they'd grown up during a time when every good idea seemed possible—public housing, public health care, *decent* public education for a change—and now that the bastards whom they'd tried to help had turned out to be such fucking *ingrates*, their desire to wallow in the corporate sludge was almost appalling to behold.

Eager now to reach his destination, Derek hurried through the small commercial district. Auburn light filled the storefronts, but the proprietors of Big Dipper Township clearly did not expect much business today. A barber sat in one of his customer's chairs, reading the paper and smoking a cigarillo. Next door, two insurance salesmen gathered around a gray aluminum desk, tossing dice and gorging themselves on junk food. A few waved at Derek as he passed, for he was a known eccentric, and this was a small place anyway.

Approaching the edge of town, he could see the roof of Julian's house through the woods. Although he hardly knew the man, Derek felt oddly reluctant to hand over such a disquieting piece of work, more self-incriminating than anything he'd written before. It was silly, he knew, but he didn't want Julian to think anything bad about him. He'd even removed some of the most disturbing passages from the manuscript. The bit about his mother was the worst. It was just too awful, even for a confession like this. He remembered those years as a black murk, a word scribbled out. Coming home for the first time after his father's death, he'd wanted to be loving and supportive, but an insistent voice urged him to misbehave, to avoid his mother's company until the end of the visit, to reject her suggestions of fun things to do, plans they'd discussed and both happily agreed to over the phone. This was a wretched fantasy, and when he finally arrived home, the feeling had passed, and he kissed her in the doorway, bags slumped on the step, and together they spent a happy weekend, and he was grateful to himself for not heeding his darker instincts because a year later she was dead, and now she was rotten.

Stepping across Julian's lawn, he held the manuscript out at arm's length, watching the pages curl in the wind. Brief flashes of black on white conveyed recollections of other bad moments. There: a *betrayal*, and with that betrayal came the memory of a night in Phoenix in the mid-eighties, when Derek had offered to visit a child at home—a tiny wreck of a boy, deathly ill, lost in a swirl of cotton bedsheets. Forgetting his appointment, he flew home a night early—he missed Donna and things were still good then—but the next week he received a letter of thanks from the boy's mother, "It meant the whole world to us, etc." and he realized with a sick thrill that she'd imagined the whole encounter—Derek Skye holding her son's hand, autographing a baseball pennant or two. For this woman, believing was enough. His actual presence was no longer necessary; like Santa Claus, he was a myth, something you told your children to help them visualize a more abstract horror, the horror of the senseless universe.

Then the pages blew, and another word, *deception*, burned in his hands like an accusation, and he could see a private room in a cocktail lounge in New York City, a pool table near the back where he and Reggie Bergman sat in two high leather chairs, Reggie with a glass of brandy and Derek cradling the restaurant's last bottle of Glenfiddich. With a look of cocksure arrogance, he cleared the pool table by himself, calling his shots and improvising aphorisms for each as Reggie dutifully wrote them down on the back of a deposit envelope. "Number three in the side pocket: never fear the future, for the future—ha!—will surely arrive . . . ," his voice rising as the cue stick turned slack in his hands, "Okay, number ten in the corner pocket: you are the center of your own universe . . . damn, write that down!" and Reggie wrote it down and the stick sailed out of Derek's hands and broke against the floor, and even though the night ended badly for both men (*Beer before liquor, never sicker*), those same empty formulations later appeared in Derek's 1980 schlocksterpiece, *You Gotta Love It!*, which wound up financing a few more years worth of equally empty, albeit comfortable, living. There: that was deception. The deliberate misuse of the public trust.

But then the pages ruffled and a new word confronted him with its bold black type. *Death*—Derek's great thesis. Projected over the lawn, he could see a multitude of cloaked strangers, their desert-colored turbans swishing in the breeze, faces concealed behind blank ivory masks. The wind carried the leader's mask across the yard, and it cracked against the sidewalk. Derek leaned over to touch one of the fragments, but the mask changed, and a puddle of milk broke under his fingers. Raising his hand to his mouth, he tasted the milk; it tasted bitter, still warm from the body. Already he could feel a solution—a warm liquid, yellow/clear—leaking from the base of his spine. The essence, now gone. The pages blew against his chest, and he knew that with a sudden toss he could release himself from this misery, but instead he stayed, locked in place, for Derek Skye was a man strapped to a conveyor belt, the floor moving, drawing him helplessly into the arms of Julian Mason, black man of the North.

Tales from
Typographic Oceans

A   Julian's heart is racing. It goes up and down.

B   Big eyes, when he read the book, the terrible manuscript. What is this man doing? This is what Julian thought. What is he doing to himself? What will his family think?

C   He'd convinced himself of one thing. He'd gone from one point to another. He wanted to be helpful. He wanted to purge himself of his earlier mistakes. But this—this was much worse. Worse than the Egg Code, because the Egg Code was never about anything to begin with. This book was a travesty, written by a demented kook. And so Julian found himself slowly changing his mind. Going from one point to another.

D   Derek's face was red when he handed Julian the manuscript. Granted, it was cold. That would account for the redness. But there was something else about the color, something unnatural. The world had stopped, and a transparency hung over the still scene, and the transparency was red, and everything behind it was red as well.

E   Three things, really. First, it was so poorly written. The ravings of a desperate soul. Second, the whole thing was offensive. What right did

Derek have to abandon his followers? And third, Julian questioned the man's sanity. He wondered if he should call the police, the suicide team (if they had one).

F Two other things. First, he hadn't had time to dress, and it was cold standing there in his bathrobe, and the wind was blowing snow into the foyer, so he figured he might as well ask the man in. Second, he hadn't read the book yet. How could he possibly know?

G *Tea?* That's fine. *I got it all ready.* Nice place. *And there's cookies in the box.* Pretty view. *The lake sure looks peaceful.* Oh, absolutely—listen Julian, let me cut right to it, because I want to get this project out by April at the latest, and that means that you need to get—well, you know the drill, you're a professional, I'm just gonna let you do your job, but what I want to say is, do what you gotta do because this is important, I'm telling you, this one's different and I want it to be just fucking amazing, you know, and whatever you've got to do, just make it incredible because it's got to be huge and it's got to be big and—whoops! ah, shit. *I'll get that.* Damn it. *Don't worry about it.* You got a napkin?

H The abbot Suger stood beneath the shadow of the church of St. Denis. Spreading a parchment, he squinted at the words on the page. The scroll was an invoice for the construction of the narthex, with its double towers and its great rose window suspended over the entrance, a strange combination but one which the abbot felt drawn to as if by the hand of God. His fellows were not openly critical of these unconventional plans, but he knew what they were thinking—that the towers were too high, that they would soon collapse in a ruin of stone and stained glass. Suger knew better. The building was sound, and the foundation would hold. This, then, was God's great triumph: the ability to build tall churches. In this twelfth century after the birth of our Lord, the works of man must reflect a grandiose reaching for the heavens. The abbot gave a quick word of thanks, knowing full well that the brotherhood would eventually come around. In the years ahead, all of France would catch the mania. Even the scribes sensed this new thirst for increased verticality, and as the abbot reexamined the invoice, he noticed how the *h* of the old Carlovingian minuscules had already started to reach beyond their small dimensions, their high extenders mirroring the twin towers at the top of this fine new church. The abbot smiled. Here was his confirmation. As the words go, so goes the world.

I Candace Mason is a pale, semi-transparent specter growing from the basement of her son's house. A column of blue light marks off her territory, along with a faint music that sounds like a Glenn Miller tune played too slowly and with too much rubato. When Julian enters the column, the light changes from blue to red, and the music fades away. For a moment he is paralyzed, and he can hear his mother's voice, a soft burbling: "Julian, how *are* you? Julian, how *are* you?" The light generates a thick mist, nearly opaque. The world outside no longer exists. He becomes nervous and can feel his heart pressing against his lungs. Soon the frozen feeling goes away, but if he dares to venture beyond the lighted column: instant frostbite! Eventually his mother lets him go.

J Eventually the type wars developed into two camps, the Roman and the Gothic. During the first fifty years after Gutenberg—the incunabula period, as historians like to call it—the Roman font began to draw away from its competitors. Thanks to the business acumen of Aldus Manutius—a kind of fifteenth-century Don King—books printed in Roman fonts began to appear all over Europe. The only notable holdout was Germany, who would pay for their reluctance nearly five hundred years later, at the close of World War II. Even today, the sight of a Gothic *J* inspires a flurry of insults and angry remarks: *"Jew-Killer! Jew-Killer!"*

K The sympathy riots began a few days after the big fires in Detroit. Julian spent the weekend working in his rooftop studio in Greenwich Village. From his window, he could gaze down at the street four flights below. The edge of the building on the corner looked two-dimensional — a line of brick, then nothing. The police officers wore helmets with Plexiglas face shields, and the troublemakers were white college students, NYU types in caftans and torn military jackets. One of the students was standing next to the wall, trying to roll a Drum cigarette with one hand and having a bad time of it, and when a cop told him to move, the kid ignored him, so the cop grabbed him by the collar, lifted him a foot off the ground, thrust him with a diagonal lunge into the wall, then pulled him away from the edge and held him a foot above his head, and Julian, looking down from his studio, dropped his pencil and said, "It's a *K*—my God, it's a *K!*"

L My pulse drops and dips. Every beat is a new surprise. Will this one be too fast, too slow, not regular enough? A few good ones in a row. Okay. Okay. Okay. (Okay). Then? Ah! There! . . . N-now . . . aahhh! . . . aaahhhh! . . . pfeehhnneeehh . . . muh-muh-muh-muh-mama . . . guh . . . guh . . . it's . . . it's . . . it's . . . it's . . . better. Wooo! Wooo! Oh, stars. Fat cheeks. A few good ones in a row.

M The men were going to die. Trapped in a pool of ice, they looked up at the steep rise to the east, where Mont Blanc towered over the Italian border, and then to the west, where a secondary peak ascended to an equal height. One of the men, Thierry, pulled out a square cut from a blood-soaked flag and held it to his forehead, whispering a prayer on the life of King François. His brother, René, reached for a wood-framed sack — its heavy truss now splintered into two neat halves — and brought out a small leather handbook. An embossed dolphin winked on the cover, its bright gold features reflecting the light from the snowy hillside. With one frozen hand, he pushed back the cover. "Where'd you steal that?" Thierry asked. "I bought it," his brother sneered back. "It's an Aldine. Cheap, you know." Thierry glowered. "Aldus was an infidel," he snarled. Pressing the book against his chest, René smiled at Thierry, and a wind from the east blew his long black hair over his eyes. "Do not curse the Italian. It is because of Aldus that peasants may die with Virgil on their lips." Turning to the first page, he hunched over the book and began to read. His brother was dead by the sixteenth stanza.

N   Derek stood in the foyer, his hands braced against the doorjamb. A tall man, he filled the entrance with his diagonal presence. "I'm so glad you've got it now," he said. Leaving the door open, he skipped down the steps and hurried across the lawn. As Julian watched him go, a complicated lie began forming in the back of his brain. His mother's voice came to him, disguised as his own: *Well, Julian, you gotta keep your word now.*

O   bury it I could bury it but that would be unprofessional no I'll just do what he says but couldn't I just play around with the format though that wouldn't be professional not the proper thing to do hell what's that they say a good typographer never calls attention to himself but what if there's no choice what if the words themselves are evil what if the words are wrong what then what does a good typographer do then does he

P   In 1957, Julian Mason stands naked in the bedroom with one arm raised, trying to make a muscle. *There!* he says, holding his breath. Joyce Ganz touches his forearm, squeezing it once and then again. Her clothes are piled on the floor, left from last night. Her own nakedness means nothing to her. *Ooh!* she laughs, and covers her mouth. *So strong! Why you want to be an artist? You shoulda been a wrestler! HA! Bullshit.*

Q   *Qu'est-ce que c'est?* Ah, this Robert Granjon is crazy, *ahhh-oui?* For twenty years, he says, "No, I no like ze Italians, with their simple letters that go chop-chop-chop across ze page. So? I make a new one, *ahhh-oui?* For ze French language. I call it *Civilité*, ze national typeface for ze people of France!" Very clever, monsieur. But this Robert Granjon, he no think straight. Ze national typeface is *nothing! Merde!* Is too hard to read, *ahhh-oui*? So in France, we stick with ze Italians. We are happy here! No more bloodshed . . . no more bloodshed . . .

R One of the few times Julian saw his daughter after Joyce moved upstate to study law, it was 1971 and Emily was thirteen, a tall girl with a big squared-off Afro and heavy eyelids that flickered pretentiously every time her father asked her a question. That day in New York, she wore a T-shirt tied in the middle to show off her belly button. Julian thought it ludicrous to waste an entire afternoon inside a downtown movie house, but Emily wanted to go and that was that. He stood underneath the theater marquee dressed in a gray trench coat—much too hot for the weather, but he was used to winter and March was a temperamental month. Joyce had given the girl enough money to pay for both tickets, but Julian said no and crammed the wad of cash back into her pants pocket. Looking up at the marquee, he exclaimed, "That's a dirty movie!" "Come on, Jules, it's not a dirty movie. It's an R-rated movie, and besides, Mom said I could." Oh boy, the magic words, Julian wasn't going to argue with that, so he followed his daughter inside, past the concession stand ("yeah . . . gimme some *black* licorice . . . I really like the *black* licorice . . . heh, kidding pal, just gimme a Pepsi-Cola . . .") and into the theater, where they sat near the front because Emily had left her glasses on the train. A love scene came on halfway through, the faces of the actor and the actress backlit so you could only see their silhouetted profiles, his profile staring down at hers, a regular rhythm, a few soft cries, the woman's breasts implied by a dim slice of moonlight. Trapped, Julian could see his daughter's face out of the corner of his eye, her little bent wrist diving periodically into the popcorn box, and he gripped the sides of his chair and told himself this would all be over soon. After the film, they went across the street to an Italian diner, where she boldly ordered a glass of wine. Discussing the film, Julian made a few genteel remarks, and Emily—sipping her grape juice—said, "Come on, Jules. Kids today have sex in the sixth grade, gawd."

S This is how Julian Mason paces from one end of the living room to the other. He starts at the northwest corner, then makes an abrupt right turn, stepping around a recliner, a rickety end table, a ceramic lamp with a pleated shade. Reaching the far corner, he swings around and heads diagonally across the room, where he stands for a moment, looking at the point where the two walls meet. Sometimes he speaks, if only to hear the hollow return of his own voice. The things he says are never interesting. *Whoo boy. Lord, lord.* Adjusting his robe, he turns around and retraces his steps, keeping strictly to the established path. He does this one hundred and sixty-one times in an hour and forty-three minutes. If you asked him what was wrong, he would say *mmmmm?*

T   J. Oporinus, Basel, May 6, 1541. I have learned of your efforts to obtain a Latin translation of the book known to the Roman Church as the Infidel's Bible. This is a worthy endeavor, yet I am certain you have also considered that Paul III will persecute your establishment with unfair levies if you publish this work. The papacy sadly refuses to acknowledge the potential benefits of the Koran to the Christian world. Educated men will not convert to heresy, but will affirm the essential wisdom of our Lord and Savior Jesus Christ. The forces of Satan will die an angry death, and we will serve as their tormentors. This publication must go forth — in Basel, or in one of the other free lands. I myself will lend my name to the introduction, as an added safeguard to your liberty. The time has come. Mohammed must speak. Your lover in Christ, Martin Luther.

U   In the memory he has of Derek Skye (and he does not know whether it is a real memory or the memory of a dream), Derek is crossing the street when a red pickup shoots around the corner. The driver leans on the brake and the truck jerks to a stop. Standing on the double yellow line, Derek waves, "Go ahead, pal. You go first." The truck grinds ahead a few feet, then makes an abrupt U-turn. Derek keeps waving as the truck roars out of sight. His hand slows; it flutters to his side. He stands there, quiet for a moment. A memory, or a dream?

U   Won't you wear this flower? *I can't.* Come on, look, you've got a nice suit. *I'm meeting a young lady for dinner.* Let me just pin it right here. *No, I'd rather not.* You don't want to wear this flower? *I have to go.* You don't want to wear this flower for peace? *You have a pleasant evening.* DON'T YOU CARE ABOUT THE CHILDREN DYING IN VIETNAM?!

W Candace Mason died in a room with six other women. Nylon shower curtains divided the room into sections. Through a thin screen, she could see the vague forms of her roommates; every night, the woman to her right sat up in bed, arms wrapped around her knees as the woman to her left blew on her soup, holding the spoon at the very tip of the handle, splashing herself whenever the spoon fell into her lap. The women spoke to each other through the semi-transparent curtains. Candace often mentioned her son, who lived in New York City. She talked about the war, how she used to take Julian out to the factories each day, and sometimes let him paint the serial codes on the hulls of the airplanes. One of the women had bad diarrhea, and the other ladies would kid about it whenever she was out of the room. In August 1970, the woman with bad diarrhea passed away, and another woman with bad diarrhea took her place. One afternoon, Julian appeared at the foot of his mother's bed, dressed in a nice hat and a dark trench coat. Candace looked up at her boy. "Julian," she asked, "do I *smell?*" He began to cry. Mrs. Mason died the next morning, and the doctors cut bright pieces out of her body and put them into bottles.

X No, I'll smother it. I'll bury the book. I can't let this happen to the children. A good typographer, yes, a good one, but no, I don't know what a good typographer does.

Y Julian Mason stands on the roof of his house in Big Dipper Township, his arms raised over his head, and he watches as the winter storm rolls in from the city, a northbound sway of illuminated cotton balls. He can smell the electricity in the air, and it makes the tiny hairs on the back of his neck bristle and twitch. High above the tower, Candace

Mason swirls in a column of blue light. A kind of warm radiance emanates from her body. Closing his eyes, Julian smiles and laughs and pumps his fists, for at last he knows what it means to be a good son.

Z   Yes, but can you withstand the diabolical forces of the mighty zee, heh? *This*, I ask you!

It Can't Happen Here

0001011101001101000110

T he house. Several apartments with high pointy rooftops. The spaces between the rooftops look like inverted rooftops. Matching rows of teeth. A cold breeze, a forceful push. The air is filled with dirt and snapped twigs.

—Rub eye? Don't rub eye?
—Rub eye.

The wind blows into Olden's mouth. His ears are rough and red and cold. His nose is wet with snot. A strand of snot flies in the wind; it flaps and flutters, clinging to his cheek.

—Wipe away strand? Don't wipe away strand?
—Don't wipe away strand.

Two surveillance men are approaching the building. Olden has been spying on them for the past fifteen minutes. Crouched in a thicket of trees, he saw the whole thing—the two cars edging up to the curb, waiting for Derek Skye to come out of his apartment. Derek looked anxious as he crossed the lawn and hurried into town. He was carrying something, Olden noticed, a stack of papers. Maybe that's what the men were looking for; the idea of a former insider writing a book certainly wouldn't appeal to the Gloria Corporation, even though Derek has written many books in his life, most of them harmless enough.

The surveillance men have now reached the front steps. They both walk with a stoop, as if expecting bullets to start flying over their heads at any moment. They knock on the door and begin to pick the lock with a specially designed, lock-picking kind of gizmo/doodad. The door swings open and one of them proceeds inside. Moments later, the venetian blinds on the second floor go from being skinny to being fat.

— Feel sorry for Derek Skye? Don't feel sorry for Derek Skye?
— Feel sorry for Derek Skye.
— Because he is an admirable man? Because you respect the work he is doing?
— See other.
— Because his predicament reminds you of your own? Because Scarlet Blessing would be unhappy?
— Because his predicament reminds me of my own, and see other.
— Because this invasion of privacy represents even greater constitutional violations that the federal government commits every day? Because, in searching the apartment, the surveillance men may inflict irreparable damage to the property, resulting in a decreased value for the landowner?
— Because this invasion of privacy represents even greater constitutional violations that the federal government commits every day, and see other.
— End of list.

The man outside walks down the front lawn and looks up the street, toward town. He then turns around and looks in the other direction, away from town. He then looks across the street and stares directly at his vehicle. His expression is stony.

— Slink back into the woods? Don't slink back into the woods?
— Slink back into the woods.

Olden hunkers down behind the stand of trees and wipes the sweat from his forehead with the palm of his left hand.

— Wipe sweat: onto pant leg? onto ground? onto other hand? onto side of face? back onto forehead? onto trunk of tree? onto invisible creature

of the woodlands? onto front of shirt? onto seat of pants? onto neck? onto hair? onto imagined likeness of Chester Alan Arthur? onto shoe? onto medallion?
—Wipe sweat onto side of face.

Looking down at the frozen ground, Olden closes his eyes as a blustery wind sifts through the trees. Pine needles fall from the branches and filter down the neck of his shirt.

—Entertain half-baked notions of guilt and complicity? Don't entertain half-baked notions of guilt and complicity?
—Entertain half-baked notions of guilt and complicity.
—Because by utilizing the current multi-communications network to satisfy your own thirst for destruction, you have taken advantage of the trust of the world community? Because by infecting the Information Superhighway with products of misinformation, you have created a greater harm than you ever first imagined, even in your most sordid, delusion-wracked fantasies?
—Because by infecting the Information Superhighway with products of misinformation, I have created a greater harm than I ever first imagined, even in my most sordid, delusion-wracked fantasies, and see other.
—Because by taking this action, you may have subtly altered the fabric of reality, thereby making the world a less secure place to live? Because you still harbor feelings of resentment and inadequacy stemming from your childhood as the son of two brilliant yet rather unapproachable mega-geniuses, parents whose love and attention you crave to such an unhealthy extent that you have resorted to this desperate gesture, a global version of look-ma-I-broke-my-new-toy-truck?
—Because I still harbor feelings of resentment and inadequacy stemming from my childhood as the son of two brilliant yet rather unapproachable mega-geniuses, parents whose love and attention I crave to such an unhealthy extent that I have resorted to this desperate gesture, a global version of look-ma-I-broke-my-new-toy-truck, and see other.
—End of list.

The surveillance man sneaks alongside the complex and disappears into the woods.

—Follow the surveillance man? Don't follow the surveillance man?
—Follow the surveillance man.

Olden tiptoes across the street and follows the man into the woods. The ground is covered with roots. He walks with his head down, breathing on his shirt; this makes his face feel warm. Icicles cover the bare tree branches, which crinkle and crack in the distance. He reaches a frozen stream bed; giant icicles pierce it in spots like vaccination needles. The stream bed sags and folds like wet cardboard when he walks across it.

—Look back at footprints? Don't look back at footprints?
—Look back at footprints.

Olden looks back at his own footprints. They are a single shade darker than the surrounding frost. He suddenly feels disoriented. He stops walking and cups his hands around his ears: seashells. The air is very cold. The tiny hairs inside his nostrils are frozen stiff. The other man is gone.

—Curse? Don't curse?
—Curse.
—Fuck? Cunt? Shit? Damn? Bitch? Hell? Damnit to hell? Goddamn fucking shit? Motherfucking goddamn bullshit fucking damn goddamn motherfucker? Goddamn sonuvabitch fucking goddamn shit? Goddamnit? Fucking goddamn bullshit? Goddamn fucking damn shit? Fuck it, fuck it straight to hell?
—Fuck it, fuck it straight to hell.

Olden stands still, considering where he is in relation to the road, the lake, other key landmarks. All around, the same tree repeats itself, like a text file copied a thousand times.

—Concoct imaginary woodland sounds to avoid confronting the hopelessness of the situation? Don't concoct imaginary woodland sounds to avoid confronting the hopelessness of the situation?

—Concoct imaginary woodland sounds to avoid confronting the hopelessness of the situation.
—Creaking branches? Chittering squirrels? Ice breaking? Cocktail making? Birds squawking? Children talking? Rodents spitting? Bamboo splitting?
—Creaking branches. Chittering squirrels. Ice breaking. Birds squawking.

Something flashes just to the left of his head. Through the trees, he can see his little one-room shack. The tower looms above the forest, its windward side covered with snow. The lake is frozen, of course; he could walk to the center from here. Coming closer, he notices two additional surveillance men, Mr. Tall and Mr. Short, poking around the house. No vehicle present. They must have come on foot.

—Consider other alternatives? Don't consider other alternatives?
—Consider other alternatives.
—Bicycle? Go-cart? Solar-powered terra-glider?
—See other.
—Dromedary? Vintage car? Helicopter? Hand-driven rail cart?
—See other.
—Stallion? A fantastic bird of some sort? The hand of Zeus? A supernatural carpet? A pogo stick? A beverage tray?
—They must have come on foot.

Olden runs toward his house, but the men grab him by the shoulders to prevent him from going inside. They say things like "Hey, man" and "Whoa there" and "Not this time." Both of them wear nice watches, loops of stretchy steel. The design in the center of the timepiece is something familiar to Olden. The tree with four trunks.

Backing away, he peers into the shack. The room is dark except for the blue glow of the monitor. The two men—tall and short—ask a few barking questions about the Egg Code. *Yeah, officers, I'm clean. Talk to my loi-yer.* Olden realizes he can't be too cavalier. Just another concerned citizen. *We all want to get to the bottom of this.* He tries to look sheepish. It's hard to do. The sheepish look. If you don't really mean it.

—Select another facial expression? Don't select another facial expression?

—Select another facial expression.

—Proud? Irate? Indignant? Indifferent?

—See other.

—Mercurial? Outlandish? Duplicitous? Doubtful?

—Stick with sheepish.

Mr. Tall reasserts himself, hefting his belt. When we say Mr. Tall and Mr. Short, we're exaggerating a little. Mr. Tall looks about six-two, six-three. Mr. Short, five-ten, five-eleven. These men have real names, real lives, real families. Olden envisions Mr. Short relaxing on the weekends. Walking the dog. He's got a golden retriever, they're running down the beach. Hair all over the place. Hip shades, the kind JFK used to wear. The golden retriever is gazing up at Mr. Short in adoration, tongue lolling. It's thinking, When is he going to throw the Frisbee?

—Imagine real names for Mr. Tall and Mr. Short? Don't imagine real names for Mr. Tall and Mr. Short?

—Imagine real names for Mr. Tall and Mr. Short.

—Buck Wilde? Dan Daniels? Ricki Fontaine? Rex Rock? Ford Brik? Billy Cougar? Dent Savage? Leif Hitler? John Boy? Clint Foxtrot? Dirk Miller? Jack Diamond? Luke Shoetree? Tarzan Laine? Zak Deal? Ted Gripp? Smash Dagger? Ben Clapp? Rob Glass? Lance Dance? Harvey Bugle? Alvin Meen? Dave Plant? Octavio—

—Cancel.

Mr. Short tells his partner to go back inside. Alone now, he warns Olden not to hinder their investigation. Ever since the Living Arrangements debacle first went public, Olden's "Egg Code" Web site has cost online retailers untold thousands of dollars. No one seems to trust the Internet anymore. The Gloria Corporation, he says, has a right to protect its own property. Hearing this, Olden tries not to smile: *Real property*, he wonders, *or cyber property?* When he asks this question, Mr. Short moves in closer and puts his hand on his shoulder. The grandfather thing. The wise old man. *Look, son. Now you're making me do something I don't want to do* . . .

—Recollect the dead face of one James Field (1910–1978)?
Don't recollect the dead face of one James Field (1910–1978)?
—Recollect the dead face of one James Field (1910–1978).
—How he looked weird without his glasses.
—The little groove running across the bridge of his nose.
—The slack jowls. The thick makeup. Trying to make him look natural.
—What if he sits up? What if he sits up right now?
—Aaahh! His head comes off. Pigeons fly out.
—People screaming. The race to the parking lot.
—His eyes are red. He vomits flames.
—You're the one he wants.

Olden twists away from Mr. Short's hand. The two men are roughly the same age. Olden could have had his job, easy. He could've worked for the Gloria Corporation. The possibilities present themselves, and he imagines another world, the comfortable life he might've led had things worked out differently. In this other place, he envisions a woman—Scarlet, perhaps—coming into the living room, carrying a tray of freshly baked cookies. The phone rings; Olden is taking a shower. The world outside is no different.

Mr. Tall emerges from the shack, clutching a fistful of evidence. A toothpick juts out between his lips. The toothpick matters; it reveals something about his personality, how he points with it as the two men stride across the driveway and slip back into the forest. *Strange*, Olden thinks, *there's nothing* in *those woods*. Puzzled, he turns and goes inside. He has a lot to worry about.

Dizzy and distracted, he feels his way across the dark room. Dust clings to the computer screen, wispy motes of something. He can't believe he's been breathing this stuff for years. In one corner of the room, he can see his windsurfer propped against the wall, the sail unraveled and spread across the floor. What a dump. He needs to move back to the city. Get a normal job. Never mind these intellectual pursuits. It would be nice to have some real friends for a change. Guys named Phil. Beers after work. *Yeah, I'll have the nachos and . . . you got Milluh Lite?* Ice hockey on the large-screen TV. Working gals and their turquoise margaritas. Men waving across the bar. *Hi, ladies!* The one on the left's nice, but lose the tie. *Phil, I think she digs you.* What do you do? *I'm in management . . .*

Too late for that. The feds are on his trail. In their eyes, he's already guilty of something. Leaning over the keyboard, he jettisons the Windows interface and the screen goes dark. Suddenly the monitor flashes; bright numbers flock in streams of zeros and ones. He prunes the data, then reboots and logs on to the Egg Code. Closing his eyes, he listens for the characteristic chatter of the CPU negotiating with its host—the handshake, the exchange of packets, the confirmation, the efficient farewell. TCP/IP in action.

—Recollect a vision of Martin Field working on the TCP/IP protocol in the late 1970s? Don't recollect a vision of Martin Field working on the TCP/IP protocol in the late 1970s?
—Recollect a vision of Martin Field working on the TCP/IP protocol in the late 1970s.
—The dining-room table covered with graph paper.
—Dad on the phone. Everyone else is eating breakfast. The smell of burnt Pop-Tarts.
—Mom lacing up her construction boots. Well, I'm off.
—Moses waiting outside, his hockey stick raised like a staff. Blade up. Wants to play.
—Where's the dog? There he is.
—Stretches its paws. Yawns. Yeeooowwwl.

Olden forces himself to look at the screen. An unfamiliar pattern grows toward the center; blue lines meet and then cross. Expecting the Egg Code, he discovers a jumble of images in its place, his original Web page scrambled beyond recognition. He rechecks the address. Nothing wrong with the URL. Words assemble, building from the top down. Blocks connect—now letters. He reads the message three times, then covers the screen with his hand.

WELCOME TO THE HOME PAGE
FOR THE GLORIA CORPORATION
OF ANN ARBOR, MICHIGAN
SERVING THE NETWORKING COMMUNITY SINCE 1966

They hacked him, the bastards.

Back outside, he lingers in front of his house and considers where to go next. A crisp leaf blows against his cheek and he takes it by the stem.

—Reduce the leaf to its veiny skeleton? Don't reduce the leaf to its veiny skeleton?
—Reduce the leaf to its veiny skeleton.

Olden picks at the leaf until all that remains is a flimsy network of connecting tendons. Dry shards the color of mulled cider stick to his thumb and forefinger.

—Make the leaf go flap-flap like a miniature hang glider? Don't make the leaf go flap-flap like a miniature hang glider?
—Do not make the leaf go flap-flap like a miniature hang glider.

Discarding the leaf, he climbs the hill and waits by the side of the road. The men from the Gloria Corporation are long gone. Over the hush of the countryside, an engine changes gears—a rush, then a crescendo as a car rounds the corner, fanning debris across the double yellow line. The driver of the vehicle is a woman with short, stiff hair, and she drives with her hands high on the wheel. The car shoots around a curve, taking all sound with it.

Olden crosses the street and follows his enemy into the forest.

Get Down! Get Down!

Simon rose out of his seat and stared over the headrest. He saw a man in the road, and then the car went around a curve and the man was gone. He tried to remember the man's face as he sank back into his seat, but all he could recall was a mane of long hair, and how it looked like dancing black snakes from a distance.

"Simon, I'm going to ask you to sit properly in your seat."

"Okay."

"I would very much prefer it if you did not sit like that."

"Mmm."

"As long as you know what you're doing. As long as you understand the consequences. Of sitting like that."

"Okay."

"All right. Then I won't worry about it."

They continued like this for some time, speeding past long stretches of woods and mailboxes that leaned on splintered posts where gravel driveways split and forked into darkness. As she drove, Lydia considered the wisdom of her decision—a decision that seemed brilliant three days ago, less so at four this morning. Simon really deserved the kind of attention only a private school could provide. Besides, both she and the boy had made too many promises to too many people, empty promises to the school board, to the head of the PTA. *Watch out for my son. He's going to be a star someday.* At a new place, at a quiet, caring institution, Simon would get another chance, a crack at normalcy. She would see to it. No more high-flown ambitions. From now on, Simon would be just another average boy. But he would be the best goddamn average boy that ever set foot in Crane City. He would study every night. This was part of the new resolution. They would study together, in the kitchen. She would buy expensive cookies and bottled milk from an actual dairy, and they would sit at the table and eat the cookies and drink the milk, and they would study, whatever, *algebra*, or the one where you draw the squares. He would excel at his schoolwork. His teachers would reward him with gold stars and lapel pins in the shapes of diplomas and graduation caps, and if they didn't, she would threaten them with legal action until they finally gave in. This was the new way. It was not too late for Simon to start behaving like an intellectual.

"Mom? What would you do if I farted right now?"

"Simon!"

"What? Fart's not a swear!"

"Don't use that language!"

"But what would you do?"

"I would be . . . very angry. And disgusted."

"Okay! I just asked!"

The car crossed the expressway and continued past a row of farm-houses with dilapidated barns the color of old skin. At the foot of one driveway, an elderly man dressed in tan slacks and a golf shirt hurled a steel rake at a small boy, forcing him to catch it. Down the road, some-one's trash bag had blown open, and a stomped-flat carton of Nestlé's Quik chocolate milk struck the car's windshield, the frayed corner get-ting stuck on a wiper blade. The carton fluttered against the glass; the tiny image of the cartoon rabbit was folded so that the ears seemed to be growing directly out of its neck.

"Mom?"

"Simon, *what?*"

"Can I say just one swear word?"

"Simon."

"Not even a bad one."

"Why are you being so silly?"

"And then I'll never say it again."

"If you *promise* to wear your hair the way I said."

"And you won't get mad?"

"Simon, please."

"Okay, okay . . . Damn."

"Good. Very nice. Now help me look."

Lydia made a right onto a dirt road, where a wood-burnt sign welcomed all visitors to the school's main campus. Broome Town—that was the name of the place, but there was no slogan, no clever quotations from Dr. Spock or the Beatles. Lydia was disappointed. She wanted a slogan, something like *Where Children Go to Grow*. Through the windows, she could see students hunched over their various activities. Trim little trees guarded the front door; thin cords forced the branches to bend into weird shapes.

Lydia parked the car and dug her purse out of the backseat. They'd probably ask for a personal check, maybe even some proof of identification. This was not a place where one minded the extra scrutiny. It added to the appeal, somehow. Not just *anyone* could get in.

"Now, Simon, you're going to have to take a test." She reached over the passenger seat and pushed open the door. "They're going to ask you some questions."

"What kind of questions?" asked Simon, not moving.

"What do you mean, what kind of questions? *Test* kind of questions, now come on. You've taken tests before."

"Yeah, but only where they let you do-over." The boy lifted the door handle, let it go, lifted it again, let it go. The mechanisms inside the door sheared and groaned. He smiled. "Look, I can make a song."

"Simon will you leave that alone!" She yanked on his sleeve. "Now listen. They're not going to let you do-over. You're going to have to think. You're going to have to guess the right answer." She held him in an awkward embrace, lugging him halfway out of his seat. "Now do this for Momma, baby. Do this for Momma and I'll never ask you for anything else. I'll never be unhappy with you again."

"I gotta do math?"

"Yes, you gotta do math. And history. They're gonna ask you all about history."

"Like what?"

Lydia sighed, releasing him. "Like what, like . . . who was Susan B. Anthony?"

"Who was Susan B. Anthony." The boy stared through the windshield, letting the question revolve inside his brain. "Who?"

Pissed, she stepped out of the car. "What do you *mean*, who? I have no idea. *Pick* something!"

She stood near the building, waiting for Simon to catch up. Once inside, they crossed a winding corridor with split levels that went up two steps and then down four, odd enclaves filled with comfy furniture, fabric sofas and ottomans shaped like giant aspirin, vending machines that dispensed only bottled water, only fresh sandwiches, only all-natural fruit pies. She stopped and pointed at the ceiling. "Listen!" she said. "Music!" Classical music played at just the right volume, something serious by Schoenberg, a string quartet, wild and dissonant. Sprawled across one of the ottomans, a young girl fingered violin hand positions in the air, each finger making its own precise movement. Another girl stood against the back wall, practicing a yoga stance. Both girls seemed to be listening to the music, focusing on every last difficult stretch of melody. This, without parental supervision! Lydia looked down at her son and smiled. She herself had enjoyed a fine education when she was his age. The private schools in the District of Columbia were lavish affairs. Children traveled with armed escorts, silent guys named Rich who sipped coffee all day and stood in the back of the room, pretending to read the show-and-tell board. The meals were all catered by fancy Washington supper clubs, and the silverware wasn't silver but at least it was stainless steel; she could still remember the clink-clink of fifty-odd sixth graders sawing through steak tartare in the school gymnasium. Most of Lydia's teachers were not American, and they spoke with thick accents, German, sometimes Hungarian. In every classroom, the sons and daughters of the world elite marked time; vaguely familiar, they resembled small, shredded versions of their famous parents.

Slightly dazed, Lydia and Simon found the main office and entered a tiny room with one desk in the center and a chair on either side. Half-drawn vertical blinds made a shadow like prison bars across the carpet. A woman sat in one of the chairs, eating a salad from a fast-food restaurant. The salad was thick with dressing; the smell of garlic stunk up the whole room. Lydia and Simon stood in the doorway while she finished her meal. Patting her lips with a napkin, she opened her purse and brought out a small compact that looked like a white seashell with a steel hinge at one end. The woman calmly reapplied her makeup, making an mmm-mmm noise as she smushed her lips together. Closing the case with a snap, she motioned for Simon to sit, then slid a booklet across the desk, along with a half-dozen pencils and a sharpener. "I'm Mrs. Olivet," she said.

"Mrs. Olivet, hi." The two women shook hands. The proctor's skin was warm and soft, and she wore thick wooden bangles around her wrist. Red letters circled one of the bangles, forming a chain.

"You've noticed my bracelet, I see." She spun the bangle, reading the message as it streamed by. ". . . *learn more so that I may grow into a person who can learn more so that I may grow into a person who can* . . . It goes on."

"Yes, that's very clever."

"Isn't it?" The woman's voice sounded dubbed, the words taken from a documentary about apples. "This examination will last approximately forty-five minutes. Would you care to wait in the outer office?"

"Oh." Lydia glanced over her shoulder, feeling rejected. "Okay! There's not a . . ." Mrs. Olivet nodded, her lips parted, wanting very much to understand, to supply the next word herself. "There's no place I can go to watch?"

"To watch?"

"A secret room somewhere. A secret room with a one-way glass."

The woman smiled, then stood and took hold of Lydia's hands. "You're nervous."

"No, I'm not nervous." Lydia balled her hands into fists and twisted away. "It's Simon. He's more comfortable when I'm around."

Mrs. Olivet, no longer smiling, looked at the boy and spoke in a soft voice. "Well, that's something we're going to have to work on. Simon is almost a young man. Young men do not need their mothers. Young men are independent, dashing and reckless. They drive their convertibles with the top down. This is what young men do. Loud music on the radio: 'We're gonna rock, rock, scream 'n' shout . . .'" She half-sung her words, snapping her fingers to some silent fifties jam. "Young men take vigorous showers. Huge handfuls of water splashing against their chests. Droplets exploding in slow motion, each drop proclaiming, *I am a man!* Young men gnaw on their food, tearing at it with their teeth like vicious beasts, vicious beasts guarding a fresh carcass. This is *my* food. Don't touch *my* food. Young men read adventure novels, grand tales from the American frontier. When they read, they bend the cover all the way back, holding it with one hand. See him now, the sexy brute. Hey, Rico! Yo, you got a problem wi'dat?" Something seemed to run out of the woman, and she herded Lydia into a reception area, where a maze of drywall divided the room into quads. "Would you like some coffee?" she asked.

Walking backwards, Lydia tripped and fell into a partition. "S-sure."

"There's coffee. The reason I ask is, not everyone likes coffee. Some people hate it. Absolutely abhor it."

"I've never noticed—"

"To the point of vomiting. If they smell it. If they even see it."

"That's—"

"Oh, yes!" Her eyes flashed mysteriously. "The fear is: I can't see what I'm drinking. You know? I can't see all the way down to the bottom of the cup. I'm just telling you what the fear is. I personally think it's absurd."

With a giggle, Mrs. Olivet closed the door and Lydia was alone. A tray of cookies looked unappetizing next to an old-fashioned coffee percolator. The coffee was strong and hot, so hot that it didn't taste like much of anything, just generically hot liquid. Lydia poured herself a cup and grabbed some cookies, holding them in her lap as she squinted at a pile of magazines. *Cosmo. Business Week.* Something with Katie Couric on the cover. She knew it at once—a *sense* of Katie Couric preceded the face itself. This was Lydia's ambition for her son—to make him a presence, a kind of psychological screen saver. What you saw when there was nothing else to see. Why him? Why *not* him? The reasons seemed arbitrary. Defeated, she now wanted an explanation, only that. Old desires turned hard inside her body. An undigested weight refused to go down.

An hour went by before the proctor finally returned, holding a scorecard in her hand. Her lips were straight and serious. She took a seat next to the coffeemaker, then hesitated, letting a difficult moment pass. "Your son is a very special boy," she began.

"Yes he is." They nodded sadly at each other, then at the floor.

"And special boys sometimes . . . have special problems."

"Okay."

"They just do. And it's up to us . . . to understand it." Wrapping her fingers around the scorecard, she formed the sheet of paper into a slender tube. "And sometimes, certain children are unable to perform . . . certain functions."

"That's true."

"It just happens. It just does, and I don't think the good Lord above knows why. And that doesn't make someone a bad person. You can be a very good person, and still not be able to perform . . . certain functions."

"Functions."

"Functions such as . . . multiplication."

"I gotcha."

"You don't have to know how to do that. And that doesn't make you a bad person." The woman reached into her blazer pocket and pulled out a roll of breath mints. One mint spilled out into her hand—white with flecks of green, like linoleum tile. "Some people can do some things. And other people can do other things. And that's what makes this world a wonderful place. We need good, strong people, who don't necessarily know how to . . . spell. We *need* them."

"We do."

"Fishermen, for example." She popped the mint into her mouth, then bit down, holding it between her teeth. "They're good people! Good, solid people. And they perform for society . . . a function . . . that some people wouldn't necessarily want to do themselves."

"Air-traffic controller."

Mrs. Olivet frowned queerly. "Air-traffic controller?"

"As another thing to do."

"No, air-traffic controllers have to know . . . trigonometry, for one thing."

"Oh."

"*Advanced* computer programming. So. Air-traffic controller would be out, unless something changed . . . pretty damn quick."

"Right."

"But what I'm saying is, there's a whole lotta things—I mean, look at Harry Truman! Harry Truman couldn't do . . . some basic thing. And next thing you know—"

"He's pres—"

"—he's president of the United States. The most respected—until recently, the most respected job in the world! And he had to deal with all sorts of things. I just saw it on TV."

"I think I missed that one."

"Incredible stuff. They had this actor playing Harry Truman. And he's walking down the street. And he sees this guy, right? And while he's standing there, this car comes—boom!—and knocks him down. And Harry Truman's standing there. The actor they had playing Harry Truman. And he goes up to the guy and says, you know, whatever, I'll take care of you."

"Nurse you back to health."

"Exactly, whatever it takes. And the guy says, Fine! Take me back to your home. I mean, I don't know, they might've—"

"Fluffed it up a bit."

"Changed it around, sure, but the way I saw it, the way I interpreted the film was—"

"Things happen."

"Things happen, and when they do—"

"You just gotta say okay—"

"And then you move on. And that's all you can do. And that's all *we* can do, as a society. But the important thing is, we shouldn't look at a given situation and say this is this or that's that. It doesn't have to be one thing or the other." She paused, a word lingering on the edge of her tongue. "This can be . . . conceivably, this could turn out to be a very good thing. But I have a sense that Simon isn't the kind of boy who would be . . . well served by the services we can provide."

"Okay. Okay."

"The scores. The scores are a problem. The scores are not very good."

"The scores are . . . poor?"

The woman nodded, less anxious now. Lydia seemed to understand. This was good. They could skim over the details. "The scores are very bad. Well below average."

"We were worried that it might be an issue. But you never know."

"You never know until you try. And you *should* try. And this is not the end of the world. This is a very small thing. In the large scheme of things."

"I suppose."

"But I'm so sorry."

"No, no."

"And if there's anything—do you have a way of getting back to . . . ?"

"Oh, we drove in from town."

"Okay, I wasn't sure. Some people have . . . things to coordinate."

"No, we're . . . we should be okay."

The ladies stood and walked across the room. Leaning against the partition, Mrs. Olivet folded her arms and sighed. It was the end of a long working day and she wanted to go home. She needed a bath. Bubbles. Steam. A bath and a big glass of sherry.

"If it's all right, I'll just let you find your way out."

"Where's . . . ?"

"Oh! He's still in the other room. He was feeling a little low, so I told him you stay here and I'll talk to Momma."

Lydia walked back into the testing room and sat down, taking Simon's hands in her own. Embarrassed, she longed to leave him here, to return home by herself, watch a movie, drink some wine, then wake up at six a.m., single and childless.

"Listen, Simon," she said. "I love you and that's not gonna change. Now we're gonna go home and we're gonna have a nice dinner."

"You're not mad?" he asked.

She bristled, detecting something manipulative in his voice. "No, of course I'm not," she said, then stood and led him out of the testing site, past the fancy vending machines, the girl playing air violin, the scores of other children engaged in their prodigious activities, arguing in Portuguese, constructing DNA models out of straws and bent paper clips, writing morose one-act plays on the backs of old calculus exams. No one looked up as they passed; no one noticed and no one cared.

It was cold outside; the car started on the third go. Driving home, Lydia turned on the radio, waited a second, then switched it off. A single note squeezed through the speakers; she recognized the song: "Hungry Heart," by Bruce Springsteen and the E Street Band, and from this she reconstructed the rest of the tune in her head. Her memory of the song was not as a linear piece of music, but rather as a single impression, all notes and all phrases heard at once. She *felt* "Hungry Heart" as a compact moment of art, and along with it came memories of the time when the song was popular, when she and Steve were still newlyweds living in Crane City and he was working four jobs, seven days a week, including a night gig sweeping up at a pharmacy, a humiliating experience for everyone involved—especially for Lydia, who had to watch her husband leave the house every night dressed in an apron and a nametag. What else did she remember from that time? Cheap furniture. Cheap wine. The magnets on the refrigerator—a watermelon magnet, a single slice of watermelon, and for a joke Steve would sometimes hold it up to his lips and pretend that it was a smiley-mouth, and Lydia would laugh and kiss him to get him to stop. The smell of Steve's socks. The smell of the hamper. The way the hamper lid squeaked when you lifted it. How a whole week's worth of their clothes fit perfectly inside the hamper. The thrill of mixing your dirty clothes with another person's dirty clothes, a person of the opposite sex. Doing the dishes together. The rack where the dishes dried. The fun of being annoyed by another person's stupid habits. Rolling your eyes in public. *Yeah, that's my husband.* But loving it, loving all of the awful things.

East of the expressway, the woods took over, and Lydia could feel Big Dipper Township pulling her toward its frozen heart, where her own home gazed out upon the water and the high tower and the ring of trees that seemed to go on for hundreds of miles. Rounding the lake, she touched her son's cheek. "Were you afraid?" she asked.

Simon scrunched his fists into his lap and pouted. "They had it too hard," he said.

"They had it too hard? What was too hard about it?"

"They asked me, they said I had to know who was the guy who made the book machine."

"Okay." She thought about it. "And what did you say?"

"I said, I dunno, I dunno who he was, and they said okay, one wrong."

She nodded as they turned up the winding drive. "That's okay, Simon. It's okay not to know things."

Leaving the car, they walked across the driveway and into the house. Motion-sensitive switches activated the recessed lighting as they moved from room to room. Simon chucked his jacket over the back of the sofa and trudged upstairs. The quiet of the house seemed volcanic—the

400 IT CAN'T HAPPEN HERE

quiet of landscapes, not of living rooms. Passing into the kitchen, Lydia opened the freezer door and took out a steak to defrost.

At six o'clock, she picked up the phone in the master bedroom and called the store. A girl named Scarlet told her that Steve had left earlier that afternoon with Mr. Pee and Mr. Carroll and had not returned. Lydia said thank you and hung up the phone. She sat there for a few minutes, seized by a weird paralysis. Sliding out of her shoes, she propped up a few pillows and rested against the headboard. If Steve was here, he would be sleeping on his stomach with his head turned toward the window, toward the edge of the bed. If Steve was here, she would be more conscious of her every movement, the way she took off her shoes, how much noise it made, the clunk of the shoes dropping to the floor. He would be lying there without his shirt on, and Lydia would be able to see the silver-blond hair on the back of his neck, and if she crept around to the other side of the bed, she could look down at his sleeping face, his mouth open as he snored or cleared his throat. She grabbed the phone and redialed the store, demanding to speak with the manager. The same girl laughed and said, "I'm sorry, ma'am, I'm doing two things at once." Lydia wedged her feet under the comforter and snapped, "Why don't you do *one* thing at once?" and the girl's tone changed from friendly and professional to stiff and mean, something along the lines of, "I'm sorry, madam, but Mr. Mould left several hours ago and I have no idea where he is," and Lydia—trying not to sound desperate—said, "Well, this is his wife and I would like to know where he is," and the girl—hoping to gloss over her earlier remark—said, "I don't know, Mrs. Mould, I'm very sorry, I wish I did, but the second we hear anything we'll—" and Lydia said *fine* and hung up.

Padding past her son's room, she leaned across the doorway and said hello. Simon looked up from his special coloring book; extra-huge crayons, the kind you'd buy for an infant, lay in piles and broken pieces. A few minutes later she came back, calling up from the bottom of the stairs, "Dinner soon!" His voice returned, unreasonably annoyed: "WHAT?!" Lydia scowled—*Oh, fuck you*—then went into the kitchen. The cat, hunched over its dinner, froze and stared, ashamed of itself. Lydia clucked softly but the thing ran off anyway, upsetting a few knickknacks in the living room. She walked over to the counter and picked up the steak. It was still hard; when she dropped it on the countertop, it made a noise like a giant poker chip. Pressing her thumb into the shrink-wrap, she felt the cold of the meat, the way it pulled at her skin. She removed her thumb and stared at her pink thumbprint, a little oval of color surrounded by frost. This was the color of flesh, of gore. The way things look when you cut them open. Her own flesh. What part would people eat? The muscles, probably. Lydia pinched her forearm. That's the choice part, right there. Ass is too tough. Too much chewing involved. The organs? More of a delicacy. A little green sphere coated with gravy. And then when you cut that open? Chambers, cavities. Undulating tubules. What hideousness we conceal. Thank God for skin. Steve's chest. Steve's stomach. The rumbling underneath. The dumb response of his genitals. Everything hacked apart. The body splayed across a bloody patch of road. A hand here, fingers curled in death. Evidence for the re-enactment. Medics swarm as wild deer look on curiously. They're waiting for leftovers. They'd eat it—oh, sure! Lap the blood. Fighting over the skull. An ear in one mouth, an ear in the other. The deer pull and the skull breaks apart. Braaayyyns! His last facial expression. Fear of the road. The wall ahead. Thank God he can't see this. Eye stalks severed.

Headlights skimmed across the driveway as Lydia dropped the frozen steak into a bowl of hot water. She leaned over the sink and saw, through the window, Steve's car parked next to hers. He climbed out and stood between the cars for a moment, his breath white and heavy in the cold air. Glancing up at the house, he gulped and slipped his keys into his pants pocket. Lydia ran out to meet him at the door. He looked horrible.

"Okay, okay."

"You've been gone all afternoon!"

He slouched across the foyer, staring vaguely at the bare dining-room table. His eyes were red and his coat was wet with slush. "Lydia, I'd like a moment to take off my jacket."

"Don't be relaxed!"

"Just a little time would be ever so nice."

"It's already—what time is it?"

"I don't know, Lydia. It's a long drive, you know? You've done it before. You gotta go all the way down and then all the way back. It takes some time. So here I am."

Closing the door, she herded him into the next room. "So now what am I supposed to do?"

"Let's all do nothing. For a treat." He sighed as he took off his jacket and let it fall to the floor. A wedge of perspiration made a dark trail along the back of his shirt.

Lydia stood directly under the blurred light of the chandelier. "I called. Some girl picked up. 'Oh, I don't know where he is!' That was helpful."

"Great, you got 'em all worked up. Let's blow up the whole world while we're at it."

"Oh, don't be ridiculous. And don't put your coat there."

Halting in mid-reach, Steve laughed and slung the jacket over his left arm. "Lydia . . ."

"Don't put your *coat* there!"

"Pffehhh. I'm gonna put it on the chair."

"Don't put it there either!"

"Where do you want me to put it?"

"That chair was my mother's and it's worth eighty-five hundred dollars."

"Okay! I won't put it there!"

"Don't you care?"

"About what—the chair?"

"The chair, for one thing, it's a beautiful piece of furniture."

"It's a great chair. I'm not saying anything about the chair."

"Don't you *dare* insinuate anything about *that* chair or *my* mother, because this house belongs to me!"

Steve's fist tightened around the jacket. "I am well aware of that, Lydia, and I'm not going to get into a big fight about it. We *all* know—*I* know. I'm a worthless, horrible, miserable person. That's fine! We're in total agreement about that."

"I'm not saying you're a miserable person, Steve. I'm saying if you touch that chair, I'm going to rip your fucking head off."

"Jesus!"

"What?"

"If you're serious about that. I need to get away from you."

"Oh, stop." She went into the kitchen and turned on the lights, but they were already on, and now they were off and so she turned them back on again. "Hang up your jacket and sit down. We're having steak for dinner."

"I don't want any steak."

"You'll eat it. It's expensive."

"I'm not hungry. I had lunch with Cam and Jim today."

"That's what you did with your day."

"That's what I did with my day. We had a nice long lunch — on the house! — and I drank a beer."

"Reckless."

"Darn right! I had a Michelob Light and a plate of nachos, and then a scoop of ice cream for dessert, and then I got FUCKING FIRED!"

Breathless, she dashed out of the kitchen. The two rooms seemed to crash together. "Oh, my God. Why on earth?"

"Listen. Let me tell you —"

"Jesus *Christ*, Steve!"

"Let me *tell* you —"

"Now we're broke!"

"Oh, we're not broke. That's an absurd thing to say. I've got severance pay, they're giving me . . . for six months."

Lydia shook her head and sat down. "What about the house?"

"The house, as far as I know . . . I don't know about the house."

"The whole point of you working, Steve, was so I wouldn't have to use my savings to pay this property tax."

"How much savings do you have?"

"That's none of your business."

Steve stood in inept silence for a moment, then slid a chair out from under the dining table. "Well, this is a good time to start using it."

"That's not what my savings is for, Steve. My savings is *my* money which *my* mother gave to *me*."

"As — I thought! — a wedding present."

"No, that's selective memory on your part. The wedding present was a ceramic mixing bowl which we don't even have anymore because you broke it in the microwave."

"*That* was the wedding present?"

"Yes, Steve, it was."

"That was not the wedding present. That was *part* of the wedding present. She gave us the bowl because she needed something to wrap up."

"What are you talking about?"

"You can't wrap up a check. That's why the bowl. So we could have something to open. She meant it as a *joke*."

"That bowl cost over nine hundred dollars."

"I stand cor—"

"Don't you even remember what it looked like?"

"I have a vague recollection of there being a bowl."

"It was signed by the potist."

"The potist?"

"It was made by a very famous potist. Who's dead now."

"Lydia, listen. I sincerely doubt that Kay meant—"

"You don't know anything about my mother! You're being very presumptuous and offensive right now, Steve. My family's estate is not your gold mine."

"And I never said it was! My God, Lydia. You have absolutely no respect for me, do you?"

Lydia smiled and stood up, heading for the kitchen. "This is where it gets to be my fault."

"No, wait, listen to me—Lydia?" He rose and followed her into the other room. "Look, I'm gonna get another job. That's not an issue. I've got a lot of connections in the sales industry."

"You and the rest of the bag boys."

"The rest of the bag boys?"

"Yeah. The Kmart bag boys. You and the rest of the Kmart bag boys."

"Okay, I don't even remotely understand that, but fine."

"You're a joke, Steve. That job of yours. A joke."

He took one step closer to his wife. Under the fluorescent lights, he looked blue and menacing. "I was district manager for the entire northern half of the state. That's no joke, Lydia. That's serious business. And I would've been zone veep by the end of the year if it wasn't for this Simon thing."

"What does Simon—"

"You know what I'm talking about. The ad campaign. Remember? That was *your* idea. Begged me to do it, and I did it because I wanted you to be happy. Then it turns out Simon's running around on the Internet with a bunch of freaky terrorists, people are asking me questions like what do I know about the Egg Code, and I'm about ready to lose my mind."

"Well, you shouldn't have listened to me, then."

"Ha! Isn't that the way?"

Steve laughed and Lydia's eyes narrowed. She tilted her head and looked at him sideways. "The way of what?"

"That's a woman talking right there."

"Yes, it is."

Pleading now, he moved toward the sink. "Six months, hon. After six months of looking, I'll have an *even better* job."

"Doing what? Earning what?"

"In sales! That's what I do!"

"You want to sell cars, Steve?"

"No, I don't want to sell cars—that's not the point."

"I can get you a job. Selling cars."

"I can get my own job. I am a store manager. And I'm a darn good one too, and if it wasn't for all this political nonsense going on downtown, I would've had Jim Carroll's job like *that!*"

"But that's not what happened, Steve. What happened was, you lost your job, you got your free lunch, your free pat on the back, and now here we are."

Steve hefted his pants, raising them up an inch and then down again. "I know that, honey. What I'm saying is, I can get a better job someplace else. Forget Jim Carroll! All those dinners with that thankless jerk. *Oh ho, Jim, you're really funny.* Drinking my liquor until two a.m. Give me a break. Forget Cam Pee! I can take this and make something happen."

"No you can't, Steve. I have zero faith in you."

He gathered himself. "Look, Lydia. People have been watching me."

"Ah-ha! I see."

"Oh, yes. People have been watching me. You ever hear of Bargain Binz U.S.A.?"

"No, Steve, I haven't."

"Bargain Binz . . . it's only the biggest . . . *place* they got out at . . . wherever that mall is. The one downtown. It's right there on the sign.

You can see it from the freeway. They just opened three branches on the east side. One in Hedgemont, one in—"

"I don't *care* where they are, Steve."

"And the other two, I don't know exactly where they are. Anyway, *that* guy, hon, the head of *all* Bargain Binz U.S.A., calls me up must be *once a week*. Be my district manager. Run my sooper stores. I'm on register, this guy's talking numbers!"

"I'm tired of this, Steve. The mediocrity." She pushed him aside, then crossed and spoke to the window. "I want you to not be a part of my life anymore. I'm willing to be civil. I'm willing to work something out with Simon. I know that you love your son. I'm not going to get in the way of that. But I don't ever want to see you again."

He closed his eyes, rotating his neck in a slow, painful circle. "Wait, now. Okay. That can't happen."

"It can happen, Steve. It just happened. I am not going to support you for one more day."

"Support me? I'm supporting you!"

"In every meaningful way, I have supported you. How many managers of Living Arrangements U.S.A. can—"

"It's just Living Arrangements."

"How many managers can afford to live in Big Dipper Township, in a house like this? None, Steve. If it was just you, we'd be living in a little shack in Skylor, no yard, no place for Simon to go to school."

"But I *worked*. I worked hard, so you could stay at home and screw around with our son. *That's* why I worked."

"No, the reason why you worked, Steve, was so you could feel in control. The big breadwinner!"

"Okay, so now *I'll* stay home."

"Not here you won't. I'll let you come back in the morning for your clothes. The rest is mine."

"But I haven't even had my dinner yet!"

"You said you weren't hungry."

"I'm not, but—"

"Then go."

"I want to stay."

"I don't care."

Shaking his head, Steve walked toward his wife, but she kept him back, crossing her arms in front of her chest.

"Look, Lydia. It's cold outside, I'm tired, I've been driving for an hour. I'll nod off at the wheel!"

"You're not going to nod off at the wheel."

"One night, and we'll deal with it tomorrow."

"No."

"Let me just take a nap. For a couple hours. Really, Lydia, I'm not faking. I'm exhausted. I'll sleep on the sofa."

"You're not putting your feet on that sofa."

Squeezing past the door, Steve ran toward the staircase and grabbed on to the banister. "Well, then, I'm gonna say goodbye to Simon. He needs to hear this from a man."

Lydia followed—fast steps in the hallway. "Simon is sick. He's sleeping."

"He wasn't sick this morning."

"He's sick, you idiot! Why won't you listen? You stupid, stupid—"

"All right, don't yell."

"Get out of this house!"

"Don't push at me."

Lydia punched at his chest with both hands, pushing him toward the front door. "Look at you, pathetic shit. Someone should break your skull with a hammer."

"Let go of my shirt."

"You fuck."

"I'll hit you, and then it's gonna hurt."

"Get out!"

Dragging Lydia across the foyer, Steve used the rest of his energy to pry himself loose, grinding his elbow into her palm until she finally let go. "All right, bye! I'm driving *far* away!"

He strained and reached for the door. Lydia pushed again; the door gave and he stumbled onto the porch step. Shivering, he held up both hands, a conciliatory gesture, but the door was already closing and Lydia was now just a pair of angry clenched jaws snarling between a six-inch gap of light.

"Stop. *Staaaahp.*"

"Shuuhhtt—"

"I wanna get my nice shoes."

"Oh DIE!"

The light in the foyer cut off with a snap. Steve leaned against the window and looked inside, but could see no movement, no sign of Lydia. Giving up, he turned and walked back to his car. Just past the yard, the frozen lake reached out to him like a white spill about to dribble over the side of a table. Realizing his new situation, he climbed into his car and started the engine, then pulled onto the main road. He drove slowly, for the road was icy and the curves were sharp. He'd come this way thousands of times before; the long commute sometimes rankled, but overall he'd loved living in Big Dipper Township. And now it was gone. Please note the changes in your course calendar. To see his own child—this was a privilege. Something given and later taken away. New rules, weekly visits. Everything subject to litigation. Have him back by six. The Friday-night anticipation. Trying not to drink, not to stay up too late. Must get up early, must leave enough time to shave in the morning. Make the ol' man look presentable. For Dad now leads a strange existence. Cold motels, rented by the week. Bad, cheap food. Grilled sandwiches. Lukewarm flirtations with the waitress down the road. *So, you a dee-vor-say?* Ordering dinner by the number. The four. The number eight. *Gimme the seventeen, no onions.* Wearing sunglasses while eating dinner in a narrow cafeteria. The old lady in the opposite booth. A quad cane. Brown stockings rolled down to the ankles. The glass of bubbled plastic. Red tint. The faint taste of detergent. Slinking off into the night. The gum machines in the foyer. All proceeds donated to the Kiwanis Club of Crane City. The stacks of free literature. Apartments. Property in Florida. Jacking off to the realtor's head shot. Getting it all over her fancy blazer. The awful room. The kitchenette. The clean ashtrays. The place in the mattress where it always dips. The pay-per-view flicks. $6.46 an hour. Soft-core pornography. *Hot Satin Nites.* Our featured selection—a Mel Gibson movie! The same clip of Mel Gibson running away from an oncoming torrent of fire shown over and over and over again. "Get down!" he's shouting. *"Get down!"*

.   .   .

Olden watched from the side of the road as Steve's car slowed around a curve and passed out of view. He'd been waiting outside for several hours, and now it was night and soon he would have to go home. The men from the Gloria Corporation were still here; he could hear their feet scurrying through the underbrush. Near. Not so near. He walked deeper into the woods, trying not to lose sight of the road, for that would mean staying out here until dawn. He could do that. After four years in the country, he was used to roughing it a little. He wouldn't be able to sleep, anyway, not until he knew what had happened to Mr. Tall and Mr. Short. There was a whole team of them lurking about, not just a few individuals. The entire organization had been dispatched to this place, making its nest amid the fruitcakes of Big Dipper Township. But why here? Why not New York City?

Reaching a break in the trees, he stared into a long column of mist. A man was standing at the far end of the column, his arms hanging at his sides, gunfighter-style. With a deft motion, Olden skipped back into the woods. He didn't hurry ahead, simply walked to where the man had been standing and looked in all directions. A small clearing opened off to the right, where he saw a gigantic tree, its roots feeding into a platch of frozen floodwater. Coming closer, he noticed that the bark was unusually smooth, like parchment. Reaching along the base, he felt a strange protuberance, about the size of his fist. At first he thought it was an old knot where a branch had snapped off some years ago. But no, it was too smooth, too properly manufactured. *Manufactured*, that was it. It was a doorknob—locked, no less. Taking a step back, he looked up to survey the full extent of the tree. High above, the moon glowed through snags of complicated bramble. Four thick trunks angled toward the same fat ball of roots. Each limb grew away from the center—a wooden cage, forty feet tall and nearly half as wide. Its overall shape recalled that of an onion, and indeed it seemed like something that belonged underground rather than out in the open.

My God, Olden said to himself. He thought about his father. He thought about Bartholomew Hasse. He thought about his small, orchestrated life.

Hoisting himself, he placed his foot on a low branch and began to climb, using his hands only to keep his balance. Near the top, the four main trunks were no longer discernible in the mass of intersecting twigs. Above a ceiling of evergreens, the air became cooler as the breeze skimmed across an unbroken expanse. All around, the tops of the pines twisted in the wind, little mad arrowheads of fuzzy green. The landscape cleared around the lake, frozen to a pale crisp. He spotted his own shack, Julian's house, a cluster of summer cottages near the water. Straight ahead—as if connected to the tree by an imaginary line—the tower stood, apparently larger from this perspective. The line streamed, passing through Olden's house at the midpoint. Even here, the equation made sense. A straight line between two points—well, that's simple. But between *three* points? This required effort, a conscious decision. A plan.

Suckass

My Darling Boy, Who's Going to Be a Dentist

1966

"He acts like he hates it, but look at him! Look!"

Doreen Mould means well. She sits on a high stool behind the register at the Warm Devotions Christian Book Store every Monday, Wednesday, and Friday afternoon, volunteering her time. A breezeway lined with potted plants connects the bookstore to the Unity International Non-Denominational Church and Community Meeting House, Shepherd Dane T. Foote presiding. Non-denominational, meaning non-denominational Christian. Meaning no Jews, no Hindus, no Buddhists and certainly no Muslims. It's not that we wish them harm; it's just that we don't approve of their beliefs and practices. Muslims are the worst.

"Steven can be hyperactive sometimes. Like when I took him to the doctor last month. I went with him into the examination room, because you never know about those people. They go off to medical school and they get all sorts of crazy ideas in their heads. So I'm standing there, holding my purse, and the doctor tells Steven to disrobe. 'Steven,' I whisper, just trying to be helpful, 'the doctor is asking you to take off your clothes, so you'd better strip and pronto! Don't worry, Mother will be right here.' Poor Steven! His face goes beet red and he starts to cry, and I say, 'My goodness, Steven, what's wrong?' and he says, 'I don't want him looking at my ding-dong!' Precious. 'Steven,' I say, 'I've seen your ding-dong and it's such a pretty little thing and you've got absolutely nothing to be ashamed of,' but I can tell that we're getting nowhere, so I reach over and I tug on his pants and—wouldn't you know?—he'd worked himself up into such a fury that he'd given himself a . . . well, you know. The darnedest thing. The doctor said he'd never seen a boy his age do something like that. Said most boys are ten years old before they can . . . well, you know."

The ladies laugh and clap as Steve sits on his own little chair and goes blink-blink. He stays quiet most of the time, unless his mother asks him to sing "A Mighty Fortress" or "One, Two, Buckle My Shoe" or "Hound Dog," and then he rises from his chair and stares down the neck of his shirt, drooling the words "You unt nun buh how daw, crin awl time" until she says, "Oh, Steven, you're making yucky-ucky," and wipes his mouth with a Kleenex. Again, the ladies laugh and clap. Their husbands are salesmen and police officers and factory foremen. It is 1966. The era of the housewife is drawing to a close, but these ladies don't know that yet. They have heard rumors of misguided young women roaming the commons at Midwestern University, handing out leaflets and chanting strange slogans, but thus far no such dissent has made its way into the suburbs. Doreen Mould, like many of her contemporaries, has no use for equal rights. Even this job is little more than a hobby, an amusement, a way to serve the Lord and to get away from the television. Doreen has no desire to challenge her husband. Warren "Barndoor" Mould is a mean man who loves his family and would do anything to protect his wife and son. He once strangled a drifter with a curtain cord because he caught him trespassing in the backyard. A nigger. The police said, We'll let this one go, Barn.

"I know what you mean, Greta. Steven sometimes has trouble controlling his bowels. Even now he'll poo his pants at least once a month, but I don't make him wear a diaper because I don't want to humiliate him. We went to the Thursday-night sermon a week ago, and I'd dressed him in his nice yellow suit because Shepherd Foote was giving the service, and I wanted to make a good impression. Not just for my sake—Steven will be an usher one day, and it's important for him to fit in with the rest of the congregation. So we're sitting in one of the pews, and Steven leans over and says 'Mommy,' and I say, 'What, and shush,' and he says, 'I made poop in my underwear,' and I say, 'Oh no, Steven, not now.' Right in the middle of the first epistle. Of course we couldn't just stay there for the rest of the service, so we stood up and hurried out of the chapel, and I took him into the ladies' room to get cleaned up. Mrs. Foote was sitting at the vanity table, doing her hair, and I said, 'Good evening, Mrs. Foote, we had a little accident,' and I took down Steven's pants—which were ruined—and I showed her, and she said, 'My, what a mess,' which it was, all down his legs and stinky too. I couldn't very well make him wear those pants out of the building, so I just told him to go bare-butt naked, and he said, 'Mommy, I don't want to,' and I said, 'Oh hush, no one will see you, and if they do, so what?' and so I carried him out through the lobby, and—wouldn't you know it—the bell choir was getting ready to play the doxology, and I figured heck, if you can't laugh at life then what good's living, so I held Steven up over my head and twirled him around and the girls in the choir giggled and I laughed and Steven was crying and I said, 'What are you crying for?' and I took him out to the parking lot and he made wee all over the car seat."

The ladies laugh and Steve sits and blinks. The only reason why he comes here every Monday, Wednesday, and Friday afternoon is because it's either that or the baby-sitter, and you never know about those people. Darn near the only ones willing to work for those cheap wages come up from Downriver or the north side of Crane City, and most of them are— what do you call it, when one of their grandparents did it with a Negro? Octoroons. *Orangutans* is what Doreen Mould calls it, and she calls it like she sees it. Not that Steve minds the long waits while his mother runs the register. The bookstore is calm and quiet most of the time, with just his mother and a few of her friends. The stock hasn't turned over in five years. Ceramic virgins. Dried flower arrangements. LP records of Perry Como or Mahalia Jackson or Lawrence Welk, but no Frank Sina- tra ever since he took up with that hippie. Motivational pamphlets: "America Is God's Country and Jesus Is Our God," "Moderation: It's the Right Thing to Do," "Explaining the Draft to Your. Young Ones." Holy Cross refrigerator magnets. Steve likes to make the magnets stick together, and sometimes he puts them in his mouth and his mother has to say stop it. Some of her friends are pretty nice, too. Mrs. Tyler is an older woman, slightly decrepit but good at making funny faces, like the one where she acts like President Johnson. *Eye'm Layn-dyn Jawhn-sun, and eye 'm an eem-buh-sul.* A sick woman, in and out of the hospitals.

Had cancer once, then she didn't. Then she did. Then she didn't. Did. Didn't. Did. Mrs. Fleet is new to the group, a young wife with pretty brown legs. Rumored to own a diaphragm. Steve once stuck his head up her long dress and his mother said stop it and Mrs. Fleet said "It's okay, he doesn't know what to look for," and Steve had no idea what that meant.

"I never spank my boy, but when I do, I believe in doing it on the bare bottom. The child won't make the connection any other way. A good, firm whack on either cheek, and then one on the crack for good measure. Last month, we went to a dinner party at my sister-in-law's house. Steven was looking at the wedding pictures on the wall, and he said, 'Who's that woman? She's ugly.' Terese pretended not to hear, but I knew he'd hurt her feelings, so I said 'Steven, you come here and take down your drawers.' Warren tried to say we'll just go, but I said, 'No, no, he's got to learn.' Steven knew I meant business, so he pulled off his pants, and I said, 'Underwear too,' and he took off his underwear and I had him lay right on the buffet table—we moved all of the leftover rib-eyes and vegetables out of the way—and I gave him three good swats, cheek-cheek-crack, and that was that. I had Terese stand over my shoulder, and I said 'You watch good now, so when you and Lance have your first one you'll know what to do.' Then I told Steven to get up off of the table and put his pants back on, and Terese said, 'Can he have some ice cream?' and I said, 'Of course he can.' He's been punished. He knows he did the wrong thing. Now he can have his ice cream."

Steve normally stays in his little seat, but when work is slow, his mother lets him wander the empty corridors of the church next door. Dane T. Foote's portrait hangs inside the main atrium, its textured surface made smooth and shiny by a thin layer of shellac. Looking at the picture, Steve knows that if Shepherd Foote ever asked him to do something—even something bad, like take money from the register or write bad words in the men's room—he would do it, he would *have* to do it, because Shepherd Foote is an important, well-respected man, and Steve understands that he must listen to him and obey his every word. Steve's favorite place to go in the entire complex is the breezeway, where the smell of car exhaust rises from the interstate, gathering in a sweet, toxic cloud a foot above the indoor-outdoor carpet. Tall potted plants reach over his head. Alone, he kneels and prays to one of them, wondering, *What if God was really a potted plant, and we all had to do what it said?*

"This was last summer, when we were driving north to Mackinac Island for the Fourth of July weekend, and about two hours into the trip I got to thinking, Hmmm, Steven sure is acting quiet back there, and I looked over my shoulder, and I said, 'What's that smell? Oh, Steven, you didn't! . . .'"

Sheesh at Rest

1999

Well, I sure don't know what to do. I told the gal at the desk, Look, I gotta get up at the crack of dawn. I don't need this noise. *We're sorry, sir*—if you were sorry, you'd do something about it, wouldn't you? Instead of standing around, *Oh, look at what Billy did to Bobby.* Finally I said to heck with it. I go back to my room, these kids are still screwing next door. I might as well watch a girlie flick while I'm at it. We'll just have ourselves a real good time, never mind that it's three in the morning and I gotta be downtown in six hours. You wanna talk about *racket*. You know, when I was that age—and it wasn't long ago—there was a little thing in the world, and you know what it was called? *Common decency*, hunh? Common decency, and we all had it and now it's gone, and I think it's a darn shame.

Course we had rock 'n' roll back then too. Oh yeah! Bob Seger and the Silver Bullet Band. I can remember them like lickety split. None of this "I killed her and I threw her in a garbage can." The rap stuff that the kids at the store listen to. No, no—I tell you what, that's a whole lotta junk. Not my style. *Not my bag*, as they say. When I was a kid, they knew how to write the rock 'n' roll lyrics. Jackson Browne. He had a way with words that I could never figure out.

But these kids, the ones next door. If I was running this place, I'd be on the phone right now, saying, "You wanna go to a flophouse, that's one thing, but this is a respectable establishment." Kids these days have *way* too much longitude. Not enough parental guidance. See, that's where

Lydia's wrong. You need a man in the house to level things off. You need a man and a woman, and if there's a kid, then all the better. I know, with me—now, my mom was a great woman, and anyone would tell you that. But if it wasn't for my dad, I would be a real loser. 'Cause it was my dad who said, Look, you better shut up, or I'm gonna smack you right in the face. And I learned from that. Those are the lessons that can help you get through life.

My approach with Simon is a little different. I never hit my son, because that's not a very modern technique. I believe in the Mahatma Gandhi principle of being fair to people. That's why I'm a good dad. I did a decent job and I worked hard—and I *always* put my family first. Not all guys can say that. You think I want to spend the rest of my life behind a cash register? No, I do not. But when you've got a family, and you've got a child who's depending on you, then you do what it takes. Before I met Lydia, I was on the fast track, man! I had brochures coming in from companies all across the country. I could've gone to Japan, worked for the Ford Motor Company. I talked to one of their recruiters over the phone. None of the other guys in my class got their phone calls returned—I did! We talked for a good long time. They were *very* interested. But I said no because—I mean, I *would've* said no, because Lydia and I were gonna get married, and I wanted to put the relationship first, which is what I *did*, and that's what I've always done—put Lydia first, put the family first, and now this is what happens.

Still, life goes on. Six a.m., rise 'n' shine! Gotta go out and get a job. Of course, soon as I start the car, the gosh-darn engine craps out. Ain't this a treat, like I need this, getting up at the crack of dawn, I just had the dang thing in for a tune-up. Now you'd think—and this would make sense, wouldn't it?—but you'd think if there was something wrong with the car, and you've already got it in the shop, you'd think they might say something about it. Just for convenience's sake. I mean, wouldn't that be dandy? Instead of two days later, I'm sitting on my rear end, having to deal with this nonsense.

I go back inside to call the mechanic, they've got some girl answering the phone, she doesn't know what the heck's going on. *Did you try to start the car, sir?* No, I put my hands on it and did a little dance—what *is* this junk? Finally I get a tow set up. Took 'em until nine o'clock, I'm sitting in bed, going over my résumé—right there on top: Steve Muld, M-U-L-D, fifty copies of this garbage. Some guy named Steve Muld's gonna get the job, eighty-seven grand plus full benefits, meanwhile I'm making shakes for $5.50 an hour, sixty hours a week, picking up change in the parking lot for a box of Wheaties and a cold hot dog. You know, I'm a reasonable person. I'm standing in the copy center, *Can I have fifty copies of this please?* You'd think, okay, look, it's Steve M-O-U-L-D on the charge card, right? And then over here it's . . . you'd think someone would've noticed that. That's part of the deal, in my mind. They got these kids working in these places, fourteen, fifteen years old, *Oh, look what Billy said to Cathy*, meanwhile the manager's got his head up his ass and I just wasted nine dollars on a bunch of crap. That's all *that* is! That's poor training.

So I say okay. I'm not gonna let this get me down. I go outside, the guy with the tow truck's there, telling me they're not gonna get to it right away because they've got all four lifts up, well isn't that fan-friggin'-tabulous, what the heck good is that gonna do me? Now I gotta take the bus, that's just great, ridin' in style—fifty alcoholics and a puddle of vomit, some old lady talking my ear off and the whole place smells like sin, you can't even breathe, now I gotta listen to some guy telling me about his daughter, he's got a picture of this little kid, tells me when he finds her, he's gonna punch her *so* hard, just you wait, mister, I'm gonna punch her so many times her teeth are gonna fall out, on and on until finally we get to my stop and I stagger outside, thank the Lord above, and my clothes are dirty and—oh! great!—there's a footprint on my briefcase!

But the good thing about getting off here instead of downtown is: *Vega knows retail*. Because downtown, what do you want? You want the twenty-four-hour drugstores and the hi-tech stereo shops. The Rent-to-Owns. And I don't mean to sound racist but it's just a fact—that's what people want down there. And I can show you the figures on that without a problem. The statistic printouts. This is all common knowledge.

But in Vega you've got a more diverse population. And that means more stores and more *different kindsa* stores. Downtown North Crane City, try selling sunglasses in one of the malls. They don't want sunglasses there because it's not a diverse enough population. In Vega you've got *three whole chains* of sunglass stores, plus the headquarters for Slick

Shades U.S.A., right across the street from the Candle Factory. I go in, totally unannounced, Hi, I'm Steve Mould, I'd like to speak to your senior representative. *Oh, I'm sorry, he's not in today.* Some woman with a hooker hairdo gives me an application. I'm like, Honey, this ain't cuttin' it! So she gets her supervisor. Finally: a man. We go up to his office, he starts asking me questions. What do I know about the company, the usual. I say, Well, I've heard about your company for a long time, and I'm very impressed with the way you do business, and I'd like to be a part of your management force. He says what do I know about sunglasses? I say that I know they're . . . pretty good. I mean, I know they're a big part of being outside and working under the sun, so in that sense I think it's incredibly important to have fashion eyewear that accommodates our needs in an ever-changing society. He says, I see you're not wearing sunglasses right now. And that's when I notice, yes, everyone in this building is wearing sunglasses, even though we're indoors and it's the middle of February and it's not even a bright day outside. I say yes, I'm not wearing sunglasses. That's very true, sir, and I respect you for pointing that out. And the *reason* I'm not wearing sunglasses is . . . I don't feel I *need* to wear them . . . in order to *prove* my qualifications for this job. I thought that was pretty smart.

After all that, I don't even get a callback. No come-back-and-see-us-next-month. This is some twenty-five-year-old kid telling me to drop off an application at the main desk, they'll keep me in mind. I know what that means—the big blow-off. Look, I say, I've got more than ten years' experience working high-level retail management. That's the real deal, pal! I sold over a million dollars in merchandise last fiscal year alone. My store led the region in opportunity-to-conversion ratios—you wanna talk about that? Three Hawley Cain Trophies for Sales and Leadership—*three!* '92, '93, and '95, right on my desk, I earned those. He's smiling at me! *Very impressive, Mister Muld—I know your CEO, we have lunch once a month.* Twenty-five years old, he's doing lunch with Cam Pee, the richest little son of a witch this side of Ho Chi Minh City, meanwhile I'm living in a rented kitchenette, weekly rates, no hot water after eleven p.m. This I don't need. *Not my style!* Steve Mould is not a charity case. If you don't need my services, fine. I'll go across the street, talk to the boys over at Groovy UV's. Can do, m'friend, can do. I'm halfway out the door, he's got a stack of coupons: Oh, don't go—look, thirty percent off, prescription flexy shades, what a deal. I don't *like* sunglasses, I say. This is what I tell him. I don't wear sunglasses. I don't like people who wear sunglasses. Hanh? I think they're all a bunch of pretentious, upper-class snobs! This is what I say, right there in the vestibule. That was a tense situation right there. I mean, I got out of there *quick!*

That's where I lose my cool. I'm a very tolerant man. I say live and let live. Peace 'n' love 'n' the whole nine yards. But you take it to a point, I'm bound to blow my top. And when that happens—watch out! 'Cause I just turn into a whole 'nother person. And that's all there is to *that*.

Of course, soon as I get out the door, my briefcase breaks. Ain't that a treat? Handle comes right off. That there is *just* what the doctor ordered. And then, the combination—I can't get the darn thing open! I'm yanking on it, got it braced up against a fire hydrant. Finally I said to heck with it. Cheap Japanese piece of . . . they make it so, if you forget the combination, there's *no chance* of getting it open. I think that's ridiculous.

So I chucked it! Goodbye to you. Steve Mould is a man. I can speak for myself. That's what these young kids don't know. Twenty-two, twenty-three years old, think they're gonna take over the world—well you're not! All you've got is yourself. And the best schools in the world aren't gonna help you. If you can't look at a man—if you can't look at him *right in the eye* and say: I'm good. I can get the job done. Then you don't even deserve to be alive.

So I start walking. I figure while I'm in Vega I might as well check out the old store. Place looked about the same. They've got some woman working there now. I hope she does a good job with it. She's got a decent team, and that's all that matters. Even the troublemakers had their moments. As long as everyone focuses on the task at hand. And for the most part, we did that, when we were really working together. '96, '97. That was probably our high point. The early part of '98.

I'm standing in the parking lot, thinking maybe I'll go in, take a look at the joint. I had to hold myself back. There's a mystique associated with certain people when they go away, particularly when that person is well respected and well liked, and I don't want to distract anyone from what they've got to do. This new gal's got enough on her hands. If I went inside, it might cause certain employees to question—well, maybe things *weren't* so bad when Mr. Mould was here, that sort of thing, and I don't want to get into that. Nope, time to give somebody else a chance.

It's pretty, though, where you can see the whole store from far away. They need to fix their aisle banners.

I'm all set to leave when I see one of my old cashiers coming off shift. I always liked Scarlet, despite the obvious sexual chemistry between us, which as a married man really got on my nerves. Anyway, that's in the past. Time to lay off the women for a while. I wave and say hi, no big deal, just on my way to the mall, doing a little shopping for my wife. She looked disappointed, so when she offered to give me a ride, I said sure, what the heck. We're pulling out of the lot—it turns out, she just gave her two weeks' notice. I'm about ready to go through the roof. That's time wasted! You get on over to store sixty-one, I tell her. I'm being the father figure now. Women like that sometimes. You talk to Jim—he'll put you in with Rick Mars at the zone HQ. Nope, not interested. Already she's got this new job—dancing, right? A bunch of girls onstage. Well, good for you. Still, that's no reason to stop working. I mean *really* working. You try putting in fifty hours per week as a first key assistant. That's *serious business*. You gotta do the drawers twice, three times on the weekends, you gotta deal with part-time cashiers who don't know what the heck they're doing, and you gotta make sure the back door is closed at all times—it's a big job! Then she tells me how much these gals make. Six nights a week, but only four hours per night. It's unbelievable—sixty-two thousand dollars a year. That's more than we pay our regional reps, and those fellas are trained professionals! Most people can't handle that kind of responsibility. You have to have an associate's degree from a *certified community college*; you have to attend the six-day Power of Potential conference in Calumet City, Illinois; on top of that, you've got to pass an eye examination, which a lot of the guys can't do!

So what I tell Scarlet is, just be careful, that's all. If you take care of yourself, everyone else will leave you alone. That's how I became store manager. I said to heck with this, I'm just gonna do my job. And this was in the days when guys were stealing merchandise left and right. Oh yeah! Living Arrangements in the late eighties, early nineties was not a very nice place to work. Used to be, three-quarters of the store managers were heavy-duty drug users. And I'm talking serious stuff—not just a little reefer, but cocaine too. They've cut that number way down.

Finally we pull up to the mall. I get out, shake her hand. For a minute there, it looked like—well, never mind. In my opinion, one-night stands are a bad idea. How do you get rid of the girl without hurting her feelings? That's the conundrum. Sometimes it's best just to play it safe. Stick with what you know. Take me, for example. I'm a manager. That's what I'm good at. And that's *still* what I'm good at. To heck with Cam Pee, Jim Carroll, all those guys. The furniture business is in for a big surprise, anyway. In two, three years, everyone's gonna be selling kitchen gadgets. Now's the time to get in on the ground level, take a drive down to the home office, *Hello, my name is Steve Mould,* wait for someone to make you an offer, you say I'll think about it, then BAM! two days later you're running the entire region. I can do that, no problem. I'll ask for a catalog, do a little research first. I wonder what it pays? Clerk—that's probably three-fifty a week. I can't swing *that* for very long. A month, maybe. A month, then I'll call for an appointment, talk to the senior veep. He'll recognize my name. These guys all know each other. I'll have to lay low for the first few days. Don't want to give myself away. Once they see you've got potential, they start to wonder: What's *he* doing here?

XXII

Fuck
Technology

I Had an Unpleasant Conversation Today

Kenneth West sat in his office, his feet on the desk. "I'm not interested in your excuses. All I know is, I've got five separate attorneys working on this, I'm buried in lawsuits, and I can't *deal* with it anymore!"

Gray leaned forward in his chair. "If you've got lawsuits, Ken, then just give them to the legal department and forget about it."

Lifting a manila folder, T. Kenneth gestured at a stack of papers and threw it back on the pile. This motion suggested a task of great magnitude, futile to even contemplate. "It's gonna take five years to pay this thing off, Gray. I've got to *stick* with this company. I can't just pack up and leave."

"You should've thought about it when you—"

"Oh, don't give me arrogance. I'll take care of myself, and that's the end of that. You give me arrogance, we end this discussion right now."

"I'm not being arrogant, Ken! My God!" Gray knitted his eyebrows, shaking his head. "What is your *problem?*"

T. Kenneth swallowed and started again. "If we have a disagreement on certain issues, that's fine. But we've already made some decisions here—"

"You don't find this a little unprofessional?"

He began to speak, paused, then laughed bitterly. "I am not here . . . to defend my actions. That's not what I'm here to do. I am so angry with you right now that I can't even . . . *talk.*"

"Well, how do you think I feel?"

"Probably pretty angry! And that's understandable, but the facts are the facts."

"Oh, come on. You know as well as I do, if you can show an eleven-year-old kid on television *simulating masturbation—*"

"He wasn't simulating masturbation."

"Yes, he was. I know—I wrote the script. What I *didn't* do—"

"He wasn't simulating masturbation. That certainly wasn't my understanding, and if I'd had even an *inkling—*"

"You would've said, 'Rah-rah-rah! Let's make some money!' It's okay, Ken, you don't have to pretend. But when a client asks me to use their own talent because someone on the board of directors gets a blow job, then I have to do it!"

"Not necessarily. You have an obligation to do your homework. It's not the client's job to research their own staff."

Waving both of his hands, Gray stammered a bit, his raised eyebrows expressing a lack of comprehension, an eagerness to understand. "Wait a minute. Let me, let me . . ."

"That's *our* job! To make sure all the bases are covered."

"It's not the client's job . . . ?"

"The kid was moonlighting, for Christ's sake! Not only that, he was working on a subversive project which you *knew* would cast a negative light on this company."

"I guess I don't get it. Why is it okay for me to put a kid in a leopard-print G-string—"

"Because bad taste is one thing, subversion is another. Bad taste doesn't mean anything. You of all people should know that. No one feels threatened by it, no one takes it seriously and no one cares. This is different. Cam Pee won't even talk to me anymore. He gets a stack of angry letters in the mail, and now he wants to keep me in court for the rest of my life."

"Then *why* did you . . . when this campaign started—"

"I was *very* supportive."

"You were very supportive."

"Because the client was happy and I assumed that everything was in order."

"And *that's* good leadership?"

"It may not be. I am not a perfect person, Gray. And God *knows*—"

"It's got nothing to do with being a perfect person. If you have a situation where a client is not forthcoming—"

"Then you talk to them. You talk to the store manager, you talk to the kid, you talk to the kid's mother."

"If I'd actually done any of that, Ken, you would've said why are you wasting your time—"

"I would've said good for you, because—"

"You would not have said good for you."

"—because I'd rather have it done properly than six months later, here we are, every day I've got to see this nonsense on the evening news and everyone's running around saying why the hell didn't you *do* something about it?"

"So I gotta be the fall guy."

"So *you're* the fall guy, Gray. If you want to put a real fine point on it. That's right."

"So why don't you acknowledge that?"

"Acknowledge what?"

"Why don't you *publicly* acknowledge—"

"You want me to go out there—"

"If you're going to terminate me, Ken, I'd think you'd at least have the decency to—"

"I'll do it right now!"

"Good!"

"I'll send out an e-mail."

"Fine."

"You can write it yourself."

"I don't work here anymore, that's not my job. I don't have to do that."

T. Kenneth glanced at his computer screen just in time to see the message docket change from eight to fourteen. "Well, I can't do it now, I've got . . . too many things going on. Give me till five."

"I want it spelled out, because this is my reputation we're talking about, and if I'm the fall guy—"

The conversation lurched; both men seemed to check themselves before moving on. "Gray, when I say that you're the fall guy, yes, that's true. But that's not the whole story."

Gray's facial expression changed from one look of amazement to another. "So you're saying I botched it."

"I'm saying that you, in part . . . yeah."

"And I can't make a mistake?"

"Of course you can, but when it becomes a legal issue, then I have to take action. I'm gonna be tied up with this thing for the rest of the year. That's at least nine months' worth of lawyers, and suits, and countersuits. We may not even have a company when this is all over!"

"Well, you can't blame me for that."

"Why not? You were the one who went out there—"

"Under your direction."

"That's implicit! I'm the goddamn CEO. That still doesn't absolve you from—"

"A good leader would assume responsibility for—"

"What, you want *me* to resign?" Touching his chest, T. Kenneth hunched over the desk, his eyes wide with good intentions.

"I don't want you to resign, I want you to take charge of the situation in a way that's fair."

"I'm being very fair to you. I'm not suing *you!*"

"Why would you sue me?"

"Because of the incredible damage your behavior has done to this company."

"Oh, that is the most horseshit—"

"I'm sorry you feel that way."

The tempo picked up; both men snapped, shouting at each other.

"Since the day I walked in here—"

"I've been very nice to you."

"—you've been nothing but an obnoxious, overbearing—"

"Fine!"

"And I dealt with it, because I didn't care!"

"And now here we are! Isn't this wonderful? We can all sing and shout and dance around."

"Oh, no, that's great! I can do that just fine, so long as you know—"

"I don't need to know anything!"

"—that it's a *goddamn bullshit*—"

"Lower your voice or get out of here."

Gray stood up; his chair tumbled over, striking a display of glass knickknacks. "You, and all of this . . . hoopla crap! *It's all garbage!*"

"Good! I'm happy! I'm real glad!"

"Yee yee yee!"

"We can all go home and jump out the window!"

"And if it wasn't for your incompetence—"

"Gray, I'm about *five feet away* from—"

"You wanna punch?"

T. Kenneth leaned over his desk; he could smell Thousand Island dressing on Gray's breath. "Oh, boy, you need a slap."

"Let's do it!"

"Oh-kaay, oh-kaay."

"Cah-mon. Cah-mon."

"Let's stop. You get out."

"Fucking idiot."

"That's right!"

"Look at you. You don't know the first thing about . . . *life!*"

"I know I don't."

"Gimme my arm!"

"Here, move, move."

"Don't touch me, you retarded piece of shit!"

Walking quickly, T. Kenneth guided the other man down the hallway and into a freight elevator. Gray rode alone, smiling at his own reflection in the copper-burnished doors. He'd deliberately prolonged the conversation, not out of any conviction, but simply for the fun of it. It was fun to argue, he felt, especially from the perspective of sheer apathy. Besides, he had no reason to disagree. After all, he'd gotten what he wanted, and now he could return to his former life of failure and exile—two essential criteria if one wants to say something meaningful and put it on the page. Success had stolen his ambition, and now he had it back. He had to tell Olden.

He arrived in Big Dipper Township thirty minutes later, driving east across the state highway. Spring had come early to the country; the trees were still bare, but the lake had thawed to a blue shimmer. The sunshine was very warm; patterns of hot and cool flashed across his face as he headed along a winding road, then turned off and steered down a hill, where a narrow drive stopped short of the lake.

The front door to Olden's shack was open, the entryway partially blocked by a pile of clothes. Gray parked his car and approached the house, calling out his friend's name. Inside, the place looked abandoned. Olden's computer lay in pieces, its broken monitor leaking snarled cables. Someone had taken a mallet to the hard drive; its vented panels bulged near the center. Stepping over the mess, he felt something under his shoe—a square of plastic, the letter *F* printed on one side. Other letters lay nearby, here an *M*, there a backspace button, the 7, the Tab, the Scroll Lock. Butchered, the keyboard hung from its coiled cord, rotating solemnly as it dangled over the edge of the nightstand. He picked up a few letters; they seemed to wriggle in his hand. Leaning outside, he tossed them onto the front porch, where they struck the step and ricocheted in all directions.

Back inside, he found the telephone and called the police. A dispatcher took down his report. "We will be there in under ninety seconds," she said, talking away from the receiver.

"Fine, do you need me to answer any—"

"Stay where you are. Do not attempt to leave the premises. If we do not arrive in under ninety seconds, it does not mean that we are not coming."

"It does not mean that you are *not* coming."

"It does not mean that we are not coming. That's what I said. What did you think I said?"

"Just that . . . it doesn't mean that . . . This is the police, right?"

"This is the police. My name is Frieda Moore. I am a dispatch officer for the Township Consortium."

"Township Cons—"

"Big Dipper Township, Big Lake Township, Clay Township, English Fire Township—"

"Okay."

"Yellow Dog Township, Diamond Township, Steelcutter Township—"

"Do you need me to stay on the line?"

"Indian Township, Union Pride Township, The Sorrow of 1951 Township, and other . . . selected . . . townships."

"I'd like to go now." He hung up the phone and walked outside. Something about the woman's voice bothered him; she'd spoken as if his was the only call she'd received all day. Whatever agency she represented—and it wasn't the police, he was fairly certain—wanted to bury Olden bad enough to keep a constant watch over his house. It made a guy feel kind of *important*.

Gray smiled, thinking about his friend. Olden always was a bit of a crank. Did *not* get along with the rest of the art-school kids. Girlfriends were never a problem—there were always plenty of those. This was one of life's great wonders, the attractive madman. Recent assassins, murderers, sex fiends—a good-looking bunch, if you take away the obvious rejects, the four-hundred-pound no-necks, the Jesus types. Given another brain, another political orientation, Olden Field would've made a nice PR man. And why not? The beautiful should not be made to suffer, this Gray felt very strongly. We subsidize intellectuals; why not pinup dolls? The extra cash might've kept Olden out of trouble. Buy the rebels' loyalty. This network nonsense was not worth fighting for.

Sirens came from all directions. A man's voice made an announcement, but the sound was garbled, too far off. Looking away, Gray turned toward the lake, now alive with sunshine. The distant shore was black, hidden by the glare. Staring into the light, he could see a windsurfer gliding over the water. Powerboats circled on all sides, keeping at a cautious distance. Gray smiled without understanding, sensing only pure excitement, the thrill of seeing it happen. He cursed in admiration as his friend passed under the shadow of the tower.

Am I Being Perfectly Clear?

http://www.eggcode.com

One of the most popular features of twentieth-century architecture is the glass brick. Glass bricks are dense hunks of glass, specially treated with chemicals to distort the passage of light. Often they're used in tandem with cinder blocks to create a sturdy, bomb-shelter effect. We associate glass bricks with factories, office complexes and high school lavatories. In some cases, they're used to spruce up an otherwise bland den or recreation room.

Today, the glass brick owes its tarnished reputation to an early association with subsidized housing and left-wing politics. In this era of mass production, glass bricks have assumed the position once held by stained glass over eight hundred years ago. In medieval times, artisans used bright colors to conceal imperfections inherent in the glass-making process. The results were glorious. Stained glass panels depicted scenes from the Savior's life, His rage in the marketplace, His courage in the desert. Even now, these windows form our impression of a time when only one church ruled the known earth, when no division existed between the religious and the secular, and when political leaders transmitted the words of Christ Himself.

But whereas the stained glass panel was born out of spiritual devotion, the origin of the glass brick is more sinister. Seeking to make a religion out of the State, the early Socialists—who praised mechanization with the fervor of angry disciples—razed the

Byzantine churches and replaced them with modular units, squat shoeboxes of concrete and glass bricks. In this way, Soviet leaders projected a humorless image of themselves, their people, and their grim, pre-fab culture.

Americans seized upon this idea as well, hoping to transfer the same loyalty once given to religion onto the government. During the Eisenhower Adminstration, glass bricks began appearing all across the country—in post offices, induction centers, vaccination clinics, even modern churches. Great chapels, once bright with color, now emitted a pale gush of light. God's love, so ran the thinking, can only be expressed through indirect means. Extending the metaphor, we must also consider the power of the Union in this same, half-seen way. The vague promise of the American Dream

Transfer interrupted!!!

This Is the
Exciting Part

The surfboard slowed as the skeg dragged in the sand. Olden jumped off, closing the rest of the way on foot. His skin felt hot under the shell of his wet suit. His long hair itched, plastered damp against his head; reaching up, he yanked off the hood and let it hang around his neck. The air was cold and the breeze was stiff—a nice day for surfing.

Just ahead, the tower looked like a giant piece of coral, blanched by the sun. He hurried around to the front of the building. Once inside, he crept along a narrow corridor, stopping where a crack in the wall revealed a sliver of daylight. Peering out, he saw five agents circling in three bright red speedboats, their eyes blank behind opaque sunglasses. One of them cradled a rifle against his leg.

Turning away, he continued down a dank and cavernous incline, the only light coming from a cast-iron grate overhead. A low rumble deep within the tower made the whole place seem alive. Squeaking in his wet suit, he leaned back and caught his breath. An absurd thought—to stay here forever, to starve himself inside the heart of the machine—made him smile for a moment; he pictured his skeleton chained to the doorway, heaped like bones inside a prison.

Past the corridor, he entered a large antechamber—abandoned, by the looks of it. A shallow pool bled up from the sandy ground. He crouched and stirred the water with his hand. It felt thick and oily, like scum in a shaving basin. Footsteps crossed overhead, and he hurried into the next room.

Up a short flight of steps, the hallway widened into an inner sanctum, poorly lit by three forty-watt bulbs. Moving carefully, he stepped over a pile of black wires to a large steel cabinet, key still in the lock. Curious, he turned the key and the door swung open, banging against the wall. Inside the cabinet, a Cisco 7500 hummed like a sump pump, the numbers on the digital display barely fluctuating as the signals hurtled in and out of the machine. Behind the console, a steel plate gave the manufacturer's specifications in raised letters—ultra-fine stencil, stamped from behind. Reaching out, he traced the panel with his fingers: a capital G, one big curve and then a tail, straight across. He knew these letters without thinking; he knew them like a bad smell. *G-L-O*. And then three more. *R-I-A*. Stunned, he took his hand away from the cabinet. His face looked steely and certain. "I don't know what I'm doing," he said to himself.

Busy now, he built a makeshift barricade, piling two tables in front of the entrance, a chair, a wastepaper basket, boxes of files, some books and steel binders. Footsteps echoed in the corridors, lost and apprehensive. Checking his watch, he planned out the next few minutes, wanting only enough time to do his job and then get out.

Bent over the machine, he yanked the console away from the wall. Silver steel hoses stretched and went slack, still connected to the back of the box. The whole configuration reminded him of the cheap stereo equipment in his parents' apartment, circa 1975. Resolved, he plunged both arms into the box, relying on feel and years of experience. Many of the screw heads were rusty, and they broke into a mica-brown powder that stuck to his fingers.

Inside the router, the sound of a cooling fan slowed and then stopped as the network began to shut down. Given the Gloria machine's tremendous capacity for sending information, several hours would likely pass before the system corrected itself. It hardly seemed worth the effort. The network was a fickle beast; after all, the Gloria router had held on to its lead by only the slimmest of margins. The drunks and deceased had come out to cast their votes, and this was who they'd picked: Random Router the First, a digitized freak from the Midwest. Alive, the Gloria machine kept its grip on the Internet, maintaining the hierarchy, *creating* it by virtue of its lone, renegade force. Once unplugged, the system kicked in, searching for another leader. In the end, the identity of the router did not matter, for what defined the system was not the charisma of the individual, but rather the system's own inherent need for a master. Even now, another rack-mounted machine in Ithaca, New York—or Houston, or San Francisco—was ready to be sworn in, his hand on the Bible, the bloodstained widow at his side. In the end, Olden wondered, who was being exploited? Maybe no one. Maybe his original premise—that people could do better, that they wanted more from life than mere gloss and convenience—was naive to begin with.

Suddenly enraged, he walked up to the router and smashed it with his foot. Another kick, and a crack appeared. Attracted by the noise, a voice outside called for reinforcements. Not satisfied, Olden seized the machine and threw it against the wall, where it fell behind a stack of computer manuals. He could feel his anger drifting away, replaced by a sleepy euphoria.

Unconcerned, he watched as a pair of armed men struggled past the barricade. One of them aimed his gun, but Olden didn't raise his hands, just walked toward them, grinning. "You need some help over there?" he asked.

The barricade caved in and scattered across the floor. The men looked bumbling and pathetic, and they handled their guns like amateurs, unused to dealing with this sort of thing. Their pants were covered with splinters, as if they'd just come down from a giant tree.

Bored, Olden listened to his rights, hearing the words for the first time, the whole speech—obscure clauses and sub-clauses, a full minute's worth. He shrugged; none of this seemed to matter. "Sounds like I've got a lot of rights," he said.

"Rights my ass," one of the agents said. It was a stupid thing to say—no one laughed, no one cared.

XXIII

A Brief History
of the Internet

The Third Death

1968

There were three important deaths in the year 1968. The first two, you already know about. The third man to die (strictly speaking, the second) was Macheath Tree, who passed away on May 5th—a date chosen, like the other two, for its well-balanced proportions. 4/4. 6/6. A tidy sequence of loss . . .

In this season of academic rage, Harvard is a relatively calm place. The campus is littered with refuse—paper cups, cigarettes, pages from a botany textbook. Dr. Tree regards the ruined text and clucks his tongue. He gets through to some of them—the students, that is. Maybe one per semester. The others are merely bodies, blank faces. Their purpose is to provide context, nothing more. *Distinguishing himself from the crowd, the brilliant young botanist quickly ascended to the rank of full professor.* Macheath's institution spends millions of dollars each year managing the crowd. The best students take care of themselves.

Today's drama has little to do with Dr. Tree. Macheath is a harmless man, with six daughters and a wife who teaches cryptology at MIT. For years, the Trees have kept to their jobs, despite many other offers, most from the federal government. Since the early sixties—even before that, some might say—the Department of Defense has been developing a transcontinental computer network, loosely based on the work of Paul Baran, a computer scientist from the RAND Corporation of Southern California. Baran's model calls for a distributed system of interconnected nodes, fully redundant and able to withstand all but the most unlikely acts of domestic terrorism. It's a novel concept, and the government has taken great pains to safeguard the project in the months and years before implementation. As an expert cryptologist, Macheath's wife is one of the more essential consultants not yet on the DoD's payroll. Watching her husband die, we must imagine Kay's anguish, her widow-wild confusion, her need to flee Boston and start life over in a new town. These things are important. They were all taken into account when this murder was planned.

The herbarium at Harvard is special to Macheath. Glass cabinets display dried poppies and centuries-old seedlings preserved in amber. He comes to the gallery, not to study, but to escape. His home life exhausts him with its constant routine of marriages and engagements, heartbreaks and adolescent fury. Stalling across campus, he spends hours talking to the curator—an old woman who, oddly enough, knows little about botany. He finds it rather unsettling, her lack of understanding, and he forces himself not to wonder about it, preferring to enjoy the simple pleasure of her company.

"You should see our garden back home," he says, closing the heavy museum door behind him. "My wife and I exchange flowers once a week. Nerves, I suppose. She worries she might not have me around much longer." He runs out of words as they move into the corridor.

The curator, laughs, embarrassed. "You dramatize, Dr. Tree."

"I know my wife," he insists. "Kay is a smart woman. She'll make an excellent widow someday."

"Dr. Tree," the elderly woman protests. "Now you're being silly."

They reach the gallery, where tall windows look out over a green part of campus. Long cabinets bank the walls; artificial roses lie under glass, resting on heaps of dark velvet. The curator moves behind the counter and slides a panel to one side.

"I'm sure you'll appreciate this." Reaching into a display case, she removes a glass bud and places it on the counter. "Just came in, on loan from Oxford." Her eyes flash ironically. "Look at the size of that stamen!"

Macheath hesitates, suddenly uncertain of the woman's name. "Why, thank you . . ."

She takes off her glasses and folds one stem, then the other. "Gloria," she says, smiling at him.

"Gloria. Yes, of course." His fingers curl around the bud. "Yes, I'd agree—this is . . . quite . . . a . . ." His body tenses as a bright stream of blood spreads across his hand. The broken stamen, filling its host with poison, drops and shatters against the floor. He stoops, gesturing at the mess. "Oh, my carelessness . . . I'm . . . sor—" He falls in stages, grabbing the counter, the woman's dress. Dark blood spills over his chin, staining the collar of his nice striped shirt. One last sound eases from the back of his throat as his hand clutches at nothing, then turns up, palm open. A bit revolted, the curator steps around the body, finds a note inside her pocket and dials the number. The words she says into the phone are measured and precise; she whispers in fragments, as if speaking to a computer.

Dateline:
Washington, D.C.—
July 27, 1974

s the network expanded, liasons from the Defense Department began to worry about their commander in chief. Every strategy, every means of delay, had failed entirely. If 1973 was a year of manic, near-constant activity, 1974 was the Year of the Vultures—slow, ominous, and inevitable. Some insiders had even begun to mention the dreaded R-word in their conversations with the President. The only way Nixon could salvage his reputation, they advised, was by burning the tapes and resigning, sacrificing himself in the name of presidential confidentiality. But he had to move quickly. With each passing day, the certainty of his impeachment loomed closer and closer. It was either leave now or wait until morning for the bandits to arrive. For these reasons, Richard Nixon's behavior on the twenty-seventh of July was something less than coherent, and those on hand to witness the presentation of the Presidential Medal of Freedom to famed cryptographer Kay Tree were treated to a classic demonstration of Nixonian mania and despair.

Kay and her youngest daughter, Lydia, were greeted in the White House briefing room by Nixon and two of his top aides, Stephen Bull and the omnipresent press secretary, Ron Ziegler. Unlike many medal recipients, Dr. Tree was certainly no stranger to the president. They had first met in the mid-sixties—an odd period for Nixon, sandwiched in between his humiliating defeat by Governor Brown in '62 and his narrow victory over Humphrey in '68. Reduced to private service, Nixon had spent this time building the contacts he would later tap for favors, both personal and political, as president. Much as he detested the academic world, he appreciated Dr. Tree's usefulness to the administration. Still in development, the ARPANET project required special precautions to ensure the president's beloved "national security." As far back as 1968, Nixon was urging Dr. Tree to move to Washington, bribing her with the promise of a job at the Pentagon. Kay resisted these advances until May of that year, when her husband died under questionable circumstances. Distraught, she accepted Nixon's offer and soon was working in conjunction with the Advanced Research Projects Agency. Over the past six years, the original charter had broadened to include a variety of different networks, most incompatible with one another. The new challenge was getting these networks to speak the same language. In accomplishing this, the project attained its ultimate goal: an invincible web of technology, encompassing all sectors of corporate and commercial life. This award, then, represented more than just one woman's extraordinary achievements. Big money was involved — big money, and the potential to make a lot more of it.

The White House briefing room was a barren, cavernous place. Nylon curtains sectioned off a tiny area from which the president liked to spy on the press. Dismissing Bull and Ziegler, he smiled at his guests and invited them to sit.

"Excuse me, Mr. President," Lydia asked with a proper curtsy. "May I play with King Timahoe?" King Timahoe was a flop-eared Irish setter, the White House's copper-colored mascot. Even at fifteen, Lydia still loved to play with dogs.

"Lydia wants to teach King Timahoe a trick," Kay explained, then reached over and covered her daughter's mouth. Lydia twisted away.

"Oh?" Nixon's face went slack. The curtains, still settling, clacked on a metal track. Making an effort, he smiled up at his guards, his teeth weathered and brown with age. "Oh, ha! Wants to teach the dog a trick. By all means." He snapped his fingers at a young officer dressed in full ceremonial garb. "You, uhh . . . I forgot your name."

"Corporal Terrence R. Daley, sir!" the officer called out.

Nixon winced a little, the sound getting to him. "Right, right." He waved his hand dismissively. "Take the young Miss Tree out to see King Timahoe. I think it's sunning in the yard with Pat."

The officer nodded and left through a gap in the curtains. Watching the young girl follow, Nixon smiled and patted his cheeks. She seemed like a good kid. He always believed that a strong woman should know how to stick up for herself. Pat was a fighter—stable, impervious. He'd tried to instill these same values in his own daughters, urging them to never settle for mediocrity, to marry up, to hold out until the best proposal came along. Nothing would've made him happier than to see Trish or Julie married to a future president of the United States. Ed Cox, maybe not—but David Eisenhower, may*be!*

"Kay, what can I get for you?" He motioned toward a tiny wet bar, where an array of liquor bottles stood in a scattered assortment. "A little Drambuie? Maybe a nice mimosa for the summah-time." He snapped his fingers and jerked his head from side to side—his unfunny impression of a swinging hipster.

"Nothing, Mr. President, thank you." Kay blushed, then lied: "I've been sick for the past few weeks. Doctor's orders."

"Aw, what do those dumb Jews know?" He laughed but quickly dropped the subject, obliging himself with a swig of whiskey. Kay looked down; all who knew the president were well aware of the depths to which his excessive drinking could lead. "You'll have to forgive me," he said. "Things have been rather hectic around here lately."

"I appreciate you doing this, sir."

"Doing what?" His eyes flashed dangerously. Kay had seen that look before, in those old photos of Nixon the prosecutor trying to trap a Red in a lie.

"Coming down here. Going through with this ceremonial nonsense. I'm sure it's probably the last thing on your mind."

"Not at all." He slicked back his hair, which seemed to hover over his head like a mantle. "This is the job, you know . . . the presidency! Hand out awards. Smile at the little girl. Never mind what the Russians are doing—it's not important. That's for the Congress to decide."

Kay interrupted, determined to keep the president on course. "Listen, I know you don't want to talk about this, but a lot has been going on lately, and my people need to know whether their resource commitments will still be honored in the event of an executive shake-up. The specs on the TCP configuration have all been drawn up, and I'd like to start working on an encryption plan before we go ahead with the protocol."

Nixon straightened in his seat. Even with the administration crumbling around him, he still managed to keep a few steps ahead of his advisors. This was the great irony, after all the sins of Watergate: Nixon was a *good* president. "There's not going to be any executive shake-up, Kay. We're going to ride this through. The Congress may despise me, but the American people don't."

"You've got a lot of supporters out there." Kay—a mother, after all—reached out and patted his hand.

"Of course I do." He crossed his legs, his pants riding high above his bare ankles: the president had forgotten to wear his socks today. "Do you know what this is all about? This is about the eastern liberal establishment sticking it to Dick Nixon. I tell you, Kay—and you ought to know because this is your old stomping ground—but I can smell a Kennedy *all over this*."

"Well . . ." Kay hedged, resisting the drag of Nixon's paranoia. "Who knows . . ."

"I did not like Jack," he asserted, clenching his jaw. "I *respected* Jack. I respected his intelligence. But I did not like him. Bobby was the devil incarnate, and I did not shed one genuine tear when he died. But Teddy . . . Teddy is a punk." His face softened as he remembered all the slights and insinuations that had plagued him, probably ever since grade school. "Those Kennedy boys sure knew how to work the media. That's always been the Republican Party's problem—bad public relations. You'd think that the Democrats were the party of creativity and progressive thought. What did Jack Kennedy ever do for the space race? 'We will put a man on the moon'? Give me a break. NASA was an Eisenhower program. ARPA was an Eisenhower program. All of those scientists were Eisenhower appointees. Eisenhower did more for science and creativity than any other president this century. Turn on the TV, all you hear about is how dull the fifties were." He looked up at Kay; his pupils were big, and Kay thought for one terrible moment that the president was stoned. "The 1950s were the most adventurous decade in this nation's history. The liberals don't want you to know this. They'd rather have their big bongo freakout."

"You're absolutely right, Mr. President." Staunchly apolitical, Kay kept her responses limited to what Nixon wanted to hear. "For too long, the Republicans have been painted as the party of warmongers. Eisenhower loved his scientists more than his generals." Getting no response, she went on: "That's how it worked in those days. Researchers always knew that if you needed money, the best source was the Defense Department." She stopped, suddenly unsure of herself. "Are we . . . ?"

Nixon frowned, unable to grasp Kay's meaning; a light dawned, and he laughed, slapping the table. "No! God, no. This room is squeaky clean. Just like the rest of my administration."

For ten minutes, they discussed plans for the network project—a national priority, Nixon believed, and one he preferred to keep a secret. The liberals in the news media always misinterpreted anything remotely connected to the Defense Department. Their careers depended on making the president look like an idiot. The beauty of the network, he realized, was that it allowed other voices to challenge the liberal stranglehold—*educated* men, passionate about their country; generals and physicists and engineers, not these glorified cue-card readers who understood nothing beyond their own ambition. Most journalists were too dumb to understand network technology; bored by the subject, they'd go on to something else, leaving the government to conduct its business where it really belonged—in private.

Wrapping up the conversation, he pressed a floor-mounted button with the heel of his shoe and buzzed Lydia back into the briefing room, followed by King Timahoe and the two aides. Lydia's clothes were stained with grass, and Kay could see russet-colored dog hair sticking to her fingers. She must have given the poor thing quite a workout. Lydia always preferred the company of animals to humans. Animals obeyed, plain and simple; they were a kind of living art.

"Excellent," Nixon said, barely noticing the dog. "I think we're about ready to join the reporters in the other room." From his desk, he brought out a velvet jewelry box and set it on the table. The copper-plated medal inside looked chintzy, mass-produced.

"Wait!" Lydia wailed, kicking King Timahoe in the rump. "You haven't seen my trick yet."

"*Your* trick?" In a playful mood, Nixon moved around the desk and stood over the girl. Most children disliked the president, sensing an awkwardness that no amount of effort could disguise. "I thought it was King Timahoe's trick."

"It's my trick because I showed him how to do it," Lydia said, coaxing the dog into an empty chair. Going through her pockets, she pulled out three acorn shells and arranged them on the desk, inches away from the creature's paws.

"Ah, a shell game," Nixon laughed, playing to the adults in the room. "Well, do your worst. I've always been a sucker for certain failure."

With Lydia's help, King Timahoe clumsily mixed the shells. Nixon reached for the one on the right, adding a little joke — "Always loyal to the cause" — as he flipped it over and looked inside. "Nope . . . Guess I'll have to compromise. I don't like to do it, but I'll move to the center." Nothing under that one, either. Confused, he winked at Kay and smiled. "Ah, well, the lefties win again." When the third shell came up empty, he turned to Lydia and asked, "Well, where's the pea?"

"He's just a dog," she said, rolling her eyes. "He can't do it with the pea."

On cue, King Timahoe yawned, yapping its mouth. Both Bull and Ziegler lurked in a far, dark corner of the room, other things on their minds.

"That's wonderful!" Nixon laughed. "Oh, I *like* that trick." Taking the medal from the box, he gently draped it around Lydia's neck. "Little Miss Tree, I hereby proclaim you an honorary Republican for life!"

Reaching behind her head, she freed her ponytail from the strap as a noisy group of reporters began to assemble on the other side of the curtain. Someone pointed at their watch and said, "Let's go." Solemnly and without a smile, Lydia followed Kay and the president into the next room.

Women in Science

1988

Old and alone, Kay rode in the back of a taxi heading west on I-94, past the outskirts of metro Detroit. Her contact was a Gloria representative named Jersey Crater, who taught at the University of Michigan, just ten miles down the road. Together, the university and the GC managed the NSFNET backbone; IBM and MCI both contributed equipment, man-hours, headache and worry, their efforts aimed at constructing a network of 1.544 Mbps T-1 fiber optics, able to serve thirteen sites across the country. For nearly twenty years, the network had remained the domain of special interests—academics primarily, plus a few thousand enthusiasts who traded tips on public-access bulletin boards. With the new system in place, things would change. It was time to go commercial.

The headquarters for the Gloria Corporation were set back in a thicket of spruce and pine. A low sign marked the entrance: GLORIA, it said, a squat little box, glowing from within. Once inside, Kay was greeted by Crater, an unhealthy-looking young man who walked with a stoop, stopping sometimes to shake his leg before moving on. "Bad circulation," he muttered as they rode the elevator two flights down to sub-level B. "This job'll kill you."

Past the elevators, they entered a computer room, where a half-dozen technicians gathered around a drafting table. Quiet men, they smiled at Kay with exaggerated formality, then returned to work. Near the back of the room, she noticed a little girl dressed in rugged clothing—overalls, black leather boots. Her hair was cut short, and her big round face quaked tearfully as she sat cross-legged in her chair. "Daddy," she cried.

"Hey, K-ster," Crater said, picking her up and setting her back down on a counter. Catching his breath, he rifled through a messy pile of charts and pulled out a stack of graph paper. "Katie's going to help us out today," he explained. "There's a problem with the access port. We need tiny hands."

Working quickly, he sketched a diagram, lines and crosses representing wires and circuits. The girl hopped down and peered at the drawing. "That's not what it looks like," she said.

The pen slowed; Crater frowned, annoyed. "What do you mean?"

She pointed at the diagram. "Look," she said, grabbing a pencil. "Here's the NOC—right here, see—so if I divert the signal, then we're screwed—"

"Don't say 'screwed.'"

"I *always* say 'screwed.'"

"Not anymore you don't." Crater smoothed the page, including both Kay and Katie in the conversation. "Here's the deal. Right now there are two systems running. The old NSFNET and the new one. The old one's a piece of junk, so we're going to take it down. This is where Katie's little-bitty fingers come in." Turning in his chair, he tried to kiss his daughter's hand, but she snatched it away and glared at the ceiling.

Kay flushed. Neither she nor Macheath had ever talked down to their kids. Lydia in particular would not have tolerated it. Now almost thirty, her youngest daughter lived in Crane City with her husband and their first child, Simon, who'd turned one just a few days ago. A nervous mother, Lydia had nearly lost the baby; throughout the pregnancy, the fetus seemed to dangle on a wire-thin cord, forever on the verge of liquid oblivion. Even now he looked sickly, undersized. Kay secretly felt sorry for the boy. *Lydia as a parent!* Good luck, kid, you'll need it.

Across the table, Crater and his daughter were still arguing over the diagram. Settling on something, Katie led the way to a low opening in the wall, about two feet across. The other researchers followed, bringing their coffees as they gathered around the hatch. A steel panel blocked the entrance. On his knees, Crater unscrewed the four corners and the panel banged to the floor. Dull green light filled a narrow tunnel that tilted out of view.

Kay moved through the crowd, pulling the little girl to one side. "Have you done this before?" she asked.

"Not exactly," Katie explained, snorfling between words, her nose running. "But when I was six? And my dad took me to New York? That was almost the same thing, because I had to set up all these High Speed Network Relays, and my dad said, 'You don't know what you're doing, you're just a little *gurrrl*,' and I said, 'Nunt-unh, I know better than you—wanna see?' and so I showed him, and the lady from the university was really impressed, and she gave me this award called *Women in Science*."

"Oh, well . . . that sounds real . . . good . . ." Dazed, Kay stepped aside as an in-house photographer took a few pictures for the quarterly newsletter. Tiny Katie stood in front of the opening, holding a miner's helmet under her arm. Kay stayed out of the way; when the little girl smiled at her, she smiled back.

"Now listen," Crater said, tightening a leather utility belt around his daughter's waist. "This is important. Don't touch the T-1 connection—"

"I *won't*."

"Let me finish." Miffed, he raised his hand; Katie stood on one leg, unimpressed. "This equipment is very expensive, and I don't want you to break anything. That means no guessing, no screwing around."

"I'm not re*tar*ded," Katie sang out as the researchers smiled and sipped their coffees.

"Don't be funny," her father said. "Just remember, those LSI-11 Fuzzballs have got to go. All six of them. And be sure to test the NCSA link before you come out. Otherwise we lose the Midwest."

Saluting, Katie dropped to her knees and peered down the tunnel. "It's cold in there," she said, then crawled inside, moving ahead in short bursts, sliding one leg, then the other. Reflected light bled along the walls before shivering into darkness.

"How long will this take?" Kay asked, trying not to sound like a grand-mother.

Crater appeared unconcerned as he monitored his daughter's progress over a walkie-talkie. "Half an hour, maybe," he shrugged. Catching a look from Kay, he added, "It's warmer near the bottom."

"I'm sure." Feeling anxious, Kay gazed into the empty hatchway and listened. Katie's sliding kneepads made a soft noise, like a bird's wing brushing against a window.

"This is the last time," Crater assured her, playing with the dials of his walkie-talkie. "When we revamp the network for good, we won't have to worry about this stuff anymore."

"For good?"

"Sure. This upgrade won't last the decade. That's why we set up the Network Operations Center. Too many problems—renegade routers freaking out, sending bad signals. They're like bratty little kids. Everyone's got to be number one." He looked at his watch, then raised his walkie-talkie and pushed the button. "How you doing down there, hon?" Finally, a soft voice answered, "It smells."

"She sounds scared," Kay said, cursing herself for worrying about the kid. *Let her learn*, she thought. Wandering away, she found a small break room and poured herself a cup of decaf. Nothing happened for a while. Nervous, she went back to Crater, who was speaking into the walkie-talkie. "What's going on, K-ster?"

"I'm busy!" a high voice raged. Her father winced and put the radio down.

After a few minutes, Kay began to fidget, so she kneeled to peer inside the tunnel. It extended back about ten feet, then split into five corridors, each attached to the same main branch. It looked, she imagined, like the inside of a heart.

Soon the floor of the tunnel began to shake. "Hold on," she called out. "She's coming back up."

She backed away as Katie appeared, her face smudged with mud. She looked pale and tired, as if she'd been gone for days. Cheering, the researchers lifted her out and propped her against the wall.

Crater came up from behind, hefting a bottle of champagne. "Think I should let her have a sip?" he asked, smiling at Kay.

For a moment, Kay felt like scolding him; this kind of behavior—so reckless, so arrogant—was something unique to the federal government. Seeing the little girl, however, she changed her mind. "First get her some oxygen," she said. "Then the champagne."

Crater laughed, and Kay felt an odd gratitude toward the man, considering the network, the years ahead. Strange times posed strange questions. She wondered whether she, too, would have the courage to send her own child into the heart of the machine.

The Planning Stages

October 13, 1989

Lydia:

Here's twelve thousand dollars, which should take care of your third-quarter payments, plus any extra cash you might need to cover the moving expenses. I hope you and Steve and darling Simon are enjoying your new home! I've set your mortgage at seven percent over thirty years, which should average out to about $2,750 per quarter, which is quite reasonable given the location. I'm dealing directly with the banks out here in Washington, but if something happens to me you'll need to know who to contact. My financial advisor is Mitchell Frenkle, and you can reach him at the P.O. Box listed below. When I die, I've ordered Mitch to manage this account, because I know how busy you are, what with a new child in the house and probably many more on the way. I trust that you will not need to relocate anytime soon. Steve may find the commute inconvenient at first, but in time he'll come to enjoy the drive. It is my wish that you will remain in Big Dipper Township for many years. Simon will have children of his own one day, and it's every family's dream to own a house and then pass it along. I'm sure you'll learn to appreciate your little piece of wilderness. God knows, you deserve it.

Fondly,
Your Mother

June 8, 1989

Dear Ben:
Do we have a problem here? I gave you a certified check for forty-eight
thousand dollars, and you told me over the phone that you'd have the
deeds carried over by the end of the month. It's a week already, and I've
got Kay Tree coming into my office every single day, and she's worried
about getting hit with the property taxes come April. I SYMPATHIZE
WITH HER ENTIRELY! There's no reason why this should take so
long. We will handle the background check—that's our job, not yours.
That property has been sitting vacant for nearly three years, we've got a
family all set and ready to go, and I'm starting to get pissed off! There is
no zoning issue so far as I can tell. Those are residential homes, and if
the people from the Gloria Corporation want to buy up the whole state,
then that's their problem because they can't do it! They already own the
fucking airspace, but that doesn't mean they can just swoop right in and
nullify our contract. So you ignore their memorandum, all right? That's
my advice to you. I want this resolved by the thirteenth. If you need to
get in touch with me, go through Kay, who's still got her place up in
Georgetown. Do it. Now.

Mitch.

April 19, 1989

Dear Mitch:
As far as the husband goes, you don't have to worry about him—he's an
idiot. Lydia is a smart woman, but far too self-absorbed to ask any
questions. Besides, she needs a break. She's been living in that miserable
city for too long. Now, with the money situation, we have to do a few
things. We already know what's in our budget—that's not a problem.
But this is a long-term expenditure. We're not going to be in power for
much longer, and we need to make sure that some new broom isn't going
to come in and screw up our accounting system. We'll have to do a
money transfer—it's very easy, just a matter of punching in a few
numbers, but it'll make a big difference. Gloria will probably pressure

the local agent to hold a public hearing, but that's a lot of hot air and Ben Donaldson should be able to handle them. Ben has set up hundreds of acquisitions through the DCA, and he's our best contact in the private sector. As far as we're concerned, this is a standard property purchase, and even if the Gloria Corporation tries to launch their own investigation, they should hit a roadblock fairly early on. It's important, however, that we keep this space filled, at least until the situation changes. We already know about this Hasse character—what he's doing out there, I don't know. It's a matter of equal representation—they have their man on the case, we have ours. Anyway, let's keep in touch.

My love,
Kay

March 28, 1989

Kay—
Got it. Okay. Let's go.

—Mitch

3-26-89
START TRANSMISSION:
00010100010111010101101010101101010001011010101010101010
10000101011101110011010101010101010101010101001101010101
01011010100101010101010101010100101011001010101010100
01011101010011101010101110101010010100110101110101001
10111010101010101100100100010011010101101110101001101
01010001010111010100010101010101010101010101010001000
10011001001001010100011010101010101010101011010101010100
10101010101010101011001010101010101010101010101011010
—END.

Back to the Womb

Parthenogenesis

1999

L ydia turned off the TV and lit another cigarette. It was early one April morning and a deer was shitting in the yard; steam rose from the curl of scat. Since the separation, she'd taken to staying up ridiculously late, till four or five a.m. Some nights she didn't go to bed at all, and this was one of them. At three o'clock, she'd opened a can of beer and left it on the coffee table; it was still there, half full. Taking a sip, she made an ugly face as a timer went off in the kitchen, sending a jet of cold water through the coffee percolator. Bored, she retrieved the TV remote and flashed the screen on and off. The newscaster was still going on about the trial of Olden Field, which had kept the people of Crane City entertained for the past five weeks. Lydia herself had applauded the guilty verdict when it finally came down. Peace and closure, this was all she wanted.

In the pantry, she found a clay mug and rinsed it out in the sink. This was another new habit, one of her post-Steve affectations—letting the dirty dishes accumulate until all of the place settings were used up. This particular mug was a glazed ceramic with a fat gargoyle-handle that made it hard to hold. She turned it over and read an inscription carved with a toothpick:

THE SOUL-SPIRIT 'CASSIDY'
PROTECTS AGAINST ILLNESS
AND FEAR
HE IS A GOOD SHAMAN

The percolator, still in the midst of its noisy cycle, spat hot coffee onto the counter as she poured herself a cup. Replacing the carafe, she tried lifting the mug but the handle was too awkward and the whole thing fell and cracked against the sink. The gargoyle itself did not break, just stared up at her with a skeletal grin, a puddle of steaming coffee making a devil's breath around its horny head. Outraged by the arrogance of this ridiculous mug, she seized the gargoyle and hurled it across the room, where it broke into fragments against the kitchen table. Disgusted, she pulled a dirty mug out of the dishwasher and filled it with more coffee from the carafe. It was 6:58 in the morning. She hoped she could make it through the day in one piece.

Finishing her coffee, she threw a robe over her clothes and stepped into her shoes. The robe had been strewn across two chairs like a painter's tarp, and indeed the whole house looked dusty and disheveled, with dining chairs tipped over in the hallway and half-empty wineglasses sitting on the floor where she'd fallen asleep. This was Lydia's month off; she deserved a little break, some time away from her adult self. Steve didn't appreciate the mess, and he'd complained about it when he'd stopped by to reclaim toiletries earlier in the week.

("You're not to touch that, Steve."

"What the heck are you talking about? I'm just trying to find my shaving kit!"

"You're not to touch the mirror, Steve. That was the choice you made when you—"

"When I what?"

"That was your choice. And now this is my house."

"Lydia, my shaving kit is inside the medicine cabinet. All I want to do is . . . If it offends you so much . . ."

"You're not to touch the mirror, Steve. If you touch it, I will call the police and you will never see your son again."

"Oh, that's ridiculous."

"It's not ridiculous. Technically, you don't even belong here. Technically, you shouldn't even be on the property. You should be hovering an inch off the ground, making no contact with any physical object whatso—"

"Well, how the heck am I supposed to get my shaving kit?"

"Come here. I will get you a pair of tongs.")

Cold wind filled her robe as she slid open the screen door and went outside. The deer did not run off, just kept nosing around in its own excrement. At the edge of the yard, she turned and faced the house. Simon's bedroom window was a bright square of sunlight. In recent days, the boy had taken to staying inside all morning. That was okay, she felt; he needed his rest, too. It had not been a good year for either one of them. Over the past month, his behavior had turned increasingly erratic, for no reason she could understand. There was the separation, true—that would upset anyone, especially a child; but it didn't explain the odd conversations, the empty stares, the daily regressions. Eleven years old, Simon sometimes acted three.

("Stop looking at the chandelier, darling."

"It looks like bugs."

"It does not look like bugs, now finish your food—and don't turn the plate. I put that plate there for a reason."

"I hate it."

"You hate what—the food or the plate?"

"Both."

"You don't like Christian Dior?"

"Not a lot."

Lydia bit into her fish. She chewed with her mouth open. "Well, I've got news for you, kiddo. Those plates—when I'm dead and gone, those plates—when you get married, those plates—"

"This tastes like bricks."

"It does not, it was very expensive and it took a long time to prepare."

"I ate a brick once."

"Somehow I'm not sur—"

"Mommy?"

"Yes? Watch your sleeve."

"What's a chair?"

"What's a chair, what do you mean what's a chair?"

"Heh-heh. Answer."

"You're sitting on one."

"Chair! Chair! Chair!")

Peering up at his window, she thought about the next few years.

Simon was nearly a teenager now; calmly, she wondered if the boy jerked off. Brass trophies stood on the window-ledge: #1 SON, WORLD'S GREATEST KID—die-cast figurines of Grecian athletes dressed in loincloths, $4.99 a pop. Simon vaguely resembled the figures on the top of each pedestal, just a little less developed in the chest and abs. Give him some time. And then what? Another child, perhaps. Simon was a good kid—handsome, with nice teeth and photogenic eyebrows—but Steve was his father, half of his life-blood, and she longed to go inside and remove all of the bad bits, the black and ugly remnants. She cherished the Lydia part of her boy, only that.

("Here, baby, I saved you the soap."

"Oh, wow."

"Brand-new."

"It's heavy."

"I just took it out of the package."

"Smells!"

"Good, hunh?"

"Like magic creatures."

"That's 'cause it's extra special."

"Heck yeah."

"Have a nice bath."

"Thanks!"

"Don't walk on the carpet.")

Near the driveway, she loosened her robe and undid the top few buttons of her blouse. Her breasts surprised her; they looked super-huge, pornographic. She'd never breast-fed her child; the thought of it made her feel like a beast of burden, all rough teats and nipples. In recent years, she'd regarded her breasts as little more than a minor annoyance. Even so, it felt good standing in the backyard with the wind flapping against her skin, and she found herself undoing another button, then another, all the way down to the bottom. The linen tips swung apart and her stomach instinctively tightened as the cool air swept across her chest. A strange desire to make love turned in midair like a fancy bird, then flew away. Outside, her body felt different, and she wanted to take everything off, her suit, her skirt and shoes. Half-naked, she wondered what she looked like from a distance.

Simon screamed.

Closing her blouse, she ran inside and hurried up the steps. Simon was convulsing in bed, the sheets cast aside, a splatch of foamy blood covering his upper lip as his legs slapped against the mattress. His eyes were wide open, and his little bald penis was hard and red; a stream of marbled fluid shot from the tip, some striking his stomach but most of it landing on the sheets between his legs. The room lurched as she picked up the phone, remembered the number and dialed.

"EMS."

"Yes, there's something wrong with my son. He's bleeding. *Was* bleeding. He's not bleeding now."

"This is a medical emergency?"

"*Yes*, I—I can't talk. I can't—"

Distracted, she stared at the puddle in the middle of the bed, thick and cloudy with sperm. Leaning closer, she touched it, dragging a bead, the stain forming little wrinkles that trailed like a mass of parentheses, then stretched and snapped. She flinched, drawing away as the dispatcher repeated her last question. Breathless, she hung up the phone and waited for the medics to arrive. The nearest hospital was three miles south on the expressway. She and Steve had driven there once when he'd insisted that he was having a heart attack, but when they arrived, a dubious nurse told them to wait in the lobby, and so he picked up a copy of *Hi-Tech Fisherman* and began leafing through the pages, glancing occasionally at a caption or a sidebar, and Lydia snapped, *If you're having a heart attack, why are you reading the magazine?* and Steve said, *Fine, I won't read it then!* and angrily tossed it back onto the table, his face screwed up in a childish pout. Remembering Steve's face, she looked at her son; it sickened her, the idea that she'd once made love to his father, that together they'd produced this compromise, this disappointment. Shamed, she brought her hand to her chin. Simon lay still, breathing softly, thorns of dark blood clustering around his nose and mouth. His lips moved in a way that suggested a limited degree of awareness.

The medics let themselves in through the front door and tramped upstairs, carrying a stretcher and a fire-retardant blanket. There were three of them, two men and a woman. The woman was black and rotund, with dark whippy hair that seemed drawn on, like a cartoon character's. Her partners both were strong and tall, a good-looking pair. The woman examined the naked boy as the men hefted him onto a stretcher and moved down the hall. Lydia followed, stopping at the top of the stairs. One of the men called up to her: "Would you like a brochure?"

"Brochure?"

"About your son's illness."

She looked down at Simon, who was now mashing his tongue against his upper lip, tasting the blood. "What's wrong with him?"

Bracing the stretcher, the medic reached inside his jumper and pulled out a shiny leaflet. "It's just a general brochure."

"Oh, right."

"It's not about any one—"

"I get it." She took the brochure and thanked him. "I'll be right there. Just let me grab my cell phone."

The medics proceeded downstairs; the sound of unfamiliar activity filled the house, dimming as the front door opened and closed. Fetching her purse, Lydia started to follow, but a new thought occurred to her, and she turned and went back to her son's room. The splotch of semen had not yet dried, and it trembled when she sat at the foot of the bed. Cautiously at first, she held her hand over the stain, not touching it, feeling only the vague warmth of thermal energy, ions fading in the air. Great possibilities revolved in her brain, and she saw a purer version of herself—not perfect, no, but close, a three-quarter clone. Curious, she cupped her fingers around the thick, viscous fluid and imagined busy sperm-heads butting up against her skin, insane with a need to break through. A soft whisper grew inside her head. From afar, a new market beckoned. Beauty pageants were never an option for the boy—but for a Lydia Junior, perhaps!

Raising her dress, she pulled her underpants aside and held her labia apart with her middle and index fingers. Gently, she guided her wet hand between her legs. The walls of her vagina stretched as hot liquid formed a pool near the base of her cervix. A weird shudder ran through her body. Electric! Gooey inside, she sat up straight and crossed her legs. With this seed, she would start again.

Rights My Ass

t was noon by the time Gray arrived at the prison, having stopped in Vega to pick up a tasteless little present—Derek Skye's new book, *Life Is Fair*. He'd never been inside a prison before. The low, brick-brown building looked neither menacing nor sternly reassuring. It looked like a wall, solid all the way through.

The guard near the visitors' entrance was eating his lunch, a garden salad in a plastic tray. Gray passed his book through the security clearance, then followed an escort into a room divided by a wall of Plexiglas. The escort was a short guard named Dale. As they waited for the prisoner to arrive, he offered Gray a stick of bubble gum. The gum was stale and had the medicinal taste of non-minty mouthwash.

After a while, Dale cleared his throat and said, "Normally, while we're waiting, I like to talk about racecars."

Gray feigned interest. "You . . . you do?"

Dale sniffed. Jaw set, he seemed to suppress an awful responsibility. "Yep. When people come in here? I sure do."

Crossing his legs, Gray focused on the other half of the room, where an open door marked DO NOT CROSS RED LINE led into a corridor of yellow tile. Looking back at the guard, he said, "You like the racecars, huh?"

Dale took off his sheriff's hat and held it in his lap. "Yes, sir, I really do. I think they're just super."

A few minutes passed before Olden was escorted into the room by a guard with a leathery brown head. His wrists were not bound, and his uniform was a loose jumpsuit of parti-colored scraps, harlequin bright.

"I've been trying to get a new lightbulb for over my bed," he said, leaning over a microphone bolted to the counter. Dale tapped Gray on the shoulder and handed him a bulky pair of headphones. Olden waited for Gray to put them on, then repeated himself, adding, "They make you sign a bunch of forms, and I guess I filled out the wrong one."

"When did it burn out?"

"Two days ago. Two fuckin' days."

Gray reached into his jacket and pulled out the Derek Skye book he'd purchased earlier that morning. He squinted at the Plexiglas wall, searching for a slot, some place to slide the package through. "I brought you this book."

"What is it?"

"Something stupid. Here . . . where do I—"

"Oh, you have to give it to the guard on the way out. Dale'll take care of it. He's cool."

Gray raised one side of his headphones and relayed the compliment to the guard, who shrugged and said *Who gives a shit?*

"I don't think he appreciates it."

"Has he talked about the racecars yet?"

"Oh, yeah."

"He does that with everyone. That's his little thing."

Gray laughed; it made him feel ashamed of himself, but he didn't know what else to do.

Olden continued: "They don't normally have him working out where you are. Most of the time, he's in here with the other guards. That guy knows everything there is to know about the Baltimore Orioles."

"Yeah?"

"Yes, he does. Dale's got it down. Ask him something."

Gray looked over at Dale and said *So, he says you know a lot about the Baltimore Orioles,* to which the guard replied *I know a little bit, sure,* and Gray thought for a moment, then asked *Who's their best player?* but Dale only shook his head and said *There's just no way to answer that question, sir.*

"Some other time, I guess."

"Yeah, maybe. Most of the guards in here are pretty cool. This isn't really where they keep the hardened criminals."

Again, Gray laughed. *Why am I laughing?* he wondered. *What's wrong with me?* Controlling himself, he asked, "How long are you going to be stuck here?"

"Who knows? I could use some time off, anyway." Olden touched the Plexiglas wall, his fingertips turning white where they pressed against the glass. "It's not that bad, Gray. It's not luxury living, but it's okay. Besides, it's fun hanging out with my dad." Martin Field, Gray remembered, had been imprisoned here for the past five years. "And I'll have more energy when I get out. I might even start up a new version of the Egg Code."

Gray glanced at the two guards, worried for his friend's sake, but Dale was too busy picking his teeth with the side of an American Express card, and the guard with the leathery head was more interested in staring at the ceiling, pointing at it first with one finger, then two, then three, then four, then none, then one, then two, then three, then four.

"I won't call it the Egg Code, though," Olden said. "I think I proved my point. Technology can't change the world. Things are what they are. It doesn't matter what *typeface* you use, for God's sake."

Gray swallowed; something hard and shaped like a ball stayed inside his throat. The vague need to apologize faded as the conversation followed a lazy course. Both men enjoyed talking about Scarlet Blessing's new gig at the Casa d'Freak in downtown North Crane City. Scarlet— another name, like Martin Field, from the not-too-distant past.

At half past twelve, Dale placed his sheriff's hat back on his head and tightened the chin strap. It was time to go. The two friends waved good-bye and promised to meet again in a few months. Leaving the room, Olden followed the guard with the leathery head down a hallway illuminated by bright fluorescent panels; one of them flickered far ahead, but the men turned before reaching it and entered a small library, where about a dozen or so prisoners sat around laminated tables, reading law manuals and potboilers donated by the Citizens' Action League. The librarian was a resentful, ugly man named Curt who warded off conversation by hiding behind a copy of *The Wit and Wisdom of Oscar Wilde*. He spoke with a heavy Swedish accent, and his favorite catch-phrase was "Put the book . . . down!" which he delivered with action-movie zeal at least once every hour. Standing in the doorway, Olden noticed his father sitting at one of the computer terminals near the back of the room. A few of the prisoners looked up from their reading as he walked by.

"Hey, O-Nice!" said a long-haired prisoner in an orange jumpsuit. On the cover of his book, a cowboy wrangled an angry steed as a woman in a red dress clung to his waist. Smiling, the prisoner bobbed in his seat. "O-Nice . . . eatin' the *rice* . . . like sugah an' *spice* . . . gonna sell it for a *price* . . . don't worry 'bout the *mice* . . . 'cause he's got some *lice* . . . gonna give it to 'em *twice* . . . his favorite drink is bourbon and *Slice* . . . when he goes to the shrink, he says gimme some ad-*vice* . . ."

"Why are you reading that crap, Cleet?" Olden asked, nodding at the book.

The man laughed, smoothing the part of his mustache with his pinky. "Yo, we got some sex going on, bay-bee! Love in the fields, know what I'm saying? Love in the fields."

Olden shook his head, not understanding. "Love in the fields?"

"Yeah!" Closing the book, Cleet pointed at the author's photo on the back cover. "I'm talking about some full-frontal, butt-wild, au naturel, muthafuckin'—"

Curt's voice boomed over the rustle of pages. "Put the book . . . down!"

Cleet glared at the librarian and thumped his chest with both hands. "Ey, ey, ey, I'm talking to my friend! You wanna take that away from me? You wanna take that away from me?"

Setting aside his copy of *The Wit and Wisdom of Oscar Wilde*, Curt nodded at a pair of his muscle-shirted cronies, who descended on the man and yanked him out of his chair. Cleet kicked with both feet, his long hair making wild, wet-mop whipping motions as he struggled to break free.

"You are the best!" he screamed, pointing at Olden as the guards dragged him out of the room. "Attica, bay-bee! Attica, '71!" Raising his fist, he disappeared around the corner, still calling out: "You are the best, bay-bee! I'ma sell you some cigarettes, cuz! I GOT THE HOOK-UP! I GOT THE HOOK-UP! I'ma sell you some cigarettes . . ."

The commotion faded as Olden returned Cleet's fallen chair to the table. Another prisoner—a stubby, baby-faced fella with a Revolutionary War–era musket tattooed on his fat cheek—picked up the romance novel and shook his head. "Brother got to know," he said, "when you start to strut, that's when you get beat down."

Olden nodded and joined his father by the computers. Startled, the older man looked up from his work. Martin Field had changed considerably since '94. The GC had been right to prosecute, petty as it seemed; the routing tables he'd stolen had ultimately led to thousands of dollars' worth of vandalism and computerized hijinks. It wasn't much money, but after so many years, the Gloria Corporation had learned to look after every dime.

At least being in prison had brought Martin closer to his son, and every few days they would meet in the library to discuss his upcoming release. As the time drew near, Martin's fears increased. He didn't want to leave. There was too much unresolved in the outside world. "Don't worry about it," Olden assured him. "Mom'll take care of you."

Martin closed his eyes. "I can't ask her to do that." As always, he felt nervous talking about this. Even after five years, he still thought about Donna Skye—her legs, her tits, the improbable fact of ass-fucking her in a motel near the airport. "I mean, I feel very bad personally."

Olden looked at his own face in the dark computer screen. "Mom admires you a lot."

Martin tried to smile; he felt dishonest, even doing that. "You think so?"

"Sure! I mean, she works for the fucking navy. She knows how this country operates. You did the right thing."

Martin shifted in his seat; his son's political views had never made much sense to him. "Well, to the extent that I did anything at all, I just . . . I don't know."

"Sure you do! You were saying to people, Look, this network is fragile. It's not what those dipshits were going on about in the early sixties. Paul Baran and all that. Yes, theoretically it's true. When you have a distributed network, the chances of taking out the entire system in one shot are almost nil. Who cares? That's the cold-war mentality right there. Yes, it can survive a full-force attack from the Soviets. *Most* cases of subterfuge aren't that obvious. These are computers we're talking about here. There is always going to be an anomaly. That's just the nature of systems. And it doesn't matter how fine the margin is. The fact that the anomaly exists renders the whole thing corrupt. That's what you pointed out. And that's why you're here today."

His father laughed nervously. "Olden, I'm glad that you've taken such an interest in my work."

Olden shrugged—a ho-hum expression, maybe yes, maybe no. "Well, that's just because you finally decided to stop working for the DoD. TCP/IP is the Esperanto of the computer age. It's economic fascism."

"I don't know, Olden. These are old issues. I've lost interest in them. But you're still quite young, and I would suggest if you feel that something is wrong, then you should devote your energy toward bringing about change. That's what the people of my generation did, and that's just . . . America."

Olden started to rant. "I've already done all I can. I showed 'em— right here in the Midwest! In this stupid town. Why there? Who owns the property? That's what I want to know. Who owns that tower? Most of the land out there is private, even the little dump I was living in. That all belonged to Bartholomew Hasse. Does *he* own the tower?"

Martin looked away; his words traveled over a treacherous ground. "Mr. Hasse owned several pieces of property in that area, but the tower was not one of them. The tower was the reason why you were out there, because he suspected of the likely candidates, it was our best bet, according to the information we had."

"Which *you* supplied, right? The routing tables. You at least explained them to him. Hasse couldn't decipher that information on his own."

The dangerous ground broke under Martin's feet. "Well, the actualities are a bit muddled. Mr. Hasse certainly wanted you out there. I don't think he ever suspected you'd try to demolish the thing. What he needed was a presence. An interested party. Someone on the scene who felt the way he did."

"Which was?"

"Which was . . . well, personally I think his only concern was money. To him, the Internet was a threat to his publishing business. But he knew you were idealistic, and that you loved books. I guess those things go hand in hand."

Restless, Olden let the conversation drop. Anything was better than hearing his father pontificate about technology and the generation gap. Whatever gap existed between the two of them had nothing to do with generations. Olden's point of view was informed by a reluctance to identify himself with any of his peers, anything not contained within his own self-ratified constitution. It was a losing battle, but being in prison made it easier.

Saying goodbye, he waited by the door for an escort, then led the guard with the leathery head down a corridor, past a series of bad smells, to the cell block on the north side of the building. Prisoners held their hands out as they walked by.

"By the way," the guard said, hefting his keys. "I put your blue form through." He unlocked the gate and winked. "You got your light back."

"All right, my man." Olden smiled at the star-badge on the man's chest. "Hey, what do they call you around here anyway?"

Gently guiding Olden back into his cell, the guard shut the gate and turned the lock. "You're not gonna believe this, but—" Down the hall, someone screamed "GIMME MY SHOE!" but the guard just clacked his teeth and said, "Most folks 'round here don't even know my name."

"No?"

"No sir. Most folks just call me 'the guy with the leathery head.'" The guard's black eyes glinted under the brim of his wide hat. "You b'lieve that?"

"That's a good one."

Taking off his hat, the guard leaned forward and said, "My head look leathery to you?"

Olden shrugged. "Not particularly leathery."

"My point exactly." The guard replaced his hat and started down the hall. A few prisoners called out to him, and someone even yelled, "HEY, SERGEANT—YOU GO HOME AND FUCK YOUR WIFE? YOU GO HOME AND FUCK YOUR WIFE?" but the guard just muttered, "You don't talk about my wife," and continued on. Olden climbed up onto his bunk and found something waiting for him on the pillow—a thin book with a simple white cover. He opened the book and held it in his lap. There, under the glow of a bare sixty-watt bulb, a few black shapes burned across an otherwise empty page. Like a blind man, he ran his fingers over the letters. The letters pressed back:

LIFE IS FAIR

XXV

Throat

The Rightness
of Dying

pproaching the end of my little indulgence, I feel it might be useful to give an account of my parents' demise, just as a kind of after-dinner liqueur, something dark and weighty to contemplate before driving off into the night. You don't know much about my mother. Rarely have I written of her, for she is not the point here, and neither am I. The point is *you*, wonderful you, you with your various grievances, some great and some small, grievances which I have sought to address in my own shallow way over the past twenty-five years.

My mother, who died in 1972, never had the chance to attend one of my Cheer the Heck Up weekend seminars. The cause of her premature death was a massive knife wound to the stomach. It was a kind of double suicide inflicted upon the same person; having swallowed thirty-seven aspirin tablets, she then attempted to cut them out with a grapefruit knife. I can only assume—for my mother was a peaceful woman who would rather cut her steak with the side of her fork than use a knife—the pain was so unimaginable that it overcame her ability to reason. The instant she felt that horrible burn, all intellectual reservations about suicide were soon forgotten, and she could only think of relief at any cost. In retrospect, the forced-extraction method was probably not a good idea. Well, live and learn. In fact, the method of her suicide has always puzzled me. I can't imagine her swallowing thirty-seven of *anything*. My mother was never a glutton. Always left a little on the plate. Good God, she even swallowed the *cotton*.

When I was a kid, my mother presided over an assembly of other neighborhood women, serving as their local guidance counselor—an unofficial responsibility, but one which tends to seek out those cursed with the gift. At my age, I was able to eavesdrop without drawing attention to myself, and thus heard many sad tales of neglectful husbands, surly teenagers, chemical addictions: subjects which, in my own chosen profession, would become all too familiar. One summer evening, the ladies decided to buy her a cake, a half-assed token of their appreciation. I remember opening the front door, looking up, then standing aside as they presented her with a plain white box, the name of the local bakery stamped in black. It was a nice gesture—probably set 'em back a buck or two—but when we opened the box, we were horrified to discover a big gash tearing through the various layers of cake and frosting. Someone had *stepped* on the cake. A few of the women fainted, collapsing splay-legged onto the couch. My mother said something along the lines of *Oh, it's all right*, but the head of the committee would have none of it, and in a mad march of indignant rage, the procession stomped out of the house, swearing vengeance on the bakery up the road. My mother and I waited for them to return until well past ten, when she woke me up with a slice of cold apple pie, and we sat there in my room, sharing the slice, sharing the same fork, my mother lying next to me, her legs wadding the sheets, big swirls bunched near the bottom. The incident was quickly forgotten, and unless I'm forgetting a few stray words scattered in the breeze, that was the last kind thing anyone ever tried to do for the woman until the day she died.

For what ultimately happened was this. I grew up and went off to school, and the month I received my master's degree from Midwestern University, my father died of a heart attack. Mother spent the first few weeks sitting in the basement, talking to herself, sleeping in a chair. My parents were always affectionate around each other, and shared a passion for board games. There was one game—I don't think they make it anymore—where if you landed on a certain spot, your opponent got to say "You're in the dungeon!" Consigned to my bedroom, I would hear this nasty phrase repeated over and over, sometimes well past midnight, the words followed by an interval of soft and sloppy kisses. I quickly decided that the dungeon was a pretty good place to be.

After the funeral, I moved back to live at home and eventually started taking night classes at U of M, all the while wondering why none of the neighborhood women bothered to stop by anymore, now that the man of the house was gone for good. I sometimes ran into them at the grocery store; in those days I did all the shopping, since my mother was too fragile to leave the house. These women—whose husbands still beat them, but lovingly now, tinged with a hazy awareness of their own mortality— would smile at me in the aisle, and without even mentioning my mother's name, they would launch into a neurotic screed about their own irrelevant dramas as I stood there with the image of my mother superimposed over the canned goods, my mother politely enduring daylong tales of marital woe in her long, solid-colored dress, offering her best advice, bearing their burdens on her weak, all-too-human shoulders, and I thought, *Oh, you miserable cunts, you bitches, you cunts.*

Over time, I've learned to suppress my feelings. Even without the grapefruit knife, without the thirty-seven aspirin tablets, surely my mother would be dead by now. Nothing matters in the end. There are some of us who are meant to die violently. Better to do it with a knife than with a pension. My father, when he died—good God, almost thirty years ago—I'm sure he was afraid of death, much as you are. He felt his heart closing in on itself, felt the dizzy weight pressing against his chest every time he got out of a chair. After he died, his body continued to digest the linguine primavera inside his belly for another few hours until finally not even that worked anymore. Knowing my mother, I'm sure she put a little sprig of parsley on the plate—just for decoration's sake— but I imagine he might've swallowed it anyway, a sweet little gesture, something to please the ol' gal, his last token of love spread out across the walls of his stomach.

Anyway, he died, and I wonder if there might be a lesson in all of this, some bit of wisdom we can apply to our own deaths-in-the-making. It is my job to find the lesson in everything.

Um. Okay.

Here's a shot. Death is . . . I want to get it perfect. Death is the goal. Death is the right thing at the end of everything. Imagine your life as a fast trajectory moving toward a large, unavoidable target. You're not going to miss it. There's no skill involved. Picture it as a literal target, if that helps you to get the idea. A real bull's-eye, except that the eye is as big as the target itself, and there's no penalty for drifting off course because there are other bull's-eyes to the right and left and up and down and even *behind* you to catch you when you fall. You have nothing to worry about. You want to worry, worry about the dishwasher, and the fact that it hasn't worked since last month. But don't worry about death. Because it's gonna happen. The only thing you've got to do is keep looking. Keep looking at death. And to my younger readers, you keep looking too. You especially—you've got more time to do it right, to hit death confidently and with class. Keep it in your sights at all times. Learn to like it. No, learn to love it. Never cower. Never fear. Look toward your death, poor people of America—therein lies your emancipation! The target will take care of everything. This is the great one-point plan, the secret I've been hiding from you for all these years. Money, sex, frustration—no longer will these things have the power to hurt, to corrupt. Emptiness will become a thing of the past. In this nearby place, the fruitcakes will rule. And I will have succeeded at last.

Broke

Unable to read anymore, Donna Skye put down her magazine and stared out the window. It was spring, almost summer, and someone across the lake was working on his boat, listening to bright, melodic guitar-rock on the radio. She drained the rest of her chardonnay, set the empty glass down and padded up the stairs. Back in bed, she reached for another magazine, then sighed and left it on the nightstand. The light coming through the window moved across her body, and when she closed her eyes, she could sense the sun going in and out of the clouds, orange and then black, a malarial back-and-forth.

Half past one in the afternoon. Why sleep now? Why *now*, for God's sake?

Sitting up, she scurried off the bed and across the room. The bed was an evil thing. It wanted her soul, the empty remains. Donna Skye was a forty-eight-year-old woman who drank and slept all day. No! That wasn't her at all. She was a published author, a big seller by some accounts, and while the press had ridiculed her first attempt, she could still take pride in accomplishing what she'd set out to do. Even as a little girl, Donna was never supposed to exert her own will. Derek's story was similar to hers; both of their courses were predetermined a long time ago — hers by her father, his by suicide.

And now? They shared something else: bad reviews. She hadn't read the book yet, a bit put off by the write-up in *The New York Times*. The critics all suggested a failure so profound only a genius could pull it off.

They'd always hated his work—hated's not the word, they *ignored* it, because his followers were not apparently well educated and therefore worthy of academic study but not respect. They ignored him, and now . . . to chastise him this late in the day? *That* was the real crime. Leaning against the closet door, she hoped her husband (*still* her husband!) hadn't read the papers. Derek was having a hard year. This wasn't what he needed. He needed *her*, the perfect unit they made together. Removing her purse from the door handle, she slung the strap over her shoulder and fled down the stairs. She had to see him.

When she reached Derek's apartment, it was not yet two in the afternoon. She parked and sat in the car for a few minutes. What to say? The first thing, plan it out. Derek, honey, I know you don't want to see me but—no, just "Derek," no "honey." Crossing the front path, she noticed that the door was open—little door, little hallway, a bachelor's pad, no place for a man over fifty (God! she'd missed his birthday). Derek, I'm sorry I missed your birthday. Let's go away from this place. The steep stairs leading up to the top flat, *clam! clam! clam!*, drives the neighbors crazy every time he comes in at night, stumble-bumble at two in the morning. Where are you, my little bleached bimbo? Some sixteen-year-old sassyslut—probably got the crabs, not that he cares, so long as it's nice 'n' tight. *Pound*-mmmm! *Pound*-mmmm! Bedsprings snapping. What the minions don't see. The legions, the clamoring fans. The phone ringing at six a.m. Sure a long way from Crane City. His hand on my back. Long limos outside. You folks ready to dee-part? Barking orders. The push of bodies. This is my wife, Donna Skye. You must feel so honored. Yes, ladies, I *am* honored. No question is too personal. Coffee chats in motel reception rooms. 2:30–2:45. Tea with Mrs. Skye. White letters on a black signboard. THE DEREK SKYE SIX-DAY SEMINAR—yes, that's fine, but this is my *husband* we're talking about! Reaching the top step, she pushed her way into the apartment, expecting some reaction, a turn, a shocked stare, a stammer, b-but Donna, don't Donna me, the words filling her mouth, too much to say and not enough time, not for this, not the blood, smears on the floor, on the walls, red stains on white Formica, fingerprints (swirls and grooves), falling, falling, elongated fingers, sloppy marks, darker pools on the carpet, soaked fibers, still spreading, Derek's hand clutching the blade, a straight-edge, a little notch halfway down, sharp steel fringed in blood, tiny red tongues, and his own tongue pushing, trying to speak, whisperwhisper, wouldn't the pain . . . ?, *how can a person do this to himself?*

"Dahn-nah." Derek coughed and a black geyser of blood shot into the air, covering his face with an ugly warm splatter. One pale tube twisted from an anchor deep inside his throat. With his neck hacked open, he looked thirty years older; his whole face seemed to sink toward the hole.

Donna rushed into the kitchen and, trying not to panic, called the police, her hands trembling, arms wrapped up in the cord. Hanging up the phone, she hurried back into the living room and fell down next to him. "No. Ohno ohno. Oh please. Oh please God."

"Muhh-nuhhh."

"Unnh? You want . . . ?"

"Mmmmuu." Derek's movements were slow and aimless. His spread arms reached for things and fell back, a weak grab.

Frantic, she dug her fingers into the wound, pulling out a terrible wad of veiny, salmon-colored gore—sloppy, with loose strands connecting it to the body like a rooty section of turf. Looking into her husband's eyes, she saw a new intensity there, something focused and immediate. She leaned in, brushing his cheek with her long hair. "Whuwhuwhu-baby, tell me."

Derek's eyelids fluttered. A strange weight seemed to be tugging on one side of his mouth. "Muhn-nyeh."

"Oh Derek I love you."

"Myaaairr!"

His expression hardened. A final word escaped, speaking directly from whatever part of his dying presence still remained. "Unfair," it said.

His fingers curled as one hand dropped and turned over. Donna looked up at the ceiling (the fan stirring slowly, stuck in a low gear). She wept, her eyes closed, head tilted back. Derek's absence changed everything; her voice seemed higher, thinner than before.

For ten minutes, she stayed at his side. He'd turned into an object, one of many inside the room: a cloth sofa, two pillows, a table, an extension cord . . . Derek's body. The smell of cooking in the downstairs apartment rose through the floor. The carpet was sloppy with blood.

Two policemen appeared in the doorway, not moving as a team of medics stormed up the steps and raced into the room. They stopped, looked down, then away from the body. An officer approached her, cupping his hands around her shoulders as the medics rolled Derek's corpse onto a stretcher. A bit of the dead man's neck hung over the edge of the cart; the lead attendant discreetly scooped it up and stuffed it back into place.

"Ma'am, would you like a sedative?" The officer searched Donna's eyes for a response; finding none, he signaled to his partner, who produced an Altoids tin filled with tiny round pills. Donna placed one of the pills under her tongue and allowed the men to lead her out of the room. They carried her to the bed, then stood sentry as the drug took hold. A narcotic sensation, rather like a hand pressing down on her face, came over her, and she soon fell asleep.

Waking, she noticed no loss of time. Both officers were staring at her, and she could smell the chemical odor of industrial-strength carpet cleanser, thick and noxious in the air.

"Mrs. Skye? How are you feeling?"

"Oh . . . I . . ."

"Do you know where you are?"

Donna nodded as one of the two men turned and left the room. Through the wall, she could hear voices, some nearby, others crackling over a walkie-talkie. The one remaining officer brought a notepad out of his coat pocket. "Your husband has been taken to a nearby hospital," he said.

She laughed, wiping her face on her sleeve. "What for?"

He nodded, head bobbing from side to side. He was a middle-aged man with gray hair and a sick complexion the color of uncooked ground beef. "Well, we need to . . . . examine the situation to determine just what happened."

"I don't have to—"

"Oh, no. You can stay right here. We won't ask you to do that."

"I can't stay here." Running her hand across the mattress, she noticed the little dips and lifts, the places where the springs pressed against the surface. "I don't live here, you know. This isn't my house."

"I see." He rifled through his notepad, finding a clean page. "This is where your husband lived."

"Yes, that's right."

"Alone?"

She looked down at the bed. Narrow. Enough room for a lover. "As far as I—"

"As far as you know. I understand, Mrs. Skye. I understand entirely. So you would visit him . . . ?"

"N-no." She closed her eyes, confused. "We rarely saw each other. This past year we . . . no. I just happened to . . ." Frowning, she looked back at him. "Don't you have to write this down?"

The officer straightened. Thoughtlessly, he closed his notepad. "Oh, I . . . I have a very good memory. I just . . . I get very nervous, you see."

"You do."

"I find it terribly upsetting." His lips began to tremble. "Particularly when . . . ch-children are involved."

Donna swallowed hard. She felt a sudden desire to touch the man's arm. "Oh, well . . . Derek and I never—"

"No, I mean, children, when children get into unpleasant situations, I find it terribly upset—" His voice broke. The other officer ran into the room; looking around, he smiled at the woman on the bed.

"Come on, Cliff," he said, drawing the cop out of his chair. Cliff followed in a blind daze, head down, shaking. The notepad fell from his hands. Pushing him into the next room, the second officer apologized. "I'm sorry, ma'am. We're just going for a little walk."

Donna sat for a moment and listened to the sound of weeping as it faded down the stairway; then she picked up the notepad, set it on the bed and left the room, closing the door behind her.

When she got outside, the ambulance had already pulled away, blowing the stoplight at the top of the hill. The sedative she'd taken now reasserted itself, but instead of making her sleepy, it overwhelmed her with a swirling abundance of information. A dizzy feeling made the ground seem uneven, and she could almost sense the curve of the earth.

Unable to drive, she left her car and started back on foot, but every time she focused on something specific—a signpost, a newspaper dispenser—it betrayed her by melting into vagueness. An expression formed upon her face, pleasant and withdrawn. For the first time she began to resemble—not her father, but her mother, whose life had also been smothered by circumstances. Her mother had worn this expression for more than sixty years. This was the expression Donna would wear for the rest of her life.

Survivors

Thank You

ow that's not something you see every day. Must take a half hour, forty-five minutes just to get to the hospital. No thank you, brother. When I go, I go . . .

Whoo, those socks sure *stink!* Somethin' foul . . .

People live too long anyway. I've got nothing left to prove. My mother knows I done good. That there's money in the bank, when you start talking about computers and the Internet and such. A few weeks of work on that typeface, boy, and *ding?* I even said to the man, *You want to buy the copyright from me, that's fine, because I'm on a fixed income and I could use the extra money.* No one ever went to hell making an honest dollar. That's what they call, "Good gettin' when you can get it . . ."

I need to call that woman from the registry tomorrow. They keep getting the name wrong. It's C-A-N-D-A-C-E. Three times, I told 'em. That's the most important part . . .

I ain't kiddin' about them socks . . .

That's all for my mother, boy, because my mother gave me everything I have, and I didn't do nothing, I was too busy looking after myself, and selfishness is what makes a man old and lonely and nothing to show for himself at my age . . .

At least I did one thing right. *Candace Mason.* All those women, back in Pittsburgh. Building bombs, trying to keep it together. They're all dead now. Thank God I got a way to remember . . .

Best pull the blinds, here. No one want to see *my* naked body . . .

That siren's stuck on the hill. Whoever it is, he's a goner. When I go, they won't even need the ambulance, 'cause I'm just gonna be *dead*. Might as well take me away in an ice cream truck. I mean it! No great tragedy in dying anyway . . .

Now who's that good-looking guy in the mirror? Heh. I look like a pile of garbage . . .

Sssss, that's cold. Should've warmed up by now.

Oh, I see what I did . . .

Mmmmm . . .

Get rid of some of this *stank* . . .

Try to go to bed early tonight. Six o'clock. The six o'clock special. Winding down the track. Clickety-clack, clickety-clack. Ain't never coming back . . .

John Steinbeck Was
a Friend of Mine

Across the water, Gray Hollows was gazing at the tower in the middle of the lake. It looked the same as it had a year ago, when he'd first visited his friend in the country. Now he'd come—not for Olden's sake, of course, but for his own. The tower had been calling out to him for weeks, sending messages. There was a machine inside the tower, just as there was a machine inside his head. But Gray's machine was different; Gray's machine was ungovernable, a complicated tangle of axons and data-processing centers, all signals programmed to fire at once. *This* was high technology: Gray's brain, not the Gloria 21169.

In a flash, then, it came to him: the lake was not a lake, but a pool of blood, and the tower was not a tower, but a snapped vocal cord, stretched taut to the sky.

Charged with this new energy, he turned from the lake and walked back to his car. The drive into Crane City was quick, and he guzzled cold coffee the whole way, riding on recycled energy. By the time he pulled into the lot behind his apartment, his eyes were throbbing with a weird blue light. Running upstairs, he burst into his unit and heaved his electric typewriter onto the kitchen table, plugging the cord into the wall. Great writers never used computers, and Gray wanted to be a great writer.

The typewriter spat and zizzed as the ribbon cartridge slid along a beam. Reaching for the phone, he dialed long distance and waited for three and a half rings. His mother picked up; in the background, he could hear a loud banging, metal against metal.

"Mom?" His hands shook as he spoke; nervous, he typed a mess of nonsense letters, then tore out the page and started over.

"Gray, your father's outside . . ."

"That's okay Mom, just tell him—"

"Herbert!" Her voice faded. He pictured the room, the stretch of the cord. Bath slippers, a robe. *Sure, save the sports section.* Coffee on the counter. *Ow! Whaddaya doin'?*

"Tell him, I lost my job."

"You did? Oh, he won't be happy to hear—"

"Tell him I'm going to write that book, the one I started when I was a kid."

"I don't know what he's—"

Reaching under the table, he lifted a fresh stack of typing paper and broke the seal. "Remember that book, Mom?"

"He's been out there with a hammer for the past—"

"I'm gonna do it. I just wanted you to know. I'm getting started right now."

"Well, you certainly are adventurous!"

He took a new sheet from the stack and guided it through the roller. "HA HA! I *am*, Mom! I'm gonna put it all down. The whole story. I'm going to tell as much as I can."

The banging stopped. Through the connection, Gray heard angry footsteps slapping against linoleum. His father's voice: *God-damnit!* He could see his mother standing with her finger in her ear, trying to hear over the racket. "Well, write a good one," she said, brighter now. Her voice drifted in and out of range. "Make it as good as *Of Mice and Men.* That's my favorite."

Gray smiled. He loved his mother, her easy tastes. This was his responsibility. To write *someone's* favorite book. To make it as good as *Of Mice and Men.* For his mother's sake. He would do his best. "I like it too, Mom. It's very tightly written."

Shuffle shuffle.

". . . okay . . . here comes your father . . ."

The Rules

Welcome to the home page for the Gloria Corporation of Ann Arbor, Michigan. We're glad you could stop by. We've had a lot of exciting new developments over the past few months. Feel free to look around, and remember, if you have any questions, we're just an e-mail away.

For a complete listing of related Fuck You!!!!

Okay, folks, haven't got much time. We've had a lot of exciting new developments, too, and the next few months promise to be just as thrilling, if you like watching a former superpower collapse under the weight of its own hubris. So here's some advice—

THE EGG CODE'S TOP TEN RULES
FOR NOT BEING A PEASANT

1. Do not put too much credence in the words of rock stars, sports players, fashion models and professional celebrities.
2. Do not have contempt for people who are more successful than you are. Learn from them instead.
3. Do not believe in UFOs. UFOs do not exist.
4. Do not allow yourself to become overly suspicious of the federal government. In doing so, you are shunting personal responsibility for your own bad decisions.

5. Do not buy too many useless products. Look around your room. There are many useless things here. Why did you buy them?
6. Do not support the toy industry. Do not allow your children to play video games.
7. Get two sources for everything.
8. Do not watch too much television, and stay away from the Internet.
9. Do not believe in the afterlife. It doesn't get any better than this.
10. Idealize no one. A hero is not a person, it is a way of life.
    (Oh, and I forgot . . .)
11. Read.

There, that's it. Gotta run now—eight o'clock bed check. Back to our regular program.